The Slaver Wars Retaliation

The Slaver Wars Book Five

Raymond L. Weil

DEDICATION

To my wife Debra for all of her patience while I sat in front of my computer typing. It has always been my dream to become an author. I also want to thank my children for their support.

.

The Slaver Wars: Retaliation

Chapter One

Blue-white spatial vortexes suddenly formed in system 884-K and Second Fleet flashed into being as the vortexes collapsed into dark nothingness behind them. In just a matter of a few moments, the entire fleet had exited hyperspace. Where before there had been nothing, now a full sized Federation warfleet had flashed into existence. Battlecruisers, battlecarriers, strikecruisers and their support ships moved quickly into position.

"Status!" barked Admiral Amanda Sheen as she gazed across the Command Center of the 1,200-meter Conqueror Class Command battlecruiser WarStorm. The Command Center buzzed around her as the crew worked with increased activity checking their consoles and preparing for battle.

"Jump complete," reported Commander Samantha Evans as the ship's systems stabilized and the sensors came online. The main viewscreen on the front wall cleared of static and a sea of unblinking stars appeared.

"No enemy contacts within engagement range," Lieutenant Benjamin Stalls reported as his sensors probed the immediate area around the fleet for any threats and then began searching further out.

"Battle Carrier Endurance is launching the CAP," Commander Evans added as she listened to fleet communications over her mini-com. "All ships are at Condition One and ready for combat."

"Enemy ships detected!" Lieutenant Stalls called out as his sensors probed deeper into the enemy held system and two red threat icons suddenly flashed into being on the main sensor screen. "Two Hocklyn escort cruisers at eight million kilometers and closing. They have detected us."

Amanda nodded; she had expected this. The stealth scouts had reported that this system held a moderate size Hocklyn base protected by a small fleet of warships. Over the past two months, Operation First Strike had rolled over Hocklyn controlled space, destroying every Hocklyn base they came across. Thus far, the Hocklyns had not managed to throw a fleet in front of Second Fleet to cause them to pause in their reign of destruction.

They had freed a number of former slave worlds as well as destroyed all Hocklyn bases across an eight hundred light year front and extending over three hundred light years into Hocklyn controlled space. Amanda's current orders were to continue probing into Hocklyn space until they mounted a defense capable of stopping her.

"Sensors are detecting more ships farther in-system," Lieutenant Stalls continued. "The enemy base is now on sensors."

Amanda gazed at the holographic tactical image now being projected above the plotting table and the red icons it was displaying. She walked over to stand next to it and gazed warily at the enemy fleet's disposition.

"They're getting smarter," Commander Evans commented as she looked at the display from Amanda's side. "All of their ships are outside of the planet's gravity well and will probably jump away as soon as we reach engagement range. This base is a small one, so I doubt if they will stay to protect it. They seem to be getting self conscious about their fleet losses recently."

"If they do jump out, it will make it that much easier for us to destroy their base," Amanda replied in a cold and determined voice. She felt no compassion for the Hocklyns, not after what they had done to her home worlds. In her mind, she could see the old Federation dying under the brutal nuclear bombardment of Hocklyn warships. Over fourteen billion people had been massacred as the Hocklyns killed without mercy.

"What's the makeup of their fleet?"

Lieutenant Stalls carefully studied one of his data screens before replying. "One war cruiser and four escort cruisers, plus the two that are currently closing on our position."

"A small force for one of their bases," Commander Evans stated and then added with a note of concern in her voice, "I don't like this; something doesn't feel right. Why haven't they already jumped out?"

"Me neither," Amanda replied as she turned toward the communications console. "Lieutenant Trask, have you detected any outgoing FTL communications from the Hocklyns?" She wondered if the Hocklyns were setting a trap for her fleet. She knew that, at some point in time, they were bound to mount an attempt to stop Second Fleet from rampaging through their territory.

"No, Admiral," Lieutenant Angela Trask replied as she checked her communications console once more. "Just standard communications and nothing going out of the system."

"So they're not screaming for help," Evans commented with a growing frown, her eyes focusing intently on the admiral. "Why not?" In other systems they had attacked, the Hocklyns had sent out frantic calls for help as soon as Second Fleet put in an appearance.

"They knew we were coming," Amanda stated, her eyes widening at the realization. "They must have detected the stealth scouts somehow."

Amanda knew this was something that Admiral Streth had been deeply concerned about. While the Hocklyns didn't have the technology to detect the Federation's stealth scout ships, there had always been the remote possibility that the AIs did. This seemed to indicate that the AIs might have furnished that advanced technology to the Hocklyns.

"They may be setting a trap for us," warned Commander Evans, looking with growing concern at the admiral. "Lieutenant Stalls, keep a close watch on sensors, it looks as if the Hocklyns may have been expecting us. We may have a welcoming party showing up shortly."

Amanda activated her mini-com and changed it to ship-to-ship to communicate with all the commanders of her fleet. "This is Admiral Sheen," she said in a calm and commanding voice. "We were sent out by Fleet Admiral Streth to see how far we could push into Hocklyn space until they could mount a force powerful enough to stop us. I believe they are about to make that attempt." She paused and looked over at Lieutenant Stalls. "We think the Hocklyns may have detected our stealth scouts and are preparing to launch a major attack against Second Fleet." Amanda glanced inquiringly over at Lieutenant Stalls.

"Nothing yet, Admiral," Stalls reported with a shake of his head as he watched his screen fixedly "Sensors are still clear of any new threats."

"We will maintain our current position until further notice," Amanda continued, keeping an eye on Stalls and the tactical display. "All ships will stay at Condition One. Battlecarriers are to prepare their Anlon bombers for a shipping strike against enemy fleet units. If this is the enemy's attempt to stop us, all ships are to be ready to jump back to our failsafe position in system 920-J. If an AI ship is detected all ships are to jump immediately, even without direct orders from the flag. The preservation of your ship is your first priority if an AI is involved."

"You don't want to engage an AI?" asked Evans, surprised.

They had four of the heavy strikecruisers in the fleet, which had the new computer program and heavier forty-megaton Devastator Three missiles. Ariel and Clarissa had both said the new computer systems and missiles could destroy an AI ship. The two friendly AIs had already demonstrated that in the attack on the main Hocklyn fleet base when two AI ships had jumped in and engaged the fleet. Ariel and Clarissa had destroyed both AI ships, much to the surprise of their commanders.

"No," Amanda replied as she went back to her command console and sat down, deep in thought. "The AIs know they inflicted heavy damage on First Fleet the first time we tangled with two of their ships. If not for Ariel, First Fleet would have been annihilated. We don't want them to know that we have updated the tactical computers on the strikecruisers and increased the explosive yield of the Devastator Threes from twenty megatons to forty."

"We're going to set our own trap, then," spoke Evans, nodding in sudden understanding.

"Yes," Amanda replied, her deep blue eyes gazing at her executive officer. "Admiral Strong is setting up a strong point in the bears' home system. It will be a death trap for the Hocklyns and the AIs if they dare to attack it. Admiral Streth is doing the same thing at the main Hocklyn base we captured. Between the two, we hope to bleed the Hocklyns heavily before we retreat back toward Federation space. I intend to do the same thing here if possible."

Amanda turned back and gazed at the holographic tactical display as she weighed her options. "Commander Evans, place the fleet into defensive position Alpha Four and move us toward the Hocklyn base at five percent sublight. I don't want the fleet to be stationary if this is indeed a trap."

"Yes, Admiral," Evans replied as she moved to the plotting table to carry out the order. She noticed the increased tension in the Command Center as the crew realized that shortly they might be engaged in major combat.

Amanda leaned back in her command chair and thought about what had brought them to this point. Fleet Admiral Johnson had talked the new Federation of Worlds into activating the entire Ready Reserve Fleet and turning it over to Fleet Admiral Streth. Admiral Streth and sixty-seven others had been in cryosleep for nearly four hundred years waiting to be awoken to lead the human worlds against the Hocklyns.

After being brought out of cryosleep and going through training to adapt to this age and the new Federation, Admiral Streth had led five fleets deep into Hocklyn space in a daring First Strike against the Hocklyn Slave Empire. So far, it had succeeded beyond their wildest dreams. The goal of the attack had been to buy the new Federation some much-needed time to switch to a war footing and finish the defenses needed to protect the inhabited planets. Amanda had been one of those in cryosleep.

Long minutes passed and still nothing new was showing up on the sensors. All seventy-four ships of Second Fleet were now in a defensive formation and slowly moving in system. Half a dozen small Talon fighters flew on the outside of the fleet searching for any unseen threats that might have slipped by the fleet's sensors.

Amanda's mind turned to her husband who was back at New Tellus working on the massive asteroid fortresses. At least he was safe from harm. The fortresses were so powerful that not even an AI ship would have an easy time taking one out. Amanda hadn't seen Richard in over three months, and that was a long time for a married couple to be apart. The long nights without him were very lonely.

"Contacts!" Lieutenant Stalls called out as his sensor screen began to light up with red enemy threat icons. "Enemy ships emerging from hyperspace at two million kilometers."

Immediately the alarm klaxons began to sound and red lights began to flash, indicating that engagement was imminent. Commander Evans strode over to the command console and turned the alarms and flashing lights off.

"At least they didn't jump in too close," Evans commented, taking a deep breath as she studied the new data appearing in the tactical hologram.

Amanda activated her mini-com so she could speak with the two battlecarriers. "Commanders Marsh and Reynolds, you are not to launch your Anlon bombers until I give the order. Your fighters should be ready to launch at a moment's notice if the Hocklyns deploy theirs."

5

Amanda's penetrating gaze returned to the main sensor screen as even more red threat icons continued to appear. She could feel her pulse beginning to race; this was looking as if it was going to be a major battle. Somehow, the Hocklyns had managed to rush a large fleet of ships to the system. From the very beginning of her push deeper into Hocklyn space, she had expected this to happen eventually. It just surprised her that it had taken so long.

"How did they respond so quickly?" Commander Evans asked as she turned back to face the admiral. "There are no major bases close by for a fleet of this size to have come from."

"We have been steadily advancing in this sector, destroying one fleet base after another," Amanda replied as she thought about what the Hocklyns must have done. "I would guess they stationed several large fleets in our path and just waited for us to put in an appearance."

"No more enemy fleet units are appearing," Lieutenant Stalls reported. For the last few seconds, the number of Hocklyn ship units in the system had remained constant.

"What are we up against, Commander?" Amanda asked as she looked over at Evans and the tactical hologram.

"It's a big fleet," Evans stated as she studied data on a computer screen. "It looks as if we're facing six dreadnoughts, twelve war cruisers, and forty-eight escort cruisers."

Amanda nodded. It seemed as if the two fleets were evenly matched in numbers, but Second Fleet actually had more firepower. She could take the Hocklyn fleet although not without suffering heavy ship losses, but she couldn't retreat without at least challenging the enemy. Admiral Streth had a plan, and it was her job to make sure it worked. She let out a deep breath, knowing what was expected of her.

"Advance on the enemy fleet," Amanda ordered in a grave and determined voice. "Increase sublight speed to thirty percent and stand by to engage. Switch to formation Beta Two and prepare to fire all weapons upon my command!"

The human fleet turned and sped toward the waiting Hocklyn fleet as the individual ships adjusted their position into a more offensive orientated formation. On board the warships, crewmembers prepared for battle. Missiles were placed in readiness and targeting systems activated. Pulse laser turrets swiveled until they faced the enemy, and energy shields were brought to full power.

On board the 1,200-meter Hocklyn Dreadnought IronHand, Commodore Krilen smirked as the human fleet turned to engage him. He had long waited to get his opportunity to crush these vermin. He had heard the rumor running rampant throughout the fleet that the humans had destroyed two AI ships, but he had discarded that as just a rumor. No one could damage one of the master's ships. He suspected it was a ruse from the High Council to encourage Hocklyn Commodores and War Leaders to fight harder against the humans.

Krilen turned toward First Leader Angoth. "Launch our war wings; it is time to destroy these humans."

"It will be a great day for honor," Angoth replied as he carried out the order.

Angoth's six-digit hand strayed to the blade he always carried at his waist. He was tall for a Hocklyn at well over two meters and wore light gray colored battle armor as was customary for all Hocklyns in positions of leadership. His skin was a light green, looking almost scaly. His eyes were large and set wide apart on his head

"A great day for honor indeed," answered Krilen as his cold, dark eyes focused on the tactical sensor screen. He had long wanted to test his battle skills against these upstart humans.

Almost instantly over four hundred small fighters launched from the Hocklyn ships and accelerated rapidly toward the approaching human fleet. Each fighter was armed with two small missiles to be used against the human support ships. The missiles contained high explosive warheads and, if enough impacted a ship's screen, it should collapse under the bombardment.

"Enemy fighters inbound," Commander Evans reported calmly as she saw the blossoming red threat icons on the tactical display and understood instantly what it meant.

"They have launched close to four hundred fighters," Lieutenant Stalls reported, his eyes growing wide at the number. His sensor screen was now covered in red icons.

"Launch our own fighters," Amanda ordered as her eyes narrowed. She leaned forward, gazing intently at the tactical display.

From the two battlecarriers, over three hundred Talon space superiority fighters launched, their targets the inbound Hocklyn fighters. The fighters were armed with Hunter interceptor missiles and two 30 mm cannons.

"Entering extreme combat range," Commander Evans reported as the two fleets narrowed the gap between them.

"Slow to combat speed and prepare to engage," Amanda ordered evenly, fastening her safety harness.

In order to stay within engagement range of an enemy, it was necessary to drastically reduce ship speeds. Also, at higher speeds, enemy weapons could play havoc with a ship's space drives, particularly exploding nukes.

-

In space, the two opposing fighter groups met and threw themselves into battle. Space quickly lit up with tracer rounds and missile flares as the Hocklyn and Human fighters tried to destroy one another. Bright, fiery explosions began to go off as missiles and cannon fire found their intended targets. Fighters on both sides died as they vanished in sudden flaming blasts. The human fighters were all equipped with two Hunter class interceptor missiles and they were using them to their advantage. Only a few of the Hocklyn fighters were equipped with interceptors.

Squadron leaders were trying to direct their fighters to optimize the use of the Hunter missiles, but the two opposing groups were so intermixed that the weapon of choice was the Talon's twin 30 mm cannons. In just a matter of a few moments, the battle had devolved into a swirling dogfight of wildly turning and gyrating fighters.

-

"Optimum missile range," Lieutenant Mason reported from his tactical console on the WarStorm. "We have firm target locks."

Amanda nodded. "All ships, fire!" she ordered firmly over the ship-to-ship channel.

Her eyes strayed briefly to the main viewscreen, which was focused on the fighter battle. The screen was full of small explosions designating the deaths of both Hocklyns and Humans. She winced inwardly, knowing she was losing a lot of brave pilots.

Both fleets fired their missiles almost at the same time. Seconds later, massive explosions as well as occasional nukes struck the energy screens of the two opposing fleets. Waves of blistering energy cascaded across the energy screens of both Human and Hocklyn ships whenever a nuke went off. Then the two fleets entered energy weapons range, and the real battle began.

The human capital ships were equipped with power beams and pulse lasers. Space was suddenly full of violet and orange-red beams of light as the powerful energy weapons struck the Hocklyn's energy shields. More than a few of the powerful beams struck and penetrated, carving deeply into the armored hulls and inflicting heavy damage. The Hocklyn's own blue energy beams responded, striking human shields and occasionally penetrating. Numerous missiles were now detonating against energy screens on both sides, causing them to waver. Railgun rounds began to add their destruction to the melee as both sides opened up with every weapon they had at their disposal.

Admiral Sheen gripped her command console, feeling the WarStorm shudder as missiles and railgun rounds began impacting the ship's potent energy screen. She knew the screen would be lit up from the exploding ordnance.

"All ships engaged," Commander Evans reported tensely as she watched the tactical display. "We are still closing the range."

Amanda blinked her eyes and gazed around the Command Center, taking stock of the situation. The crew seemed calm and were going about their jobs in an efficient and deadly manner, though she could sense an undertone of anxiety. She felt the WarStorm shudder again as another powerful enemy missile slammed into the ship's energy screen.

From the WarStorm, two deadly power beams flashed out from the bow, striking an enemy war cruiser. The eight dual pulse laser turrets on the upper hull locked on, adding their firepower to the power beams trying to knock down the war cruiser's powerful energy screen. Klave and Devastator class missiles launched from the missile tubes, blasting the Hocklyn screen with a rain of high explosives and nuclear fire causing it to waver. A Klave missile slipped through the screen impacting on the hull blasting a glowing hole in the side of the war cruiser.

Several blue Hocklyn energy beams struck the light cruiser Capella, penetrating its energy shield. Almost instantly two Hocklyn nuclear missiles arrived, slamming into the hull and detonating, splitting the valiant ship into two sections. The Capella's self-destructs engaged blowing the separate sections into oblivion as their nuclear energy was released.

A human battlecruiser was battering down the energy shield of a Hocklyn war cruiser using its power beams and regular Devastator missiles. The shield suddenly collapsed, and the Hocklyn war cruiser vanished as nuclear explosions tore it apart.

"Light cruiser Capella is down," Lieutenant Stalls reported, his face grim. He hated those words; ones he had spoken too often since they had embarked on Operation First Strike. He also knew, sadly, that he would continue to say those words in the future as the war waged on.

"Shift all of our battlecruiser's fire to the war cruisers," ordered Amanda, wanting to inflict as much damage on the Hocklyn's heavier units as possible before she was forced to withdraw. Admiral Streth had ordered her explicitly not to risk heavy damage to her fleet. They were too far away from home to receive reinforcements.

The firing intensified as the larger capital ships shifted their targeting to the enemy war cruisers. In less than a minute, a brilliant light flared across the main viewscreen as another 1,000-meter Hocklyn war cruiser died in a series of fiery explosions. Even as it did, the loss of human ships continued to mount. Missiles penetrated ship screens damaging large sections of armor. Occasionally, railgun rounds and energy beams would slip through adding to the carnage.

A human destroyer died as heavy weapons fire slammed into its energy shield, causing it to fail completely and leaving the armored hull unprotected. Hocklyn missiles, energy beams, and railgun rounds pummeled the helpless destroyer, leaving it a riddled wreck. The ship finally exploded in a fiery ball of energy as a nuclear missile detonated, finishing off the small 400-meter ship. Other human ships were also dying as they fell prey to the heavy fire from the enemy.

"Monarch cruiser Amethyst is down," Stalls reported as the green icon representing the cruiser flared up and vanished from his screen. "Light cruisers Britta and Corales are down. Destroyers Stalker, Findley, and Dragon are down."

Amanda winced as Lieutenant Stalls continued to call out destroyed human ships. She knew that many others were receiving grave damage from the heavy fire from the Hocklyn warships. They were beginning to lose too many ships. It was nearing time for her to order Second Fleet to withdraw.

Commander Evans continued to fight the WarStorm. The ship's power beam and pulse laser batteries were firing non-stop. Occasionally, she would use a Devastator missile to knock down a Hocklyn energy screen. She gasped nervously as she felt the WarStorm shudder from several high explosive missiles impacting the shield. The shield held, and the WarStorm continued firing. If only they could use the more powerful Devastator Threes, this battle would be over quickly.

"Hard to port and bring all of our pulse laser batteries to bear on that war cruiser," Evans ordered as the WarStorm continued to close on the enemy ship. "Stand by with Devastator missiles; I want to fire all tubes upon completion of the turn."

In space, another war cruiser exploded and then another as their shields failed under the powerful onslaught of the human battlecruisers. Hocklyn escort cruisers were dying as the human destroyers and light cruisers pummeled them with every weapon they had at their disposal. Space was becoming littered with dead and dying ships.

The fighters from both sides continued to gyrate in their deadly game of cat and mouse as dozens of fighters from both sides were annihilated in bright, fiery explosions. For every two Hocklyn fighters that died, a Human fighter was lost. Missile trails and tracer rounds were everywhere, and space was lit up from the battle.

The WarStorm rocked as a Hocklyn missile penetrated her wavering screens and impacted the heavily armored hull. Amanda's eyes flashed to the damage control console, seeing several red lights blink on indicating damage to the area of the ship the missile had impacted.

"Commander Evans, I believe it's time for us to withdraw," stated Amanda, feeling they had done what they needed to do. They had bloodied the Hocklyns, but Amanda couldn't afford any more losses to Second Fleet. She had to obey Admiral Streth's orders to keep her command intact even though she would like to stay and finish off this Hocklyn fleet. "All ships change course to 230 by 12 and accelerate to 30 percent sublight," she ordered over the ship-to-ship channel. "All fighters are to return to the carriers. We will jump in ten minutes."

Instantly the human ships turned one hundred and eighty degrees and began accelerating away from the Hocklyns. The human fighters quickly disengaged and headed for their respective carriers. Unfortunately, not all of the human ships could escape. Two light cruisers and four destroyers had suffered catastrophic damage to their jump drives and, rather than be boarded by the Hocklyns, they turned with a vengeance and rammed the nearest Hocklyn ship.

The Hocklyns were ill prepared for this tactic, even though it was one of their own doctrines. A powerful Hocklyn dreadnought died as one of the light cruisers struck the Hocklyn ship almost head on, engaging the self-destructs on both ships. Both vanished in a series of powerful and deadly nuclear explosions.

Amanda watched the valiant deaths of the left behind ships on the main viewscreen in the Command Center, feeling pain as the ships sacrificed themselves one by one in blazing explosions as they rammed enemy ships. This was a war where neither side surrendered. She felt her eyes grow moist knowing that thousands of Fleet personnel had just died under her command. It was a part of being an admiral she absolutely hated, the need to send brave men and women to their deaths. Taking a deep breath, she turned to face Commander Evans.

"All fighters have reached the carriers and have landed," reported Evans, knowing how the admiral was feeling. War was difficult for everyone, especially the sacrifices that had to be made to keep the human race safe.

Amanda nodded and activated the ship-to-ship communications once more. "All ships, jump to system 920-J," she ordered. "Commander Evans we will be the last ship to jump."

"Yes, Admiral," Evans responded. She knew the admiral would not leave until all of her other ships were safely away and the last fighter picked up.

In space, spatial vortexes formed in front of the individual ships of the human fleet and the ships dove into them, vanishing into hyperspace. As soon as a ship was gone the vortex collapsed, leaving no trace of it ever having existed. In less than forty seconds, the entire fleet had left the Hocklyn system.

Hocklyn Commodore Krilen gazed in anger at the sensor screen as the last human ship vanished. "They run!" he cried in frustration, his hand slapping the chest plate of his body armor.

"We will find them," First Leader Angoth replied as he stepped up closer to the commodore. "I suspect they have not gone far. Shall I order some of our escorts to jump to the nearby systems to find where they have fled?" Angoth wanted to finish the battle; there was still much honor waiting if they could destroy this human fleet.

Commodore Krilen stood upon the command pedestal as he thought the suggestion over. He had lost a number of ships, including a dreadnought and four war cruisers. While he had hurt the human fleet, he had lost more ships than he had expected, and many others had suffered extensive battle damage. He also had orders from the High Council not to sacrifice his ships needlessly.

"No, Angoth," replied Commodore Krilen, taking a deep breath. "For today, honor has been satisfied. Let us repair our battle damage and await reinforcements, then we will seek out the humans and destroy them."

"As you command," replied Angoth, keeping the disappointment out of his voice. "Much honor was gained today in this battle."

Krilen let out a deep, cold breath as he thought over the battle; he knew that if the humans had not run they could have probably destroyed his fleet even though it would have cost them substantially. He wondered why they had disengaged. He put the thought from his mind, for now he needed to see that his own flagship was repaired. The 1,200-meter dreadnought IronHand had suffered several missile strikes during the battle, and its armored hull was covered with numerous scars.

The WarStorm dropped out of hyperspace and exited the swirling blue-white vortex in system 920-J. Around the WarStorm other ships were also appearing. In moments, the entire fleet was safely in the system and forming up on the flagship.

"Get me a report on ship losses and damage," Amanda ordered as she let out a long sigh. They had made it safely away from the battle, and she knew it would take the Hocklyns some time to find them if they sent out their escort cruisers in a search pattern. Some of her ships needed to initiate major repairs before they jumped again.

The battle was over, and she knew that she had won. It had been costly, but it had served its purpose in allowing the Hocklyns to feel that they had stopped the human advance into their space. If all went as planned, the Hocklyns would spend some time consolidating their positions before pushing back into the space the Federation had taken away from them.

Commander Evans spent a few minutes speaking to various ship commanders and reviewing parts of the recent battle to determine their exact losses. When she was finished, she turned toward Admiral Sheen. "We lost one Monarch heavy cruiser, five light cruisers, and seven destroyers."

"Hocklyn losses?" asked Amanda, recoiling inwardly at the ship losses. They had lost more ships than expected. Some of the commanders of those ships she had come to know very well. It seemed as if in every battle now she lost someone she knew.

"One dreadnought, four war cruisers, and twelve of their escort cruisers," Commander Evans replied. "If we could have just used the Devastator Threes we could have destroyed their entire fleet!"

Amanda stood up and looked over at Evans. "The time will come when we can use those missiles. For now, we will stay in this system for twelve hours to conduct repairs, and then the fleet will go to the Careth system. Admiral Strong has constructed two fleet repair bays on their orbiting space station where we can repair our more heavily damaged ships. I will be in my quarters if needed. Take the fleet to Condition Three until we are ready to depart."

"Yes, Admiral," Evans replied as she prepared to pass on the orders. She knew she would be extremely busy for the next few hours.

Amanda walked through the WarStorm still feeling numb from the losses in the battle. It had been necessary, and they had achieved their goal, but she still hated losing people; she always would. Sometimes she still wished she were only an executive officer as she had been for Fleet Admiral Streth on the old StarStrike back in the original Federation.

Reaching her quarters, she went inside, sat down on the large comfortable couch, and closed her eyes. She sat there for several minutes as she thought about her actions in the recent battle; there was nothing she could have done differently.

Opening her eyes, she gazed across the small room at a picture of her parents that hung on the far wall. It was a photo of happier times when her parents had lived on Krall Island on Aquaria. It showed them standing in front of their vacation home on the popular resort island. She wondered what her parents would think if they could see her now. Closing her eyes again, she soon fell into a troubled sleep. In her dreams, she could see the worlds of the old Federation burning as the Hocklyns nuked the helpless planets.

Amanda awoke and was startled to see that nearly six hours had passed. The battle must have taken more out of her emotionally than she had thought. Standing up, she went into her bedroom and taking off her uniform, quickly took a refreshing shower. Stepping back out, she looked at herself in the large bedroom mirror. Her brunette hair was cut short, and her blue eyes stared back at her. Her stomach was flat, and she had all the right curves but not excessively. She was thirty-nine years old and had been in the Fleet since she was twenty. With the medical treatments available in the Federation, she was still considered to be very young.

She kept to a rigorous exercise routine to keep in shape. She knew that her husband Richard liked her figure, and just thinking about Richard made Amanda realize just how lonely she felt. As an admiral, she could not allow herself to get too close to members of her crew. The only people she felt she could confide in were Commander Evans and a few others in the Command Center that had been on the old StarStrike.

After putting on a clean uniform, Admiral Sheen walked back through the flagship heading toward the Command Center. Whenever she passed a member of the crew, they halted and stood at attention as she passed. It took her a few minutes, and then she was back in the Command Center. After stepping through the heavily armored hatch and past the two marines that guarded it, she took her place at the command console in the center of the busy room.

"Ship repairs to the WarStorm are complete," Commander Evans reported upon seeing the admiral. "Other ships report that they are making substantial progress and we should be ready to jump in a few more hours. I also made up a list of the casualties in the recent battle. It is ready to be sent to the Federation so next of kin can be notified."

Amanda nodded and then noticed how worn out the commander looked. Amanda wondered how long it had been since Evans had gotten any sleep. "Samantha," Amanda spoke in a sympathetic voice. "Go to your quarters and get some rest; I can handle this."

Commander Evans nodded. She was too tired to argue. It only took her a moment to leave the Command Center and head toward her quarters.

Looking around, Amanda noticed that there had been a shift change during her absence. She saw that Lieutenant Karen Ashton from the old StarStrike was the only first shift officer still present. Amanda walked over to the lieutenant and touched her gently on the shoulder. "Lieutenant, aren't you supposed to be off duty?"

"Yes, Admiral," replied Ashton, looking up. "I did take a few hours, but I wanted to get the next few jumps plotted."

Amanda nodded. Lieutenant Ashton was one of the best navigation officers in the Fleet. "Once you're finished Lieutenant, go get some rest."

"Yes, Admiral," the young blonde replied with a nod. "I just have one more jump to plot and then I'll go."

Amanda returned to her command console and spent the next few hours talking to various commanders in the Fleet checking on the progress of their repairs. She felt pleased at the progress that was being made. Some of the internal damage was being routed around to bring ships back up to full operational status. Other damage, particularly to the armored hulls of the ships, could only be mended in a repair bay and would have to wait until they reached the safety of the Careth system.

A few hours later, Amanda was satisfied that everything that could be done had been finished. All the ship commanders felt confident that they could now make it to Careth. It was time to leave this section of Hocklyn space.

"All ships, prepare to jump," she ordered as she sat back down behind the command console.

She looked at the main viewscreen and could see blue-white space vortexes beginning to open. For close to two months, Second Fleet had been going from one small battle to the next. It would be good to give the crews some time off. Amanda knew that several resorts had been built on the bears' planet for the human crews of the warfleets. The only thing Amanda regretted was that Richard would not be there to share her leave time.

Moments later, the WarStorm entered a swirling spatial vortex and vanished. This part of Operation First Strike was complete, and now the second part would begin.

Chapter Two

Admiral Sheen breathed a deep sigh of relief as they made the final jump into the Careth system, home to the bears. The bears were actually called Carethians but, due to the fact that they vaguely resembled Earth bears, the nickname had stuck. The bears had accepted the nickname after learning about the ferocious animals that lived upon Earth.

"We're being hailed by the light cruiser Fury," Lieutenant Angela Trask reported as she sent the WarStorm's ID codes to the light cruiser. This was now standard procedure for any ship or fleet entering a human held system.

Amanda knew the Fury was assigned to Fourth Fleet, commanded by Admiral Jeremy Strong. "Inform the Fury that we will be going into orbit around Careth for some downtime and ship repair. Admiral Strong already knows we're coming." Amanda had previously notified Strong about the damage Second Fleet had received in the battle with the Hocklyns. He had assured her that he would have the two repair bays as well as the four fleet repair ships ready to receive her ships.

Angela sent the message and then turned toward the admiral. "The Fury says we have permission to micro-jump to Careth and that we will enjoy the new resorts. The commander of the Fury says the bears have done a fantastic job building the accommodations for us to enjoy on leave."

"I heard the new resorts are on one of their oceans," Commander Evans commented with a broad smile. She definitely needed to work on her tan, and she couldn't wait to get down to the planet. It had been a tiring and stressful two months not knowing when they would stumble across a major Hocklyn fleet. It would be good to get her mind off the war for a few days.

"Set up a micro-jump to just outside of Careth's gravity well, and once we arrive we need to set up yard time for our ships that need to be repaired," Amanda ordered with a nod.

She knew it would be good for her ship crews to have some extended leave. It would improve morale as well as improve their efficiency and help to relieve the stress from the last battle. Amanda knew she could certainly use it.

There were ten planets in the bears' home system, with the fourth being located in the Goldilocks zone and home to the Carethians. The bears had been slaves under the Hocklyns until Admiral Strong had destroyed the two escort cruisers guarding the planet and freed them. Now the bears were becoming staunch allies and helping to build massive defenses above their world in preparation for the eventual return of the Hocklyns.

More blue-white vortexes formed in front of Second Fleet, and the ships entered them only to exit new vortexes a few seconds later closer to the bears' home world. It had taken them three days to travel from the scene of their last battle to the Careth system.

On the main viewscreen of the WarStorm, the massive space station in orbit around Careth appeared. It had grown tremendously in the past two months as the bears and the humans labored intensively on it. Setting close to it were four massive fleet repair ships that had been working non-stop expanding the station. It originally was two kilometers across and supported a large landing bay for small shuttles and freighters. Now it had grown to more than six kilometers across and contained two large repair bays for fleet ships as well as new landing bays for fighters and bombers. The construction was ongoing, and the station was still far from being completed.

On the tactical hologram, the planet seemed to be surrounded by blue and green icons. Amanda knew the blue icons were defensive satellites, though she noticed with surprise that a number of these were unusually large. She would have to ask Admiral Strong about those. The green icons were Admiral Strong and Admiral Stillson's ships. Amanda was surprised to see that the Ceres relief fleet was still here; she wondered what else had changed during her two-month absence. She also noticed that a big part of Admiral Kimmel's supply fleet was in orbit around Careth.

Admiral Strong was on board the large space station meeting with Grayseth, Admiral Stillson, and Admiral Kimmel. They had been discussing the continued expansion of the space station as well as the offensive and defensive weapons it was to be equipped with. Ariel had been vital in this as she could quickly evaluate their plans and suggest changes. The dark haired AI was currently busy on the Avenger and had not been able to attend the meeting.

Jeremy's mini-com went off in his right ear, informing him that Admiral Sheen's fleet had just arrived outside of Careth's gravity well and was proceeding toward orbit. "Second Fleet has just arrived," he informed the others. "They suffered a lot of damage in their recent battle and are in need of major repairs."

"That means the Hocklyns will be arriving soon," Admiral Stillson commented in a grave voice, leaning back in his chair and looking at the others. "We still have much to do before we're ready for a major battle."

"We need to speed up our timeline," Jeremy stated, determined to defend the bears' home system. He had become very close to the bears in the last few months and had no intention of leaving them undefended. "Let's assume we have between six to ten weeks before we see an attack here. That means we need to have the station completed and its weapons ready six weeks from today."

"That will be a major undertaking," Admiral Kimmel spoke with a deep sigh as he thought about the resources he had available. "But with the help from Grayseth's people, I believe it is doable."

"My people will do whatever is necessary," Grayseth spoke in his powerful voice. "We will never be slaves to the evil ones again!"

"We will stand with you," Jeremy promised solemnly, staring at the large figure of Grayseth. The bear would easily tower over Jeremy if they were standing next to each other. "In this we will hunt together."

"We will hunt together," Grayseth repeated, his large brown eyes glowing in affirmation.

"The new fighters and bombers from Ceres will be arriving in two more days," Admiral Stillson added as he looked down at a computer pad he was holding. He had just received a communication from Admiral Teleck before coming to the meeting. "They are also sending twenty-four more of the new defensive battle stations."

Grayseth grinned at this information. To most, the grin would have been frightening at the sharp teeth it revealed. "The new fighters and bombers will be well received by my people," Grayseth spoke.

The new fighters and bombers had enlarged cockpits and controls so the bears could operate them. Already, hundreds of bears were working in hastily assembled simulators to prepare them to fly the new ships. When the Hocklyns returned, Grayseth's people would join the humans in space to defend their planet.

Jeremy was pleased to hear about the battle stations; they would add considerably to his offensive and defensive capability. "We will also be positioning all of our destroyers in the same orbit as the defensive satellites," Jeremy added as he thought about the plan to defend the planet. "The destroyers are too vulnerable in a fleet action. They will serve better if we use them to protect the satellites. Admiral Sheen lost seven in her most recent battle with the Hocklyns."

"We will also have ships to add," Grayseth spoke as he thought about the work being done in the secret underground cities on Careth. "We are adapting your technology to many of the smaller ships we built in secret. They will be ready in six weeks."

Jeremy had seen the small ships of the Carethians. The bears had established a number of deep underground cities they had kept secret from the Hocklyn occupiers. They had almost been ready to attempt to overthrow the Hocklyns and free their world when Fourth Fleet arrived and did it for them.

The small ships were one hundred meters long and carried a crew of twenty with powerful sublight engines. They were equipped with heavy railguns and were now being modified to add energy shields and several small missile tubes. The bears were being given a smaller class of Klave missile tipped with a tactical nuclear warhead. Jeremy also knew that the bears had nearly two hundred of these small ships.

"We will meet in two more days when the new supply fleet from Ceres arrives," Jeremy informed them as he stood up. "I need to meet with Admiral Sheen and arrange for her ships to be repaired and crews to take leave on Careth. I also need to go over the weapons plans for the station with Ariel."

"The resorts are ready for your people," Grayseth rumbled. "We are pleased that you approve of them."

"You have done a fantastic job with the resorts," Jeremy responded with a friendly nod. He had gone down to Careth with Grayseth and inspected them. Grayseth had insisted that Jeremy give his approval before they were opened. "Our people really appreciate what you have done for us."

"It's the least we could do," Grayseth responded. He liked these humans; in many ways they were much like his own race. Grayseth hoped this alliance was the beginning of a long and trusting friendship.

A few days later, Amanda was down at one of the seaside resorts the Carethians had built for Humans to use. She had been pleased to find that the resorts were very plush with all the amenities. Even more surprising was the fact that a number of Federation civilians had been brought in to help operate them. Amanda suspected it was because the

Carethians had felt other Humans would know more about what would be expected at the resorts.

Amanda was lying on a lounge chair next to the water with Samantha Evans, sipping a relaxing glass of iced tea. It was nice to get away from the fleet and burden of command. Only this morning had she finished with the arrangements to have all of her damaged ships repaired. She had spent nearly two days setting priorities and meeting with Admirals Strong and Kimmel. She knew her ships were in good hands and she could relax.

They had only been on the beach a couple of hours when Amanda noticed someone was blocking the sun. She looked up and her mouth fell open in amazement. Her husband Richard was standing there, with a big grin on his face.

"Richard!" she screamed in astonishment, jumping up and wrapping her arms around him. "Where did you come from?"

He laughed and untwined himself from his wife's arms after giving her a long, passionate kiss. "I came with the supply fleet that arrived earlier today. Admiral Streth sent a message that he thought you would have some leave time in another week or so and suggested that I come out with the fleet. Since he couldn't afford to let you come back to New Tellus to take leave, here I am."

"That's so much like Admiral Streth," Amanda spoke, her eyes glowing with excitement at seeing Richard. "He always seems to be watching out for me."

Richard looked over at Samantha and saw that she had stood up and was watching them with a happy smile. The commander was wearing a modest, white two-piece swimming suit and looked very alluring in it. "Hello, Commander; how are you doing?"

"We're on leave, so please call me Samantha," Evans replied pleasantly and then, with a knowing smile, she added. "I'm glad you could come out to see Amanda. We have two week's leave coming, so you two should be able to get reacquainted very well."

Amanda blushed at what Samantha was implying. She was so glad to see Richard; this was just what she needed! "Richard, sit down and tell Samantha and I about what's been going on in the Federation. What are people thinking about this war?"

Richard sat down next to his wife, holding her hand, and began. "As you know, we have a chain of communication buoys between Fleet Admiral Streth's main base and New Tellus. We've been getting an update each day on the progress of Operation First Strike, and it's been the hot topic on all the media channels. The admiralty is highly pleased, and the civilians believe that Admiral Streth could walk on water if he so desired."

"I wouldn't be surprised if he could," Samantha commented with a grin. She came from Harmony and had always been taught that someday Admiral Streth would be awoken and lead the humans to victory over the Hocklyns. So far, he had done a pretty good job of it.

"But the Hocklyns are bound to counterattack, and then what will they think?" Amanda asked and then proceeded to tell Richard about her most recent battle.

"So they finally managed to stop the advance into their space," Richard spoke in understanding. "We knew that would happen sooner or later, and the civilians know that First Strike was just to buy time for the Federation to finish arming itself and get all the planetary defenses set up."

"We have some big battles ahead," commented Samantha, knowing that many of the ships in Operation First Strike might not make it back home once the Hocklyns launched their counterattack.

"We're going to lead the Hocklyns back to the Federation," Amanda said worriedly, still finding it hard to believe that Richard was sitting next to her. "I wish we didn't have to do that."

"That has been the plan all along, for us to lead them back to New Tellus and attempt to destroy them," added Samantha, hoping that her home world back in the Alpha Centauri system was ready. She knew there had been plans to put some massive defenses in orbit to go with the ones already there. Only Earth had a larger human population than Harmony.

"We're ready for them," Richard replied confidently. "If they follow you back to New Tellus, they will die there!"

"I hope you're right," Amanda responded, her blue eyes focusing on her husband. She felt sure New Tellus could handle the Hocklyns, but she wasn't so sure about the AIs. The AIs still frightened her after what they had done to the original Federation.

Samantha listened to the two talk for a while longer, then stood up and wandered down the beach. She knew the two needed some alone time, and she would make sure they had plenty of it.

Jeremy was in the newly completed Command Center in the space station speaking with Grayseth. Both bears and humans, in almost equal numbers, staffed the large room. At the moment, he was waiting for the commander of the newly arrived supply fleet to make an appearance, if it could be called a supply fleet. Looking at one of the numerous holographic tactical displays, he was amazed at the warships that had accompanied the fleet. Some he had expected, but not the sheer number that had put in an appearance.

There were thirty supply ships in the fleet, including several of the new fleet design being built at New Tellus. There were four battlecruisers, eight battlecarriers, six of which had brought the new defensive battle stations, six Monarch heavy cruisers, six heavy strikecruisers, twenty light cruisers, and twenty destroyers. What was even more surprising was that all the ships except the supply ships were obviously from Ceres. Jeremy knew Ceres had a large supply of warships in its construction and ship bays; they had spent the last one hundred years building ships non-stop just for this war.

"An admiral has come on board from the new fleet," Grayseth reported as one of the bears working communications sent the message over to him.

Jeremy nodded. A fleet that large would have to have an admiral in command. He was curious to see who it was and why no one had said anything.

After a few minutes, the heavily guarded hatch to the Command Center swung open, and Jeremy's eyes widened when he saw who was standing there. He instantly snapped to attention as he watched Admiral Teleck step into the room; he was one of the last people that Jeremy had expected to see. He was in charge of all of Ceres's military forces and had been primarily responsible for promoting Jeremy to the rank of rear admiral.

"At ease, Admiral," Teleck spoke with a friendly smile as he strode up to Jeremy. "This space station is impressive."

"Thank you, Sir," Jeremy replied as he relaxed. "I wasn't expecting to see you." Then, gesturing toward Grayseth, Jeremy continued. "This is Grayseth, the Carethian's military commander."

"Live long and hunt together," Admiral Teleck spoke, acknowledging the bear.

"Live long and hunt together," Grayseth replied, pleased that this great admiral had studied their customs. It spoke well for the humans and their leaders.

"Do we have someplace we can talk?" Admiral Teleck asked. "Grayseth may come with us since this involves his world."

Jeremy nodded and led the admiral to a small conference room just off the Command Center set up to accommodate both Humans and Carethians. He wondered what was going on that it required Admiral Teleck to put in an appearance this far from home.

After Jeremy and Grayseth were seated, Admiral Teleck turned to them and began speaking. "I spoke to Fleet Admiral Streth, and we both feel that the Hocklyns will begin moving back into the captured territory in just a matter of weeks."

"We thought that also," Jeremy replied, nodding his head in agreement. "We are working on a timeline of at least six weeks before they reach us here. We hope to have the station done as well as all the orbital defenses."

"That sounds reasonable," Teleck responded. Then, in a more serious tone of voice, "Jeremy, what are your plans? I have spoken to President Kincaid and Fleet Admiral Johnson and we have reached a decision. This was not an easy decision for any of us, and it could have some grave consequences for the morale of the Federation once it becomes known. We will not force your fleet to withdraw from Careth when Admiral Streth retreats from this section of space. The decision will be up to you."

Grayseth looked over at Jeremy and spoke in a solemn and controlled voice. "Admiral Strong, you have become a good and trusting friend. Thanks to you, my world is once again free and growing strong. Across our entire world, our young are once more being taught the old ways and traditions. We will resist the evil ones when they return. We cannot in good faith expect you and your people to stay and face what may be a losing battle."

Jeremy was silent as he listened to Grayseth, knowing the bear was speaking from his heart. He knew that without his fleet, the bears had only a slight chance of holding off the Hocklyns, and if an AI ship appeared that chance dropped to zero. If he were to return to the Federation and Careth was destroyed by the returning Hocklyns, Jeremy knew that he could never live with himself knowing his fleet might have made a difference.

"I will not leave," Jeremy spoke, his eyes meeting the large brown ones of Grayseth. "In this battle we will be one and hunt together. Our enemy is the same and must be stopped; the Hocklyns will not be allowed to return to your world." Jeremy had long since made this decision; he would not leave the bears to face the Hocklyns alone. He knew the crews of his fleet felt the same.

Grayseth reached out, placed his large hand on top of Jeremy's, and nodded. At this moment, a bond was formed; one that nothing would ever break apart.

Admiral Teleck nodded. He had expected that answer from Admiral Strong even though there would be much concern in the Federation when it was discovered that Jeremy and the other special members of the Avenger had elected to stay behind and defend the bears. He strongly suspected that when the civilian population discovered Admiral Strong's reasons for staying behind and defending the bears there would be a massive upwelling of popular support for his decision. It was the kind of stuff that created heroes.

"I want you to know that Ceres is fully behind your decision, as well as the president and Fleet Admiral Johnson," Teleck spoke. It showed the growth in Jeremy as an admiral, and that pleased Teleck immensely. "When I leave, a number of the ships in my fleet will be remaining. They are all from Ceres and crewed by volunteers who know they might not be seeing home again for quite some time."

"Thank you, Sir," Jeremy replied, his eyes opening wide. He had never expected to have more than Fourth Fleet to defend the bears' home system with.

"Admiral Stillson's fleet over the past two months has been brought back up to full strength. After a few personnel changes, his fleet will also be remaining. I will be leaving you two battlecruisers, two battlecarriers, four Monarch heavy cruisers, four additional heavy strikecruisers, ten light cruisers, and all twenty of the destroyers that came with my fleet."

"Thank you, Sir," Jeremy spoke in a stunned voice as he realized all the extra firepower this would give him.

It made holding the bears' system a real possibility. He could really use the strikecruisers, since with their new programming and more powerful Devastator Three missiles they were the only ships capable of taking on an AI ship and winning. This could be a game changer for the Careth system.

"Jeremy," Admiral Teleck spoke in a more serious voice, his eyes taking on a grim look. "We will not be able to spare any more ships without seriously affecting Ceres's ability to defend itself. There will be two more trips made with supplies and twenty-four additional satellite battle stations, and then you will be on your own. We placed additional FTL communication buoys in place as we jumped to allow you to communicate with the Federation. Keep in mind that once the

Hocklyns and the AIs retake this section of space and advance on the Federation, you will be cut off with no safe way to return to Federation space."

"I understand, Sir," responded Jeremy, accepting the fact that it might be quite some time before any of his crews saw Federation space again. He knew and understood that once the Hocklyns arrived they might be on their own for a long time.

"Your people are honorable," Grayseth spoke as he realized the ramifications of what Admiral Teleck and Jeremy had just done. "You may have just assured my people's survival. We will never forget this. From this day forward, we will fight at your side until the evil ones are defeated."

"You're welcome, Grayseth," responded Admiral Teleck, gravely. "We will honor your alliance with the Federation and do everything in our power to ensure your world remains free. Now, let's discuss just how we are going to defend this system from the Hocklyns."

Amanda was in the resort with Richard lying in bed and just enjoying each other's presence. As they lay there in the afterglow of their lovemaking, he began to tell her of the decision by the higher ups to allow Admiral Strong to remain and attempt to defend the Carethians. He also informed her that Admiral Teleck had come with them.

"Admiral Teleck!" Amanda spoke, sitting up. "If Admiral Teleck is here then I need to go up to the station and report."

"Not until tomorrow," Richard said, pulling her back down beside him. "He will be here for a week or more before it's time for us to leave."

Amanda nodded. She was pleased to know that she had Richard for at least a week. She rolled over and kissed him. He reached for her and soon they were lost in each other once more as their heated passion took over.

In the Command Center of the space station, an alarm sounded. An unauthorized hyperjump had been detected in a nearby system by a hyper detection buoy. The officer in front of the console instantly notified his commanding officer, who came over and studied the data.

"Looks like one ship only," the captain commented as he studied the information. He instantly notified the major who was currently the senior officer in command. "We have an unauthorized hyperjump in system 211-M, only two light years away."

The major called up the data on his command console as one of the Carethians came over, and the two discussed it. It took only a moment for them to notify Admiral Strong who instantly ordered two light cruisers to be immediately dispatched to the system. Everyone knew that this could be a Hocklyn armed scout sent to probe the human defenses.

The major also ordered the station to go to Condition Three until the validity of the threat could be ascertained. While it wasn't likely, there was a slim possibility of this being the prelude to an attack.

The light cruisers Kallen and Sidney emerged from two swirling spatial vortexes into system 211-M and instantly began searching for the unknown ship. From the data they had from the FTL detection buoy, the unknown should be within two million kilometers of their exit point.

"Nothing," Lieutenant Dalk reported as his sensors came back negative.

Commander Linnert of the Kallen frowned and wondered if the hyper detection buoy could have been wrong. "Keep an eye on your sensors; something isn't right." He then turned toward his executive officer. "Keep the ship at Condition One until we determine for sure there is no threat." He passed the same order on to the Sidney.

The two 700-meter Federation light cruisers were motionless in space as their powerful sensors scanned the area around them. For twenty minutes, they held their positions as their sensors swept the system.

A little over one million kilometers away the stealth destroyer New Ashton had gone to Condition One upon detecting the two Federation warships. The ship had come from the Old Federation world of New Providence on a mission to find the Humans that were fighting the Hocklyns.

"Are you sure they're Federation light cruisers?" asked Commander Strone, looking over at the sensor operator.

"Yes, Sir," the lieutenant replied with excitement in his eyes. "It's a definite computer match even though there are some slight differences."

Strone nodded. That was to be expected since the last time they had seen a Federation light cruiser was over four hundred years ago. He had been sent to this section of space to see if it was indeed Federation ships that were fighting the Hocklyns. There had been much debate back on New Providence about how this could be possible. It had seemed extremely unlikely that the ships that Fleet Admiral Streth had escaped with could have built up a sufficient population and tech base to mount such an attack. However, if their sensors were right, there in front of them were two Federation light cruisers.

"Very well, prepare to come out of stealth and send our ID codes to the two cruisers," he ordered, reaching a quick decision. "Let's hope they still recognize the old codes and don't open fire." He knew his lightly armed destroyer would be no match for a light cruiser, let alone two of them.

"Hostile contact at one million kilometers," Lieutenant Dalk called out as a red threat icon suddenly appeared on his sensor screen."

"Crap," muttered Commander Linnert, seeing how close the enemy was. "Contact the Sidney and tell them to prepare to engage." If this was a Hocklyn scout ship or escort cruiser, they needed to destroy it as quickly as possible.

"Hold," the communications operator suddenly called out, her voice sounding confused. "I am receiving ship IDs from the unknown contact."

"Ship IDs?" replied Linnert in astonishment, turning his gaze toward communications. "Who are they?"

"I'm not sure," replied the ensign, sounding confused. "The ID codes are old Federation. The ship is called the New Ashton."

"New Ashton," spoke Lieutenant Dalk, turning pale as he recalled his old Federation history. "That was the capital city on New Providence!"

"Ensign, try to raise that ship," ordered Commander Linnert, suspecting a Hocklyn trick. "Ask them to explain who they are and what they are doing here!"

Jeremy was still in his meeting with Admiral Teleck and Grayseth when his mini-com activated. His eyes narrowed and his heart rate quickened as he listened to the impossible report. After a moment, he looked over at Admiral Teleck, wondering how he would receive this news. It was like a person long dead suddenly turning up alive and healthy.

"Admiral Teleck, there was an unauthorized hyperjump into a nearby system a short time ago," he began. "I sent two light cruisers to investigate in case it was a Hocklyn armed scout."

"Yes, I recall you doing that," Teleck responded. He hoped it had turned out to be a false alarm.

"The light cruisers have found a ship," continued Jeremy, finding it hard to believe what he was about to say. He took a deep breath and then continued. "It is a Federation destroyer from New Providence. They claim they have come here searching for us."

"New Providence!" Admiral Teleck repeated, his eyes growing wide in astonishment. "That's impossible! The population of New Providence was wiped out by the Hocklyns. There are no survivors in the old Federation."

"Nevertheless, that's what they claim," Jeremy replied evenly. "The two light cruisers are bringing the ship here. They should be ready to jump shortly."

Admiral Teleck leaned back in his chair as he thought about what this might mean. Could humans have actually survived in hiding back in the old Federation? He knew there had been a serious attempt to do so on New Providence. If there were any survivors in the old Federation, New Providence would be the logical place. What would this mean to the new Federation and the war effort if this ship was actually from where they claimed?

"Contact Admiral Sheen and Admiral Andrews and get them both up here," ordered Admiral Teleck, reaching a quick decision. "Admiral Andrews is from New Providence and Admiral Sheen went there on a secret mission during the New Horizon incident. Perhaps they can shed some light on this situation. I also want the supposed origin of this ship kept a secret. If anyone asks, it is a new Federation ship that has just returned from a secret mission. If there are survivors on New Providence we can't let that become general knowledge for their own safety."

Jeremy nodded. He would also contact Ariel on the Avenger. She was very familiar with the old Federation and might be of some help. Jeremy suspected if this ship was really from New Providence that the war was about to get even more complicated and much more dangerous.

Chapter Three

The 400-meter destroyer New Ashton had docked to the space station, and Admiral Strong and Admiral Teleck were waiting for the people on board to make an appearance. Two full squads of marines, as well as a squad of heavily armed bears, were waiting for the hatch to open. Admirals Sheen and Andrews were en route from the surface of Careth and would be arriving shortly. Both had been stunned when they had been informed that a Federation destroyer from New Providence had put in an appearance.

"How can this ship actually be from New Providence?" Jeremy asked as he kept his eyes glued to the hatch. Everything he had heard in the past stated clearly that the old Federation worlds had been wiped out.

"General Allister stayed behind in a number of hidden military bunkers," Admiral Teleck answered. "They were going to attempt to hide from the Hocklyns and save as many civilians as possible. At the time of the New Horizon incident, Admiral Sheen was sent on a mission to find out if anyone had survived. As you know, she was detoured while searching for your ship, but she did finally complete her mission. They found a few survivors on Aquaria, but none on any of the other planets. We thought General Allister had failed. Now it seems he may have succeeded after all."

"Imagine staying hidden from the Hocklyns for all of these years," responded Jeremy, shaking his head. He couldn't comprehend how difficult that would have been. "It seems as if it would be almost impossible."

"I would have thought so too," Teleck replied his eyes focused on the hatch of the small destroyer. "But it seems as if somehow they managed to do just that. Keep in mind that Grayseth's people have underground cities on Careth that the Hocklyns never found."

The hatch opened, and a man and a woman stepped out. One was obviously the commander of the ship from his fleet uniform and insignia, but the other was a civilian.

They came to a stop in front of the two admirals, and the commander came to attention and saluted. "I am Commander Strone of the New Providence destroyer Ashton, and this is Maureen Arden of the New Providence Senate."

"At ease, Commander," Admiral Teleck responded. "I am Admiral Teleck, and this is Admiral Strong. We represent the new Federation of Worlds which is based on our old Federation."

"Then you are Federation survivors?" Senator Arden spoke, her eyes widening at the revelation. "We hadn't thought that was possible."

"Yes and no," Admiral Teleck responded. "Let's go to a conference room where we can be more comfortable and talk privately. We have two other admirals we are waiting for who will be joining us shortly."

The four went to a conference room and were soon joined by Amanda and Richard. Then it was time for revelations.

Senator Arden began first by giving a brief description of the situation in the old Federation of Worlds and what they had done to survive. "Immediately after Admiral Streth left the Federation the Hocklyns returned with a vengeance. They scoured all the planets looking for human survivors and eradicating them whenever any were found. On New Providence General Allister stayed hidden, only sending out occasional patrols to bring in scattered groups of survivors. Despite the Hocklyns believing they had killed everyone, they continued to monitor the Federation worlds. Even today a routine patrol goes through each system weekly, scanning it."

"Those early years must have been tough," Amanda spoke as she recalled what General Allister had planned to do. She was in awe that his plan had actually worked.

"The last time I spoke to General Allister he thought there was a remote chance that he could remain hidden. I am glad to see that he succeeded," added Richard, recalling his days in the shipyard above New Providence.

"You spoke to General Allister?" Senator Arden repeated, her eyes growing wide in astonishment. "That was over four hundred years ago!"

"Yes," Admiral Teleck said, and then explained. "After Admiral Streth arrived in Earth's solar system a number of key personnel went into cryosleep to be awakened when it was time to renew the war with the Hocklyns."

"Earth?" said Senator Arden, looking confused. "I have heard that word mentioned in old legends. It supposedly represents the world from which we originated. I thought that was just a fairy tale; everyone did."

"Earth's real enough," Admiral Teleck responded. He then proceeded to explain to the two what had transpired with Earth and the establishing of the new Federation.

"You mean to tell me that Admiral Streth is still alive!" Commander Strone spoke, his eyes widening in awe at the thought of meeting the legendary admiral of the old Federation.

"Yes, and you will be meeting him at his base before you continue on to Earth," Admiral Teleck promised. Then he looked at the two. "I assume you want to go on to the new Federation and speak to its leaders."

"Yes," replied Senator Arden, feeling excited at the prospect. She was anxious to see this new Federation for herself. If it was as powerful as Admiral Teleck had indicated they would have much to talk about.

Commander Strone nodded his head. He had seen all the powerful Federation warships that were around this planet. The battlecruisers and the battlecarriers had been impressive sights on the New Ashton's viewscreens. The largest warship New Providence had were destroyers; it wasn't practical to build anything larger in the underground construction bays. It was impossible to launch a battlecruiser or carrier from the surface of a planet.

The meeting went on for several more hours, and both sides were amazed at what each had to say. It seemed that humanity was much harder to kill than the Hocklyns had realized.

On the border of Hocklyn space, an AI ship prowled. The 1,500-meter sphere of death floated silently in the system it had just jumped into. Its mission was quite simple, find several human ships and engage them in order to discover everything they could about the human's weapons and technology level. The reappearance of humans had deeply shaken the AIs.

They were well aware that in the distant past their creators the Altons, had brought the humans to the Federation worlds to prevent the AIs from spreading out across the galaxy. Now the humans had attacked one of their proxy races with worrisome success. This was a war the AIs would have to take a direct hand in, for the humans could be a serious threat as they had already demonstrated by destroying two AI ships.

Over a period of hours, the AI ship remained motionless as it extended its powerful sensors to encompass several nearby star systems. After detecting nothing, the AI ship vanished into a white vortex and jumped farther into the region of space the humans had taken from the Hocklyns. Several former slave worlds might have human ships still in orbit. They would search those and see what could be found.

Jeremy had returned to the Avenger to speak with Ariel. The ship's AI was a good friend as well as a protector. As he entered the Command Center, he was surprised to see Kelsey sitting at the command console. There were only a few crewmembers on duty since the Avenger was docked to the space station, and most of the crew was down on the bears' world on leave.

"Trying to take my job?" Jeremy teased as he walked up to her.

"Jeremy!" Kelsey spoke in a pleased voice. It had been several days since she had last seen him. Kelsey knew he was working extra hours with Grayseth setting up the defenses for the bears' planet. She blinked her blue eyes at him and smiled. "I might be; think I can get promoted to admiral?"

"Perhaps," he replied grinning. "I thought you were down at the resort with the others."

"It's boring without you there," Kelsey replied in a quieter voice so no one could overhear. "Katie and Kevin have a room together and haven't been coming out too often."

"About time," Jeremy spoke. Glad that his two friends were becoming closer. Katie and Kevin made an excellent couple. "What about Angela?"

"Last I saw of her she was hooking up with a good looking marine captain she met while scuba diving." Then, looking at Jeremy with a pleading look in her eyes, "Are you going to be able to take any time off? I still have the room reserved for us at the resort. The food there is great, and they have several fruit drinks that are very similar to that one you liked on New Tellus."

"It's possible later this week," answered Jeremy as he thought about his busy schedule and everything he needed to do. He would really like to spend some quality time with Kelsey. "I might be able to come down and spend a day or two. Right now something else has come up that I have to deal with."

"The ship from New Providence," Kelsey said, nodding her head in acknowledgment.

"How did you know?" demanded Jeremy, frowning as he looked around making sure no one else had heard Kelsey's comment. "Where that ship came from is supposed to be a secret."

"I told her," spoke a voice from just behind him.

Spinning around, Jeremy saw a beautiful young woman with dark eyes and black hair that barely touched her shoulders. "Ariel, that information is classified!" Jeremy knew that very little escaped the talented and inquisitive AI.

"I have told no one but Kelsey," replied Ariel, crossing her arms over her breasts defensively.

"Neither the Hocklyns nor their masters, the AIs, can ever learn where that ship came from," Jeremy warned them in a serious voice. "The ship will be going on to Earth shortly, and all records of it ever being here will be erased from our systems."

"A wise decision," Ariel commented, her eyes focusing on Jeremy. "It would be ill advised to leave information that could someday reveal to the Hocklyns that there are still humans on one of the old worlds."

"What have you been able to find out about the ship they came in and the story about survivors on New Providence?" asked Jeremy, knowing Ariel had been snooping. He was still having a hard time accepting that a large group of survivors could have survived four hundred years deep in Hocklyn space without ever being discovered.

"Their ship is a stealth destroyer and very similar to our own newer stealth scouts," Ariel replied. She'd spent some time breaking into the New Ashton's core computer in order to confirm their story on her own. She had been concerned that this could be an elaborate ruse by the AIs to gather intelligence. She also made sure that there were no traces of her tampering with the New Ashton's computer system. "They do indeed come from New Providence, though a lot of pertinent information is missing from their core computer."

"A precaution to prevent the Hocklyns or AIs from learning where the humans are on the planet in case the ship was captured," suggested Kelsey, intrigued by what Ariel was saying.

Jeremy nodded; it all made sense. He was just relieved to know that the New Ashton ship was legitimate. Looking over at Kelsey, Jeremy felt a stirring of desire inside. He knew he needed to take a few days off and spend some time with her. Later this week he would arrange it; for now he needed to return to the space station for another meeting with Admiral Stillson and several bear engineers. They were going to be discussing the heavy pulse laser batteries that were going to be installed on the space station. Ariel had worked up a set of detailed specifications for the engineers to follow.

Before he left, he turned to Kelsey. "I promise I will try to take some time off. Keep the room at the resort and I will see what I can work out."

"You need the time off," Ariel said, looking intently at Jeremy. "Humans need to spend time alone with each other; it's what they do. Besides, you need to spend time with Kelsey; she needs you."

"Ariel," admonished Kelsey, shaking her head in dismay at the AI. "You're getting too personal, and you have been reading too many of those old romance novels in your files."

"Sorry," Ariel replied her deep dark eyes focusing on Kelsey. "I read the romance novels because that is one aspect of humans that I still don't understand very well."

"You're doing fine, Ariel," Jeremy spoke with a grin. "Just don't do anymore snooping in the New Ashton's computer files."

-

The AI ship jumped to a system that contained an inhabited world that only a few short months back had been under Hocklyn control. The four AIs in the ship's Control Room hovered just above the floor their tentacles carefully adjusting instruments as they scanned the system.

"Human ships detected," one of the AIs spoke as the glowing orb that served for a head brightened. "Two of their light cruisers are in the system just outside the gravity well of the inhabited planet."

"So they can escape if Hocklyn ships are detected," a second AI suggested as it swiftly calculated the best method to take out the two human vessels.

"We will set our energy beams to disable their jump drives and then allow them to engage us as we analyze their weapons," the command AI ordered. "Once we have gathered all the necessary data, we will destroy them and return to Kenward Seven where the Hocklyn fleet is being rearmed."

As soon as the decision on a course of action was made, another white spatial vortex formed in front of the AI ship and it vanished. A few seconds later, it reappeared a bare 2,000 kilometers away from the two unsuspecting human light cruisers. Instantly, two beams of deadly white light flashed out, striking the human ships and disabling their jump drives. The AIs had accomplished their first goal and the human ships were trapped.

The two Federation light cruisers were on patrol just outside the gravity well of a small planet that Fifth Fleet had freed from the Hocklyns a short six weeks back. It had a small population of less than twenty million, and there was a moderate sized space station in orbit. Attempts had been made to speak with the inhabitants of the planet, but so far they had refused to respond to all attempts at communication. A number of the experts felt that it was due to a fear of reprisals from the Hocklyns when they returned.

The light cruisers Sphinx and Goliath were in the system watching for any signs of returning Hocklyn ships. If any were detected, they were to jump out and report the Hocklyn's presence using their FTL transmitter and then wait for further orders.

"Sensor contact," the sensor operator suddenly called out on the Sphinx as a bright red threat icon suddenly blossomed on his sensor screen. "Range to unknown is 2,000 kilometers."

"Crap, they're already in engagement range!" Alex Bartley, the executive officer, exclaimed as he looked up at the sensor screen.

"Go to Condition One and prepare to jump," Commander Rodriquez ordered. He passed the same instructions on to the Goliath. "Do we have an identity on the unknown?"

"Oh my God!" the sensor operator spoke with obvious fear in his voice as the red threat icon suddenly changed to orange. "It's an AI ship."

"How soon can we jump?" demanded Rodriquez, glancing over at Bartley. "We have no chance against that thing." An AI ship was the last thing they had expected to encounter.

"Two minutes," replied Bartley, shaking his head in alarm He knew what this meant. "Communications is reporting that all FTL channels are being jammed."

The Sphinx suddenly shuddered and seemed to leap to one side, and its hull made a terrible groaning noise. The lights dimmed and then brightened.

"What was that?" demanded Commander Rodriquez, looking over at damage control. "Were we hit?"

"They took out the jump drive," Bartley replied his face turning ashen as he realized they would not be leaving the system alive. "The Goliath is reporting the same thing."

Rodriquez nodded in understanding as he accepted their fate. "Load Devastator missiles in all tubes and prepare to fire. Helm, take us toward the AI. We're going to ram this ship down its throat. Tactical, fire everything we have at that monstrosity, including the kitchen sink." The commander then contacted the Goliath, ordering it to follow him in. He did not intend to let either ship fall into the hands of the AIs.

From the two light cruisers, sixteen Devastator missiles blasted out of the missile tubes and hurtled toward the 1,500-meter sphere that was the AI ship. The two ship's heavy bow pulse lasers began firing sending orange-red beams of light to impact harmlessly on the powerful energy screen of the AI. Then the Devastator missiles struck, and sixteen ten kiloton nuclear explosions rolled across the AI ship's energy screen in blinding nuclear fire. In one or two places, the screen flickered slightly, but that was all.

Inside the AI ship, the four AIs in the Control Center watch impassively as the two human cruisers threw every weapon at their disposal against their ship's powerful energy screen. One of the AIs checked the recording devices that were cataloguing and evaluating the weapons being used against the ship. Nothing these two human ships had were of concern or could be considered a threat.

Commander Rodriquez frowned as he realized the AIs were not returning fire. They were just sitting there, allowing his two ships to pummel their energy screen. Gathering intelligence on our ships and weapons, Rodriquez realized as the railguns on both ships opened up, striking the AI ship's screen with even more ordnance. They were firing explosive shells, and bright explosions crawled across the AI's screen.

In space, the area between the two ships was full of tracer rounds from the railguns, missile trails, and the orange-red beams of the lasers. Even the pulse laser batteries on the upper and lower hulls of the two Federation light cruisers were now firing.

Rodriquez shook his head, seeing how their weapons were having little effect against the AI. If he could get the Sphinx close enough, he intended to ram the huge 1,500-meter sphere. "Increase sublight speed to forty percent!"

"We have all the data necessary on these two ships," one of the AIs spoke as it studied some recording instruments. "It is time to end this."

One of the others moved forward and touched several controls with two of its tentacles. Instantly, the AI ship's potent energy weapons fired.

The deck heaved under Commander Rodriquez, sending him sprawling to the floor. Struggling to stand, he stumbled back to the command console hearing cries of pain and fear from the crew in the Command Center. Smoke and small fires were everywhere, and alarms were blaring loudly on the damage control console. Red lights were blinking on in rapid succession, indicating serious damage to the ship.

"We're done for," Bartley reported as he reached the command console. His right arm was hanging limply at his side, and blood was running down the side of his head. "The main fusion reactor is down, and Engineering is reporting we are running on the auxiliary. Shields are at twenty percent and dropping."

On the sensor screen, the green icon representing the Goliath suddenly blossomed and then faded away.

"Goliath is down," reported the sensor operator in a dull and frightened voice. "Its self-destructs activated."

"We can't let them board our ship," Commander Rodriquez spoke as he pulled a key from around his neck and inserted it into his console, gazing intently at Bartley. He knew his plan to ram the AI ship was now doomed to fail. Loss of the main reactor had shut down the ship's sublight drive.

"No, they will not have the Sphinx," his executive officer agreed as he reached for his own key and inserted it with a blood covered hand into its slot. Then, looking at Commander Rodriquez, Bartley nodded his head.

Both Federation officers turned their keys at the same time, and the two nuclear self-destructs in the Sphinx detonated simultaneously.

"They destroyed their ships," one of the AIs spoke as the bright glare of the nuclear explosions washed across their energy screen. "There will be nothing of value to recover."

"We have what we came for," the command AI responded. "It is time for us to return to Kenward Seven with the data we have gathered."

Moments later, another white spatial vortex formed and soon afterward, the AI ship was gone. It had completed its mission and eliminated two human ships. The human commanders would never know what had happened in this system.

At Kenward Seven, Fleet Commodore Resmunt gazed at the main viewscreen in the War Room of the dreadnought Liberator. On the screen was one of the massive fleet shipyards that built and maintained the Hocklyn fleet. The structure was over twenty kilometers across and had forty bays capable of building and repairing any warship. There were four of these massive shipyards in orbit around the planet.

Kenward Seven was a large world, rich in natural resources as was the entire system. Millions of Hocklyn slaves toiled on the planets, moons, and asteroids mining the resources and building the equipment needed by the massive shipyards. It was not uncommon for several thousand slaves a day to die in mining or construction accidents.

"How goes the refit?" First Leader Ganth asked as he stepped up next to the command pedestal, placing his right hand upon it. Ganth stood two meters tall and was powerfully built for a Hocklyn. He had won several honor duels in the past during physical combat.

"Another six weeks and it will be done," Resmunt responded in his rasping voice as he turned his dark eyes toward the First Leader. "Then five weeks to travel to the sector the humans have taken from us."

"There will be much honor for all of us when we return to fight," Ganth responded, pleased with the new weapons they had been given by the AIs. "How many AI ships will be accompanying the fleet?" Ganth didn't like the AI's presence, but against these new humans they might very well be needed.

"I don't know," answered Resmunt in his cold grating voice. "I'm not sure the AIs even know yet."

"What War Leaders will be going?" Ganth continued to ask. Since being driven from their main base by the humans, Fleet Commodore Resmunt had allowed Ganth more freedom to speak his mind.

"That is being decided by the High Council," Resmunt replied with a hint of aggravation in his voice. He would rather pick his own War Leaders than have the council do so.

Resmunt turned his gaze back to the viewscreen. It had changed to show several dreadnoughts settling into orbit above Kenward Seven. Shortly, he would be in charge of the largest warfleet ever gathered in the long history of the Hocklyn Slave Empire. If he succeeded in his campaign and destroyed the humans, then he would return to the home system in triumph. Perhaps he could even win a seat on the High Council.

"The AIs have ordered us not to sacrifice our ships to uphold our honor," continued Resmunt, agreeing with the decree from the AIs. "The humans are too powerful, and there will be no shame in withdrawing to preserve our ships if the tide of battle goes against us."

"That will be difficult for many First Leaders and others to accept," warned Ganth, tapping the blade at his waist. "They may not obey those orders in the heat of battle. The accruing of honor has been a big part of our military for untold generations, and it cannot stop overnight."

"I fear you are correct, First Leader," replied Resmunt, nodding his head in concern. "I am afraid in the coming war, we will lose many ships needlessly."

"We have a large empire and thousands of warships," continued Ganth, knowing even though their fleet here at Kenward Seven was large, there were many more ships that could be called upon from within the Empire if needed. "We can afford the losses, and I suspect the humans cannot. We are opposed by a few worlds at most, and once we have destroyed their fleets those worlds will fall and be destroyed as the AIs have demanded."

"You are right, of course," agreed Resmunt, seeing the logic in Ganth's words. "The fleet we are gathering will be an iron fist aimed at the heart of the humans. There will be many opportunities for our warriors to gain honor in the coming battles. In the end, the humans will fall before the might of our Empire."

"Honor will be ours," Ganth responded.

"Honor will be ours," Fleet Commodore Resmunt replied.

He just hoped everything worked out as First Leader Ganth had said. However, there was something about these humans and the way the AIs were going about this war that made him feel uneasy. He wished he knew what it was about the humans that worried the AIs. Resmunt stood at the command pedestal for a long time as he thought about the coming war. Deep inside of him something just didn't feel right, and he knew it concerned the humans.

Chapter Four

Deep in Hocklyn controlled space was the heavily populated capital world of Calzen. On its surface in the ornate halls of the High Council Chambers, the ten members of the council were meeting.

"The fleet we're sending against the humans is ridiculous," Councilor Jarles complained as his cold, dark eyes looked at each of the other councilors seeking support. "We have stopped the expansion of the entire Empire for this foolish war against these few worlds."

"We can't anger the AIs," Councilor Ruthan spoke up with deep concern in his voice. "They have already attacked us here as punishment for our failure to contain and report the presence of more humans. We can't fail again!" The recent attack by the AIs on the orbiting habitats had deeply shaken the councilor.

"Our warriors grow restless from this inaction," Jarles continued in disagreement. "Honor cannot be found unless we start to expand again. There are still tens of thousand of possible slave words waiting for our fleets to arrive; surely we don't need all of our ships to fight these humans."

"None of your family's habitats were destroyed in the recent AI attack!" snarled Ruthan, angrily. "You would be speaking differently if they had been." His own family had seen one of their ancestral habitats destroyed and tens of thousands had died.

"Enough!" roared High Leader Nartel, wanting this petty bickering to come to a stop. "The AIs have ordered us to undertake this war against the humans. They are to be annihilated. We have no choice but to obey, and once we have completed this war, the Empire will begin to expand once more. Many of our fleet units in the bordering sectors of the one the humans have attacked are being moved to protect our Empire from more attacks. Need I remind everyone on this council that the AIs are furnishing us with even more powerful weapons and shields for our ships?"

High Councilor Berken stood and looked around at the other council members. He folded his sinewy arms across the chest plate of his ceremonial light gray battle armor. "High Leader Nartel is right. With ships that are more powerful, we will be able to expand the Empire at an even greater pace than before. I want to remind all of you that we wouldn't be in this current situation if it wasn't for former

High Leader Ankler and his distant relative who kept the survival of the humans a secret."

"He paid with his life for his insolence," Ruthan spoke, his large eyes flashing red. "Our former High Leader got what he deserved!"

"I agree with Berken," High Councilor Desmonde added, rising to his feet and ignoring High Councilor Ruthan. "We need to decide on the War Leaders that will be accompanying Fleet Commodore Resmunt when he is finally ready to launch his attack on the humans. The sooner we can launch this attack, the sooner we can put this behind us."

"War Leader Versith of the dreadnought Viden is an excellent tactician," Berken spoke, thoughtfully. He had met the War Leader on several occasions and had been impressed by his knowledge of tactics.

"Former High Leader Ankler's son Jaseth is the Second Leader on the Versith," Ruthan reminded the councilors with a deep frown. "That may pose some problems in the future, particularly if he does well in this war."

"He has fought enough honor duels recently to be allowed to maintain his position," Nartel spoke, his eyes narrowing.

If Second Leader Jaseth were to achieve much honor in the coming war, it could pose a problem for Nartel later on. That was a situation he would deal with if and when it occurred. He could always assign Jaseth to some far and distant outpost in the Empire. Things like that had been done in the past.

"War Leader Osbith of the dreadnought BattleHand was with Resmunt at the fall of his base," Desmonde reminded them all. "He should be included since he has already fought the humans and his ships are currently being updated."

Nartel nodded and then spoke. "We have some very dependable War Leaders at Kenward Seven already. War Leaders Daseth, Zenth, Perth, Crytho, and Hilden will remain in command of their fleets. In addition, Commodores Aanith and Maseth will serve as Fleet Commodore Resmunt's second and third in command of the attack fleets."

"How soon before the attack is launched?" asked Councilor Jarles, knowing he had no choice but to support the war against the humans. The sooner the war was over with and the human worlds destroyed, the sooner they could begin expanding the Empire once again.

"The fleets will be ready in six weeks, then another five to travel to the sector the humans took from us," High Leader Nartel answered. "Once we have driven them from that sector we will continue onward to conquer and destroy their worlds."

"Do we know where their worlds are?" Desmonde asked, his black eyes growing even wider.

"We know where one of their worlds is located," High Leader Nartel replied. "The others will be close by. There will be enough ships in the attacking fleets that it will not take long to locate them."

"How many AI ships will be accompanying the fleet?" asked Ruthan, nervously. The AIs scared him because of what they could do to the Empire if they were displeased. They had already demonstrated their wrath and Ruthan didn't want to risk seeing that happen again.

"At least five," Nartel replied as he recalled what the AIs had said previously. "Perhaps more."

The council spent hours more discussing the upcoming war and then finally departed the Council Chambers. Only High Councilor Berken remained.

"Why are the AIs so afraid of these humans, High Leader?" demanded Berken in his rasping voice as the six digits of his left hand rested on the light gray battle armor that covered his chest. The two had known each other for many years and had kept few secrets from one another.

"I don't know," replied Nartel, shaking his head. "Something happened in the remote past that made the AIs feel these humans could pose a threat to them. In our first encounter with the humans four hundred years ago, we were not allowed to attempt to conquer their worlds. The AIs demanded that we destroy them immediately and even sent two of their warships to ensure that happened."

"And we failed because Ankler's ancestor allowed a large number of humans to escape," Berken commented with a deep frown spreading across his face. "If the AIs are afraid of these humans, shouldn't we be worried about the possible consequences of this upcoming war? I wish the AIs were more open about why these humans pose such a threat. Granted they have powerful warships, but our Empire should be able to crush them when the full force of our fleet is marshaled against their worlds."

"The human ships are more powerful than ours," Nartel conceded. "That gave them an initial advantage in our first engagements against them and when they attacked our Empire.

However, with the new weapons and updated energy shields the AIs are giving us we should be on an even footing. Our Empire is large, and I can't imagine the humans being able to stop us once we attack. We have the resources of a major portion of the galaxy; the humans can only have a few worlds to draw upon."

Berken nodded and then, standing up, exited the High Council Chambers. Nartel retired to his office and stepped out onto the balcony. It was nearly dark, and he gazed upward toward space. He could still see the shattered remains of the habitats the AIs had destroyed when they had decided to punish the Hocklyn High Council for not telling them about the humans. Millions of innocent Hocklyns had died due to High Leader Ankler keeping the humans existence a secret from the AIs. It would still be several long months before all the wreckage was cleared from orbit.

Nartel would not make that fatal mistake. He would send the most powerful fleet ever assembled by the Hocklyn Slave Empire to destroy the humans. Perhaps after they had won the war, the AIs would allow the Hocklyns to colonize the new worlds they had agreed to earlier and then abruptly taken away. If not, then High Leader Nartel would have to pass a law limiting the number of births allowed to Hocklyn families, one that would be highly unpopular and probably have to be enforced by the Protectors in the Hocklyn military.

Nartel let out a deep, rasping breath and touched the blade he always carried at his side. It had served him well in numerous honor duels in his younger days. He wished he knew what secrets the humans held and why the AIs were so determined to see them destroyed. There was a mystery there, and he hoped someday to know the answer.

Fleet Admiral Hedon Streth stood in the Command Center of the Vanquisher class battleship StarStrike behind his command console. He gazed at the busy crew as the ship continued to orbit the planet he was using as his primary base. The StarStrike was the only battleship ever built by the Federation and now, with the new programming that Clarissa, Ariel, and Lieutenant Johnson had designed, was capable of engaging an AI ship and winning. The StarStrike was 1,600 meters long and had a crew of 2,900. It was the most powerful fleet vessel the Federation had ever built.

The day before, he had spent a considerable amount of time talking to Senator Arden and Admiral Teleck about the events on New Providence. Since Admiral Streth knew the locations of most of the secret military bunkers from back when he was at New Providence with General Allister, the senator had confided in him that there were over 60 million people in the deep underground cities on the planet. Hedon had just shaken his head in amazement when he heard the numbers. It was unbelievable that so many people could have stayed hidden from the AIs and the Hocklyns for so long.

It made him feel good knowing one of the original Federation worlds had survived. It made him even more determined than ever to return home one day and make all the old Federation worlds safe for humans once more. From New Providence, they could spread out and repopulate the old worlds. Perhaps one day he would be able to rebuild that cabin by the lake on Maken. There was not a day that went by that he didn't think about that or his brother Taylor. However, before that could happen, he had to destroy a major portion of the Hocklyn fleet and if all of his plans came together, he might just be able to do that.

His original plan had been to fortify all six of the former Hocklyn planets they had been using as fleet bases and bleed them above each one in limited fleet actions. Now he'd changed his strategy. He was only fortifying the main base and doing so heavily. He had emplaced layer after layer of defensive satellites in orbit above the planet and set up a carefully concealed trap that would make the Hocklyns pay heavily to retake the base.

On the planet's surface at the spaceport, he had built concentric rings of offensive weapons. High-powered lasers, missile launchers, and railgun batteries provided the offensive threat he needed to heavily damage or destroy any Hocklyn ship that entered the atmosphere. There were also numerous Hunter interceptor missile batteries to take out enemy missiles, assault shuttles, or fighters. The entire system around the spaceport was automated and had several failsafe devices wired into it. Once the Hocklyns managed to destroy ninety percent of the offensive and defensive weapons, the failsafes would activate. Four ten-kiloton nukes would detonate, destroying the spaceport complex and ensuring that the Hocklyns would never be able to use it in the future.

He had twenty-four of the defensive battle stations from Ceres to command his defensive satellites. He had placed all twenty-four in one of the outer satellite rings. If things worked as he hoped, the Hocklyn attack would falter against this section of his defenses, giving him an excellent opportunity to attack their fleet.

At the moment, he was meeting with Admiral Adler and Admiral Gaines to discuss some recent reconnaissance information the stealth scouts had returned with. There was another operation he had decided to set in motion to further weaken the Hocklyn Fleet in this sector. The scouts had been tasked with observing the area of space that bordered the Hocklyn Empire in order to detect any major Hocklyn ship movements.

"The fleet that attacked Admiral Sheen is continuing to reconquer their freed slave worlds one by one," commented Hedon, motioning for the two admirals to follow him. He walked over to one of the large tactical holograms and had the two officers sitting in front of it project an image of the area of space the fleet had freed from the Hocklyns.

"Once they conquer a world they land a large number of Protectors on the planet to ensure it stays under their control," he continued. "From what our stealth scouts have reported there has been some minor fighting on several of the worlds, but nothing major."

"At this rate they will reconquer all of their former slave worlds in just a matter of a few weeks," stated Admiral Adler, frowning heavily. "Are we going to allow that?"

"No," responded Hedon, drawing in a sharp breath. "I believe that the Hocklyns may have been furnished with some advanced technology from the AIs which allow them to at least partially detect our stealth scouts. As a result, I have ordered them to stay at least ten million kilometers away from any Hocklyn ship or installation on their reconnaissance missions. However, from the way this large Hocklyn fleet is moving I believe we can predict its next few targets. I want to destroy it before it reaches the bears' system. It is vital that they don't discover what Admiral Strong and the Carethians are doing, at least not yet."

"What are your orders?" Admiral Adler asked as he studied the hologram. Even he could see from the systems the Hocklyn fleet had already reconquered what its next few targets would be.

"Jacob, I want to destroy or damage this fleet as much as possible," Hedon spoke in a determined voice, his eyes focusing on his old friend. "If we can do that, they might not bother us again until they're ready to launch their counterattack. They already believe they have stopped our advance into more of their territory."

Admiral Gaines studied the hologram for a moment and then pointed to a system that was eighty-two light years away. "That system would make an ideal place to bushwhack this Hocklyn fleet. It's far enough away from their current border to prevent them from getting reinforcements, and we can make it there in four jumps."

"I agree," Hedon spoke with a nod of his head. "This will be a joint operation involving Second, Third, and Fifth Fleets. Second Fleet and Fifth Fleet will be leaving their destroyers behind. Only Third Fleet will retain their destroyers to serve as protection for the carriers. During this attack, Second and Fifth Fleet carriers will be reassigned to Third Fleet."

"When do we attack?" Jacob asked, ready for battle. He also wondered how far along Second Fleet was in having all of its ships repaired from their previous battle. It was still in the Careth system undergoing repairs.

"The Hocklyn fleet should arrive in system 664-L in four more days," Admiral Streth replied. "Your fleets will leave the day after tomorrow."

Jacob nodded and then turned to Admiral Gains. "I will contact Admiral Sheen, and we will come up with a tentative battle plan. We need to mousetrap this Hocklyn Fleet and drive it back out of our space or destroy it."

"I agree," replied Gaines as he thought about the fleet units they would have available.

Admiral Sheen would be in charge of the combined Second and Fifth Fleets, while Admiral Adler would carry out the carrier operations. They would have sixteen battlecarriers available for this battle. Their force was powerful enough that they should be able to hold fleet losses down to a minimum. Gaines would be acting as second in command behind Admiral Sheen of Second and Fifth fleets while Admiral Adler would be in overall command.

Hedon watched the two seasoned admirals leave the Command Center. Letting out a deep sigh, he went back to his command console and sat down. He wanted badly to take the StarStrike and command this battle, but he had full faith in his admirals. It was also necessary for him to remain here and finish getting this system ready for the inevitable Hocklyn attack.

The next day Admiral Streth was in a shuttle with Admiral Teleck, Admiral Andrews, Colonel Trist, and Colonel Anne Grissom. Grissom was from Military Intelligence on Ceres and Hedon had added her to his crew at the start of Operation First Strike. They were currently touring the defenses that were being put in place around the planet. The New Ashton had left for Earth the day before under the escort of two battlecruisers and four light cruisers. The rest of the supply fleet and the ships that had come with Admiral Teleck would be leaving shortly.

"We have four rings of defensive satellites," Colonel Grissom informed them as they gazed at the tactical display in the special shuttle. She had helped design the makeup of the satellites in the different rings, taking into account Hocklyn tactics and the type and number of ships they might be facing.

The shuttle had been designed specifically to inspect the planet's defenses. In its main cabin, there were two large tactical holograms. One was currently showing the defenses around the planet, and the other was showing the fleet units in the system.

"The outer ring is not as thick as the next one," Admiral Teleck noted as he gazed at the tactical display. "Is there a reason for that?"

"The outer ring is seeded with Klave missile platforms," Grissom replied as she looked respectfully over at the admiral. "Each platform has six Klave class missiles with a one-kiloton nuclear warhead. There are one hundred and twenty of these platforms hidden amongst the defensive satellites. Their primary task will be damaging or taking out the Hocklyn escort cruisers."

"Where will your fleet be, Admiral?" Richard asked as he looked at the defenses. He could well recall how he had felt when he was aboard the space station above New Providence as the Hocklyns attacked. They had been hopelessly outnumbered, and he had expected to die. He hoped Admiral Streth wasn't putting himself in the same position.

"The fleet will be positioned just inside the gravity well of the planet," Hedon answered as he studied the planet's defenses, which he had helped design. "We will lure the enemy down toward the planet and then retreat to a position between the second and third defensive satellite layers. We have to make them believe we are trying to defend the planet and don't intend to abandon it."

Admiral Teleck nodded and then asked his next question. "The outer layer doesn't look as if it is defended very well. What's to stop the Hocklyns from destroying it and blowing right through it with their ships and fighters?"

"Our fighters will give the outer layer cover until the platforms fire their missiles, at which point they will retreat to the second layer." Colonel Grissom explained.

"I notice the defensive battle stations are all in the second outer layer," Richard said as he studied the makeup of the satellites. "Is there a reason for this?" He suspected that Admiral Streth had a number of surprises set up for the Hocklyns. He wondered if this was one of them.

"We have more of our laser satellites in this layer as well as another one hundred and sixty missile platforms," explained Hedon, nodding his head.

"But these missile platforms are different," Colonel Grissom interjected with a wicked smile. "They are much larger and instead of being equipped with Klave class missiles, all the platforms are equipped with ten Devastator class missiles, each with a ten kiloton warhead."

"I wondered what you were doing with all of those missiles," spoke Admiral Teleck, recalling all the questions that had been raised back home when Admiral Streth had requested nearly two thousand additional Devastator missiles.

Admiral Teleck looked at all the defensive satellites that had been deployed. Between Admiral Streth and Admiral Strong, they had been sent a major portion of the Federation's defensive satellite production for the last two months. A number of Federation planets and mining colonies were still screaming, demanding to know where their defensive satellites were.

"Besides the defensive battle stations, we will have forty of our destroyers mixed in, adding their defensive fire to that of the satellites and battle stations and ensuring their maximum survival," Admiral Streth added. "We hope to inflict significant damage on the Hocklyn fleet at this juncture."

Admiral Teleck stepped over closer to the tactical hologram, inspecting the deployment of the laser satellites and the missile platforms. "We are doing something similar at New Tellus, but on a much larger scale. What happens when the Hocklyns manage to penetrate this defensive layer?"

"Then it becomes a major fleet action," replied Hedon grimly, knowing he might lose a major portion of his fleet at this point in the battle. "We will engage the Hocklyn fleet in a running skirmish as we make for the edge of the planet's gravity well. Our Devastator Three missiles should allow us to blow right through the Hocklyn fleet, inflicting heavy damage upon it. Once we reach the edge of the gravity well we'll jump and begin our retreat back toward New Tellus."

"What about AI ships?" asked Richard, worriedly. He had witnessed firsthand back at New Providence what they could do to a fleet and satellite defenses. "What if they jump a large number of them inside the gravity well, or even inside the satellite defensive rings?"

"We will have our heavy strikecruisers in position to respond if they do," Hedon replied evenly. "If it's only a few we can handle them, but if the AIs bring a major fleet we could have problems."

The AIs were the big unknown in his plans. He hoped after showing that they could destroy an AI ship that the Hocklyn's masters would hold back and let the Hocklyns do most of the fighting in this system. If they did become involved, then his losses would become much higher.

"I assume they have all been updated with the new program that Lieutenant Johnson and Ariel designed?" Admiral Teleck asked.

He had already made sure the new program was being installed in all the new strikecruisers coming off the production lines, as well as the older ones in the Federation. It had been necessary to slightly upgrade all the older strikecruiser's computer systems to handle the new program.

"Yes, Sir," Hedon replied with a nod. That had been one of his first priorities since they were so far from the Federation. "Clarissa and Ariel have checked the programming on all of our strikecruisers and confirmed that they are ready. Our two AIs are fully confident that the new program and heavier Devastator Three missiles will allow us to destroy an AI ship."

"I hope so, Admiral," Teleck replied grimly.

A lot was riding on that assumption. Clarissa and Ariel had already demonstrated that they could destroy an AI ship. The new program was still untried and, until it was, there were some questions as to whether it would actually work, even though the two friendly AIs and Lieutenant Johnson swore that it would.

They continued their tour, inspecting the next two defensive rings, then went down to the planet to look at the defenses around the spaceport. The alien slaves that had been working at the spaceport had been transported off a few weeks back and taken to their home planets. It had been difficult to convince a few of them to go; only after explaining that the spaceport was going to be destroyed by nukes had they agreed to leave. The former Hocklyn slaves intended to stay hidden on their home planets and hope the Hocklyns would believe they had all died in the nuclear explosions at the spaceport.

The next day, Richard was aboard Admiral Teleck's flagship and on his way back to the Federation. They had left a large number of warships behind in the Carethian system. Richard hated leaving Amanda, knowing the next time he saw her it would be after the big battle in the system Admiral Streth was planning to defend. He knew his wife would be playing an important role in that conflict. He just prayed she would come through unharmed and make it back to the New Tellus system safely. Unfortunately, when she did, he also knew that the Hocklyns and the AIs would be right behind her.

Commodore Krilen stood upon the command pedestal in the War Room of his flagship, the dreadnought IronHand. He had a look of deep satisfaction upon his face as they had just finished landing Protectors on the next slave world in his campaign to retake all of the former Hocklyn worlds the humans had freed. He was surprised that the humans seemed to be avoiding contact. Since that first battle, their ships had been strangely absent. It was just as well; with each world that he put back into the Hocklyn Empire, his honor grew. If things continued, he would be a full Fleet Commodore when this was over.

"What planet is next?" Krilen asked in his cold rasping voice as he gazed at his First Leader.

"There is another inhabited planet in a system eighteen light years distant," First Leader Angoth replied. "It produced agricultural goods for the Empire before the humans destroyed the two escort cruisers and the space station that was in orbit."

"Very well," Krilen replied as his dark eyes looked at the large viewscreen on the front wall of the War Room. "Prepare all ships to make the jump. We will land our Protectors on it and then continue on to the world of Careth. It is a high tech system and will bring us much honor when we bring it back into the Empire."

It was a shame the humans had destroyed the space stations above so many of the slave worlds. All would have to be rebuilt at tremendous expense to the Empire. Of course, the cost of rebuilding the space stations would eventually be passed on to the inhabitants of the planets the stations orbited.

The fleet had been heavily reinforced since its initial engagement with the humans. Part of that was due to the fact that the High Council had felt there was a possibility of a major engagement as Krilen's fleet proceeded deeper into the space the humans had taken from the Hocklyn Empire. Krilen had strict orders not to approach any of the six former major fleet bases. It was felt that the humans would be waiting at these strong points to attempt to stop the Hocklyn advance.

The fleet currently under his command was composed of eight dreadnoughts, fourteen war cruisers, and sixty escort cruisers. Krilen also had stern orders to withdraw rather than suffer major losses. With the current size of his fleet and after the earlier battle with the humans, he was not too concerned. He felt confident that he could handle anything the humans threw at him.

Fleet Commodore Resmunt gazed at the latest report from Commodore Krilen. He was continuing to advance unopposed through former Hocklyn space retaking slave world after slave world. He shook his head, knowing that Krilen was becoming too overconfident. This was the biggest danger when fighting the humans, which Resmunt had learned the hard way after nearly having his fleet annihilated. Resmunt had seen what the humans were capable of and was worried that they were luring Krilen into a trap. He debated sending Krilen a warning but strongly suspected the commodore would ignore it. The commodore would have to learn his lesson the same way Resmunt had.

Looking at the main viewscreen of his flagship, the dreadnought Liberator, he looked with distaste at what was on the screen. A 1,500-meter AI ship was setting in orbit above Kenward Seven after returning from human occupied space. The AIs were even now evaluating the new weapons systems that were being installed on Hocklyn ships against what they had learned about human technology. From what Resmunt had heard so far the AIs seemed certain that the new weapons and energy screen would be effective against human warships.

"The AIs seemed satisfied with our progress," Ganth commented as he gazed impassively at the screen. "The shipyard the AI is in orbit next to has reported that they will be leaving shortly."

"Let them go," Resmunt hissed; he had no love for the AIs. "As the worlds of this galaxy are our slaves, we are slaves to the AIs."

"It is dangerous to speak that way," Ganth cautioned, though he felt the same about the metal monstrosities. "We have no choice but to obey them. There is no power in the galaxy that can stand up to their ships and technology."

Resmunt nodded. He thought about the coming war with the humans. They had already demonstrated that they could destroy an AI ship. What if they were a much bigger threat to the AIs than the High Council believed? The commodore let out a deep breath and shook his head. Those were dangerous thoughts and best left alone. It was his duty to get his fleet ready for combat, and that time was rapidly approaching. There was much honor waiting in the future for all members of the Hocklyn military, and he intended to get his share. That seat on the High Council was beckoning, and Resmunt intended to have it someday.

Chapter Five

Fleet Admiral Karla Johnson was on Earth visiting with President Kincaid about the current status of the fleet and preparations for defending the Federation. The president was also briefing the Darvonian ambassador as to the current status of Operation First Strike and the likelihood of a Hocklyn attack. The Darvonian star systems were sixty-eight light years from Earth and consisted of their home system, six highly developed colony worlds, and fourteen additional worlds that were under development. They had numerous scientific and mining outposts in twenty more star systems and a highly advanced exploration program.

The Darvonians had actually made contact with the Federation when one of their exploration ships had found the human colony of Bliss at Epsilon Eridani. They had become good trading partners, and it was not unusual to see Darvonians on all of the planets of the Federation. The Darvonians were similar to Humans in many ways and had even grown to like Earth music, which was in high demand on the Darvonian worlds, along with other forms of Earth entertainment. In return, art from the Darvonian worlds was highly prized by Earth collectors. Some of their paintings were truly breathtaking and had taken the art world by storm.

Of even greater importance was the fact that they had the next largest warfleet after the Federation. The Darvonians preferred smaller warships and had 440 ships slightly larger than a Federation destroyer. They also maintained twenty command ships, which were similar in size to a Monarch heavy cruiser. After being informed of the threat the Hocklyns posed to them, the Darvonians had updated all of their ships as well as surrounded their key worlds with dense minefields as well as defensive satellites.

"This coming war is worrisome," spoke Ambassador Flay, raising his eyebrows. "My government is deeply concerned about what will happen if we have to face an AI ship. Currently we have nothing that can stop one."

President Kincaid looked over at the ambassador. He had known the Darvonian Ambassador for quite some time. Most Darvonians were the same height as humans with a red tinge to their skin. They were also bulkier, had six digits on their hands, and no hair upon their heads. Their eyes were widely set with large, flaring nostrils.

"We may have a remedy for that," President Kincaid responded. He had already discussed what he was going to propose with Fleet Admiral Johnson. They could not afford for one or two AI ships to show up and wipe out one of their allies. "Your people have done everything we have asked to prepare for this war. As you may have heard, Fleet Admiral Streth successfully destroyed two AI ships in his battle above the Hocklyn's primary fleet base."

"Admiral Johnson has briefed me on that," responded Flay, nodding his head slightly toward the admiral. "But you also suffered considerable fleet losses in doing so."

"It was a learning experience," President Kincaid confessed with a deep sigh. He didn't want the ambassador to know just how close the AI ships had come to stopping Operation First Strike and wiping out First Fleet. "We did manage to destroy the two AI ships and have adopted a new strategy to ensure that we can do so in the future. Admiral Johnson, will you please inform the ambassador what we are willing to do."

"With your government's permission, we will position two small fleets in your space," Fleet Admiral Johnson began. "The fleets will each consist of one battlecruiser, two of our heavy strikecruisers, and four light cruisers. The heavy strikecruisers will be equipped with the technology and weapons needed to destroy an AI ship. We are also willing to allow your military to place observers on the battlecruisers if you so wish."

Ambassador Flay leaned back in his chair and placed his right hand upon the president's desk as he considered the offer. The fingers on his hand were slightly longer than a humans, and he was unconsciously tapping his index finger upon the wood of the desk. "I will have to speak to my government about this," he said as his eyes narrowed in thought. "I assume the battlecruisers will be the flagships of the two fleets?"

"Yes, Ambassador," Admiral Johnson replied. "We will allow your military to decide upon the best locations to position the two fleets to protect your worlds from the AIs."

"Keep in mind Ambassador, that we expect the AIs to attack here before they engage your worlds," President Kincaid added. "If we can stop them, your worlds may never need to worry about facing an AI ship."

"Perhaps," Ambassador Flay replied thoughtfully. "But it would be comforting to my government and our people if we knew we could handle one if it became necessary. I believe my government will accept your offer as long as we can place observers upon the flagships. I will make the recommendation to my government to accept the offer and get back to you once I receive their response."

Fleet Admiral Johnson watched the ambassador depart and then turned back to face the president. "The Kessels and the Zanths have already agreed to accept our fleets. What concerns me are the Albanians; they're still refusing to believe that the Hocklyns and the AIs are a threat."

President Kincaid leaned back in his chair and rubbed his brow with his left hand, then looked over his desk at the Fleet Admiral. "Karla, the Albanians have acted strangely ever since we told them about a potential attack. They have closed off their borders and are now refusing trade of any kind. In the last few weeks, even their research and exploration ships have remained within their area of space."

"Sir, they can't be expecting the Hocklyns and the AIs to leave them alone," Karla said, her hazel eyes looking worriedly at the president. "Even with their advanced technology, it will mean nothing if they have no warships with which to defend themselves."

"And that's the big question," Kincaid replied as he stood up and walked over to a large map of the galaxy that showed Federation controlled space, their allies and, of course, Albanian controlled space. The space the Albanians controlled was larger than what the Federation and its allies controlled combined.

"Why are they ignoring this war? They have to know what will happen to them if we lose," Karla asked as she came to stand next to the president. "They have sixteen highly developed worlds and numerous smaller colonies as well as their mining operations and scientific outposts. They have more to lose than anyone."

"Their embassy here is still open even though the one we had on their home world has been shut down at their request," Kincaid informed the Fleet Admiral. With a deep sigh, he turned to face Karla. "I just feel we are missing something with the Albanians. They have been in space far longer than any of our allies and have explored a major portion of this section of the galaxy. There is even speculation that they may have visited Earth centuries before the Federation survivors arrived."

"They are a mystery," admitted Karla, feeling frustrated that the Albanians would not take an active role in the war. "Their science could give us the key to defeating the Hocklyns and possibly the AIs; I just don't understand how they can refuse not to get involved."

"They are an old race," Kincaid replied in a tired voice. "They don't believe in war, and we have to respect their wishes or we're no better than the Hocklyns."

"You're right," Karla responded with a deep sigh. "It would just be nice if we had weapons based on their technology."

Over the last several weeks, anxiety had been growing in the Federation as its people realized that the Hocklyns would soon attack the Federation worlds. For centuries, they'd heard about how dangerous the Hocklyn Slave Empire was and what had happened to the worlds of the old Federation. They also knew that Admiral Streth had been brought out of cryosleep to lead the Federation to victory. President Kincaid doubted if even the legendary admiral of the old Federation could pull off that miracle, but at least it gave the people a reason for hope.

"How are we doing on preparing for the attack, and what's the latest from Fleet Admiral Streth?"

"Admiral Streth has already bought us over three month's worth of time to prepare," Karla replied as she recalled the latest reports coming in from Operation First Strike. "Production of new warships has been ramped up, and we are building hundreds of new defensive satellites daily."

"What about the new defensive battle stations that Ceres has been building?" Kincaid asked. "Have we started production on them yet?" He knew how important they could be in protecting the satellite defensive grids around all the Federation worlds. The new battle stations would also go a long way toward calming the nerves of several of the Federation senators, including Senator Fulbright.

"Yes," replied Karla, nodding her head. "We have four production lines operating at New Tellus, and we are producing thirty of the new battle stations per week. We will begin emplacing them as soon as the crews finish their training."

"Have the first ones sent to Serenity and Bliss; perhaps that will quiet down Senator Fulbright," President Kincaid ordered as he thought about the most recent complaints from the senator. "He is sure his world is going to be destroyed by the Hocklyns."

"I will pass on the order," replied Karla, knowing the president needed to keep the senators satisfied that everything was being done to defend their worlds. Serenity was the smallest colony in the Federation with only 200 million people, and Bliss had slightly over 680 million. Even so, it was the Fleet's responsibility to defend them and Karla would make sure they were adequately protected.

Karla had made certain in recent weeks that the satellite defense grid above both Serenity and Bliss had been properly strengthened. There was a small fleet assigned to each world and if the Hocklyns attacked, the two fleets should be able to hold out until help arrived.

"When does Admiral Streth expect the Hocklyns to launch their counterattack?"

Karla let out a deep breath. "Another six to ten weeks," she replied, recalling Admiral Streth's latest report. "When they do, Admiral Strong will be staying behind and helping to defend the Carethians. Fleet Admiral Streth will begin a strategic retreat back toward New Tellus."

"Will we be ready?" asked President Kincaid, his eyes focusing intently on the Fleet Admiral, fearing what would happen to the Federation when the Hocklyns and the AIs finally arrived.

He knew everything possible was being done to prepare, but the Hocklyns were a galaxy-spanning empire and the AIs were even worse as they controlled everything behind the scenes. He had seen the videos of the deadly AI spheres in action as they attacked the old Federation fleet. They had been unstoppable. President Kincaid didn't want to see that type of destruction befall any Federation world. He had recently gone on a tour of the Fleet Academy on the Moon and had been impressed by what he had seen. Hundreds of heavy weapons emplacements had been built on its surface as well as countless flight bays for thousands of Talon fighters and Anlon bombers. The Moon would serve as a Sword of Damocles against the Hocklyns and the AIs if they dared to attack Earth.

Karla was silent for a long moment. She knew nothing was certain in war, and when the Hocklyns and the AIs attacked New Tellus not even the best military minds were certain of what the results would be. They had spent years preparing and could only hope that they had done enough.

"We will be as ready as we can be," Karla finally replied in a somber voice. "It depends on the number of AI ships that take place in the attack."

President Kincaid nodded. "Thanks for the briefing Karla. I have a meeting with the Federation Council later to brief them on the current situation. Senator Fulbright will be demanding assurances that his colony will be safe, as usual."

"Assure the senator we are doing everything possible," replied Karla, hoping it would be enough.

President Kincaid watched the Fleet Admiral leave. He walked back over and sat down at his desk, feeling the burden of his office weighing heavily on his shoulders. He prayed that Fleet Admiral Streth would return safely, but what concerned him the most was that Admiral Strong and the crew of the Avenger would be staying behind and would be cut off from the Federation. It would be a huge blow to the Federation's morale if something happened to any of those five young officers on that ship. In many ways, those five and Ariel were the Federation.

Several hours later, Fleet Admiral Johnson was on her way to Ceres to meet with Governor Malleck and Admiral Kalen. As she approached Ceres, she was surprised at how heavily the defenses had been reinforced over the past six weeks. There were seventy-two of the new satellite defensive battle stations in orbit around the asteroid as well as several thousand defensive satellites. Add to that all the heavy weapons that were emplaced on the smaller asteroids that guarded the approaches to Ceres and it might very well be the most heavily defended colony in the Federation.

Once her meeting was over, she would be returning to New Tellus to go on an inspection tour of her new battleship that was under construction. The engineers had told her it would be another two months before the ship was ready to leave the dock for its space trials. She just hoped the Hocklyns and AIs waited long enough for it to be completed.

Jeremy rolled over and opened his eyes. The sun was just beginning to shine through the window of the resort room that he and Kelsey were in. Jeremy sat up, being careful not to wake Kelsey as she was still sound asleep. She should be after the way she had worn him out in their lovemaking. He let out a deep breath of disappointment, knowing that today was the last day he could spend down at the resort. For the last three days, he had left Admiral Stillson in charge of working with the bears and taking care of the day-to-day routine of organizing the defense of an entire solar system. There were so many details that needed to be taken care of.

"Are you leaving?" Kelsey asked sleepily as she gazed up at Jeremy with half open eyes.

The last three days had been wonderful, and she wished that they could continue. However, she also understood that Jeremy had an important job to do and that job was going to occupy him more and more in the coming days and months. Special times like these would be few and far between.

Jeremy smiled and leaning down kissed Kelsey on the lips. She smiled back and her arms slid around Jeremy, pulling him down partially on top of her.

"Do you have to leave now?" she asked, enjoying the warmth of Jeremy's body on top of hers. She wiggled suggestively as her hands moved gently up and down his back.

"You know I do," replied Jeremy, disentangling himself from Kelsey's arms and sliding out of bed. "Admiral Sheen's fleet is departing shortly, and I need to be on the Avenger for that."

Kelsey nodded; feeling disappointed but understanding that Jeremy had to go. "The rest of us will be coming back up in a few days. Katie is going to do some work on the new computer system in the station, and Kevin is going to be assisting her. Angela will be setting up some encrypted communication codes for use when the Hocklyns attack, and Ariel and I will be working on refining our in system jumps even more. She thinks it might be possible to emerge from hyperspace less than a hundred kilometers from an enemy ship."

Jeremy nodded. "We all have jobs to do and this resort has been great. Perhaps we can come back down in a few more weeks, but we have a lot of work to do in the meantime."

Kelsey was silent as she watched Jeremy get dressed. So much had changed since their time on the New Horizon, and the five of them had continued to grow even closer. Kelsey had already decided that she wanted to spend her life with Jeremy, and she was fairly certain he felt the same. They just had to defeat the Hocklyns and the AIs first.

After Jeremy left, Kelsey closed her eyes and thought about her parents. Her father and mother had been such a big influence in her life, and she wished they were here to share how she felt about Jeremy. She knew her mother would be extremely happy, and her father would definitely approve.

Ariel was busy running battle simulations in an effort to find the best strategy to take out an AI ship. She knew that if the Federation was to survive, the AIs had to be stopped. Ariel was currently standing in the Command Center of the Avenger next to Lieutenant Charles Preston, the ship's tactical officer.

"That was interesting," Preston commented as he watched Ariel's latest simulation on one of his tactical screens. "You managed to take out the AI ship with no losses to the fleet, how did you do that?"

Ariel put her hands on her hips and turned to face Lieutenant Preston. She had discovered that humans reacted better when she spoke to them face to face. She was wearing a standard dark blue fleet uniform with no insignia. "I placed four Devastator Three missiles in a twenty-meter area on the AI's energy screen and then sent two more through the resulting twelve-meter hole to impact and explode on the ship's hull. If you noticed, I used three strikecruisers, with two of them hitting the screen over a larger area with Devastator Threes."

Lieutenant Preston did some additional checking and then turned back toward Ariel. "Your ships did receive some damage," he informed her. "It's moderate, and all three ships are still capable of another attack, but as the AIs learn that the strikecruisers are a danger to them they will start to make their destruction a priority. Each subsequent attack is going to be more difficult and dangerous."

Ariel nodded in agreement. She folded her arms across her breasts and pondered what the lieutenant had just said. He was right of course, once the AIs realized that only the strikecruisers and the StarStrike were a danger to them they would place a high priority on their destruction. She would have to run more simulations on how best to increase the survivability of the strikecruisers. Even as she thought about this, she saw Jeremy enter the Command Center, nodding at Lieutenant Preston she walked over to the command console where Jeremy had gone.

"Hello, Admiral," Ariel spoke in her pleasing, female voice.

"Hello, Ariel," replied Jeremy, smiling.

Ariel was a mainstay; for all of his adult life she had been around. Even when he had been serving on the light cruisers after the New Horizon incident she had been waiting for him any time he returned to the academy on the Moon.

"Admiral Sheen and Second Fleet will be departing soon," Ariel informed Jeremy, knowing he would want the current status of Second Fleet's departure.

"Were all the repairs completed?" Jeremy asked as he sat down and looked across the Command Center. It was only partially staffed as they were still docked to the space station.

"Except for two light cruisers that will remain in the repair docks," Ariel reported as she called up the latest status on the two crippled warships. "They still like another forty-eight hours before the engineers are finished with the repairs. Both ships were heavily damaged in the last battle with the Hocklyns and were fortunate to be able to make it here."

Jeremy nodded as he ordered the communications officer to contact Admiral Sheen on the WarStorm. Jeremy spoke briefly with the admiral, wishing them luck in the coming battle and promising that her other two ships would be repaired shortly.

"Put Second Fleet up on the tactical display," Jeremy ordered as he walked over to the plotting table.

Instantly, the tactical hologram lit up with fifty-nine bright green icons representing Second Fleet. Even as he watched, the fleet began moving away from the protection of the bears' planet and toward the edge of the planet's gravity well where Second Fleet would jump to their rendezvous with Admiral Adler and Admiral Gaines. The fleet's destroyers would jump to Admiral Streth's position while the remainder of her fleet would jump to the rendezvous point.

Amanda was sitting in her chair behind her command console on the WarStorm watching as the fleet neared the edge of the gravity well where they could jump. The last several weeks had been interesting, to say the least. Richard showing up with Admiral Teleck had been a shock and the time they had been able to spend together at the resort had been fantastic. The beach resorts the bears had built upon their planet to allow the humans of the fleet to take leave were wonderful. They were very similar to the ones on New Tellus and Earth itself.

Commander Evans had taken overseeing to the repairs of the fleet and had insisted that Amanda spend all of her time with Richard. Samantha had reminded Admiral Sheen, in no uncertain terms, that she could handle the repairs and that the admiral needed to spend this time with her husband as it might be months before they saw each other again.

Amanda had relented and agreed to stay at the resort. Well was she aware that when she did see Richard again, a Hocklyn and possibly an AI fleet would be just behind her. She would be bringing death and destruction with her.

"Ready to jump," Commander Evans reported from her position at the plotting table as the fleet cleared Careth's gravity well.

"Very well," replied Amanda, looking over at the commander. "Order the jump and let's go kick some Hocklyn ass."

In front of the fleet, spatial vortexes began to form. The ships of Second Fleet entered the vortexes one by one and jumped into hyperspace. Behind them, the vortexes collapsed and vanished as if they had never been. Admiral Sheen watched until only the WarStorm was left, then her ship entered the vortex in front of it and she felt the familiar nauseous feeling in the pit of her stomach as the ship made the transition from normal space to hyperspace.

On the main viewscreen, she gazed at the swirling dark purple colors of hyperspace and felt some comfort. Ships could not be attacked in hyperspace, and they would be in no danger until they exited the spatial vortexes. Amanda knew that Admirals Adler and Gaines would be waiting for her, and once Second Fleet arrived, they would finish planning their attack on the Hocklyn fleet.

Jeremy watched as the WarStorm vanished from the tactical display and Second Fleet was gone. He let out a deep breath. For some reason, he had felt more secure with Admiral Sheen and her fleet in the system. He knew it was because she was a highly experienced admiral and well trusted friend of Fleet Admiral Streth.

"Admiral," Ariel spoke quietly as she stepped closer. "Grayseth is on the station and wants to launch some of the new Talon fighters and Anlon bombers. He says he has a number of pilots that have finished their training on the simulators and are anxious to try out the real thing."

Jeremy smiled. He was curious to see what type of pilots the bears would make. He had a suspicion they would be fearsome pilots and would give the Hocklyns fits in combat.

"Tell Grayseth I will be over shortly," Jeremy replied. This should be interesting.

He would also be talking to Commander Susan Marks of the battle carrier Retribution. It might be a good idea to pair up some of the bear pilots with human ones for the next part of their training. Susan was an expert when it came to training pilots from her previous experience a number of years back as head instructor at one of the flight schools at New Tellus. She had already been instrumental in programming the simulators the bears had been using.

On board the space station, Grayseth and a number of bear pilots were in one of the station's large flight bays, inspecting the new fighters and bombers that had been dropped off by the supply fleet. Many more would be coming on the next two supply missions, giving the bears an even greater opportunity to protect their world.

The new fighters were sleek, though the cockpits and controls had been enlarged to allow a bear to operate the deadly little spacecraft. Grayseth looked at where two of the human's Hunter interceptor missiles could be placed beneath the small stubby wings of the fighters. They could operate in the atmosphere of a planet, if necessary, though they were more at home in space.

"The humans make excellent fighters," one of the pilots spoke as he ran his large hair-covered hand gently over the hull of one of the ships. "They will serve us well in our war with the evil ones."

Several others nodded in agreement. Grayseth wished they could make fighters such as these on Careth, but the technology was too far advanced. It would take too much time to build the factories to make all the parts necessary to construct a fighter. No, for this they would have to depend on the humans and, so far, the humans had been very generous in their aid.

"We will hunt together," one of the pilots spoke solemnly as he looked at the sleek fighters and bombers that were lined up in the bay.

"Yes," replied Grayseth, feeling pride for his people. "We will hunt together and make the evil ones pay for what they did to our world and our colony. The people of Careth will never be slaves again!"

Jeremy had just entered the flight bay and heard the conversation between Grayseth and his pilots. He knew the bears spoke the truth. They would fight until they either won or their world was destroyed, and Jeremy had already sworn to himself that he would do everything in his power to prevent Grayseth and his people from dying. The bears were worthy allies of the Federation, and they would stand together against the Hocklyns and the AIs. They would either live together in victory or die together in combat. There could be no other way.

Chapter Six

Commodore Krilen looked at the main viewscreen, which showed the blue-white world beneath his orbiting flagship. The IronHand was 1,200 meters of death. The ship was heavily armed and wedge shaped, with a width of 400 meters. Heavy railgun turrets covered the hull, as well as thick protective hatches over the missile launching tubes. On the bow of the ship were two heavy energy beam batteries capable of cutting through any ship's armor. Krilen was confident that his fleet could handle anything the humans might throw at him as long as he stayed away from the former Hocklyn bases they had captured.

"The Protectors are landing now," First Leader Angoth reported as he stepped over to the command pedestal. "They are reporting no resistance and expect to be in full control of the planet within a matter of hours."

Krilen nodded and spoke. "Excellent; the humans still refuse to give battle. With each former slave world we land our Protectors on, the more honor comes to our fleet."

"Honor is ours," Angoth replied in agreement. Someday soon, he would be a War Leader and have his own fleet. Commodore Krilen was causing the fleet to accumulate honor rapidly, and all the warriors of the fleet were very pleased.

Krilen gazed at the viewscreen as he thought about his campaign so far. It had gone better than expected. Once again, there had been no human ships in the system to offer resistance, so his fleet had gone into orbit of the planet unopposed.

"The system of Careth is next," he spoke, wondering if human ships would be waiting for him there.

Every system they took control of only added to the honor that was steadily mounting for the fleet. It also pleased him that the majority of that accrued honor would fall upon him. It still confused him that the humans were offering no resistance. Why free all of these worlds and then do nothing to defend them? Perhaps their fleet was not nearly as powerful as Fleet Commodore Resmunt had claimed. He had always been an outcast, and it amazed Krilen that the commodore was still in the fleet.

"Careth is home to a very aggressive species," Angoth warned as his left hand strayed to the blade he always carried at his waist. He clenched the hilt of it with the six digits of his right hand. "There will be much fighting for our Protectors. There will be honor waiting for them on the planet's surface."

Angoth would enjoy going down to the surface of the Carethian's planet with the Protectors to bring it back under Hocklyn control. From what he had studied in the ship's computers about the Carethians there would be heavy resistance when the Empire returned to their world. Hand-to-hand combat with a worthy opponent brought quick honor. Perhaps the Commodore would allow a few warriors from the flagship to join the Protectors in subduing the Carethians.

"Yes, honor will be waiting," repeated Commodore Krilen in agreement. "If the humans are interested in protecting any of our former slave worlds, it will be Careth. I intend to send a couple of escort cruisers forward to see what awaits us in that system. Thus far, they have avoided contact with our fleet since that one action, and that may stop when we reach Careth."

"A wise precaution," Angoth rasped out with a nod. "So far we have seen little resistance from these humans. Why free so many worlds if they will not stand in their defense? These humans have no honor or they would not have allowed us to retake world after world unopposed."

Commodore Krilen nodded his head in agreement. He drummed the long sharp nails of his hand against the command console that was in front of him. Nothing about these humans made any sense. When he had started on this conquest, he had been cautioned by the High Council to be prepared to meet heavy resistance. However, that resistance had never materialized except for that one engagement. Since then there had been no sign of human ships. Each system he had jumped his fleet into he had expected to meet some resistance. It was almost as if the humans had vanished.

First Leader Angoth left the command pedestal and walked across the War Room to study the tactical screen. In his opinion, Commodore Krilen had grown lax in his concern for the safety of the fleet. In the early conquests, a major portion of the fleet had stayed just outside the gravity well of the planet and only a few war cruisers and escort cruisers had gone in to orbit the targeted planet. They would then land their designated Protectors and, after a few orbits, move back out to rejoin the fleet. However, in the last few conquests Krilen had allowed the entire fleet to enter the gravity well of the target planet. Angoth feared that if these humans were indeed as dangerous as the High Council claimed, then Krilen could be playing right into their hands.

-

Admiral Sheen gazed at the latest reports sent back from the stealth scouts that were observing the Hocklyn fleet in system K-445. It was obvious that the commodore in charge of this fleet had little fear of an attack or he wouldn't have taken his entire fleet into the gravity well of the planet. Amanda could feel the adrenaline rushing into her system as she prepared to launch her attack. She had forty-eight ships in Second Fleet, and the Hocklyn fleet was composed of eighty-two warships. Her ships had better weapons and shields, but the Hocklyns would make up for that by their sheer numbers.

"What's the plan?" Commander Evans asked as she gazed at the data being put up on the tactical display. "We have them trapped in the gravity well of the planet. That is a tactical error on the part of their commodore."

"The only problem is we don't know if they have reinforcements close by," Amanda spoke quietly as she studied the disposition of the Hocklyn fleet. "We have used our stealth scouts to search some of the nearby systems, but they haven't found anything. Either the commodore in charge of that fleet is overconfident or we are missing something. Either way, we dare not allow Second Fleet to go to far into the planet's gravity well in case we need to withdraw quickly. We will jump in and allow them to come out to us."

"What about Third and Fifth Fleets, when will they be jumping in?"

"When we call for them," replied Amanda, relishing the anticipated shock on the Hocklyn commodore's face when the other two human fleets appeared. If they jumped in with all three Federation fleets, the Hocklyns might scatter and attempt to escape; this way she could lure them into engaging Second Fleet. "Have the fleet go to Condition One and prepare to jump. We will be jumping to just outside of the planet's gravity well."

Moments later the Condition One alarms sounded and lights began flashing red. The WarStorm was about to go into battle as her crew rushed to their battle stations. Missiles were readied and railgun rounds loaded into their magazines.

-

Commodore Krilen was just about to retire to his quarters when the alarms on the sensor console went off and red warning lights began flashing. "What is it?" he demanded, looking intently at the Hocklyn sensor operator. "Why are those alarms sounding?" If this was a malfunction, some Hocklyn technician was gong to lose some of their honor.

"We have unknown ships emerging from hyperspace just outside of the planet's gravity well," the Third Leader who was operating the sensors reported.

Krilen whirled around to face First Leader Angoth. "Are those human ships?"

Angoth studied the data for a moment on his tactical screen before replying in his cold rasping voice. "Yes, Commodore; they are indeed human. Sensors show forty-eight human warships have jumped into the system."

"Forty-eight," Krilen responded as he thought over his options. "We have eighty-two ships and twenty-two of them are capital ships. The humans have made a grave error if they intend to attack this fleet."

"We are in the gravity well of the planet," Angoth reminded Krilen, knowing this was a tactical disadvantage. "We should exit it before engaging the humans."

"We have superior numbers and firepower," Commodore Krilen admonished as he studied the tactical screen. "It does not matter whether we meet these humans inside the gravity well or out, we will destroy them!"

Krilen could already taste the honor that was waiting for him in this battle. He had the humans outnumbered, and he had heavier firepower. There was no doubt in his mind that after this battle and a triumphant return home he would be raised in rank to a full Fleet Commodore.

"The human fleet has formed up and is moving slowly toward the planet," spoke First Leader Angoth, feeling the rush of blood through his veins and the thirst for battle. "They will be in combat range in twenty minutes if we hold our current position."

"Let us go and meet them," Krilen ordered his cold dark eyes gazing at Angoth. "Allow them to enter the gravity well where they will be trapped from escaping. Ready the fleet for battle, much honor awaits us today."

"Honor awaits us,' Angoth repeated as he began passing on the commodore's orders. He still felt it would have been wiser to meet the humans outside of the planet's gravity well.

"The Hocklyn fleet is forming up and coming out to meet us," Commander Evans reported satisfied that the first part of the admiral's plan was working.

"Lieutenant Stalls, what is the makeup of the Hocklyn fleet?" Admiral Sheen asked as she gazed at the tactical hologram above the plotting table. She could see that a number of the red threat icons were large, indicating Hocklyn capital ships. It was obvious that this fleet had been heavily reinforced since her previous encounter with it.

Benjamin spent a moment as he checked the data on his sensors and then transferred the information over to the tactical display. "I make it eight dreadnoughts, fourteen war cruisers, and sixty escort cruisers."

Amanda nodded. "Have our two carriers pull back to wait for Admiral Adler." That still gave Second Fleet a heavy hitting force of six battlecruisers, four heavy strikecruisers, eleven Monarch cruisers, and twenty-five light cruisers. It was enough to hold the enemy and inflict some serious damage until she summoned Admiral Adler and Admiral Gaines.

"Hocklyn fleet will be in engagement range in seventeen minutes," Lieutenant Stalls reported.

"Here we go again," Angela Trask mumbled over her private communications link with Benjamin. "This is starting to seem familiar."

"Admiral Sheen will get us through this," Benjamin promised confidently as he watched the myriad of red threat icons steadily nearing the fleet.

"I hope so," replied Angela, feeling nervous about the coming battle. She looked over at Lieutenant Ashton at Navigation and noticed that she was looking pale also. At least she wasn't the only one that was worried.

"I wish we could use the Devastator Threes in this battle," Commander Evans spoke quietly from her position next to Admiral Sheen. "With them we could take this Hocklyn fleet out by ourselves."

"I know," Amanda replied, totally in agreement. "But we want the Hocklyns to think we have a very limited supply of those weapons. Admiral Streth has strictly forbidden their use unless an AI ship is involved."

Commander Evans turned and walked back over to the plotting table and gazed speculatively at the tactical hologram being displayed up above it and then looked over at Tactical. "Lieutenant Mason, load an even mix of Klave and regular Devastator missiles in our launch tubes and prepare to fire. All railguns to be armed with high explosive rounds for maximum effect against the Hocklyn's energy screens. Prepare to fire all heavy pulse laser batteries and our power beams upon my command. Pick out the nearest dreadnought as our primary target."

"All ships except the carriers are to launch their fighters," Amanda ordered as she listened to Commander Evans prepare the WarStorm for battle. The two carriers would wait for Admiral Adler to arrive before launching their bomber strike. She could feel her pulse quickening as the time for combat neared.

Moments later, two hundred and eight Talon fighters blasted forth from the flight bays of Second Fleet and hurtled toward the Hocklyns. The squadron leaders quickly formed up their commands into a solid wall in front of the advancing human ships.

"Humans have launched their fighters," First Leader Angoth warned as numerous new threat icons appeared on the main sensor screen.

"Launch our war wings," ordered Commodore Krilen, feeling the blood rush that impending battle brought. "They are to destroy the inbound human fighters and then target the smaller human support ships with their remaining missiles."

"Honor awaits us," Angoth spoke as he passed on the orders.

From the Hocklyn ships, five hundred and forty sleek deadly fighters launched and, after quickly forming up, headed toward the human fighters in a massive wave.

"Our fighters are going to be outnumbered two to one," Commander Evans warned Admiral Sheen as she saw the massive cloud of Hocklyn fighters headed toward them. "They won't last long against those numbers!"

"Damn!" Amanda swore as she looked at the tactical display. She knew she was supposed to wait until Admiral Adler arrived before launching the fighters and bombers from the two carriers, but she couldn't stand by and let her fighters be destroyed. "Contact the carriers and order them to launch their fighters to join ours. They may keep one squadron each back for their own protection."

It only took a few moments and two hundred and eighty Talon fighters launched from the carriers Endurance and Clayton. They quickly formed up and then rushed to join their fellow pilots who were already closing with the horde of inbound Hocklyn fighters.

"Combat range in two minutes," Commander Evans reported as the distance between the two fleets continued to close. Second Fleet was moving forward at a reduced speed while the Hocklyns were coming full on. "Fighters engaging now!"

In space, the two opposing fleets of fighters suddenly filled the void between them with hundreds of small interceptor missiles. Dozens of fighters on both sides died in sudden fiery explosions as missiles slammed home, annihilating their targets. Fighters swerved in mad gyrations as they attempted to dodge out of the way of the small deadly missiles launched by both sides.

"Break and hit them now!" the strike commander called out over the squadron's linked com system. "Stay with your wingman and let's take these fighters out. No heroics, just do as you were taught and what we have done in practice. Make your shots count!"

Instantly, the two groups of fighters split apart as hundreds of individual dogfights broke out. Initially the human fighters were on the losing end from being so badly outnumbered and were losing two fighters for every Hocklyn they managed to destroy. Then the reinforcements from the battlecarriers arrived, and the odds rapidly shifted.

Space was full of flying interceptor missiles and tracer rounds as pilots from both sides tried to destroy their enemy. Damaged fighters died quickly as there was no mercy from either group. If a fighter was damaged or lost power it was only a matter of seconds before a missile would slam home, blowing the fighter into pieces. The fighter battle moved over to one side of the two closing groups of warships. To remain between them when they opened up with their heavy weapons would be suicide.

"Combat range!" Commander Evans suddenly yelled as the Hocklyn ships opened fire.

"Return fire!" Admiral Sheen ordered her pulse racing. "Lieutenant Trask, send an FTL message to Admiral Adler and inform him that we are engaged."

Amanda felt the WarStorm shudder as inbound ordnance struck the energy screen. The intensity in the Command Center picked up as the battle began in earnest.

From the WarStorm multiple missiles arched up and away from the battlecruiser as their targeting systems locked on a Hocklyn dreadnought. Large, dual pulse laser turrets on the upper and bottom hulls locked on the enemy dreadnought and fired. Multiple orange-red beams flashed out to impact on the dreadnought's energy screen. Then the missiles arrived, covering the Hocklyn ship in raging nuclear fire. Multiple ten-kiloton Devastator warheads detonated against the Hocklyn screen, releasing torrents of nuclear energy.

"Fire power beams!" Commander Evans ordered Tactical, seeing the energy screen on the dreadnought was wavering. "Target their midsection."

From the WarStorm, two power beams of violet energy leaped out and smashed into the energy screen of the dreadnought. The screen wavered and then partially collapsed where the power beams hit. Both beams instantly struck the dreadnought's armor, penetrating deeply into the hull and setting off secondary explosions within the ship. The dreadnaught seemed to stagger and then the energy screen strengthened, stopping the raging power beams.

All the ships of both opposing fleets were now within weapons range, and the space between the two became filled with orange-red laser beams, deep blue energy beams, and the violet color of power beams. Mixed in were fiery explosions from missiles being knocked down by interceptors as well as from close in defensive fire. The human ships were equipped with defensive laser turrets and these were firing nonstop, destroying numerous inbound missiles before they could impact on their energy screens.

As heavy as the defensive fire was, occasional missiles were still striking the human ships as well as numerous railgun rounds. Energy screens were aglow with nuclear explosions and exploding railgun munitions. The light cruiser Malken was suddenly hit by two nuclear missiles as well as several energy beams. Her energy shield wavered and then collapsed under the bombardment as a Hocklyn dreadnought pummeled the light cruiser with its heavy railguns. Explosions crept across the ship's armor, and then a violent explosion blew the cruiser apart.

"Light cruiser Malken is down," Lieutenant Stalls reported in a grim voice.

"The fleet's taking a lot of damage," Commander Evans reported as the WarStorm shook violently as a heavy nuke struck her energy screen. "Admiral Adler had better get here soon!"

"Press the attack," Amanda ordered her face covered in determination. "Switch missile tubes to Devastator missiles only!"

Lieutenant Mason acknowledged the order and swiftly made the adjustments. Commander Evans passed the order on to the rest of the fleet.

In space, strike commander Major Livingston grimaced as his wingman's fighter exploded in a fiery ball of flame. Everywhere he looked, there were tracer rounds and bright missile flares from interceptors. "We have the advantage now since the fighters from the carriers have arrived," he spoke over his com to the various fighter squadrons. Concentrate on the enemy and let's thin them out."

Turning sharply the major dove down toward a Hocklyn fighter, pressing the firing button for his two 30 mm cannons. Instantly tracer rounds arched out toward the enemy fighter, striking it just behind the pilot's canopy. The fighter exploded, and Livingston had to pull up to avoid flying through the fiery remains. He was just locking on to his next target when a Hocklyn interceptor missile struck his fighter. The human fighter exploded in a ball of light, taking the strike commander along with it.

Commodore Krilen swore as one of his dreadnoughts vanished from the sensor screen. The battle was growing more intense, and both sides were losing ships. He felt the IronHand shake violently, and the lights in the War Room dimmed briefly.

"We're taking damage," War Leader Angoth reported as several red lights flared up on the damage control console. "We have several compartments open to space."

"We have them outnumbered," replied Krilen, feeling that victory was within his grasp. "Have our ships focus their fire on the enemy capital ships; we can finish off their lighter units later."

The Hocklyn fleet turned every weapon on the human's heavier ships filling space with deadly ordnance. One of their targets was a Monarch heavy cruiser, which had become cut off from the rest of the human fleet. Its energy screen was suddenly overwhelmed as a dozen deep blue Hocklyn energy beams struck the screen simultaneously. The shield collapsed as two Hocklyn nuclear missiles arrived, detonating against the ship's heavy armor. For a moment, the ship seemed to shrug off the deadly nuclear explosions, but then the hull melted away, allowing the raging nuclear inferno to incinerate the engine room, as well as the ship's main fusion reactor. The Monarch blew apart as its nuclear self-destructs went off.

Admiral Sheen watched the main viewscreen as it showed the Monarch's destruction. All that was left of the cruiser was a fiery mass of wreckage and glowing gas. She knew with a sick feeling in her stomach that over eight hundred people had just died on that ship.

"Monarch cruiser Dresden is down," Lieutenant Stalls reported stone-faced. Those frightful words had been repeated too often in the last several minutes as more human ships had fallen to the Hocklyns.

Just as he finished saying the words, his sensor screen lit up with numerous green icons that were flashing into being. "Admiral Adler and Admiral Gaines have arrived," he reported with relief.

Commodore Krilen stared at the main sensor screen in anger. More human ships had arrived and very shortly he would be heavily outnumbered. If he didn't do something quickly, he was in danger of losing his entire fleet. He was trapped in the gravity well of the planet and would have to fight his way through heavy opposition to extricate his fleet. He realized now that it had been foolish to take his entire fleet into the gravity well to begin with. His own overconfidence was going to be his undoing. His dream of becoming a Fleet Commodore was evaporating before his eyes.

"Honor is before us," First Leader Angoth spoke as he gazed at the new human arrivals. He knew that victory against such numbers was not possible. The human weapons were too good, and their energy screens were just as strong as Hocklyn screens, if not better. They would die with honor today.

"I think not," replied Krilen, making a swift decision. "The High Council has ordered us to preserve our fleet at all costs and not to sacrifice ships needlessly. Have all ships form up into our standard defensive formation. We will fight our way out of the gravity well and then jump to safety."

Angoth stared at the commodore in shock. He had heard of the new orders not to sacrifice ships to preserve Hocklyn honor, he had just never expected to experience it. "As you command," he replied as he began carrying out the order.

The offensive fire from the Hocklyn ships lessened as they maneuvered into a more powerful defensive formation. They were almost in a sphere, with the escorts on the outside and the heavier ships on the inside. The Hocklyns began disengaging from the human ships and started accelerating toward the edge of the planet's gravity well in an attempt to escape.

—

Admiral Adler saw instantly what the Hocklyns were doing. There had been some discussion as to whether the Hocklyns would stand and fight to the last ship or try to preserve their fleet. Now they knew the answer.

"Launch our bombers," ordered Adler, looking over at his executive officer Colonel Timmons. "Target their escorts while Admiral Gaines engages the heavies."

—

Major Karl Arcles felt the acceleration as he flew his Anlon bomber out of the Wasp's large flight bay. All sixteen battlecarriers were launching every bomber they had in a desperate attempt to hit the Hocklyns before they could clear the planet's gravity well and escape. Arcles quickly formed up the Wasp's squadrons and then set course for the Hocklyn warships.

"I thought you promised we wouldn't be in a bomber again," Captain Lacy Sanders complained from her seat behind the major. She loved flying the new fighters, but she passionately disliked the bombers.

"This is war, Captain," Karl replied with a grin. "Besides, we get a chance to fire nukes at a Hocklyn ship. I knew you wouldn't want to miss out on that."

"Boys and their toys," Lacy muttered as she activated the forward energy shield for the bomber.

—

From the sixteen carriers, over 1,500 hundred bombers launched. Several squadrons of Talon fighters also launched to serve as escorts. In a massive wave, they set course for the Hocklyn ships.

"Bomber strike away," Colonel Timmons reported as the tactical display lit up with a cloud of green icons representing the outbound strike. Timmons studied the screen for a moment before turning toward the admiral. "Our bombers will reach the Hocklyns two minutes before they clear the gravity well and can jump."

Admiral Adler nodded; he then sent orders over to Admiral Gaines to follow the bomber strike with his fleet. If the timing was right, they should be able to take out the majority, if not all of the Hocklyn ships.

Commodore Krilen snarled in frustration at the main sensor screen as it told its deadly story. The humans had launched their small bombers toward his fleet. Thirty-eight of the newly arrived warships were following in the bombers' wake to finish off any Hocklyn ships that survived the bomber strike.

"They will reach us with both the small bombers and their fleet reinforcements before we can clear the gravity well," Angoth reported as he studied his tactical screen. Then, standing straight and putting his right hand upon the center of his chest armor, he turned and faced the commodore. "Honor comes for us today."

"Honor be damned!" Krilen cried as he thought desperately about how to preserve his fleet. It was obvious the humans had laid a trap for him due to his own carelessness in entering the planet's gravity well. There had to be a way out of this!

"Order all escorts to move forward into a wall shielding our dreadnoughts and war cruisers from the human bombers," Krilen ordered as he thought of a possible solution. It was desperate and would cost him most of his fleet, but it should allow his heavier units to survive.

"That will leave us open to attack from the fleet we have been engaging," Angoth warned. The two fleets were still firing upon each other, though the fire had lessened as the Hocklyn fleet began to pull away and flee toward the edge of the gravity well.

"Do as I say," Commodore Krilen ordered in a cold and determined voice. "All dreadnoughts and war cruisers are to be prepared for high speed maneuvers upon my command!"

"Close the range," Admiral Sheen ordered as the Hocklyn fleet tried to disengage from Second Fleet. "We must not let them escape!"

On the tactical display, she watched as the Hocklyn escort cruisers moved ahead of the heavier ships to meet the incoming wave of Anlon bombers. Her own ships were now closing the distance between the two fleets, even though it was evident the Hocklyn fleet was rapidly accelerating toward the edge of the gravity well of the planet in an attempt to escape. Missiles and railguns were finding fewer targets at the increased speeds even though energy weapons on both sides were still highly effective.

Amanda winced as another of her light cruisers exploded as deep blue energy beams from two Hocklyn dreadnoughts tore the smaller ship apart. Her fleet's own energy weapons were focused on a war cruiser, blasting through its screen and ripping into the armored hull. She felt satisfaction as the damaged ship's self-destructs finally detonated, shredding the ship into thousands of small glowing pieces.

Major Arcles swore as a railgun round from one of the Hocklyn light cruisers slammed into his bomber's forward shield. The shield seemed to waver briefly as the round spent itself.

"Shield's holding," reported Lacy, nervously, as she studied her instruments. "But just barely. We can't take too many more hits like that. Can't you dodge a few?"

"We're almost within range," Karl replied as he swerved the bomber to avoid an inbound interceptor missile. He watched as Lacy fired off several counter measures, drawing the missile farther away from their bomber.

His eyes focused intently on his tactical display, and suddenly four green lights blinked on his targeting console indicating he had a good lock on the escort cruiser that was firing on his bomber. Karl juked the bomber several times in sharp curves and then when he was sure he was close enough, released the bomber's four Shrike missiles. Each contained a one-kiloton nuclear warhead.

Looking out his cockpit window, he saw a sudden fiery explosion as an Anlon bomber was destroyed by Hocklyn defensive fire. It wasn't the first bomber to die, and it wouldn't be the last. "All bombers return to the carriers as soon as you've fired your missiles," he ordered grimly. "Don't stick around to see if you get any hits."

Lacy looked out the cockpit window, feeling nauseous. She saw numerous explosions where human bombers were dying. Shaking her head, she refocused her attention on her instruments. She could see that the Hocklyns were firing a lot of interceptor missiles toward the bombers in an attempt to destroy them before they could launch their deadly payloads. Pressing several buttons, she launched additional counter measures as well as two small decoys that should serve to attract any inbound missile. Hopefully, that would allow them to clear the combat zone. After this, she was determined that there would be no more bombers for her!

Commodore Krilen grimaced as a nuke penetrated the IronHand's energy screen and detonated against the dreadnought's heavily armored hull. The entire ship shook violently, and the damage control console became lit up with numerous red warning lights.

"The hull has been seriously compromised," First Leader Angoth reported as he listened to reports coming in from around the ship. "We've lost a number of railgun batteries as well as four of our missile tubes, and we're venting atmosphere."

Krilen looked closely at the sensor screen, which showed the human bomber strike decimating his escort cruisers. "All dreadnoughts and war cruisers are to switch to heading 120-90 by 30," he ordered his cold eyes looking at the main viewscreen, which was lit up with exploding ships. "When we reach the edge of the gravity well all ships are to jump to system K-416."

"What about our war wings?" asked Angoth, knowing that they would all be destroyed if they were left behind.

"Honor comes for them today," Krilen replied in a grave voice.

Amanda had ordered Second Fleet to continue to close with the fleeing Hocklyn capital ships. It was now obvious to her that the commodore in charge of this fleet was going to sacrifice his escorts to allow the dreadnoughts and war cruisers to escape. Admiral Gaines could not change his course in time since it would allow the surviving escort cruisers to close on the battlecarriers. He would have to eliminate them first before he could turn his fleet toward the fleeing enemy capital ships.

"Twenty seconds to the edge of the gravity well," Commander Evans reported as weapons fire from the WarStorm and two strikecruisers tore apart another enemy war cruiser. She watched as its red icon expanded and then vanished from the tactical screen.

"They're going to get away," Amanda spoke as the Hocklyn fleet crossed the edge of the planet's gravity well and began to vanish into white spatial vortexes as they jumped into the safety of hyperspace.

"Not many of them," Commander Evans responded. She studied some data on the tactical display and then turned back toward Admiral Sheen. "Only four of their dreadnoughts and six of their war cruisers managed to jump into hyperspace. We got the rest of them."

-

The surviving Hocklyn escort cruisers saw that the dreadnoughts and war cruisers had jumped into hyperspace and realized that they were now on their own with no hope of escape. Without hesitation, the sixteen surviving escort cruisers redlined their subspace drives and targeted the approaching human ships. Even though they were all heavily damaged, just the mass of their ships alone would be deadly weapons. Honor would be served in their sacrifice.

The escort cruisers charged toward the inbound human fleet, but Admiral Gaines had been prepared for this. A massive wave of Devastator missiles launched as every missile tube in Fifth Fleet was emptied. Escort cruiser after escort cruiser died as nuclear fire consumed their ships, but five of them managed to burst through the rain of nuclear fire and hurl themselves upon Fifth Fleet.

Admiral Gaines looked in sudden shock at the main viewscreen as he saw a burning Hocklyn escort cruiser growing impossibly large on the main viewscreen. His flagship shook violently and he was thrown out of his command chair, landing painfully against the plotting table. Lights in the Command Center went out, and he could see numerous fires breaking out as consoles shorted out and died. In the distance, he could hear explosions and people screaming out in terror and pain.

The emergency lights in the Command Center came on, but the ship was now shaking uncontrollably as explosions rocked the battlecruiser. He didn't have to check the damage control console to know that his ship was mortally wounded. It was at that moment that the self-destructs in the flagship activated, blowing the ship apart and ensuring its total destruction.

-

Admiral Sheen looked on in shock as the main viewscreen showed the death of Admiral Gaines's flagship. "It's gone," she said in a stunned voice. A Monarch cruiser and two light cruisers had also been destroyed in the final suicide attack.

Commander Evans said nothing as she stared at the viewscreen. Everyone in the Command Center was silent as they watched the burning wreckage of what had been Fifth Fleet's flagship.

"Admiral Adler is ordering us to rendezvous with Fifth Fleet, and you are to take command," Lieutenant Trask said suddenly into the silence.

Amanda nodded and turned wearily to Commander Evans. "What's the status of our fighters?"

"The fighter battle is over, and all the Hocklyn fighters have been destroyed," the commander reported.

"Order the fighters to return home and set course for Fifth Fleet," Amanda ordered. "We need to initiate repairs and prepare to return to Careth. Some of our ships will need to go back into the repair docks. Also, get me a status on our losses."

After a few minutes, Second Fleet rendezvoused with Fifth Fleet and Admiral Sheen carefully formed the two fleets up into a defensive formation while repairs were made. Admiral Adler was busy with the carriers as they were involved in rescue operations for any surviving pilots from the fighters and the bombers.

"I have our losses," Commander Evans reported as she walked over grim faced to Admiral Sheen. "We lost one battlecruiser, three Monarch cruisers, and twelve light cruisers. We also lost one hundred and thirty-four fighters."

"What about Fifth Fleet?" Amanda asked. "What were their losses?"

"One battlecruiser, one Monarch cruiser, and two light cruisers, all from the suicide attack. They also lost four hundred and sixty-two Anlon bombers."

Amanda knew the battle could be considered a major victory for the Federation, but it had left a sour taste in her mouth at the way it had ended. "How long before we can jump?" she asked, leaning back in her command chair and rubbing her forehead.

"Two hours and all ships should have sufficient repairs made to make it back to Careth," Commander Evans replied.

Amanda nodded. She had spoken briefly with Admiral Adler. She was to jump both fleets back to the bears' system and then send all the undamaged ships to Admiral Streth's location. Admiral Adler would go straight to the fleet base to speak to Admiral Streth about the recent battle and Admiral Gaines death. Amanda let out a deep breath and thought about all the fleet personnel that had just died. Sometimes she wished she wasn't an admiral, and she knew that all of those deaths would haunt her for a very long time. It was moments like this that she really wished Richard were near. Amanda knew she was in for some sleepless nights.

Chapter Seven

President Kincaid was in his office being briefed by Fleet Admiral Johnson on the latest battle in Operation First Strike. The two had been discussing the losses suffered by both sides and possible ramifications.

"I believe the Hocklyns were just feeling us out," Admiral Johnson spoke as she handed the president a list of ship and personnel losses. "There were no AI ships present and the weapons and energy screens that these ships possessed were no more powerful than those we have faced in the past."

"Then these ships hadn't been updated by the AIs?" Kincaid asked as he studied the losses suffered by Second and Fifth Fleets. He shook his head at the loss of so many valuable ships and personnel. "How did Admiral Gaines die?"

"No, the ships hadn't been updated," replied Karla, letting out a heavy sigh. She had felt deeply saddened when she heard of Admiral Gaines death, having known the older admiral for quite some time. He had been a veteran of the fleet and highly dependable. "Admiral Gaines died when his flagship was rammed by a heavily damaged Hocklyn escort cruiser."

Kincaid nodded. He leaned back in his chair and gazed gravely over at Fleet Admiral Johnson. "I am sorry to hear of the admiral's death. From what I know of his record, he was a good officer. Did he have any family?"

"Just a younger brother, who is also an officer in the Fleet," Karla replied. "I took it upon myself to personally notify him of his brother's loss." It had been a difficult conversation for Karla, one that had become too common in recent months since the Hocklyns had first attacked Gliese 667C. She had staff members that were normally responsible for notifying families of combat deaths, but in this instance Karla felt that she needed to be the one delivering the message.

"Will this latest loss by the Hocklyns delay their counterattack?" President Kincaid asked as his eyes focused on the Fleet Admiral. "They lost nearly their entire fleet."

"I doubt it," Karla replied in an even voice. "I believe and so does Fleet Admiral Streth that when the AIs are finished upgrading a sufficient number of Hocklyn ships, they will launch their counterattack immediately."

"Are we certain the AIs are upgrading the Hocklyn ships? They could just be gathering a massive fleet to attack us," Kincaid suggested. He didn't like the idea of facing advanced weapons from the Hocklyns. He also knew the Hocklyn fleet vastly outnumbered the warships the Federation had available. It was one of his greatest fears that no matter what they did the Hocklyns would just overwhelm the Federation with their superior numbers.

"We're fairly certain that is happening," Karla replied with a nod of her head. "The AIs will want to be certain of our defeat, so they will equip the Hocklyns with weapons similar to ours or perhaps slightly more advanced to ensure their victory."

The phone rang on the president's desk, and he frowned at the interruption. He had left strict instructions that he was not to be bothered unless it was an extreme emergency. Reaching down with his right hand, he picked the phone up. After listening for a minute, he put it back down and looked over at Fleet Admiral Johnson with a strange, disbelieving look upon his face.

"That was Senator Barnes from Ceres," Kincaid began in an unsteady voice. "Four battlecruisers have just jumped in from New Tellus and are on their way to Ceres. They are escorting an unknown ship similar in size to one of our fleet destroyers."

"Why?" asked Admiral Johnson, feeling confused. No one had informed her of any of this. "Where did the ship come from?"

"That's the strange part," Kincaid replied in a lower voice as if he was afraid to repeat what he had just been told. "The ship is supposedly from New Providence."

"New Providence!" spoke Fleet Admiral Johnson, rising to her feet and her hazel eyes growing wide. "That's impossible!"

"Nevertheless, that's what they claim, and they have a recorded message from Admiral Teleck confirming who they are and that they are to be taken to Governor Malleck on Ceres immediately."

"I need to go to Ceres," Karla said, still trying to make sense of what the president had just told her.

There were no survivors in the old Federation worlds; Admiral Sheen had confirmed that years ago on her search mission when she had been sent back to the old Federation. They had only found a few on Aquaria and none anywhere else.

"I'm going with you," replied President Kincaid, reaching for his phone. He would be canceling all of his appointments for the next few days. If this ship was indeed from New Providence, it could be a game changer.

-

On Ceres, Governor Malleck and Admiral Kalen were waiting in the massive ship bay as they watched the destroyer enter and then dock smoothly in the designated berth. Two full platoons of heavily armed marines quickly lined up outside of the ship's main hatch waiting for those inside to disembark.

"From New Providence," murmured Admiral Kalen, gazing at the ship awestruck. "Is it possible?"

"So they claim," Governor Malleck responded in an even voice. "Admiral Teleck, Fleet Admiral Streth, Admiral Sheen, and Admiral Andrews all spoke to the commanding officer and this Senator Arden. They are all convinced that this ship is indeed from New Providence."

"That means there are survivors in the old Federation," spoke Kalen, wondering how they could have escaped detection by the Hocklyns all this time. "It also suggests that General Allister succeeded in saving a significant number of people."

"If our historical records from that time are correct, he could have saved several hundred thousand," replied Governor Malleck as his eyes remained focused on the hatch of the ship waiting for it to open.

Even as they spoke, the main hatch slid open and half a dozen heavily armed marines stepped out, followed by the commander of the ship and a woman. They stopped in front of the Ceres marines, and then the sergeant in charge of the small guard detail snapped to attention and saluted the captain in charge of the waiting marines.

"Let's go meet our guests," Governor Malleck suggested as he began walking forward. "I imagine they have one hell of a story to tell us."

-

The next day, President Kincaid, Fleet Admiral Johnson, Governor Malleck, Admiral Kalen, and Doctor Evelyn Reynolds were all seated at a large conference table with Senator Arden and Commander Strone. Senator Arden had been describing in detail the early days on New Providence shortly after Admiral Streth left the Federation with the survivors he had gathered.

"We had a dozen stealth scouts in the military bunkers," Senator Arden explained as she looked around at the attentive group. "For several years during the Hocklyn occupation the ships would go out at night and fly to the other worlds of the Federation searching for survivors. We rescued over twelve thousand people before it became too dangerous. The Hocklyns were intensifying their efforts on all of our worlds to wipe out any large groups of survivors. We finally realized that if we continued with the rescue operations it would only be a matter of time before one of the scouts was either captured or led the Hocklyns back to New Providence. General Allister hated discontinuing the rescue efforts, but he felt there was no other choice, not if he wanted to keep the hidden military bunkers a secret."

"We finally had to stop the rescue efforts and wait," Commander Strone added. "For ten years the Hocklyns searched our worlds, killing every survivor they came across. They only left a few scattered pockets of survivors in remote isolated areas such as the mountains, and most of those died due to a lack of supplies or adequate protection from the weather."

"When the Hocklyns finally left we sent our ships out again, but all they found were empty worlds, except for Aquaria," added Senator Arden, sadly.

"Krall Island," exhaled Admiral Kalen, feeling excited at hearing what had happened back on the Federation worlds. "We sent a cruiser back to the Federation years ago to check for survivors. They found a few still living on Krall Island on Aquaria."

"Yes, Krall Island," Commander Strone confirmed with a nod of his head. "We contacted them, but they declined to come to New Providence; they wanted to live out their lives on the island. As for your cruiser, when it appeared over New Providence the leaders of our world at that time feared it might be a Hocklyn trick to try to draw us out of hiding, so we did not respond to its hails."

"That explains a lot," spoke Governor Malleck, looking over at Fleet Admiral Johnson and President Kincaid. "Our people have long wondered what happened to those that stayed behind on New Providence. It is good to hear that you survived."

"How did you learn of us and know where to find our fleet?" President Kincaid asked. He knew they had to have had some clue or it would have been like hunting for a needle in a haystack. The galaxy was a large place and the new Federation only inhabited a small fraction of it.

Senator Arden and Commander Strone glanced at each other and then the senator spoke. "Two Hocklyn escort cruisers were passing through our system, and we intercepted some of their communications. They told of a massive battle that had been fought against other humans and that two AI ships had been destroyed. We came to find those humans, believing they were those that had escaped with Admiral Streth. You can imagine our shock when Admiral Teleck told us about Earth."

"We were even more shocked to learn that Fleet Admiral Streth was still alive and leading your fleets," Commander Strone added. "Even back on New Providence he is a legend."

"Admiral Streth is special," agreed Governor Malleck. "Our young children have always been taught that someday he would be awoken from cryosleep and would lead us to victory over the Hocklyns."

Senator Arden nodded, not feeling surprised. "I just hope that's true."

"New Providence is well inside the Hocklyn Slave Empire at the moment," President Kincaid said, his eyes focusing on Senator Arden. "There must be another reason you came this far risking exposure to your world."

"We want to join the war effort," spoke Commander Strone, stunning the group. "We can put a massive satellite defensive grid up above New Providence at almost a moment's notice. We have constructed a large fleet of destroyers that can be put in place to ensure the survivability of that defensive grid."

"But we don't have a weapon that can destroy an AI ship," Senator Arden spoke in a deadly serious voice, her eyes looking pleadingly around the group. "We need that weapon from you or our world will have to remain hidden, and we will not be able to join the war effort." She paused and looked intently at each person at the conference table, then continued with intensity in her voice. "We have remained hidden for over four hundred years! We are ready to come out, reclaim the surface of our world, and show the Hocklyns that the old Federation isn't dead. We just need the weapon you used to destroy the AIs."

President Kincaid closed his eyes and let out a deep breath. This was something he hadn't been expecting. He also didn't know about the feasibility of giving Devastator Three missiles to New Providence.

"The weapon you're speaking of is a Devastator Three missile, and it is a highly technical weapon and expensive to produce," Admiral

Kalen ventured to speak, not wanting to give out any technical details without permission from President Kincaid.

"The weapon and delivery system are so complicated that in order to take out an AI ship we only have one class of ships that can even deploy the weapon effectively," Fleet Admiral Johnson spoke as she thought about the recent upgrades to all of the heavy strikecruisers.

"This is something we will need to discuss," President Kincaid finally said as he weighed the request in his mind. "We could probably give you a supply of the weapons, but the delivery system is going to be a problem."

"Could our defensive battle stations be modified to deploy the Devastator Threes?" asked Governor Malleck, looking over at Admiral Kalen.

He knew the admiral was more familiar with the technical side of the new missiles than anyone else at the table. If the battle stations could be modified it might be feasible to send a large number to New Providence to strengthen their defensive grid as well as provide an effective counter weapon against the AIs.

"It's possible," Kalen admitted with a heavy frown on his face as he thought it over. "It would take a total redesign to make them work."

"What's so special about these missiles that we can't produce them ourselves?" Senator Arden asked, not understanding the problem. After all a missile was a missile, just the warheads were different.

Admiral Kalen looked over at President Kincaid who nodded. "The Devastator Threes have a miniature sublight drive as well as an inertial dampening system installed. They arrive on target almost instantly when they are launched."

"How did you ever do that?" Commander Strone asked as he realized the extent of the technology the new Federation was using in these missiles. He realized with a sinking feeling that this was a type of weapon that would take New Providence years to put into production even if they had the specs.

"We had hundreds of years to develop the weapon," Admiral Kalen responded as he recalled the numerous failed tests until they finally got the missile to work properly. "Getting the sublight drive small enough to use in a missile was the big problem."

"So we can't build it?" asked Senator Arden, looking over at Commander Strone with disappointment in her eyes. She had hoped to see the day they could emerge from their underground cities and step out on the surface of their world once again.

"No, at least not yet," replied the commander, shaking his head. "It would take us several years just to develop the technologies to build such a missile even if we had the plans."

"So, what are we going to do?" Senator Arden asked as she looked questionably around the group. "We are tired of hiding underground."

"Let us show you and your people around the new Federation," suggested President Kincaid, putting a smile on his face. "The people from the old Federation that came with Admiral Streth helped to build it. That way when you return home you can tell them what their ancestors helped to create."

"In the meantime, we can have our scientists discuss your situation and what we can do to help," Governor Malleck added as he thought over what might be possible. "We don't want to expose New Providence to the Hocklyns if you can't defend yourself. You may have no option but to remain hidden for a few more years until we can do more from our end."

"I understand," Senator Arden responded with a heavy sigh of disappointment. She had hoped for so much more, but guessed she would just have to wait and see if the scientists in this new Federation could come up with anything. Then she looked over at President Kincaid. "We would like to see your Federation; at least it will give our people back home hope even if we can't join the war effort."

"I will make the necessary arrangements," President Kincaid promised with a friendly smile. "I believe you will be impressed."

Admiral Race Tolsen gazed at the large viewscreen on his new flagship, the Conqueror Class battlecruiser Defiant. He had just completed over four months of physical therapy from the injuries he had suffered when his former flagship, the battlecruiser WarHawk, had been destroyed in the Gliese 667C system. For months afterward, he hadn't been sure if he would ever step foot upon a warship again.

"Admiral Bennett did a fine job building the Defiant," Colonel Arnett commented from her position at the plotting table where she was watching as the fleet came together into a standard defensive formation. "She is the latest design with more powerful weapons and shields."

"I just hope its good enough, Colonel," Admiral Tolsen replied as he sat down in his command chair behind his console. "When

Admiral Streth brings the Hocklyns back here we will be in for one hell of a battle."

The viewscreen switched to show a view of New Tellus Station, the largest shipyard in the Federation. New Tellus Station was sixteen kilometers in length and eight in width, and contained six massive construction bays each of which could produce any size ship the Fleet required, as well as twelve repair bays. It was also covered in offensive and defensive weapons with the firepower of twenty battlecruisers. Two hundred defensive laser satellites and sixty missile platforms also surrounded the station. Two full squadrons of fighters were on constant patrol along with half a dozen destroyers.

In the distance, he could see one of the vast asteroid fortresses. They were anywhere from sixteen to twenty-two kilometers in diameter and covered with massive offensive and defensive weapon systems. Each fortress was fully capable of dealing with a Hocklyn invasion fleet on its own.

"Those fortresses are impressive," commented Colonel Arnett, seeing what Admiral Tolsen was looking at. "They're built to take a lot of punishment." Arnett had toured one recently and been extremely impressed.

"We may need them when the Hocklyns and the AIs finally reach us here," Tolsen said as he looked over at the tactical display, which was showing his assembling fleet.

His new fleet was much more powerful than the previous one. He had six battlecruisers, three battlecarriers, six heavy strikecruisers, twelve Monarch cruisers, and thirty light cruisers. All fleet destroyers had been assigned to support duty in the satellite grids to help ensure their survival. Destroyers had been found to be too vulnerable when fighting Hocklyn warships.

There were four fleets of similar size based in the New Tellus system in anticipation of a Hocklyn attack. Similarly sized fleets were also present in Earth's solar system as well. There were also several squadrons of light cruisers constantly out on patrol to serve as a quick reaction force for any unknown ships that might jump into the system. Each light cruiser squadron was commanded by a Monarch heavy cruiser.

"All ships are now in formation," Colonel Arnett reported as the last two light cruisers moved into their positions.

"Very well," Admiral Tolsen responded, ready to finally get underway. "All ships, twenty percent sublight, and let's move out of the gravity well."

The fleet slowly accelerated and moved away from New Tellus, the light cruisers forming a screen around the heavier units with the battlecruiser Defiant at the center. This was a strong defensive formation aimed at protecting the more powerful ships in case of a sudden and unexpected attack.

A little later, Colonel Arnett looked over at Admiral Tolsen. "We have cleared the gravity well and can assume standard patrol speed."

"Accelerate to forty percent sublight and move out toward our patrol area," Admiral Tolsen ordered. Inside the gravity well of New Tellus, ships were restricted to only using twenty percent power on their sublight drives.

"We have ships dropping out of hyperspace," Lieutenant Brent Davis spoke from sensors, then after a moment, added. "It looks like Admiral Teleck has made it back."

"Have we confirmed that it's Admiral Teleck's fleet?" Tolsen asked sharply. He didn't want his people taking anything for granted.

"Yes, Sir," Davis replied. "The light cruiser Arniss has confirmed their ID codes."

"Very well," replied Tolsen, nodding his head in approval. "Continue on course."

Currently there were two warfleets always on patrol in the outer system of New Tellus with two others waiting just inside the gravity well of the planet. All the systems within twenty light years of New Tellus had multiple FTL detection buoys in place. Tolsen had known from previous reports that Admiral Teleck's fleet would be jumping into the system. He had wanted to know how his young sensor operator would respond to numerous ships suddenly appearing. The young man had performed his job well.

Admiral Teleck breathed a sigh of relief as his fleet dropped out of hyperspace in the New Tellus system. Once he dropped off the now empty supply ships, he would be returning to Ceres to take some days off.

"New Tellus Defense Fleet One is just leaving the gravity well of the planet," his sensor operator reported as numerous green, blue, yellow, and violet icons lit up the screen.

"That would be Admiral Tolsen's new fleet," his executive officer commented.

"Yes, it is," replied Admiral Teleck, smiling.

He knew that Admiral Tolsen had gone through a long recovery period after being injured at Gliese 667C. He was glad to see that he had returned to duty. It was also comforting to know that he'd fought the Hocklyns in the past and was an experienced admiral. They would need that experience when the Hocklyns attacked New Tellus.

"Ready to get back to work?" asked Teleck, looking over at Admiral Andrews who was standing just behind him watching the big viewscreen which showed several of the other ships of the fleet.

Richard nodded as he replied. "Yes, it was great to get to see my wife and spend some time alone with her, but being on the front lines and speaking to several of the Carethians really brings everything home."

"Those bears are going to be staunch allies if Admiral Strong can hold their home world from the Hocklyns," Teleck spoke. He too had met and talked to several Carethians. Grayseth, their leader seemed very straightforward and trustworthy.

"I think he will," Richard replied as he recalled what he had learned while on the bears' planet. "With the defenses they are setting up, the AIs and the Hocklyns might be hesitant to accept the losses it will take to conquer the system."

"If we can defeat them here at New Tellus then Admiral Strong may not have to face a massive attack at all," responded Teleck, agreeing with Richard's assessment. That would allow the bear system to remain intact and serve as an advanced base for future Federation attacks on the Hocklyn Slave Empire. It could also serve as a jumping off point to free the old Federation worlds.

"We have permission to micro-jump to just outside the gravity well of New Tellus," the executive officer reported as she turned toward the admiral.

"Plot the jump and take us in," Admiral Teleck ordered.

He was anxious to get home and curious to see what had happened when the ship from New Providence had arrived at Ceres. He could well imagine the uproar it must have caused when it was discovered that there were millions of survivors still in the old Federation.

Richard was back in the Command Center of his massive asteroid fortress. In the center of the large room was an upraised dais with an enormous console. Directly in front of the dais were a dozen plotting tables with tactical holograms floating above them. There were four fleet officers sitting at each one operating the computer controls and data screens. Farther across the room, upon the front wall, six massive viewscreens showed various views of the New Tellus system. Currently they were focused on several of the other fortresses, New Tellus Station, one of the other shipyards, the large fleets in orbit, and New Tellus itself.

Looking at the blue-white globe that represented the planet reminded Richard of what New Providence had looked like the last time he'd been there. That, of course, had been when his wife had taken the original WarStorm on its mission to search the old Federation for survivors. They had only found the few on Aquaria, even though he now knew there had been millions of survivors hiding beneath the surface of New Providence.

"Status," he spoke, gazing over at his second in command, Rear Admiral Drew Hazleton.

"All systems functioning normally," Hazleton reported as he stood up and relinquished the command chair. He moved over and sat down at a second command chair on the left side of Richard.

"Fighters and bombers?" asked Richard, knowing that the pilots were flying regular practice missions almost daily.

They were also responsible for patrolling the space inside the gravity well of New Tellus. At any one time, over one hundred Talon fighters were out on patrol along with several wings of bombers. All were fully armed and ready to react at a moment's notice.

"Routine training only, Sir," Hazleton replied as he recalled the latest pilot training schedules. "Patrols have been normal with no incidents."

Richard nodded as he leaned back in his chair and gazed about the large room. Several hundred trained men and women were busy in the large Command Center that was the heart of the New Tellus's defenses. From here, Richard would command all eight of the massive asteroid fortresses, five of the shipyards, and the defensive grid around the planet. Fleet Admiral Johnson would command New Tellus Station and the fleets that were based in the system.

The surface of the asteroid was covered with defensive railgun and laser batteries. Each was capable of individual tracking and eliminating an inbound target. There were also numerous interceptor missile batteries capable of taking out inbound missiles and enemy fighters. However, the biggest thing was the fortresses' offensive capability. Massive pulse laser and power beam turrets dotted the surface. There were also multiple missile launchers capable of firing Klave, Devastator, and Devastator Three missiles. Richard was confident that if any Hocklyn fleet came near his command asteroid he could destroy it. Everything could be controlled from the Command Center or the two auxiliary Command Centers hidden in other parts of the asteroid.

The only real danger to the fortress would be from an AI ship. Since Ariel and Clarissa had managed to destroy two of them, it had become necessary to make some changes. Ariel and Lieutenant Johnson had written a new computer program that should allow the advanced computers on the heavy strikecruisers and the StarStrike to be able to take out individual AI ships. That same program had been more difficult to install on the fortresses as it had taken a major modification to the computers and the targeting systems for the Devastator Threes. It had finally been accomplished, but Richard didn't know how well it would work until they tested it against an actual AI ship.

Later, after making a tour of various sections of the fortress, Richard retired to his quarters. They were quite spacious and in some ways could almost be considered lavish. He sat down in a large leather recliner and picked up a book he had been reading before he had left with Admiral Teleck. The book was from Earth and had been written by someone called H.G. Wells. The name of the book was The War of the Worlds. It reminded him of several books he had read in his youth back home on New Providence. Reading allowed him to relax and not focus so much on Amanda not being close by. It worried him that the next time he saw her a massive Hocklyn and AI fleet would probably be following her home to New Tellus. He just hoped his fortresses were ready. He opened the book to the page marked and began reading.

Chapter Eight

Fleet Commodore Resmunt was reading Commodore Krilen's report of his fleet's battle with the humans. He was on board his flagship, the Liberator, and wasn't too surprised at what the report told. It was becoming more evident with every battle that the humans were better tacticians than the average Hocklyn War Leader or Commodore.

"Another trap," he hissed as he looked over at First Leader Ganth. "These humans have a propensity for setting traps for us, and we seem to fall right into them."

"They nearly wiped out Commodore Krilen's fleet," Ganth rasped, his large dark eyes narrowing. "How could he allow himself to get caught in a planet's gravity well?"

"It is our own fault," Resmunt replied as he tapped the chest plate on his light gray battle armor with his left hand. "For far too long we have not faced an enemy worthy of battle. We have been taking victory for granted after so many centuries of easy conquests. The human's technology is better than ours, and after what was done to their original worlds, they now seek revenge against us. They have trained their fleet commanders very well."

"Our weapons are being updated by the AIs," Ganth reminded the Fleet Commodore. "Surely we will be more than a match for the humans in future battles."

"Perhaps," Resmunt replied as his cold dark eyes gazed at his First Leader. "Before we launch our attack all the War Leaders must understand the danger these humans represent. We can't afford to underestimate them anymore, or we could face defeat."

"Defeat!" Ganth echoed his eyes growing even wider in disbelief. "We will have AI ships with us; surely victory and much honor will await us."

"Our War Leaders will have to fight against humans who are just as good as they are and perhaps better at directing a fleet battle," replied Resmunt, firmly. "I learned much in our own battle against the humans, and I will not let them trick me again. We will have overwhelming forces in this next battle, and we must use them to our advantage."

"Several of the War Leaders that have been chosen are some of the best in our fleet, such as Versith of the dreadnought Viden," Ganth pointed out. He had served with War Leader Versith on a short tour many years ago when he first joined the fleet.

"We were lucky to get War Leader Versith," Resmunt responded in agreement. He had studied Versith's record and been duly impressed by the level of strategy the War Leader was capable of.

There were several of the other War Leaders he was not happy with. Some were obviously political appointments by the High Council, such as War Leader Osbith who had been with him when the fleet base had fallen. Osbith knew nothing of strategy and directing a fleet in battle.

"There are two other things that concern me," Fleet Commodore Resmunt continued as he thought about the coming war. "The new weapon the humans used to destroy our space station above the fleet base, as well as the two AI ships and their small bombers which have wrecked such havoc with our warships."

"The humans must not have too many of those new weapons or they would have used more of them against our fleet," First Leader Ganth pointed out. "They must have a very limited supply and only used them in desperation when the battle was going against them."

"That would explain why they waited so long to deploy them," Resmunt conceded as he thought over what Ganth had said. "If their supply of these weapons is limited, perhaps the threat from them will not be so great."

"Their small bombers are another matter," Ganth continued in his rasping voice. "I have spoken to a number of the First Leaders on the war cruisers that will be accompanying the fleet. We can add five more of our fighters to each of our war cruiser's flight bays and ten to the flight bays of our dreadnoughts. I would also suggest that we only equip our fighters with short-range interceptor missiles to combat the human bombers. That will allow each of our fighters to carry four of the small missiles. If we can destroy the human bombers before they can launch their payloads of nuclear missiles then they will be of no threat to the fleet."

"It might be a good idea to hold some of our fighters back," Resmunt spoke as he thought the idea over. This was a good suggestion coming from his First Leader. "We won't launch them until the humans launch their bombers. In all of the previous battles, our fighters have been engaged against the human fighters and could not respond to their bomber attacks."

"We could launch only a portion of the war wings to engage the human fighters, but hold others back until needed against the bombers," Ganth suggested.

Commodore Resmunt looked over at First Leader Ganth. His suggestions were worthy ones and could bring Ganth even more honor. "Make it so," he ordered. Resmunt wanted every advantage he could have when he faced the humans again.

Aboard the dreadnought Viden, War Leader Virseth looked at the ship's main viewscreen, which showed the massive fleet being gathered above Kenward Seven. It was the largest fleet the Hocklyn Slave Empire had ever assembled.

"The humans will die when the might of our Empire falls upon them," spoke Second Leader Jaseth in a heated voice.

He still felt a smoldering hatred for the humans because of the ruin they had brought upon his family. His father, High Leader Ankler, had been executed by the AIs, and they had lost the majority of their family's holdings. Jaseth would not rest until the human worlds were crushed beneath the might of the Hocklyn fleet and all humans were dead.

War Leader Virseth gazed worriedly at the young Second Leader, suspecting what he was feeling. Virseth had been good friends with Jaseth's family for a very long time and had taken Jaseth on as a Second Leader on board his flagship after the young Hocklyn had completed the first part of his military training. If Jaseth could keep his wits about him, the young Hocklyn would make a fine warrior and rise swiftly in the ranks.

"Jaseth, be wary of your anger," Virseth cautioned, his large black eyes focusing on the young Second Leader. "Anger can blind you at times and force you to miss what is obviously in front of you. I suspect this will be a long war and not decided by just a few battles. There will be plenty of time for you to extract vengeance for what happened to your family."

Jaseth nodded, knowing the veteran War Leader was right. He reached down and touched the hilt of the blade he always carried at his waist. "I just hope to have the opportunity to use my blade against the human warriors. It calls out for human blood, and it shall have it!"

"In time," replied Virseth, knowing he would have to keep a careful eye on Jaseth. "For now we must make sure our section of the fleet is ready for battle. I need a status report on how far along the shipyard is on finishing the upgrades to our fleet's weapons and energy shields."

Jaseth nodded. While the raging anger against the humans was always with him, he knew he still had his duty to fulfill. He turned and strode away from the command pedestal to carry out his orders.

"Jaseth is full of much anger," First Leader Trion spoke as he stepped over closer to the War Leader. "It clouds his judgment and could some day pose a danger to the ship."

"He is young and has lost much," Virseth replied as he watched the young Hocklyn going about his duties. "We will keep an eye on him and make sure he stays on the right path. He has the makings of a fine warrior if he can only control his anger."

High Leader Nartel was seated in the High Council Chamber along with the other councilors of the Hocklyn Slave Empire. For once the councilors were quiet as if waiting for their own deaths. The reason for their silence was simple; at any moment, they were expecting an AI to come through the council chamber doors.

"What can they want this time?" Councilor Ruthan asked in a subdued voice, almost as if he was afraid the AI could hear him speaking.

"Our obedience," High Leader Nartel responded, his cold eyes focusing on the troublesome councilor. "They ordered this meeting and directed that all of us be here."

"They brought four ships," Councilor Berken spoke in a nervous voice. "Never have they entered the heart of our Empire with four ships before."

"To impress us," Councilor Jarles suggested, his cold dark eyes looking at the High Leader. "They want to impress upon us the importance of this coming war with the humans." Jarles was not pleased with this latest development. Expansion of the Empire had ground to a halt as preparations were made for war. All across the frontier ships were being pulled back and positioned in case they were needed against the humans.

Any further discussion came to a halt as the massive council chamber doors swung open and four AIs came in. As usual, each one was of a different shape. Tentacles waved in the air, and their heads were a glowing orb of what looked like pure energy. They floated above the floor using some type of anti-gravity, exuding power and ultimate authority.

"We have come to speak to the High Council," the first AI to enter the room spoke in a powerful and commanding voice.

"We are yours to command," responded High Leader Nartel, rising to his feet. The AIs made him nervous as he knew they carried some type of deadly energy weapon with them, the same weapon that had been used in these very chambers to execute High Leader Ankler only a few months back.

"The fleet at Kenward Seven is almost ready for the war against the humans," the AI spoke as it came even nearer to the conference table. "That fleet is to be followed up by a second fleet of your regular warships to ensure that no humans escape as they did before. Failure in this will have severe consequences for your Empire. No human must survive this war; they and their worlds must be annihilated!"

"It will be as you command," replied High Leader Nartel, trying to keep his eyes focused on the AI. The AIs were frightening, and it was all Nartel could do to not look away.

"We have scanned the area of space the humans took from you," the AI continued in a nearly emotionless voice. "They have gathered themselves around two worlds. One is the world of Careth, and the second is Fleet Commodore Resmunt's former fleet base. The humans at Careth will obviously attempt to defend the planet; however, those around the fleet base will undoubtedly flee back to their home worlds when faced with your fleet and our ships. We will follow them and destroy those worlds as we find them."

"What about Careth?" High Leader Nartel forced himself to ask. "What is to become of it?"

"Your follow up fleet will be used to annihilate it!" the AI commanded his mechanical voice rising in intensity. "Destroy the system! The Carethians have been exposed to the humans for too long and must be eliminated."

"It will be so ordered," Nartel replied evenly. He knew from reports that the Carethians were highly advanced and destroying that system with the humans present might prove to be both difficult and costly. They would also be losing a valuable slave race.

"There will be ten of our ships accompanying the main fleet," the AI added as it came over and hovered close to Nartel as if trying to make a point. "The humans must be driven back to their worlds!"

"With the new weapons you have furnished us, it will be done," Nartel spoke as he took a step back. It almost felt as if he could feel an electrical charge coming from the AI.

"It had better be a successful campaign," the AI warned. "We will not accept failure! You have already experienced once what happens when we are displeased."

The AI turned and left the council chambers, followed by the other three. None of the other AIs had spoken, but their presence had been enough to shake the council.

"Ten AI ships," Ruthan breathed in shock. "Never have they gathered such a force."

"It's the humans," Berken stated as he looked at the other councilors. "For some reason they greatly fear them."

"Something from the remote past," High Leader Nartel suggested as he gazed at the now closed doors. He was relieved the AIs were gone. "We must prepare the second fleet to attack Careth as well as sweep the area the humans took from us for any of their ships that might escape our initial assault upon their main fleet."

"We should send a large number of scout cruisers along with the second warfleet," Councilor Ruthan added, his eyes still showing fear at being so close once more to an actual AI. "They can be used to search the area for any humans that the main fleet may have missed."

Nartel nodded; this was a good suggestion and he would order it to be done. "Commodore Krilen will be advanced to the rank of Fleet Commodore and placed in charge of our follow up fleet. He has faced the humans and learned how they fight. He will not make the same mistakes again in battle or his honor will greatly suffer."

"Make sure that Krilen understands the importance of his mission," Berken spoke in his rasping voice. "He must understand what the price of failure will be, not just upon him but upon all of us."

"It will be stressed," Nartel assured the councilor. Nartel would make sure that Krilen had a large enough fleet that failure would be impossible. Krilen would sweep Careth and the humans defending it into oblivion.

The meeting broke up, and High Leader Nartel went up to his office. Going in, he stepped over to the balcony that allowed him a view of the capital and the sky above. It was late afternoon, but the sunlight seemed dim due to all the artificial structures in orbit. Enough light came through to allow some plant growth but as he looked over the massive city, which ruled the Hocklyn Slave Empire, there was very little green to be seen. The air was clearer than normal today, and he could see across most of it. Millions of Hocklyns lived and worked in the capital, ensuring that the Empire continued to grow and that a firm grip was maintained on the thousands of slave worlds that served the Empire.

Nartel wished he knew why the AIs seemed to fear the humans so much. Granted they were fearsome warriors, but they could be killed as had been demonstrated by Hocklyn warships. Looking upward toward space, Nartel thought about the new law he was about to propose. Strict population controls for the entire Hocklyn race that would be highly unpopular. Several members of the High Council would oppose it, even though there was no other choice.

In twenty more years, their population would outgrow the ability of the ten star systems they called home to feed and house them. There would be widespread starvation as it would be impossible to bring in and process the food and resources the increasingly massive population would need. It would also become impossible to build sufficient habitats quickly enough to match the estimated population growth.

There was a slim hope to avoid this if the AIs would grant them the right to colonize more star systems as the High Council had previously proposed, but High Leader Ankler had destroyed that hope once before. Perhaps if the war against the humans was a success, that hope could become a reality once more. Nartel thought long and hard and decided it might be best to wait until the war with the humans was over before he brought forth a vote on his new law. He couldn't risk a possible uprising of the civilian population while this new war was going on.

Nartel let out a heavy sigh of frustration. These humans had ruined everything, and they had to be dealt with. He turned and went back to his desk, sitting down. Taking his blade out of its sheath, he examined it closely. It was made out of the strongest metal, and its hilt was decorated in fine jewels. The blade was sharp enough to cut easily through the light battle armor worn in honor duels. Sighing deeply, he put the blade away.

It was a shame this war couldn't be decided by an honor duel between him and the human leader. Leaning back, he closed his large eyes as he thought about the AIs and their demands that the humans be destroyed. They were keeping something about the humans a secret and Nartel would give almost anything to know what that secret was.

Jeremy was aboard the Avenger studying the latest readiness reports of his fleet as well as the bears. Another shipment of the new fighters and bombers had arrived and been delivered to the bears on the massive space station. The Carethians were flying numerous training flights daily as they tried to ramp up their flying ability to match the humans. Each day, several squadrons of human fighters would engage an equal number of bear fighters in war games. So far, the humans were undefeated, but the bears were rapidly closing the gap as they gained experience.

"The supply fleet today brought an additional quantity of Devastator Threes," Colonel Malen reported, pleased with the number they had on hand. All the battlecruisers and strikecruisers now had an adequate supply plus there was a large reserve on several ammunition colliers that were in orbit beneath the satellite grid. A Monarch cruiser and four light cruisers were also guarding the two ammunition ships to ensure nothing happened to them.

"I sent a request to Governor Malleck about equipping the space station with power beams," Jeremy said, looking over at his executive officer.

Colonel Malen's eyes widened as she thought about what Jeremy had just said. "President Kincaid won't like that," she commented, pursing her lips. "He may feel as if you're trying to go around him."

"I know," said Jeremy, allowing frustration to enter his voice. "But we need those power beams to ensure the survivability of the station. We've put a lot of heavy pulse laser turrets on it, but they're not power beams."

"Have you spoken to Admiral Streth about this?" asked Malen, feeling uneasy about going around President Kincaid. She agreed that they needed the power beams, but she wasn't sure Admiral Strong had made a good decision in bypassing the Federation president. There was such a thing as the chain of command.

"Yes," Jeremy replied. "Admiral Streth said he wouldn't object if I sent a private message to Governor Malleck. However, he was unwilling to broach the subject to the president again."

The president had already denied Fleet Admiral Streth's request for power beams for the bears. It had been a hard decision for Jeremy to decide to approach Governor Malleck, but without the power beams he wasn't sure he could hold Careth. Jeremy's eyes strayed to the large viewscreen on the front wall of the Command Center. A beautiful blue and white globe floated there. Jeremy had swore to Grayseth that he would defend the planet and stand side by side with the bears when the Hocklyns returned.

"Governor Malleck will likely give you the power beam installations," Ariel said as she appeared at Jeremy's side. The dark haired AI had a look of confidence about her as she continued. "He will not let anything happen to the Special Five if he can help it."

Kevin had overheard the private conversation between Jeremy and Colonel Malen and now Ariel. "What do the rest of you think?" Kevin asked as he gazed over at Angela and Kelsey who were at their duty stations and explained what he had overheard. This was the first time in several weeks that they had all been on board the Avenger together.

"I think we should put power beams on the station," Angela replied as she monitored the communications between various units of the fleet. "We need to do everything we can to protect the bears." Angela had become quite fond of the bears after getting to know them better. The female Carethians were very friendly, and she had met several of them at the resorts.

"I agree," responded Kelsey, fervently. "Jeremy is doing the right thing; we need those weapons! Surely Governor Malleck will agree."

She knew that by adding power beams to the orbiting space station, it would give them a more commanding presence in orbit. She was extremely worried about what would happen when the Hocklyns and the AIs finally returned. When they did, she knew they would be bringing a powerful warfleet that would be very difficult to stop.

"Jeremy has committed us to protecting the bears," Kevin spoke firmly. He had made several friends over on the space station and learned a lot about the Carethians over the last few months. He would hate to see anything happen to them. "I can't see Governor Malleck turning him down; surely they will send us the power beam installations."

He had spoken to Katie about this in depth, and she too was adamant that they do everything in their power to protect the Carethians. It was one of the reasons the young lieutenant was spending so much time on the space station doing all she could to update the station's computer systems. Kevin strongly suspected that when Katie was finished the bears' space station might have better computer systems than anything in the Federation. He smiled to himself. Over the last few months, he and Katie had grown quite close, and they had even spoken briefly about a future together.

Ariel was listening quietly to her friends talk. She enjoyed listening to them as they spoke about different things and walked over toward them. Over their private communications channel she said, "Governor Malleck wants to maintain an advanced base to be used to return to the old Federation someday. This system fits those needs quiet well. I suspect we will see the power beam equipment very shortly after he receives Jeremy's request for it."

"Especially since the ship from New Providence is now at Ceres," Angela added, her eyes looking at the others. All five of them knew about the New Providence ship and had spent a considerable amount of time discussing just what it might mean for the future.

Kelsey nodded. She suspected that Ariel and Angela were correct in their supposition. Between Admiral Teleck and Governor Malleck, Jeremy would get what he wanted. Kelsey finished her last practice jump program and turned around to look at Jeremy. He was still speaking to Colonel Malen. Kelsey felt a warm feeling inside just looking at Jeremy.

They were closer than they had ever been before and she knew most if not all of the crew knew of their relationship. For now, it wasn't a problem, but when they returned to Federation space, she knew they might be separated because of it. Not just her and Jeremy, but probably Kevin and Katie also. Fleet doctrine specifically forbid close personal relationships between members of the command crew. Letting out a deep sigh, Kelsey decided not to worry about it for now. It might be quite some time before they returned to the Federation.

Later, the six of them were in the officer's mess eating a warm meal. All except Ariel, of course, she had joined them in her holographic form to make interaction easier.

Angela looked over at Kevin and laughed. "What would you do if the cooks ever run out of hamburgers and fries?" she asked, shaking her head at the large, double meat hamburger surrounded by fries on his plate. "Katie, you have got to get him to start eating something else!"

Katie giggled and nodded. "While we were at the resort we tried one of the restaurants, and they didn't have hamburgers on the menu. I thought he was going to die!"

Jeremy smiled as he listened. "I can imagine. For as long as I have known Kevin, he eats hamburgers at least once a day."

"What did he eat?" Angela asked curiously. She had met a marine captain while at the resort and spent much of her time with him. They had made plans to get together again the next time they both had leave.

"A steak!" Katie replied to everyone's surprise. "He actually ate a steak and a baked potato."

Angela looked over at Kevin with wonderment on her face. "Did you have to choke it down?"

Kevin face turned a little red but he answered anyway. "I like hamburgers and fries, I always have, but I also don't mind a good steak every once in a while."

Jeremy nodded. He didn't mind a good steak either if it was cooked just right. He looked over at Kelsey and could see the smile on her face as she talked. Their little group was very special, and he hoped nothing would ever break it up, but he also knew that people changed over time, and someday the couples in the group would have to make some decisions. Fortunately, that time was still quite a ways off.

Ariel watched the other five and smiled inwardly. She was quite pleased with Jeremy and Kelsey's relationship and had been mildly surprised when Katie and Kevin had paired off. She hoped that someday she would have a new set of special children to watch over. But for now, they had a war to fight and win, and the odds were not stacked in their favor.

The next day, Jeremy was back on the space station meeting with Grayseth and Admiral Stillson. They were making plans on how best to defend the Carethian system when the Hocklyns finally launched their attack.

"I say we let the Hocklyns come to us," Admiral Stillson suggested as he walked slowly around a large tactical hologram that showed the space around Careth. "We don't have the fleet units to meet them in open battle. I feel we should lure them down into range of the satellite defensive grid and use it plus our ships to cut them down to size."

"Only problem is I don't want to be throwing Devastator Threes around that close to the planet," Jeremy objected as he gazed at all the icons displayed in the hologram. "We could end up taking out a large part of our defense grid ourselves."

Grayseth stood and walked over to the tactical display crossing his powerful bearlike arms. "What about the space station?" he asked. "It will be the primary target in any attack by the Hocklyns. It is above the defense grid, and with its shields you could use your more powerful missiles without the fear of damaging the grid. It will also provide some much needed protection for your ships."

"We could also order any heavily damaged ships to retreat beneath the grid," commented Jeremy, liking the idea. "That would lessen our fleet losses."

Admiral Stillson rubbed his brow with his left hand as he thought over the idea. "It just might work. However, I have another suggestion. What if we place about a dozen of the new defensive battle stations around the space station to give it some added protection?"

"We want to shoot their missiles down, particularly their nukes," Grayseth spoke as he eyed the hologram. "We now have factories on Careth turning out new laser and railgun defensive satellites. What if we put a couple hundred of them around the station as well? It would add even more protection to the fleet as well as to the space station."

"The battle stations could command them," Admiral Stillson added as he thought the suggestion over. "We could mix in some missile platforms as well."

Jeremy nodded. They had the beginnings of a plan that might just allow them to hold Careth. It all depended on one important factor; how many AI ships would jump in with the Hocklyn fleet? The AI's weapons could blast right through their energy screens and cause immeasurable damage before the Devastator Threes could be brought to bear.

"We will also have a huge advantage in fighters and bombers," Grayseth added. He had given the order to add two more large flight bays to the station. Each bay would hold two hundred additional fighters and the same amount of bombers. If everything worked out, Carethian pilots would operate all of these.

"What if we used your small attack craft at the same time we launch our bomber strike?" Admiral Simpson added. He knew the versatile, one hundred meter ships could be deadly if used along with the fleet's bombers, particularly with their newly installed energy shields.

"I will speak to the commanders of our ships," Grayseth replied as he nodded his head. "It will be wise for them to begin practicing some maneuvers with the bombers. We have enough trained Carethian pilots to begin such training now."

"We still need approval for the power beam installations," Jeremy added with a heavy sigh. If he could add them to the station, he could almost double its firepower. While it would be no threat to an AI ship, it would play havoc with attacking Hocklyn warships.

"How soon before we know?" asked Admiral Stillson, glancing over at Jeremy. He knew how important the power beams were if they wanted to hold the system.

"Soon," Jeremy replied. "The next major supply fleet is due in two weeks. If there are no power beam installations accompanying that fleet then I fear my request will have been denied."

"I was up in the Command Center earlier," Admiral Stillson said as he returned to the conference table and poured himself a glass of cold water. "The new computer system that Lieutenant Johnson is setting up is remarkable. It can lock on and fire at multiple targets simultaneously, delivering a tremendous amount of firepower. I spoke with Ariel, and she informed me that they will be able to hit a dozen targets at once using every weapon on the station. I would not want to be on the receiving end of that kind of firepower."

"That's why we need the power beams," repeated Jeremy, wishing he knew if his request was going to be granted. "Just imagine the damage we could do to the Hocklyn fleet if we had twenty such installations on the station."

"Will we have power for that many power beam installations?" Admiral Stillson asked. He knew they needed a tremendous amount of energy in order for them to be effective.

"If we get the power beams, I will install several class one fusion reactors on the station," Jeremy replied.

Admiral Stillson was silent. The class one fusion reactor was one of the Federations highest technical achievements and was only used in very secure installations. He wondered how Jeremy had managed to get a hold of them.

Jeremy and Grayseth sat down at the conference table joining Admiral Stillson for they still had a lot of planning to do. Jeremy knew they might only be able to count on another one or two supply fleets at most before the Hocklyns and the AIs arrived. It was essential that they had every supply they could possibly need before that happened.

Once they were cut off from Federation space, they would have to depend on the space station and the factories on the bears' planet to produce what they needed. All of the massive fleet repair ships would be returning to the Federation with Admiral Streth. Admiral Streth would be depending on the six repair ships to keep his fleet operational until they could reach New Tellus.

Jeremy closed his eyes briefly; he almost wished his friends were returning with Admiral Streth. It was going to be extremely dangerous to remain in the bears' system. He just hoped and prayed that they all didn't end up dying here.

Chapter Nine

The 1,500-meter sphere floated quietly in the small star system just four light years away from the former Hocklyn fleet base. The AIs on board were carefully monitoring the activity in the system and the number of ships present. They were at the extreme range of their advanced sensors, but to go any nearer to the human system might risk detection. Their current orders were to gather tactical information on human defenses and the deployment of their fleets.

"The humans have a large number of ships in the system," one of the AIs spoke as it activated another sensor with one of its tentacles.

"They are also heavily fortifying the space around the former fleet base," commented another in a monotonic, nearly mechanical voice. "My instruments are detecting numerous defensive satellites in orbit around the planet."

"We must ensure that our attacking fleet is large enough to drive the humans out of the system and lead us back to their worlds," spoke another AI as it analyzed the data coming across the screens before it.

"The Altons were clever in choosing this race to obstruct us," said the AI in charge of the mission. "Our former creators may have actually succeeded if the humans would have had more time to develop their technology."

"They will be annihilated and then nothing will be able to stop us from extending our Empire to the very edge of this galaxy and beyond," the AI at the ship's sensors responded.

"The great project will someday be completed," the commanding AI spoke as it thought about the massive construction project going on in the center of the galaxy in the heart of AI space.

"More resources are required," spoke one of the other AIs. "Our proxy races need to be coerced into speeding up the delivery of the raw materials that are needed for the project."

"Once this war with the humans is over, new quotas will be delivered to all four of our proxy races," the commanding AI informed the others as it used its tentacles to manipulate several computer screens. "When the great project is completed, the entire universe will be ours to control, and organic races will be a thing of the past."

Admiral Streth was in the StarStrike looking with great concern at the latest readings from one of the FTL sensor buoys. It had recorded an unscheduled hyperjump in a system just four light years away.

"It's an AI ship," Colonel Trist commented as the data from the buoy was put up on the tactical display. "Fifteen hundred meters and spherical in shape. The jump was detected by three other buoys in the system as well."

"Why is it there?" Admiral Adler asked as he gazed over at Hedon. "Surely we are out of their sensor range; that's over four light years!"

"Perhaps not, Jacob," replied Hedon, letting out a deep breath. He didn't like the idea of an AI ship being so close. "We haven't detected any other unauthorized hyperjumps within twenty light years, so it is here alone."

"What are we going to do?" asked Jacob, folding his arms across his chest and looking inquiringly over at the Fleet Admiral. He had a strong suspicion that Hedon wasn't going to let the AI ship just set there and spy on them, if that was indeed what it was doing.

"Clarissa," spoke Hedon, looking over at the gorgeous blonde AI who was standing close by. "What is the farthest distance we can be to use our Devastator Three missiles effectively on the AI ship?"

Clarissa was silent for a moment. Was the admiral contemplating attacking this lone AI? "The effective range of the Devastator Three missiles is close to twenty thousand kilometers," she responded as she ran some quick calculations. "However, with an AI ship the response time on their defensive systems is almost zero. To ensure the arrival of all the missiles, the Devastator Threes would need to be launched no farther than eighty-five hundred kilometers away from the AI."

"If we jump from here we can do that," commented Colonel Trist, taking a deep breath. He had known Admiral Streth long enough to know that he was indeed thinking about attacking this lone AI.

Hedon looked back over at Clarissa, who was watching him intently. "Clarissa, if we use the StarStrike how close can you plot a jump to the AI?"

Clarissa was silent as she ran some simulations and calculated several hyperjumps to see how close she could put the StarStrike to the AI. Finally, she had the results and looked up at the admiral. "I can put the StarStrike four hundred and fifty kilometers from the AI. That will also put us well within their weapons range."

"That's awfully close," Colonel Trist cautioned. At that range, the AI was bound to get off some shots. He knew the StarStrike had a powerful energy screen, but even it could only take so much.

"If we can destroy this AI ship it might delay the eventual attack by a few days or even weeks," Hedon pointed out. "The longer we can delay this attack, the more time the Federation has to prepare itself for war." Hedon knew how vital it was to allow the Federation to finish its war preparations.

"How many ships would you use?" asked Jacob, feeling concerned. He felt Hedon should send several of the heavy attack cruisers instead of the StarStrike.

"Just the StarStrike initially," replied Hedon, knowing he was taking a big risk. However, at 1,600-meters, the StarStrike was the only ship in the human fleet of comparable size to an AI ship. "If just the StarStrike jumps in the AI may risk staying and engaging us. They already know we can destroy their ships, but I doubt if they believe that one ship is a serious danger no matter how large it is. If we jump in with a fleet, they will just jump out and report back to their base."

Jacob nodded. Hedon's reasoning was sound even if he didn't like it. "How soon after the StarStrike jumps in can I jump in with more ships?" Admiral Sheen was currently out on a reconnaissance mission close to Hocklyn space. She had taken nearly all of the stealth scouts to see if they could detect a Hocklyn fleet buildup. It would be another week before she returned.

"Five minutes," Hedon replied after a moment.

"Five minutes!" Jacob uttered his eyes growing wide. "The StarStrike could be destroyed in five minutes."

"Jacob, the AI ship may have moved since it jumped into the system," replied Hedon, knowing he was risking his flagship. "We may have to make a micro-jump almost as soon as we jump into the system if the AI is out of range."

Hedon looked over at Clarissa. "Once the StarStrike's systems have stabilized, how soon can you jump again?"

Clarissa ran some quick computations. "Forty seconds," She replied. "It will take twenty-eight seconds for all systems to stabilize and then twelve more to set the jump drive up for a micro-jump."

"They will know you're coming," warned Jacob, looking at both Hedon and Colonel Trist. "When you come out of hyperspace they will hit you with everything they have."

"It's a risk we will have to take," responded Hedon, determinedly. "We attack in an hour. Jacob, get back to your command ship and pick out four strikecruisers to come with you. Clarissa will plot your jump and load the coordinates into your ship's navigation computers."

Jacob nodded, knowing he wasn't going to change his friend's mind. "Good luck, then," he spoke as he turned to leave the Command Center.

"This is necessary," Colonel Grissom added from where she had been listening to the conversation near one of the tactical displays. The Intelligence officer was concerned about the presence of the AI ship and what they might be learning of the defenses around the former Hocklyn fleet base. "We can't let them escape with data concerning our defenses."

"Taylor would agree with this decision," Colonel Trist spoke quietly to Hedon. He knew how much the admiral missed his brother's advice. "If they can scan the system from that range, they must be destroyed."

"I know he would agree," Hedon replied somberly. Sometimes he almost felt as if Taylor was standing behind him in the Command Center. Several times, he had caught himself looking behind him only to see that no one was there. "We can't let that AI escape."

Fleet Admiral Streth looked at one of the tactical holographic displays which showed the StarStrike, the Wasp, and the four strikecruisers leaving the gravity well of the planet. He wanted to hit the AI ship before it left the system it was currently in.

"Five minutes to jump," Clarissa informed the admiral. She was standing at his side and carefully monitoring all the ship's systems.

"Clarissa, you will be in charge of the jumps as well as the attack," Hedon informed her, his eyes focusing intently on the AI.

"Yes, Admiral," Clarissa replied, pleased that the admiral trusted her with such an important mission. She just hoped when this was over that she would have some good news to send to Ariel.

Admiral Streth watched with calm nerves as the Command Center buzzed with increased activity as the crew anticipated the jump. "Take us to Condition One and jump the ship, Clarissa," Hedon ordered as he fastened the safety harness that secured him to his command chair.

In front of the StarStrike, a large blue-white vortex formed, and the ship flew unhesitantly into its center.

-

"Good luck, Admiral," Jacob Adler spoke quietly from the Command Center of the Wasp as he watched the flagship vanish into the vortex. In five minutes, he would be jumping his small fleet. He just hoped the StarStrike was still intact when he arrived.

-

The AI ship was still in the same system using its advanced sensors to monitor the human held fleet base. They had watched with interest as a small group of ships led by the largest ship in the human fleet left the gravity well of the planet. The larger ship vanished and soon after so did the other five that had followed it out.

"That large ship is the human's most powerful warship," one of the AIs operating the sensors commented. "It reportedly was involved in the destruction of our ships that attacked the system."

"One of the ships," the commanding AI spoke his orb like head glowing even brighter. "The Hocklyn Fleet Commodore reported that both of our ships were under heavy attack from numerous ships using massive nukes, which eventually led to their shields collapsing."

They continued to make their observations, collecting as much data as possible on the human held system. The command AI went from station to station checking the data that was coming in.

"Sensor contact," the AI at sensors reported suddenly. "Contact at two million kilometers."

"It's the human flagship," spoke the AI at the data gathering screens. "They must have detected us somehow."

"Impossible; they don't have that level of technology," the command AI spoke, the glowing orb above its metal body nearly doubling in size.

"Do we jump?" inquired one of the AIs standing at Navigation.

"From one ship?" the commanding AI replied derisively "Bring all weapons on line and prepare to engage the human ship. We will destroy it. This will substantially weaken the human forces."

-

"AI ship has moved," Clarissa reported as she quickly calculated the next jump. "It is two million kilometers away."

"It must have moved after jumping into the system," Colonel Trist spoke as his eyes focused on the tactical display, which was now showing the 1,500-meter AI ship. "Damn that thing is big!"

"Jumping," Clarissa spoke again as she activated the ship's jump drive and flew the StarStrike into the swirling vortex that had formed just in front of the ship.

The StarStrike exited the vortex four hundred and sixty kilometers from the AI ship. It took a few seconds for all the systems to come online, and Clarissa made sure the first system was the ship's energy shield.

"Incoming fire," she reported as a powerful energy beam struck the ship. Immediately, alarm klaxons began to sound and red lights began to flash.

"Turn the alarms off, Clarissa," Hedon ordered as his eyes focused intently on the tactical display. He could sense the sudden tension in the crew of the Command Center as the ship was struck by more Hocklyn energy beams. They all remembered what had happened the last time they had engaged and AI ship.

The ship shuddered violently as even more AI weapons impacted the shield. The screen was lit up in a brilliant display of light as energy beams from the AI ship played across its surface. Suddenly an energy beam penetrated the screen, striking the forward section of the ship. The beam cut deep into the hull, setting off several secondary explosions.

"Multiple hull breaches along the forward hull near section four," Colonel Trist reported as he scanned the damage control console. "We're venting atmosphere, and I am receiving reports of several internal explosions."

"AI ship is still firing and closing the range," Colonel Grissom warned as she watched one of the tactical displays.

"How long until we can fire, Clarissa?" demanded Hedon, looking over at the female AI. The ship shook again, but this time the energy shield held.

"I've shunted all available power to the energy screen," Clarissa replied as she prepared to fire the ship's Devastator Three missiles. "Firing in ten seconds!"

The ship was shaking badly now as the AI poured its fire against the ship's wavering energy screen, trying to knock it down.

"Firing!" Clarissa screamed as the StarStrike was hit by another energy beam that penetrated the hull and dug deep into the hull close to Engineering. The lights flickered and then steadied.

"Energy screen at sixty-two percent," warned Colonel Grissom as she gazed intently at one of the main viewscreens, which was now showing the deadly AI ship.

From the missile tubes of the StarStrike, four Devastator Three missiles left the ship. They vanished as soon as they were launched because of the tremendous speed of their sublight drives and inertial dampening systems. A microsecond later, two more missiles left the tubes.

On board the AI ship, the energy screen suddenly flared up as massive amounts of energy struck one small section of the screen. A microsecond later, the ship shook violently as two forty-megaton nuclear explosions blew two massive holes in the side of the ship.

"Ship systems compromised," the AI at damage control reported, the glowing orb above its metal frame glowing even brighter. "FTL is out, weapons are out, sensors are out, and the energy shield is down."

"Communications?" the commanding AI demanded as the ship continued to shake. The commanding AI knew the ship was mortally wounded, and internal explosions were beginning to finish the work the human weapons had started.

"All communications are out," one of the other AIs reported.

"It was a series of sublight missiles that knocked a hole in the screen," the AI at the now nonfunctioning sensors reported. "The missiles must have also been equipped with an inertial dampening system."

"We didn't suspect the humans had this type of advanced technology," the AI at the data processing screens commented. "This is a dangerous development."

The commanding AI stood still as it evaluated the situation. The humans were indeed dangerous beyond belief if they could destroy an AI ship with just one of their warships. The technology they had just used could pose a series threat to any AI ship. The commanding AI now understood why the Altons had chosen this race so far in the past to stand in the way of the AIs domination of this galaxy.

"Sublight drives are out, and the FTL drive is not repairable," the AI at Navigation reported.

The commanding AI reached out its tentacles and pressed down on two red buttons that stood out on the console near it. None of the technology in the sphere could be allowed to fall into human hands; it had to be destroyed. Moments later, multiple nuclear explosions tore the AI sphere apart as its self-destructs were activated.

"AI ship is down," Captain Reynolds spoke with obvious relief in his voice.

"Its self-destructs have gone off," Colonel Trist reported from where he was standing in front of the tactical display, which had been showing the AI ship. Now it was just showing a slowly expanding debris field.

Colonel Grissom breathed a sigh of relief. Any threat of data getting back to the AIs about the defenses they had set up above the former Hocklyn fleet base was now gone.

Admiral Streth could feel the tension evaporate from the Command Center with the AI's destruction. "Clarissa, are you detecting anything worth salvaging?" Hedon would love to get his hands on some of the AI's tech.

"No," replied Clarissa, looking over at the admiral and shaking her head. "I'm scanning the wreckage, but I am not detecting any active power sources or signs of surviving weapons. I believe the AIs have their self-destructs set to go off in the most sensitive areas of their ships that contain the highest levels of technology. They may do this to ensure that their technology remains a secret."

Hedon nodded. They had found nothing in the two previous AI ships they had destroyed several months back. "Nevertheless, I want to search that wreckage. Colonel Trist, as soon as our other ships get here I want a thorough search of what remains of that AI ship."

"Yes, Sir," Trist replied.

"I don't think we will find much," commented Colonel Grissom, turning to face the admiral.

"What about our damage?" Hedon continued. He could see several glaring red lights on the damage control board. He knew energy beams had hit the StarStrike at least twice, perhaps more. It pained him to see his flagship damaged, but this had been a necessary battle in his opinion.

"The forward hull has been compromised in several areas," Trist replied as he quickly spoke to the damage control teams who were in that area of the ship over his mini-com. "We also have a major hull breach near Engineering in section fifty-two. We have four decks open to space and the damage control team is reporting we have a six-meter hole in our hull."

Hedon winced. It was going to take the fleet repair ships at least several days to repair the damage. "What about casualties?"

"Twenty-four confirmed," Colonel Trist reported. "Another sixty-eight suffered injuries. Six of those are critical."

Hedon nodded, feeling pain at the losses. He would make it a point to visit sickbay to speak to the injured as soon as he could.

"Contacts!" Reynolds reported suddenly as five new contacts flared up on his sensor screen. Then he relaxed as they turned a friendly green. "Admiral Adler has jumped into the system."

"Admiral Adler is requesting orders," Captain Janice Duncan reported from Communications.

"Have them jump to our location," Hedon ordered. "They're going to help us search the wreckage of the AI ship."

Hedon allowed himself to relax. The threat from the AI ship was gone, and it wouldn't be going home with any of the information that it had been gathering. Reaching to his chest, Hedon unfastened the safety harness and stood up walking over to stand next to Colonels Trist and Grissom.

Colonel Trist looked over at the admiral. He had known Admiral Streth since he had first been assigned to the original StarStrike back in the old Federation. "How much longer before the big attack?" he asked.

"It's hard to say," replied Hedon, taking a deep breath. "There has been no sign of any large Hocklyn ship movements since we took out the majority of the Hocklyn fleet that had been nearing Careth. The latest reports from Admiral Sheen indicates that her stealth scouts haven't found anything either."

"Intelligence estimates we have at least several more weeks minimum," Colonel Grissom stated.

"You still think they're rearming?" asked Trist, wondering what type of weapons they might be up against when the Hocklyns finally did attack.

"Yes," Hedon replied evenly. "That's the only explanation for this long delay. The AIs want to ensure a quick victory and will undoubtedly attack in what they feel is overwhelming force. I just hope that by destroying this AI ship today, it buys us another week or so."

"It should," agreed Colonel Grissom with a nod as she turned and walked over to one of the tactical displays. She wanted to replay the AI's destruction to see if she could learn anything new.

Colonel Trist was quiet as he watched Admiral Adler's ships vanish on the tactical screen to appear only moments later twelve hundred kilometers away from the StarStrike. "Hedon," he spoke in a much quieter voice. "Do you honestly think we will ever get to return home someday?"

Hedon gazed over at the colonel. "I hope so," he replied with a sigh. "We already know there are survivors on New Providence. If we could just find a way to fortify that planet we might be able to retake all the old worlds of the Federation and bring them back under our control. If we're successful in luring the Hocklyns and AIs back to New Tellus and inflicting major damage to their fleet, that is what I intend to propose to the Federation Council."

"A return home," Trist spoke, his eyes growing wide with hope. "Do you really think it's possible?"

"We have several big battles to fight first," Hedon replied, his eyes showing that he firmly believed that he would see the shores of that small lake on Maken where his brother and Lendle had built a summer cabin. "Someday we will return home, I promise."

-

Amanda looked at the latest reports coming in from the returning stealth scouts. Hocklyn ships were few and far between. They had searched deep into Hocklyn space to a depth of nearly forty light years and had not located any significant fleet formations. They had found a few small bases, but they possessed only minor fleet units. Normally a war cruiser and half a dozen escorts were all that could be found. It had been tempting to launch a strike and destroy these small fleets, but Amanda knew that Admiral Streth wanted it to look as if the Hocklyns had stopped the Human advance into their territory.

"That's the last scout," Commander Evans reported as the flight bay reported the small ship had landed and been secured.

"Prepare the fleet to jump," Amanda ordered. It was time to return to Admiral Streth's location.

"Where are the Hocklyns?" Commander Evans asked with a frown on her face. "You would think that if they were preparing to attack there would be some sign of gathering fleet units."

"That's what frightens me," Amanda replied her eyes showing her deep concern. "The Hocklyn Slave Empire has thousands of ships at its disposal, but we just aren't seeing them."

"Do you think it's because of the two AI ships we destroyed?" Commander Evans suggested. It was the only thing she could think of.

"Perhaps," Amanda responded. "From what intelligence we have gathered those are the first two AI ships that have ever been destroyed. The AIs may have been knocked for a loop when they realized that we could destroy their ships. I fear that when they do attack it will be with a fleet much larger than anything we have ever seen before."

Commander Evans remained silent as she thought about Amanda's words. She wondered just how large a fleet the Hocklyns were gathering.

"We're going back to the fleet base," Lieutenant Stalls spoke to Lieutenant Trask over their private communication channel.

"I'm glad," Angela responded. "It makes me nervous to be so close to Hocklyn space."

"Admiral Sheen is a good commander," Benjamin replied. "She would never let anything happen to us."

"It will be over soon," Lieutenant Ashton spoke from Navigation. She had just finished entering the next hyperjump into the navigation computer. She turned her blonde head toward the other two. "Once we get back to New Tellus we will all get a nice long leave. I don't know about you two, but I could use some serious beach time."

Benjamin and Angela nodded. The beaches at New Tellus sounded so inviting, but they had a lot of fighting to do before they saw them again. Benjamin turned his attention back to his sensor screens. He just hoped they all made it through the coming months safely.

Amanda was in her quarters relaxing. It would take three more days to reach Admiral Streth's base of operations. By the time they made it back, most of her ships that were being repaired at Careth should be waiting to rejoin Second Fleet. From what she understood there were no more planned operations against the Hocklyns until they mounted their main attack.

Once that happened the fleet would bleed the Hocklyns and the AIs as much as possible and then began a fighting withdrawal back toward Federation space. The eventual goal was to lead them to the New Tellus system and hope that the massive fortifications in the system could destroy the invading fleet.

Amanda walked over and entered her bedroom. She removed her uniform and stepped into the shower. She closed her eyes as she felt the warm water coating her body, wishing that Richard were here. It was times like this that she really missed him.

After drying off from her shower, Amanda lay down on her bed and tried to relax. She was still having trouble sleeping after the deaths of so many people under her command. Many times when she did finally manage to fall asleep, she had the same recurring nightmare. In her dream, she saw the worlds of the new Federation on fire with a massive fleet of AI ships above each world.

Chapter Ten

Admiral Teleck was meeting with Governor Malleck and Admiral Kalen to discuss Admiral Strong's most recent request. It had been a heated conversation so far.

"Power beams!" Governor Malleck exclaimed with a worried frown on his face. "President Kincaid will never agree to that. How can Admiral Strong make such a request and why didn't he go through President Kincaid and the Federation Council?"

Admiral Teleck was silent for a moment as he thought over Jeremy's request. "He needs those power beam installations so he can hold the bears' planet," Teleck spoke in a soft voice. "With power beams on the space station, he might just be able to stop the Hocklyns from retaking Careth."

"Admiral Strong didn't go through President Kincaid because I suspect he has already been turned down," Admiral Kallen added. "Fleet Admiral Streth may have suggested that he go around the president and the council by going straight to us."

"I don't know," muttered Governor Malleck, knowing there would be some serious repercussions if President Kincaid ever found out that Ceres had sent such installations to Admiral Strong without permission from the Federation Council. "If his request has already been turned down by the Federation Council, how can we seriously consider ignoring their decision?"

"What if we don't send the installations and Admiral Strong and his crew are killed defending the Carethians?" Admiral Kalen asked, his eyes showing deep concern. "What would the people of Ceres as well as the rest of the Federation think when they learn that we refused to give Strong the weapons that he requested?"

"It wouldn't look good, and it would be a major blow to morale in the Federation," Governor Malleck admitted, not liking where this conversation was going. While Ceres did have some autonomy in how its forces and weapons were used, this went way above that. "Admiral Teleck, what do you suggest we do?" Malleck had always trusted the admiral's advice.

"Governor, our power beams are just one step ahead of the Hocklyn's energy beams," Admiral Teleck pointed out. "I strongly suspect that when the AIs are finished upgrading the Hocklyn fleet there won't be much difference between the two."

Malleck put his hand to his forehead and rubbed it. No matter what he did there were going to be repercussions. But there was one thing he did know; the crew of the Avenger could not be allowed to die because Ceres refused to act. He leaned back and let out a heavy sigh. "Do it," he ordered, his face showing renewed determination at what must be done. "Send Admiral Strong the power beam installations and whatever else he might need. Do it discretely; I don't want word of this to get out, at least not for a while."

Governor Malleck knew that, at some point, President Kincaid and the Federation Council would discover what they had done. When that day came, all hell would probably break loose in the council chambers and he would be in the middle of it.

"I will see to it," Admiral Teleck replied, pleased with the governor's decision, and then looking at Governor Malleck, he continued. "Keep in mind that if Admiral Strong can hold the bears' system we have a forward base to use to someday retake our former worlds."

"Speaking of our former worlds, our friends from New Providence will be back in a few more days," Governor Malleck said, feeling a headache coming on. "They're currently on a tour of the Federation as well as our allies. They will be expecting us to inform them of our decision to furnish them with Devastator Three missiles and an adequate delivery system."

"I have spoken to our engineers who designed our defensive battle stations," Admiral Kalen said, placing his hands on the conference table. "They have come up with a new design that will be able to handle Devastator Three missiles with the necessary computers and targeting systems to destroy an AI ship."

"Why do I feel I am not going to like this either?" Governor Malleck groaned, his eyes focusing on the admiral. "What are they suggesting?"

"They have designed a totally new battle station based on what will be needed to defend New Providence," Kalen informed the governor. "The new battle station will be one hundred and fifty meters in diameter and have most of the functions of the old ones with several new innovations."

"What are the innovations?" asked Malleck, knowing it was hard telling what the technicians and engineers had come up with. It was also probably going to be very expensive.

"The engineers are calling it a defensive battle station type two," Kalen continued. He had spent considerable time with the engineers and technicians explaining exactly what would be needed in the new battle station in order for it to survive. "It is fully self-contained, has an upgraded energy shield, defensive lasers, four pulse laser turrets, interceptor missiles, and twelve Devastator Three missile tubes with a standard crew of fifty. It will be powered by a class one fusion reactor."

"Crap, everything but a power beam," Malleck said, shaking his head. "Why was a power beam not included? It seems as if everything else was."

"No room for the installation," confessed Admiral Kallen, recalling the argument about whether to include one or not. "By not having a power beam it leaves more power for the energy screen."

"How long will it take to build one of these?" asked Admiral Teleck. If they could be built in time, he might suggest sending some to Admiral Strong. They were sending him everything else, why not these also? A number of these around his space station could be quite valuable in its defense.

"Three weeks until the first one rolls off the assembly line," replied Kallen, looking over at Admiral Teleck. "We currently have two assembly lines producing the type one battle station; it won't take much to change one of them over to produce the type two."

"Make it so," Governor Malleck ordered. "If this means we can someday return to the old Federation worlds then it must be done. When our people fled to Earth and then later to Ceres so many years ago, it has always been our intention to return home and free our worlds from the Hocklyns. This could be the first step in making that happen."

"What about the Federation Council?" asked Admiral Teleck, knowing that what they were proposing to do would have to be run by them and approved.

This was much different than sending power beam installations to Admiral Strong. If they were successful, this could mean opening up an entire new offensive front against the Hocklyns and AIs deep within their own territory. It would also be placing the sixty million humans on New Providence in danger. They would be depending on the new

Federation to carry through with their promise of providing the new battle stations, as well as the Devastator Three missiles.

"Let's start construction first," Governor Malleck suggested as an idea came to his mind. "If we have several completed type twos we could offer them to the Federation Council as a solution to protecting all of our planets and mining sites from an AI attack and perhaps even protect our allies. That might be sufficient incentive to get the council to agree to allow us to send them to New Providence."

"What do we tell Senator Arden?" asked Kallen, knowing the senator from New Providence would be expecting an answer when she returned to Ceres.

"I don't think its practical to deploy these new battle stations to New Providence until after First Strike is completed and Admiral Streth has led the Hocklyns and AIs back to New Tellus," Governor Malleck said, taking a deep breath and looking at the two admirals. "If we can win at New Tellus then I suggest we deploy the battle stations immediately and perhaps send Admiral Streth along with them."

"The council may not agree to deploy any ships so far from the Federation," spoke Admiral Kallen, realizing it could be a problem.

"If they don't we'll send a fleet from Ceres," Governor Malleck answered, determined to help the people of New Providence. "We still have a substantial reserve of ships in our bays, and this may be a good use for a major portion of them."

"How many of the new battle stations will we need to adequately defend New Providence from the AIs?" asked Admiral Teleck, looking over at Admiral Kalen.

"Sixteen should be sufficient, though I would recommend twenty-four if possible," Kalen replied. "Once the production line is changed over we can produce eight per month of the new type two model."

"Three months," responded Admiral Teleck, leaning back and crossing his arms across his chest. "Admiral Streth is expecting the Hocklyns and AIs to attack his position in another four to eight weeks. We can expect the Hocklyns to reach New Tellus two weeks after that."

"When I speak to Senator Arden I am going to recommend that they stay here at Ceres until after the Hocklyn attack," said Governor Malleck, hoping that would not be a problem. "If we win at New Tellus, then the senator can return to New Providence at the head of a fleet, one that will free our home worlds."

"Let's not get ahead of ourselves," cautioned Admiral Teleck, leaning forward. "There is a lot that's going to happen between now and then. If the AIs attack in overwhelming force, the Federation could face defeat."

Governor Malleck was silent as he weighed Admiral Teleck's worrisome words. The admiral was right; they mustn't get ahead of themselves. "That's why Ceres is so heavily defended," Malleck replied. "It would be suicide for either the Hocklyns or the AIs to attack us here."

Teleck did not reply. Governor Malleck, while being a very good politician, was not a military man and had never been in battle. There was no doubt in Teleck's mind that if the AIs wanted to take Ceres badly enough, they could probably find a way to do it.

Admiral Streth was holding a meeting with Admiral Sheen and Admiral Adler on board the StarStrike. They were rapidly nearing the time when a Hocklyn attack might occur.

"I want all ships completely repaired and ammunition holds filled," Hedon was saying, his eyes focusing on the other two admirals. "The defense grid around the fleet base is complete, and we are nearly ready."

"I spoke to Admiral Strong earlier, and they have finished their preparations also," Jacob added as he drummed his index finger upon the conference table. "The last supply fleet for the bears is supposed to arrive next week, but Admiral Strong is pushing for at least one more with more fighters and bombers for the Carethians."

Hedon was silent as he weighed Admiral Adler's words. "I will speak to Fleet Admiral Johnson and see if she can't arrange for another," he said after a moment. "From what Jeremy has said, these Carethians are turning into fine pilots. If they want more fighters and bombers, we need to try to furnish them if at all possible."

"I saw several of their training exercises," added Amanda, recalling how the bears seemed to take to the fighters like bees on honey. "With enough training they will be as good as human pilots and give the Hocklyns fits."

"That's good to know," Hedon commented, pleased with how everything was going. "I just hope that Admiral Strong can hold out against the coming attack. If he finds himself on the losing end of this, there is no chance of the Federation coming to his rescue."

"He won't withdraw," Amanda spoke with respect in her voice. "He is determined to defend the Carethians and is willing to sacrifice everything to do so. If Careth falls, there will be no defending fleet ships returning to the Federation." In many ways, Jeremy reminded her of Hedon when he was younger.

Hedon nodded; Admiral Strong was becoming a fine admiral and would give the Hocklyns and AIs one hell of a battle at Careth. Hedon just hoped that the young rear admiral survived.

"Once we retreat to New Tellus and the battle there is over, I intend to lead a relief fleet to Careth immediately," Hedon spoke firmly. "I won't let Admiral Strong be defeated if there is any way I can prevent it."

"I just hope we have enough ships left to form a relief fleet," commented Jacob grimly, knowing the battle at New Tellus would be massive.

"If I have to come back in just a destroyer, I'm coming back," Hedon spoke determinedly. Admiral Strong was part of his command, and he wouldn't abandon him.

After the meeting Hedon was walking through the corridors of the StarStrike; sometimes it did him good just to walk throughout the lengthy corridors in the 1,600-meter ship. It allowed him time to think and put things into perspective.

"Out for a walk, Admiral?" a pleasant female voice spoke from beside him.

Startled, Hedon turned and saw Captain Janice Duncan. She had been jogging down the corridor and come up behind him. "Yes, Captain," replied Hedon with a relaxed smile. "I enjoy taking long walks in the ship occasionally."

"I know what you mean," replied Janice, falling in beside Hedon as they continued to walk. "I do the same thing whenever I have the chance. In the months I have been aboard the StarStrike, I still haven't made it down all the corridors. This is one hell of a big ship, Sir!"

Hedon laughed and nodded his head. "Sixteen hundred meters; there must be hundreds of kilometers of corridors. I know just the other day I had to ask Clarissa to give me directions back to the Command Center."

"Speaking of Clarissa, she was telling me that you are originally from the planet Maken in the old Federation."

"Yes," replied Hedon, recalling those days long ago.

"What was Maken like?" Janice asked. She was extremely curious about the old Federation and what living there had been like.

Hedon allowed himself to smile as he recalled those days by the lake with his brother Taylor and Lendle. Without hesitation, he began telling the captain all about his days on Maken and the small cabin. For a while, Hedon allowed himself to forget that a war was going on.

Fleet Commodore Resmunt smiled, allowing his sharp teeth to show as the first of his fleets moved out of Kenward Seven's gravity well. In all, there were ten fleets under Resmunt's command. Close to seven hundred warships to conquer and destroy the humans, all with recently upgraded shields and weapons. It was the most powerful fleet even sent out by the Hocklyn Slave Empire, and it was under his command.

"Commodores Aanith and Maseth report that their fleets are ready and will soon be moving out of the gravity well," First Leader Ganth reported from where he was standing at Communications.

"So it begins," Resmunt spoke as his eyes focused sharply on the new tactical display his ship had been equipped with.

All the flagships of the individual fleets had this new holographic tactical display, which had been furnished by the AIs. There was no doubt in Resmunt's mind that the new display would allow him to better coordinate his fleet's movements, particularly in battle.

"War Leader Osbith is moving his fleet out of orbit," Ganth reported as more War Leaders checked in with the flagship.

Resmunt frowned in distaste. He wished he could have found some way to remove Osbith from command. There were three War Leaders he had very little confidence in and would have to be careful in battles as to what their objectives were. Any of the three could easily make a tactical blunder that could result in major losses to Resmunt's command. Of course, if that were to happen then Resmunt would have a legitimate reason under the Hocklyn honor system to remove them from command of their individual fleets.

Then, of course, there was War Leader Versith of the dreadnought Viden. He was the most talented of all the available War Leaders and in reality probably should have already been promoted to the rank of Fleet Commodore, but for some unknown reason Versith had preferred to remain a War Leader and command his own individual fleet.

"All fleets should be clear of Kenward Seven's gravity well in forty minutes," Ganth reported as he stepped over to gaze at the new tactical display. The display showed all ten Hocklyn war fleets as they were now all underway and moving to exit the planet's gravity well.

Even as he watched, ten new large red icons suddenly flared up just outside of the planet's gravity well and then turned to green. "The AIs are here," Ganth rasped out. With nearly seven hundred warships and ten AI ships, the humans would not stand a chance.

Fleet Commodore Resmunt walked over to the tactical display and gazed at the icons representing the AI ships with disdain. He was sure the massive Hocklyn fleet he had at his command could defeat the humans. The AIs would just sow discord in the fleet by their mere presence and what they represented. It was a harsh reminder as to who was the real power behind the Empire.

"The AIs are transmitting jump coordinates," Third Leader Vrill at communications reported.

"Transmit them to Navigation to be checked and then we will send them to the rest of the ships in the fleet," Resmunt ordered. He had assumed they would plot their own jumps. He also wondered if an AI would be coming aboard his ship and directing the coming battles, he hoped not.

"What does this mean if the AIs are plotting our jumps?" First Leader Ganth asked, his dark eyes gazing at Resmunt.

"We may be engaging the humans much quicker than I had originally planned," replied Resmunt, feeling aggravated at the AIs. He suspected they would not allow his ship's crews to rest during jumps or to retune their drives as often as Resmunt had planned.

"Coordinates are for system C-112, which is twenty-two light years distant," Fourth Leader Brack reported from Navigation.

"Nearly maximum jumps," Ganth uttered with displeasure. "Depending on what the AIs plan, we could be in human space in three weeks!"

"The AIs want the humans destroyed," responded Resmunt, staring at the ten large green icons in the tactical display and wishing they were not there. "Send the coordinates to all ships and stand by to jump as soon as all fleets have cleared the gravity well."

Ganth nodded and proceeded to do as ordered. In this war with the humans, there would be much honor to be had, if the AIs didn't interfere. Somehow, Ganth feared the AIs could care less about Hocklyn honor.

High Leader Nartel was in the High Council Chambers meeting with Councilors Berken and Jarles. "The AIs have demanded the fleet leave immediately, and that they will be plotting the jumps."

"The AIs," Berken repeated, not liking the sound of that. "It sounds as if they want to hit the humans as soon as possible."

"What about Fleet Commodore Krilen?" demanded Jarles. "His new fleet is not fully assembled yet."

"I have already sent orders rushing more ships to his command," replied Nartel, feeling frustrated with the way things were going down. "Within three weeks he will have nearly eight hundred ships."

"That should be enough," commented Berken, nodding his head.

"We are stripping all of our expansion fleets in that entire galactic region," warned Councilor Jarles, aggravated that the expansion of the Empire had ground to a halt. "I understand the necessity, but if we suffer significant losses it could set our expansion plans back for years."

"There are ten AI ships with Fleet Commodore Resmunt's fleets," Nartel reminded the other two. "Not even the humans can stand up to that type of firepower."

"They did destroy two AI ships already," Berken responded. "What if they destroy all ten of these?"

"We believe the weapons they used are in short supply," replied Nartel, recalling the latest intelligence reports he had recently received. "They only used a few in all the battles and then only in desperation. Our military analysts believe that the weapons must be extremely difficult to produce and possibly experimental; that's why we only saw a few of them deployed."

"It might also explain why the AIs are in such a hurry to attack," Councilor Jarles added. "They might fear the humans perfecting these new experimental weapons and then building them in sufficient quantities to be a direct threat to the AIs and the Empire."

Councilor Berken looked around the High Council Chambers as if wanting to ensure that they were alone. "I wonder if there is any possibility of us procuring one of these human weapons? The AIs have already attacked our habitats once; what's to stop them from doing so again?"

"What are you suggesting, Councilor Berken?" Jarles demanded, his eyes growing wide. "Surely you're not suggesting that we acquire one of these weapons and then reverse engineer it so we could build our own. If the AIs suspected we were doing something like that, they would destroy our worlds. They would wipe out the Hocklyn race just like they want to destroy the humans."

Councilor Berken was silent for a moment, knowing he had overstepped himself. "No, of course not," he responded, shaking his head. "I was merely thinking out loud. Of course we mustn't do anything to offend the AIs."

After the meeting was over, Nartel alone remained in the High Council Chambers. He was thinking about what High Councilor Berken had suggested. One of Nartel's biggest fears was what would happen when the day arrived where the Hocklyn race was no longer useful to the AIs. Would the AIs still need the Hocklyns once the entire galaxy had been conquered?

Nartel thought long and hard about the issue. What if they could get one of the human weapons? There were distant Hocklyn bases that had never even seen an AI ship. It wouldn't be difficult to pick one of the more distant ones and assign the necessary Hocklyn scientists and technicians to reverse engineer one of the weapons. If somehow they could secretly build a stockpile of these missiles and then deploy them in all the home systems, that might serve as a deterrent to the AIs. Perhaps the AIs would even allow the Hocklyns to become equal partners in the Empire. They could then expand and colonize all the worlds necessary to handle their growing population.

The problem was who could he trust to follow his orders and get one of the human weapons? Nartel knew he had at least three weeks to decide upon a plan if he decided to go through with it. The risk would be great, and he could very easily end up suffering the same fate as High Leader Ankler. This was something he would have to think upon. It was risky, but the rewards could well be worth it.

Jeremy stared in disbelief at the viewscreen as three special supply vessels from Ceres docked to the space station. They had arrived under a special escort of four battlecruisers, two battlecarriers, and six heavy strikecruisers. Ceres Admiral Kalen himself had come with the fleet and was now in the Command Center of the *Avenger*.

"There are twenty dual power beam installations of the latest type on board those three supply ships as well as four class one nuclear fusion reactors," Kalen informed Jeremy. "I also brought the technicians needed to install them."

"Governor Malleck really came through," Jeremy said, elated at the news. "You have no idea what this means."

"I think I do," Admiral Kalen replied, pleased to see how excited Jeremy was about what he had brought. Then, in a more serious tone, he added, "Jeremy, no one outside of the people on Ceres that were involved with this knows that we have sent you these power beam installations and reactors. When President Kincaid finds out there's going to be hell to pay for us going around the Federation Council."

"What can I ever do to repay Ceres for this?" asked Jeremy, realizing the giant risk that Governor Malleck and the others were taking.

"It's quite simple, actually," Admiral Kalen replied. He looked at Jeremy his eyes growing intense. "Just hold Careth and keep the Hocklyns and AIs at bay until we can return with a relief fleet. If you can succeed in doing that, the Federation Council will see the wisdom in what we did."

"Will the Federation Council agree to send a relief fleet?" Jeremy asked. "This entire region may soon be back under Hocklyn control."

"If the Federation won't, Ceres and New Tellus will," Admiral Kalen promised. "I also need to tell you that there will be another large supply fleet in three more weeks. It will contain four of the new type two battle stations as well as more fighters and bombers for the Carethians."

"Type two battle stations?" Jeremy spoke confused. He had never heard of these. "What are type two battle stations?"

Admiral Kalen quickly explained their purpose and what they were capable of. "They would be ideal to place around your space station. It would add the final piece to the firepower the station will need to defend itself."

"Will there be any more supply fleets after that one?" asked Jeremy, knowing it would soon be time for the Hocklyns and AIs to show up. It might be too dangerous to send another.

"Probably not," replied Admiral Kalen, shaking his head. "New Tellus has been sending stealth scouts to the outer regions of the Hocklyn Empire, and they have discovered an unsettling piece of information. Almost every Hocklyn warship for over three thousand light years around this section of space has been pulled back."

"That could be over a thousand ships!" exclaimed Jeremy, growing worried. "Why pull those ships back? I thought the AIs were rearming Hocklyn warships from deep within their Empire?"

"Our intelligence people suspect they are," Admiral Kalen replied with worry on his face. "We think these ships will serve as a mop up force to follow up their strike fleet. Anything the strike fleet misses or doesn't destroy completely, this fleet will finish off."

Jeremy turned pale as he realized he could be facing many more enemy ships than he had originally estimated. It might make it nearly impossible to hold the bears' planet. He took a deep breath and looked across the Command Center. Kelsey was at her station working on her navigation computer. Kevin and Katie were over at the main computer console running diagnostics with Ariel. Angela was over on the space station installing special encryption codes on the stations communication systems. He knew the whole crew of the Avenger was counting on him to keep them safe.

Jeremy had sworn to protect this system and to stand by Grayseth when the Hocklyns returned. He fully intended to keep that promise. He turned to face Admiral Kalen and spoke. "When the Hocklyns and AIs are defeated at New Tellus and you can return to Careth, you will find us waiting for you."

Admiral Kalen nodded. He had expected nothing less from Admiral Strong and the crew of the Avenger. Their parents had founded the Federation, and they were continuing in that tradition. Kalen wondered if any of them realized that when they returned to Federation space they all would be considered heroes just like Admiral Streth. In many ways, they already were.

Chapter Eleven

Jeremy watched as the last supply ship was being unloaded at the space station. Ten large supply ships had arrived with a large military escort from New Tellus. On board the ships were the last munitions and spare parts he would receive for quite some time.

"They're almost done unloading," commented Kevin. He was standing next to Jeremy in the Command Center watching the big viewscreen on the front wall. "It might be a while before we see Federation ships again." Over the years, Kevin's freckles had gradually faded, but his fiery red hair remained.

"The supply fleet brought three hundred more fighters and two hundred bombers for the Carethians," Ariel informed them as she walked over to stand next to Jeremy. "They're crated up and will have to be assembled."

"That won't take long," Jeremy replied.

He knew that Grayseth's people had become very well versed at assembling the small craft. Jeremy also didn't tell Kevin that another small supply fleet was waiting in a nearby system with additional supplies from Ceres, including the four new type two battle stations. He would leave that as a surprise. As soon as the New Tellus fleet left, they would jump in. The crews on the New Tellus ships were from all over the Federation, but the crews on the Ceres ships were from Ceres only.

"Commander Marks is on the station and she is reporting that several of the supply ship commanders have been asking about the power beam installations on the outer hull of the space station," Ariel added with concern in her voice.

She knew those had not been in the initial plans, and the installations had only been added after Jeremy had coaxed Ceres and Governor Malleck into furnishing them.

"Tell her to explain to the commanders that they are a recent addition to the station and are essential to its defense," ordered Jeremy, wishing there had been some way to hide the installations. They were just so large that it wasn't practical. He knew that when this news got back to the Federation that Governor Malleck would probably be summoned immediately to appear in front of the Federation Council for an explanation.

Ariel nodded and seemed to focus her dark eyes on a distant point as she sent the message to Commander Marks. "Commander Marks says she will do it and that she is also going to the assembly area in the flight bays to help the bears with the new fighters and bombers."

Jeremy nodded as he continued to watch the viewscreen. Commander Marks had been spending a lot of time with the bears, particularly the bear pilots as she was responsible for their training. Every day squadrons of bears and human fighters engaged each other in war games. Initially the humans had won every game easily, but recently the odds had begun to shift and now the bears were winning occasionally. It wasn't uncommon to hear the bear pilots bragging about how they had beat their human opponents. The two groups were developing a lot of mutual respect for one another and were working well together in joint maneuvers.

"How many fighters and bombers does that give the bears?" Kevin asked. Kevin had made several close friends with the bears on the station.

"Eight hundred fighters and six hundred bombers," replied Jeremy, looking over at his best friend. Kevin had changed considerably since that first day when they had met so long ago at the Fleet Academy and then later during the failed New Horizon mission.

"We'll be on our own soon," added Kevin, knowing they were over seven hundred light years from home.

He glanced over to his left side where Katie was busy at her computer station. Over the months since they had been at Careth he had fallen deeply in love with the green-eyed blonde. Katie had also changed considerably over the years. She was no longer that crazy green-eyed kid that had snuck aboard the New Horizon, even though later she had been responsible for saving all of their lives, or at least getting them off the New Horizon before it was destroyed.

Jeremy noticed where Kevin was staring and smiled inwardly to himself. He knew that once they returned to Federation space there would have to be some changes. In all likelihood, the five of them would have to be split up if they elected to continue to fight in the war. It would be difficult for all of them when that happened. Jeremy was not sure what he would do without the others around.

Looking back at the main viewscreen, Jeremy saw that the last supply ship was undocking and starting to move away. Just the day before Rear Admiral Kimmel's supply ships and the large fleet repair ships had jumped to Admiral Streth's base. Admiral Streth would need all six of the repair ships if his fleet was to make it back to Federation space intact.

Ariel looked around the Command Center. She knew that shortly the Hocklyns would be arriving and attempt to drive them out of the Careth system or destroy all the Federation ships outright. She had spent weeks running different simulations on how best to defend the bears' planet. If the Hocklyns did manage to drive them away, they would find it very costly. Ariel just hoped it would be costly enough to force them to call off their attack. She didn't think Jeremy would jump away as long as he had a single warship capable of fighting.

"How soon before the power beam installations are complete?" asked Jeremy, looking over at Ariel and marveling how not a single hair on her head was out of place. Recently Ariel had been experimenting with different hairstyles. Today her thick black hair was just above her shoulders and slightly curled.

"Another five to six days," Ariel replied. "Grayseth and Rear Admiral Stillson have engineering teams working steadily, as well as the ones Admiral Kalen left. Once they have all the installations completed and the new reactors online, they plan on two days of tests to ensure the power relays will stay operational when the power beams are fired."

Jeremy nodded. These power beam stations were the same as the ones used on the asteroid fortresses in the New Tellus system. They were twenty percent larger and more powerful than the ones on a warship. He had been surprised when he saw these being unloaded from the supply ships. He had expected the regular ones that warships were equipped with.

Ariel knew she would feel relieved when the new power beam stations were finished. With the laser satellites and missile platforms that were currently in orbit around the space station, it would make it very difficult for the Hocklyns to destroy it. She was also aware of the four type two battle stations that were soon to be delivered. Her biggest concern was keeping Jeremy and the rest of the Special Five safe. Those had been her last orders from Admiral Jason Strong, Jeremy's father, and she intended to obey those orders no matter what the cost.

Six hours later, Kevin looked at his sensor screens in surprise as eight more friendly green icons appeared. They were quickly challenged by the light cruiser Kallen and sent their IDs. Kevin was amazed to see two additional supply ships, two battlecarriers, two battlecruisers, and two strikecruisers.

"Jeremy, where did those ships come from?" he asked, looking back toward Jeremy who was sitting at the command console watching the tactical display now showing the new ships.

"Those will be the last Federation ships we will see in a long time," Jeremy replied sadly as he looked over at Kevin. "They are bringing four of the new type two battle stations and additional Devastator Three missiles from Ceres."

"Type two battle stations?" Kevin asked confused as he looked back at the tactical display. "What are those?"

Jeremy allowed himself to smile. "Ariel, put up the specifications of the new battle stations on one of Kevin's screens."

Ariel complied and soon Kevin was lost in studying the schematics of the new one hundred and fifty meter stations. "How did Admiral Teleck ever manage to send us these?" Kevin blurted. The power beams, the class one fusion reactors, and now these battle stations. It was hard to believe the Federation had agreed to send such advanced technology to the bears.

"I believe it was Governor Malleck," replied Jeremy, wondering how much trouble the Ceres governor was going to be in for doing this. From the encrypted message he had received from Admiral Teleck, he knew that Governor Malleck had done much of this without the approval of the Federation Council.

Kevin nodded as he went back to studying the new battle station. From what he could see, it would be a great addition to the defense of Careth.

A few days later, Governor Malleck was called to a special meeting in the Federation Council Chambers. Fleet Admiral Johnson and Admiral Teleck were also in attendance.

"I can't believe you did this!" stated President Kincaid, looking angrily over at Governor Malleck. "You have turned over to the bears nearly all of our most advanced weapons systems!"

"The AIs probably already possess this technology," Governor Malleck responded calmly. He had just informed the council that he had sent Admiral Strong the power beam installations and the new battle stations. "We already know that the Hocklyns are not allowed to develop new technology on their own, so there is no real danger of any of these weapons systems being captured and ever used against us."

"You still went around the council," Senator Fulbright of the planet Serenity said accusingly. "What if the Hocklyns do develop this technology? Out on the perimeter of the Federation our worlds of Serenity and Bliss could end up being prime targets. Both of our worlds have defensive grids, but only small fleets to protect us."

"I agree," replied Senator Davis of Bliss. "We have 600 million people on my world. This blunder could put all of them in danger." Bliss and Serenity were both in the Epsilon Eridani system, the fartherest inhabited human star system in the Federation from Earth.

Admiral Teleck stood up. "May I address the council? I have something to say that might alleviate this situation."

"By all means, Admiral," President Kincaid responded with a heavy sigh. This entire situation was dividing the council, and that was a situation that couldn't be tolerated at this precarious time, not with an impending attack by the Hocklyns and the AIs.

Admiral Teleck walked over to a holographic projection table and inserted a computer chip. Instantly a large, gray sphere materialized above the table. It was slowly rotating, showing numerous defensive laser turrets, as well as missile tubes. "This is the new type two satellite defensive battle station we have developed on Ceres."

"That's one of the weapons we should not have sent the Carethians," Senator Fulbright spoke loudly. His face was turning lived at the nerve of the Ceres people having bypassed the council. "You have endangered the Federation with your audacity."

Admiral Teleck ignored the interruption and continued. "The station is one hundred and fifty meters in diameter and fully self-contained. It has an upgraded energy shield, defensive lasers, four pulse laser turrets, interceptor missiles, and twelve Devastator Three missile tubes with a standard crew of fifty. It is powered by a class one fusion reactor."

Then, pausing, Admiral Teleck looked directly at Senator Fulbright. "It has advanced computer and targeting systems that will allow it to engage an AI ship, and we are willing to furnish these to place around all the worlds of the Federation."

A majority of the senators started speaking at once. Protecting their worlds from the AIs had been the biggest concern of the senators for months.

"Are you saying this battle station could destroy an AI ship?" asked President Kincaid, gazing at the hologram with renewed interest.

"In conjunction with fire from the defensive satellite grid and the type one satellite battle stations, it could," Admiral Teleck replied. "We can also furnish these to our allies to better protect their worlds."

"We would have to maintain Federation control over them," spoke Fleet Admiral Johnson, rising to her feet and coming over to the hologram to examine the new battle station in more detail. "If all the stations had Federation crews on board then I don't see a problem with using them to defend our allies' worlds. That has been their biggest complaint, that they have nothing that can stop an AI."

"We did send small fleets with strikecruisers to all of our allies," President Kincaid reminded Carla. "But I can see the advantages of using these battle stations; it would obviously make them feel more secure with something so powerful in orbit of their worlds."

"How do we test them against an AI?" Senator Malle from Mars asked, his eyes focusing on Admiral Teleck. He could easily see how beneficial these new stations could be if they were available in significant numbers. They could also free up valuable fleet units to be used elsewhere if needed.

Admiral Teleck looked grimly around the large conference table at the senators. "It's quite simple. In another few weeks, the Hocklyns and AIs will, in all likelihood, be attacking the Carethian system. We will know then if they work."

"How soon before you can deploy them to our worlds?" Senator Fulbright demanded. "We should have the first ones since our defenses are the weakest."

"We will need to set up additional production lines," Admiral Teleck answered. "These new battle stations take longer to produce than the type ones."

"We are already producing the type one battle stations at New Tellus," Fleet Admiral Johnson commented as she thought about what they could do. "How hard would it be to change over one or two of our production lines to accommodate the type two battle stations?"

"A little over a week," Governor Malleck replied. "It's not that difficult."

President Kincaid nodded. He could see how the new battle stations could be extremely beneficial to the defense of all Federation worlds. He would finish speaking to Governor Malleck later in private. While he didn't totally disagree with what Ceres had done, the governor should have spoken to him about it first. Kincaid knew he would probably have privately approved allowing Ceres to send the weapons to Careth. After all, there was still a heavy Federation presence there. He also didn't want to see Admiral Strong and the crew of the Avenger fail because the Federation had refused to give them what was needed to stop the Hocklyns and AIs.

Admiral Tolsen felt relaxed in his command chair as he gazed out over the Command Center of the Defiant. His fleet was currently on patrol at the far edges of the New Tellus system. So far, the patrol had been uneventful; he had spent much of it working his fleet and preparing them for battle. They had practiced changing formations rapidly and making short micro-jumps to disrupt the enemy's formation. He had read up on all the battles and war games that Admiral Strong had been involved in using short micro-jumps to confound the enemy.

Tolsen had nearly lost his entire fleet at Gliese 667-C, and he had no intention of that happening again. Whenever possible, he was running battle drills and had only recently watched as several of his battlecruisers supported by four light cruisers pulverized a small asteroid in a weapon's test.

"Last fleet efficiency reports show we have improved by three points over the last week," spoke Colonel Arnett, feeling pleased at the results of the last few battle drills.

"No one was shooting back," responded Race, raising his eyebrows. "Only a few of our ships have actually seen combat, and that is a game changer. I want us to be as ready as possible. We have one more week of deployment before we return to New Tellus. Tomorrow we will divide the fleet and practice a more complicated war game. The winning side will get an extra two day leave when we get back."

"I will spread the word," Colonel Arnett replied with a grin. She knew the added incentive of additional leave would spur the crews of all the ships to give their utmost effort.

Race leaned back in his command chair as he watched Colonel Arnett walk off. She was turning out to be an exemplary executive officer. In many ways, she reminded him of Colonel Beck his former executive officer who had died on the old WarHawk in the Gliese-667C system. He could still picture that horrible sight as the Hocklyn energy beams ravaged the WarHawk after its shields failed. Almost the entire command crew died, and he had been severely injured.

They had won the battle thanks to some unorthodox maneuvers by Admiral Strong and Ariel, and finally when Admiral Streth sent the rest of the waiting fleets in to destroy the Hocklyns. From what Race had seen from the videos and reports, the Hocklyns had been wiped out to the last ship. He just wished he could have been conscious to see it.

—

Jeremy was with Grayseth and Daelthon in the massive Command Center in the space station. Daelthon was Grayseth's second in command, and his short fur was a light brown in color. They were watching one of the large viewscreens as several small tugs were placing the four new battle stations into their protective positions around the station.

Kelsey was also in the Command Center as she had been visiting one of the female Carethians who was working as a navigation officer. Kelsey had made friends with several of the female Carethians, and she was currently talking to Malith about how to set up routine patrol routes for fighters and bombers.

Looking over at Kelsey, Jeremy smiled as he saw the contented look upon her face. Kelsey and Malith were fast becoming close friends, and Kelsey had even brought the female bear over to the Avenger for a tour. Malith had been uneasy at meeting Ariel, as she didn't quite understand how the crew of the Avenger could be friends with an AI after she had heard so much about how big a threat they were. Kelsey and Ariel had spent quite a bit of time explaining Ariel's origin and how she was not like the AIs from the center of the galaxy.

"With those four battle stations and the defensive satellites we have placed around the station the Hocklyns will not enjoy their return to our world," Grayseth spoke, his large, friendly eyes turning to look at Jeremy.

"With the new power beams and fusion reactors the station will be a hard nut to crack," Jeremy agreed with a satisfied nod. The new reactors greatly enhanced the strength of the energy shield as well.

"We will hunt our enemies together," Grayseth said, sounding more serious. "They will not be allowed to have our world again."

"We will hunt together, my friend," Jeremy promised, equally serious.

"We will have the new bombers and fighters assembled shortly," Daelthon added. "I've just come from the new flight bays and assembly is well underway. Commander Marks has brought a team over from her battlecarrier, and they are assisting our engineers. The new hunting wings should be ready for deployment within two more days."

Jeremy glanced over at one of the large holographic tactical displays that showed space for twenty light years around Careth. Each star system had been seeded with multiple FTL detection buoys. When the Hocklyns arrived, Careth should have some advance warning; at least enough time to get all the crews off the planet on leave and back up to their waiting ships.

Grayseth nodded, noticing where Jeremy's eyes had strayed. This human great leader was so much like a Carethian. He had strict rules of honor he followed, and when Jeremy gave his word, it was like a bond. Grayseth knew that his human friend could be counted on to stand by Careth until the end or until they found victory.

He was a little confused about the relationship between Kelsey and Jeremy. Only in private did they show their true feelings for one another. That was one area where humans and Carethians were different. Female Carethians were not allowed to risk themselves in dangerous positions as pilots or as crewmembers on warships. Only a few had been allowed upon the space station, such as Malith, and then only in positions that would not involve actual combat. Grayseth knew that with humans it was different. Their females fought alongside them and showed just as much ferocity as the human males did.

Grayseth turned his attention back to the large viewscreen, seeing that the tugs had finished positioning the battle stations. Once the stations were powered up and their crews went on board, the station's own position keeping thrusters would maintain keep them in place. Grayseth knew that by positioning the battle stations around the space station with their Devastator Three missiles it would allow the human fleet more versatility in its maneuvers when dealing with an attacking Hocklyn fleet or an AI ship.

"I don't understand you humans," Malith was saying to Kelsey as the female bear used her large hands to enter practice patrol routes for the new fighters into her console. "Your mate is over there, and the two of you scarcely acknowledge each other."

Kelsey's face flushed, and she shook her head slightly. "It's complicated," she explained in a quiet voice. "In our fleet you are not supposed to become involved with another member of the command crew as it could cause complications during combat as well as with the crew."

"I understand that, I guess," Malith conceded as she pressed several buttons on her computer. "But I have overheard members of your crew talking, and most are aware of your relationship and they are not bothered by it."

Kelsey let out a heavy sigh. She and Jeremy were well aware that most of the crew knew about their love life. They didn't make it a secret when they were down at one of the seaside resorts about spending time together. For now, it wasn't a problem, but when they returned to Federation space someday, it might be.

"What about your own mate?" Kelsey asked as she reached forward and corrected a minor mistake in the information Malith was using to plot the patrol routes. "Your mate is still down on Careth."

"He is a pilot on one of our warships,' Malith spoke with pride as she watched Kelsey make the correction. She realized quickly where she had erred. "Our ships will hunt as a pack and will cause great harm to the evil ones when they return."

"What is it like living in the underground cities?" Kelsey asked curiously.

She knew the bears had a number of hidden underground cities scattered around the planet. Even now, they remained secret in case the Hocklyns and AIs managed to destroy the orbital defenders and wreak havoc with the surface of the planet. Only Jeremy had been allowed inside of one and he had said very little.

"They are like massive, interconnected caves," Malith replied slowly. "There are few open spaces for our young to play and learn the way of the hunt. Even in the underground cities, it has been difficult to teach our young our heritage."

"I understand your heritage is important to you," Kelsey commented.

"It is what makes us Carethians," Malith replied as she set up the final patrol route on her computer. "In our early history there was much violence between different tribes. Over the years, we learned to hunt and work together, and our heritage has evolved around that. Now there are no longer different tribes, only Carethians, and we are very proud of that."

Kelsey nodded. It sounded so much like what she knew of Earth's own history until Jeremy's father had changed everything. That was what Jeremy's father had accomplished and was known for. Working with Katie's father, the two of them had united the countries of Earth, introduced the Federation survivors on Ceres, and formed the beginnings of the new Federation.

With a heavy sigh, Kelsey began showing Malith how to calculate orbits and patrol routes an easier way. It made her sad to think about those early years at the Fleet Academy and the New Horizon incident. All of them had left their parents behind when they had gone into cryosleep. True, Admiral Johnson had introduced them to some of their close relatives that lived now, but it wasn't the same. Sometimes Kelsey wished her mom were here so she could confide in her and ask for advice. Putting those thoughts to the back of her mind, she tried to focus on what she was showing Malith. She also knew that someday she and Jeremy would have a life and children together, if they survived the coming months.

Governor Malleck was back on Ceres. The meeting with the Federation Council had gone better than expected, particularly once Admiral Teleck had described the new battle stations and what they could mean. He had met privately with President Kincaid, and Kincaid had stressed that Malleck mustn't do this again. All the worlds of the Federation needed to work together if they were to survive the next few months, and Ceres must do its part.

"So you're leaving tomorrow," Malleck said, looking over at Admiral Teleck who was standing next to him in the large ship bay which held four battlecruisers, including Admiral Teleck's own flagship, the battlecruiser Ceres.

"Yes," Teleck replied. "Fleet Admiral Johnson wants me to make a tour of our allies as a reminder that we are all a part of this coming war. She feels that if they see some of our more powerful warships in their space it will help to calm fears within their civilian populations."

"How many ships are you taking?" Malleck asked. The Hocklyns hadn't hit Admiral Streth yet, so he knew they still had at least two to four weeks before the Hocklyns could arrive at New Tellus.

"The Ceres and two other battlecruisers, two of our battlecarriers, four strikecruisers, six Monarch cruisers and twelve light cruisers," Teleck replied. "All the ships are from Ceres as Fleet Admiral Johnson wants to keep her regular fleet units close by."

Malleck nodded. He was just glad that Ceres had been focusing for years on building up their fleet. "I assume that arrangements have already been made with our allies about allowing your fleet to enter their space."

"Yes," replied Teleck, nodding his head in the affirmative. "Our allies seem pleased that we are sending the fleet. I think even some in their own militaries need a morale boost."

"How long will you be gone?" Malleck asked. He wanted Admiral Teleck back before the Hocklyns attacked New Tellus.

"Three weeks," Teleck responded evenly. "If I receive word that the Hocklyns have hit Fleet Admiral Streth's base or Careth, I will return immediately."

"Just make sure you stay away from the Albanians," Malleck warned the admiral.

"We're not going out that far," Teleck assured the governor. "Besides, the Albanians have made it very plain recently that we are not welcome in their space."

"They may change their minds when the Hocklyns and the AIs arrive," Malleck responded. "They will probably be screaming loudly for help then."

"Perhaps," Admiral Teleck responded. Something about the Albanians and their response to the Hocklyn and AI menaces just didn't make any sense to him. How could such an advanced race stick their heads in the ground and hope the danger didn't find them? "Admiral Kalen will be in charge of the Ceres military until I get back."

"Have a safe trip," spoke Governor Malleck, wishing Admiral Teleck wasn't leaving. While Admiral Kalen was a well qualified commander and could handle the defense of Ceres if necessary, Malleck still felt more comfortable and secure when Admiral Teleck was around.

Chapter Twelve

Fleet Commodore Resmunt studied the latest readiness reports from the ships in his fleet carefully. The AIs were still jumping the fleet at regular intervals that would cause them to arrive in human controlled space much sooner than Resmunt had originally planned. He looked up at the main tactical display and saw that all ten fleets had completed their latest jump. The AI ships were in the center of the formation with a large gap between them and the nearest Hocklyn ship. No one wanted to be close to those 1,500-meter behemoths and what they contained. So far, none of the AIs had come over to Resmunt's flagship.

"Three more days and we will be in range of the humans," First Leader Ganth rasped as his dark eyes focused on the Fleet Commodore. "We are receiving complaints from various ships about their drive harmonics becoming unbalanced."

"I want to stop and retune our drives before we jump into combat with the humans," Resmunt spoke as he gazed with frustration at the ten large green icons representing the AI spheres in the tactical hologram. "The day after tomorrow I will ask the AIs to allow us to do so."

"What if they refuse?" Ganth asked his large eyes narrowing. "If the harmonics on several of those ships get much worse they may fail to make a rendezvous."

"I will insist," replied Resmunt, knowing it would cause him to have to deal in person with the AIs. "If they want this fleet ready for combat they will allow us the time we need to prepare our ships."

The AIs had only allowed them to stop twice this far to retune the drives. It was becoming more evident with each jump that some ships were in serious need of maintenance time. In the jump they had just finished, a number of ships had been over ten million kilometers off when they exited their jump vortexes. They couldn't afford that type of error if they were jumping into battle with the humans.

"The AIs are sending new jump coordinates," Third Leader Vrill reported. "We are to be ready to jump in one hour."

"Just barely enough time for our drive cores to cool," complained First Leader Ganth, shaking his head. "If the AIs insist we

145

continue at this pace, some of the ships will begin suffering serious damage to their drive cores."

"They are focused on destroying these humans," Fleet Commodore Resmunt grated out, his eyes darkening. "Order all ships to do what repairs they can until we reach our destination. If I didn't know better, I would think the AIs are afraid of the humans."

"Impossible!" spoke Ganth, shaking his large head in disbelief. "The AIs are made out of metal and don't have those types of emotions."

"I'm not so sure," Resmunt responded with doubt in his voice. "From what I have heard from the High Council, the AIs do at times exhibit emotions."

Ganth was quiet as he weighed that thought. Could it be possible that the AIs feared the humans and if so, what did it mean for the attacking Hocklyn fleets? It made First Leader Ganth wonder if there was something important that the AIs were not telling them.

On board the dreadnought Viden, War Leader Versith stared contemplatively at the deadly AI sphere showing on the main viewscreen.

"It is a frightening sight to have so many AI ships in amongst our fleet," spoke First Leader Trion. He had never cared much for the AIs.

"As long as they remain aboard their ships we have nothing to fear," Versith replied as he turned to face Trion. "How is Second Leader Jaseth doing?" Versith had assigned the First Leader to keep a close watch on the young Hocklyn warrior. Jaseth's emotions had to remain in check if he wished to rise in the ranks of command and perhaps someday command a warship or even become a War Leader.

"He follows orders," Trion replied evenly. The First Leader folded his sinewy arms across the chest plate of his light gray combat armor. "I still fear his hatred of these humans could endanger the ship. He will have to be watched very closely when the Viden goes into battle."

"I don't believe so," challenged Versith, disagreeing with the First Leader as his trained eyes looked across the War Room and the busy crew. "His hatred will spur him to become an even greater warrior. If this war lasts for any measurable length of time, he could well become a leader in our fleet."

"Perhaps," responded Trion, doubtfully. "But there are many in the fleet that don't care for Second Leader Jaseth and would not hesitate to challenge him to fight an honor duel if he were to leave the Viden."

"Then we will make sure he stays on the ship," Versith replied in a stern and commanding voice. He had promised Jaseth's family that he would look after the young Hocklyn warrior. His long friendship with the family had made him feel honor bound to offer that commitment.

"As you command," replied Trion, knowing that Versith was close to the young Hocklyn's family. "I will continue to watch Jaseth. But I fear that honor will be slow to come to Jaseth in this war."

Deep in the bowels of the ship, Jaseth was busy practicing with his blade. He was in a training room with a number of blade targets hanging from the tall ceiling. Stepping forward and pivoting on his left foot, he drove his blade deeply into the shoulder of his intended target. Stepping back, he swung his fist, feeling the sharp nails on his fingers dig into his palm as he struck the center of the target.

Jaseth reached out and wrenched his blade free. Since leaving the home system, his wounds had healed up, leaving only minor scars. Each day he came to this room and worked on his combat skills. He knew that, in the future, he would have to face many more honor duels if for no other reason than he was the son of the former High Leader. Many would always hold that against him regardless of what he did in the coming war.

"You drive your blade deep," rasped a voice from the open doorway.

Spinning around, Jaseth saw Fourth Leader Armith who served in Engineering. The two were not friends but did occasionally spar together.

"I seek to inflict pain on my opponent," Jaseth replied in a steady voice. "If this were a human, that blow would have incapacitated him."

"Perhaps," Armith replied as he stepped farther into the room. "But we know nothing about the human warriors and their combat skills. All we know for certain is that they have defeated us each time we have met them in battle."

"Not this time," Jaseth spoke, his eyes flashing red. "This time the humans will die. Between our ships and the AIs none of the humans will survive!"

Turning, Jaseth kicked one of the targets, sending it flying backward. "I intend to ask War Leader Versith to allow me to go down to the fleet base and test my combat skills against the humans that will be defending it."

"That job is for our Protectors," spoke Armith, shaking his head in disapproval. "The Protectors find their honor in individual combat; we find ours with the fleet."

"No!" Jaseth insisted as he placed his blade back in its scabbard. "My blade craves human blood, and it shall have it!"

Jaseth walked past Fourth Leader Armith and out of the room. He was determined that he would meet the humans in individual combat. His honor would not be denied.

Armith watched him go. Just from speaking to Jaseth, he could sense the pent up rage the young warrior had inside. Armith shook his head; the honor Jaseth yearned for was not the kind craved by other Hocklyn warriors, he wanted revenge for what had happened to his family. Armith greatly feared that no good would come of this. He would speak to First Leader Trion. Jaseth would require constant scrutiny when the Viden went into battle or he could endanger the ship with his reckless desire for vengeance.

Admiral Streth was meeting with Admiral Sheen, Admiral Adler, and Admiral Kimmel on the StarStrike. All four knew that their time was rapidly running out, and the Hocklyns and AIs could show up at any time. For several days now, Hedon had been feeling as if something momentous was about to occur. He had learned in the distant past to trust these intuitions. There was no doubt in his mind what it signified. The Hocklyns and the AIs were coming.

"James, I want you to take the supply fleet and go to system K-994 and wait for us," Hedon ordered. "Your fleet should be safe there and when we arrive I imagine we will be in need of all of your repair ships."

"That's seventy light years from here," Rear Admiral Kimmel replied with concern in his voice. "Will your ships be able to make it that far if they receive major damage?"

Hedon let out a deep breath and then replied. "Not all of them. I expect we will suffer heavily when the Hocklyns and AIs arrive, but it is the only way to ensure they follow us back to New Tellus."

"You still plan on us meeting them in the gravity well of the planet?" asked Amanda, knowing it would greatly increase their losses as they would have to fight their way out of it to jump to safety.

"We have no other choice if we want to substantially weaken their fleet," replied Hedon, knowing this decision would cost the lives of thousands of fleet personnel. However, this wasn't about saving members of the Fleet; it was about saving the new Federation of Worlds and the billions of people who were depending on them.

"Jacob, you will have all twenty-three of our battlecarriers assigned to your fleet," Hedon began as he thought for the thousandth time about the best way to fight this impending battle. "Under no circumstances are any of your fighters or bombers to attempt to engage an AI ship. I want them to focus on the Hocklyn's lighter units."

"Their escort cruisers," Jacob responded, surprised. He arched his eyebrows and looked over at the admiral. "Wouldn't we do more good focusing on their heavier units?"

"No, we will need those fighters and bombers if we want to reach the Federation with a major part of our fleet intact. I don't want them sacrificed needlessly. Your fleet will stay just inside the second satellite defensive layer with the majority of our destroyers. Forty of them will be assigned to protecting the battle carriers and the others will be scattered amongst the satellites to provide defensive fire."

"Amanda, the survivors of Admiral Gaines's fleet will be split between First and Second Fleet. We will fight a retreating battle back toward the defensive satellite grid until we can activate the missile platforms in the outer two defensive rings. Once that has been accomplished, we will form a defensive envelope around Third Fleet and fight our way to the edge of the planet's gravity well. When we reach it, we will jump."

"We're going to be leaving some damaged ships behind," Jacob warned in a low voice.

"I know," replied Hedon, letting out a heavy sigh. "We can't try to rescue them, or we could lose the entire Ready Reserve Fleet."

Everyone was silent as they thought about the battle that was soon to come. They knew that many of the people they had come to know over the past few months of Operation First Strike might not make it back home.

"James, I want your fleet out of here today," Hedon ordered in an even voice. "I don't want to risk the Hocklyns or the AIs detecting your presence."

"How many warships will be going with me?" Admiral Kimmel asked.

"Ten destroyers, one battlecruiser, one strikecruiser, and two Monarchs," Hedon answered. "I will need the rest."

James nodded. He stood up and saluted Fleet Admiral Streth. "Good luck, Sir," he spoke. "We will be waiting for you." With that, Rear Admiral Kimmel left the conference room to get his fleet ready for immediate departure.

"I had better return to the Wasp," Jacob said as he stood up, then he paused, giving the admiral a serious look. "Hedon, don't do anything heroic when the AIs and the Hocklyns show up. The Federation still needs you."

Hedon didn't reply, only nodded his acknowledgment of Jacob's words.

Amanda watched Admiral Adler leave and then she turned to Hedon. "You know they're coming, don't you," she said, her deep blue eyes focusing on the admiral. "You can feel it."

Well did she know about the intuitions Hedon had at times. He had sensed the destruction of the original Federation worlds days before they were able to return from their search mission deep into Hocklyn space. Upon their return, they had found the old Federation worlds in ruins.

Hedon was silent for a long moment. Only Amanda and a few others knew how at times he could sense events. "Yes," he spoke in a soft voice. "The Hocklyns are coming, and the AIs are with them. They should arrive in just a few more days; that's why James has to leave today."

Amanda nodded in understanding. She knew that Hedon suffered severe headaches when he had these intuitions. "We will be ready for them," she promised. Amanda for once was glad that Richard wasn't here, at least for now, her husband was safe back at New Tellus.

Newly promoted Fleet Commodore Krilen watched as the fleets making up his new command began to make rendezvous. He watched his sensor screens in deep satisfaction as fleet after fleet exited hundreds of white spatial vortexes as their individual ships made an appearance.

"Eight hundred and twenty warships," Krilen spoke in elation as the final ships arrived.

"Much honor will come from this command," First Leader Angoth stated as he watched the various fleets moving into formation.

"Enough honor for all of us," Krilen responded, pleased that the High Council had chosen this honor for him.

Only Fleet Commodore Resmunt had command of a fleet as large as this one. Krilen was confident that someday he would sit upon the Hocklyn High Council; he suspected that Resmunt might also have the same goal.

First Leader Angoth nodded in agreement. He fully expected to be raised in rank to War Leader when this campaign against the humans was over. He also suspected that Fleet Commodore Krilen had even higher aspirations for his own future.

"How soon before Fleet Commodore Resmunt arrives?" Angoth asked. He knew that along with Resmunt's fleet there would be ten of the massive AI ships.

"Within the hour," responded Krilen, recalling the latest FTL message from Resmunt. "Fleet Commodore Resmunt informed me earlier that the AIs were pushing his fleet to the limits of their jump drives. He also said they would be spending an entire day in this system to retune them and do a complete check of their drive systems before moving on to begin their attack on the human controlled fleet base."

"And our own attack?" asked Angoth, feeling anxious to engage the humans and acquire more honor.

"We attack Careth a few hours after Resmunt begins his attack," Krilen replied, his cold eyes looking across the War Room. "We have been ordered to destroy everything in the system and nuke Careth until nothing living remains on its surface."

"The Carethians were a good slave world with their technology," Angoth replied. "It seems foolish to destroy such an asset to the Empire."

"The AIs have ordered it," Krilen replied, his eyes growing even darker. "They are our masters, and we must obey. Careth will be destroyed."

"We must obey," agreed Angoth, acknowledging the AIs rule over the Empire. "After Careth, what are our orders?"

"We will sweep this entire section of space to ensure that no human ship has escaped us," Krilen answered. He had very explicit orders from the High Council concerning that. "Then we will follow Fleet Commodore Resmunt to the human worlds, ensuring that no humans have managed to elude him. We will spend some time in human space searching every star system, world, moon, and asteroid to ensure they are all dead. This time there must not be any human survivors!"

"Genocide," Angoth muttered. He had never agreed with the wholesale destruction of a race. "It seems wasteful to destroy both the Carethians and the Humans instead of making them into obedient slave races." Angoth knew the AIs must have their reasons for doing this, and it was not his position to question the masters.

"The AIs have ordered it," Krilen responded, and he would see to it that their orders were carried out to the fullest.

An hour later, Fleet Commodore Krilen watched nervously as Resmunt's fleets began to drop out of hyperspace. Hundreds of swirling white spatial vortexes formed, and Hocklyn warship after warship emerged. He noticed that a large number emerged thousands and even millions of kilometers outside the rendezvous area; an obvious sign of poorly tuned jump drives.

He took in a deep breath and held it as ten larger white space vortexes formed and the 1,500-meter AI ships emerged. All ten of the AI ships came out of hyperspace within ten kilometers of one another. Krilen shuddered and let his breath out. He had never been in the presence of an AI ship before, let alone ten of the monstrous craft. The AIs must really want the humans dead.

On the outer edge of the system, a human stealth scout was watching the emerging Hocklyn fleets. Admiral Streth had ordered all the scouts deployed toward the section of space where he thought the Hocklyns would come from.

"How can we fight that?" Lieutenant Dunbar asked with fear in her eyes as she watched her sensor screens as they continually updated as even more Hocklyn ships continued to arrive.

"That is Fleet Admiral Streth's job," Captain Allison replied as she nervously watched the glowing cloud of red threat icons on one of the sensor screens. "Our job is to observe and get this information back to the admiral."

"There are ten AI ships in that formation," spoke Dunbar, shaking her head. "Admiral Streth barely destroyed two when they attacked the fleet base the last time."

"We are better prepared this time around," responded Captain Allison, knowing it was getting close to time for them to jump out. She knew there was a distinct possibility the AI ships would be able to detect her stealth scout.

On board the AI command ship, the stealth scout had indeed been detected. The AI operating the sphere's powerful sensors turned toward the AI commander in the center of the massive room. "A human scout ship has been located," the AI reported. "It is operating in stealth mode and has been observing the arrival of the Hocklyn fleets as well as our own ships."

"Unfortunate that they have detected us," the command AI spoke as it moved slowly toward the sensor screens using its antigravity field. "I will order sphere seven to jump to the human scout's position and destroy it."

"Too late," the AI at the sensors replied as the human stealth scout vanished. "The human ship has jumped into hyperspace and is no longer being detected."

"It is not important," the command AI responded as it turned to float back to the center of the room. "Even with advanced warning we will destroy them."

Admiral Teleck was far from the Federation visiting one of their key allies. His fleet was fifty-seven light years from the Federation in the area of space controlled by the Kessels. The Kessels were an advanced culture whose science was roughly at the same level as the humans.

"The Kessel ambassador will be coming on board shortly," Colonel Kathryn Barnes reported. Kathryn was Senator Barnes' daughter and had opted to join the Ceres military rather than go into politics like her father.

"The Kessels are an important part of our alliance," Admiral Telleck responded as he recalled what he knew about their worlds. "They have four highly developed colony worlds and seven smaller ones. They also have science and mining outposts on a dozen more. They maintain a defensive space fleet of approximately 210 vessels. The Kessels have surrounded their worlds with dense minefields and defensive satellites."

"I have always liked the Kessels," Colonel Barnes replied with a smile. "They remind me of cats."

"They do have some feline ancestry in them," Teleck admitted with a nod. The Kessels were slightly shorter than humans with a thick coat of body hair. Even their faces were feline, with thick whiskers and catlike yellow eyes.

A few minutes later, the Kessel ambassador arrived in the Command Center of the Ceres. He came up to Admiral Teleck's shoulder, and his body hair was a light tan in color. "It is a pleasure to see more human ships so far from your Federation," Ambassador Ulrich spoke in a rich purring voice. "Our people will be pleased to see we have such powerful allies."

"We are also pleased that your people are staunch allies in the coming war with the Hocklyns and the AIs," Admiral Teleck responded politely.

"Your protection fleet with the strikecruisers arrived last week," continued Ambassador Ulrich. "We have stationed it in our home system as from there they can rapidly jump to any of our four main colony worlds. Our military has also assigned a force of twenty of our own warships to accompany your fleet if an AI ship does indeed make an appearance in our space."

"Hopefully that will not occur, Ambassador," Teleck said. "The AIs should attack the Federation first, and we hope we can stop them there. If we can do that, then all you will have to be concerned with is an occasional foray into your space of regular Hocklyn warships which your own fleet should be able to handle."

"As you say, Admiral, we can only hope not to have to face one of these monstrous AI ships which the Federation has shown us videos of," Ulrich responded with a nod of his head. "They are truly frightening."

"We will be jumping into your home system shortly," Admiral Teleck informed the ambassador. "Would you like to return to your own ship, or stay on board the Ceres? We have accommodations ready for you if you desire to remain."

"I will remain," Ulrich replied his yellow eyes focusing on Admiral Teleck. "It will be good for me to see how one of your warships functions."

Admiral Teleck was pleased that the Kessels were a friendly race; a lot of beneficial trade had developed between their worlds and the human ones. Since both civilizations had similar levels of technology, very few things were restricted.

Two hours later, the battlecruiser Ceres and her accompanying escorts exited swirling spatial vortexes just outside of the Kessel's home planet. On the main viewscreen of the Ceres, a beautiful blue-white world filled the screen. The planet Kessel was covered by forty percent water, with the rest of the planet consisting of nine main landmasses. Most of those were covered in green as the Kessels were very self-conscious of their planet's ecology. Everything they did was aimed at minimizing the impact of their civilization on the biosphere of their world.

"We are just outside of the gravity well of Kessel," Colonel Barnes reported as she confirmed their position with Navigation.

"Move us in at ten percent sublight," Admiral Teleck ordered. Looking over at the tactical display, he was satisfied to see half a dozen small Kessel warships breaking orbit above the planet to escort them in. It was good to see that the Kessels were taking this war threat seriously.

Admiral Teleck knew that in order for his ships to go into orbit they would have to pass through several very dense minefields. The Kessels had left paths through the mines, and these were heavily guarded by defensive satellites. In addition to the minefields, there was a massive defensive net of satellites surrounding the planet. In orbit, there were also two large, heavily armed shipyards that were used by the Kessels to produce both civilian and military ships.

Ambassador Ulrich stepped back into the Command Center with his small, catlike ears standing up sharply as he strode over to Admiral Teleck. "I see that we have arrived," spoke Ulrich, smiling as he saw his world on the main viewscreen.

"Yes, Ambassador," Admiral Teleck responded. "We will be going into orbit in a few more hours."

"We will be preparing a feast to celebrate your visit," Ambassador Ulrich said as he turned to face the admiral. "I hope you will approve."

"I am sure I will," Teleck replied with a smile of appreciation. He had heard from others that the hospitality of the Kessels was outstanding.

Looking over at Colonel Barnes, Admiral Teleck said, "Colonel Barnes, I am sure you are familiar with state dinners so you will be attending also. It will be good experience for you."

"Yes, Sir," Colonel Barnes replied. Kathryn had attended a number of state dinners with her father. This would be her first one away from Ceres and Earth.

Satisfied, Admiral Teleck turned back to the Kessel ambassador. Now if the Hocklyns would just hold off their attack on Admiral's Streth and Strong until he returned to Ceres. However, he also knew that time for the admirals of Operation First Strike was rapidly running out.

Chapter Thirteen

High Leader Nartel was sitting in his office high above the ground in the massive government building that housed the High Council Chambers. He knew from the latest communication from Fleet Commodore Resmunt if they had maintained their current jump pace that within only a matter of a few hours they would be launching their attack against the humans.

Nartel stood up, walked over to the balcony, and stepped outside to gaze at the busy city below him. Part of it was obscured by pollutants in the air as there was very little wind blowing. Looking down, he could see that the grass in front of the building was turning an unhealthy brown.

There were thirty-two billion Hocklyns crowded together on the planet. Most lived in very small rooms in large buildings designed to maximize the use of space. Some of the buildings had underground sections that housed even more of the planet's large population. Every year space grew less and less and civilian unrest steadily grew. Already, food was being rationed to the lower classes, and there was constant complaining about its lack of quality. Fortunately, a few Protectors stationed at key locations were keeping the problem from getting any worse.

The population was still increasing and would soon reach the point where it was no longer sustainable. Letting out a deep breath, Nartel knew this war against the humans had to be a success. If it was, then he would ask the AIs to allow the Hocklyn race to colonize the ten star systems they had asked about in the past. At that time, the AIs had granted access to three of them until High Leader Ankler's betrayal had wiped that promise out.

Nartel's right hand slipped down to the long blade at his waist, pulling it from its jeweled scabbard. He watched as the dim sunlight glistened off its hard metal surface. Turning it over, he could see his own reflection in the highly polished metal. Looking up, his gaze turned toward space and what it was hiding. Somewhere in toward the center of the galaxy lay the civilization of the AIs. No space faring race was allowed to enter their domain. Daily, hundreds of cargo vessels loaded with special metals and parts were shipped to the very edge of their space to be unloaded at massive space stations. What the AIs were doing with those materials was unknown, even though vague rumors hinted about some giant construction project near the massive black hole at the galaxy's core.

Nartel replaced his blade in its scabbard and returned to his desk, sitting back down. Looking over at the wall, a huge map of the known galaxy depicted the space controlled by the Hocklyn Slave Empire. Nearly a sixth of the galaxy was under their control. He was deeply concerned that the AIs were keeping something from him. There was some secret about these humans that they were refusing to reveal, and that worried him. He greatly feared what would happen if this war against the humans failed.

The last jump had been made, and now Resmunt's fleets were in position to attack the human forces. At his insistence, the AIs had allowed him a full day to prepare for the attack and some much needed maintenance on the Hocklyn warships. The long journey and multiple jumps had been hard on the fleet, and engineers had scrambled trying to get all their maintenance done before the AIs demanded they jump again.

"I have a communication from the lead AI ship," Third Leader Vrill spoke in his rasping voice. "They are reporting that all the human ships are in the gravity well of the planet and have not moved out of it since we arrived in this system."

"Strange," First Leader Ganth spoke, his dark eyes growing even wider. "I would have thought they would have positioned their fleets just outside the gravity well so they could escape if necessary. Their previous tactics seem to indicate they would not make this serious a mistake."

"Then they are dead!" spoke Resmunt, feeling jubilant. "We will jump in with six fleets and immediately engage the humans. Our other four fleets will remain just outside the gravity well and destroy any human ships that attempt to escape." Resmunt remembered how the humans had trapped him; now it was his turn.

"Honor will be ours today," intoned Ganth, feeling the rush of blood through his veins as it neared time for battle.

He knew that much honor could be gained in the coming battle. He was also anxious to try out the new energy beams the AIs had equipped the Liberator with. They were supposed to be forty percent more powerful than the previous ones. Surely, with the new weapons and strengthened energy shield, they would be more than a match for the human ships.

"Commodore Aanith will remain behind with War Leaders Osbith, Crytho, and Zenth," Resmunt ordered as he took his place upon the command pedestal. "We will jump in first and engage the humans, then Commodore Aanith will follow and stay outside the gravity well of the planet. He is to destroy any human ship that attempts to escape."

"I will pass on the orders," Ganth replied as he moved toward Communications.

Admiral Sheen was pacing in the Command Center between the large tactical hologram and the main sensor screen a few feet farther away. The FTL sensor buoys had detected a massive Hocklyn fleet just two light years distant. They had known for several days the fleet was coming once the frantic FTL message from the stealth scout had arrived. All the stealth scouts had been sent on to Admiral Kimmel's position since they would be of no tactical assistance during the coming battle. They had been waiting for several hours for the Hocklyns and the AIs to make their move.

First Fleet and Second Fleet had taken up a defensive position in the center of the gravity well, waiting for the first Hocklyn and AI ships to emerge from hyperspace. Admiral Streth was certain the AIs would jump in and try to engage the fleet first in order to inflict as much damage as possible before the Hocklyns arrived. Eight of the valuable strikecruisers along with sixteen light cruiser escorts would target two of the AI ships, hoping to destroy them quickly and force the AIs to withdraw. Then the battle would come down to the Federation ships and their hated adversaries, the Hocklyns.

"Hocklyn ships are jumping," reported Lieutenant Stalls, trying his best not to sound nervous. Glancing over at Angela at Communications, he could see that she looked very faint. "Don't worry Angela," he spoke over their private channel. Admiral Sheen and Admiral Streth will get us through this."

"I hope so," Angela replied in a strained voice. "But we never faced these kinds of odds before."

"Place the fleet at Condition One," ordered Amanda, nodding at Commander Evans. "Load Devastator Three and regular Devastators in all missile tubes. Unlimited use of Devastator threes has been authorized."

Commander Evans raised her eyebrows at this. "That will take the Hocklyns by surprise," she said with a pleased grin. "They must think we have a limited supply of Devastator Threes from the way we have hesitated using them in the past."

"They are about to find out differently," Amanda responded. They were depending on the powerful sublight missiles to even the playing field against the superior size of the Hocklyn warfleet.

"AIs are jumping," Lieutenant Stalls reported, his face turning pale.

"All ships, stand by to engage AIs," Amanda ordered her ship commanders over the ship-to-ship channel in her mini-com. "Strikecruisers are to engage AIs upon emergence."

Amanda watched expectantly as four heavy strikecruisers and eight light cruisers separated themselves slightly from Second Fleet's formation. She knew there was a good chance the AIs would jump in close to her fleet formation in an attempt to destroy Second Fleet as quickly as possible. She was depending on the strikecruisers to prevent that. They were about to find out if the new computer program and updated targeting systems would be able to take out an AI ship.

Watching the tactical display intently, she saw that four of the strikecruisers with First Fleet were doing the same thing as they pulled slightly away from their fleet formation. "All weapons prepare to fire upon my command. Power beams are to target AI ships as soon as they exit the spatial vortexes."

Amanda knew that the AI jump drives were much more efficient than the Hocklyns' or the Federations'. She sat down at her command console and buckled herself in. Moments crept by as she watched the tactical display tensely waiting for the AIs to appear. As she waited, she wondered what Richard was doing at this moment; she just hoped she lived through this so she could see him again. She could feel her pulse racing and hear her heart pounding in her ears. This would be by far the biggest battle yet.

"Spatial vortexes forming off our starboard bow," Commander Evans reported as a warning alarm on one of the sensor screens went off.

Commander Evans had scarcely spoken the warning when the ten AI ships appeared in between First and Second Fleet.

"How the hell did they do that?" Evans screamed as she saw how close the AI ships were. All ten were within one hundred kilometers of some of Second Fleet's units and within two hundred kilometers of First Fleet.

"Incoming fire," tactical reported as the WarStorm shuddered violently as an energy beam impacted the ship's screen.

"Light cruiser Wrath is down," Stalls reported as he saw the light cruiser's green icon flare up and then vanish.

"We're too close!" swore Commander Evans as reports of damaged ships started coming in.

—

All ten AI ships were firing numerous white energy beams at the two human fleets. The range was so close that very few were missing. Four energy beams from two AI ships struck a human Monarch cruiser, and its energy screen instantly failed. The beams impacted the hull, cutting easily through the ship's battle armor and inflicting serious damage. The beams played across the hull, setting off secondary explosions and eventually cutting the ship into setting off its self-destructs. The Monarch cruiser vanished as nuclear explosions consumed what was left of it.

Another light cruiser exploded in flaming wreckage as AI energy beams tore through its screens and ravaged the ship. Inside First Fleet's formation, a battlecruiser was on fire and other ships were taking damage. Second Fleet was suffering even worse as the AIs were closer.

—

"All ships return fire," ordered Amanda frantically knowing that, at this close range, the AIs could seriously damage both human fleets. They had to buy enough time for the strikecruisers to lock on and fire their Devastator Threes.

Human weapons were now impacting on the AI ship's screens as the human ships began to return fire. Power Beams, lasers, explosive railgun rounds, and nuclear missiles pummeled the AI screens, lighting them up in brilliant explosions. Nuclear fire walked across the AI's energy screens, but the massive ships seemed to shrug off the violent attacks with little effort.

"Light cruiser Terrene is down," Lieutenant Stalls reported as the damaged and dying Federation ships continued to mount.

"Strikecruisers closing on the AI ships and are preparing to fire," Commander Evans reported grimly as she listened to frantic commanders over her mini-com. "The AIs are switching their fire to the cruisers."

In space, the screens on the eight cruisers began to flare brilliantly as multiple AI energy beams bracketed them. The strikecruiser Eden's energy screen failed when the combined fire from four AI ships overwhelmed it. The valiant cruiser tried to launch its Devastator Three missiles but before the first one could clear the launch tube the ship exploded as the deadly AI beams tore the ship apart.

"Strikecruiser Eden is down," Lieutenant Stalls reported grim faced. He knew they couldn't afford to lose the strikecruisers; they were the only ships other than the StarStrike that could take on an AI ship.

"Strikecruisers are firing," Commander Evans spoke tight-lipped her eyes glued to the tactical hologram.

Instantly massive 40-megaton explosions tore into the shields on two AI ships, ripping open two small gaps. Through the gaps shot two more Devastator Three missiles, striking the AI ship's hulls and detonating in bright flashes of nuclear destruction. The two AI ship's shields instantly collapsed as two massive glowing holes were blasted in their hulls.

"Yes!" screamed Lieutenant Stalls, seeing the damage done to the AI ships on the main viewscreen. It was focused on the AI ships and the damage could be seen very plainly. Others in the Command Center let loose cries of elation at seeing the damage done to the two massive AI spheres.

"All ships, target those two AI ships," Amanda ordered, knowing they needed to finish their destruction quickly before the others could respond. They had to drive the AIs back away from the fleets.

From both First Fleet and Second Fleet heavy weapons fire poured into the two AI ships, ripping them apart. Multiple nuclear explosions marched across the two ship's hulls, incinerating metal and superstructure. Secondary explosions began to go off inside the AI ships, blowing out huge sections of the hull. In a matter of moments, the damage to both AI ships became critical, and they blew apart as their internal nuclear self-destructs were activated.

"AI ships are jumping out," Lieutenant Stalls reported with relief as the eight remaining AIs vanished from his sensor screens. Even as he spoke, red threat icons began to appear just outside of the gravity well of the planet. The Hocklyn fleets had arrived.

"Reform the fleet," ordered Amanda, letting out a deep sigh. She looked at her shattered fleet formation, knowing the AIs had hurt them. However, they had managed to destroy two of the AI ships; perhaps the AIs would hold back now, not wanting to risk further damage to their huge ships.

"We have several ships that are too damaged to fight," Commander Evans reported as she listened to the incoming damage reports from the fleet over her mini-com.

"Order them to withdraw to Admiral Adler's position and initiate repairs," Amanda ordered. They had lost too many ships in the brief engagement with the AIs.

-

The AI commander stared in surprise as the remaining fleet of eight ships came back out of hyperspace. It had stunned the AIs how quickly the humans had turned and destroyed two AI ships.

"Analyze how our ships were destroyed," the AI commander ordered as he floated nearer the ship's data collection terminals studying the data flowing across the screens. He waved his multiple tentacles at another AI and continued to speak. "The humans are using nuclear missiles equipped with sublight drives to destroy our ships. How are they doing this? Our ship's screens should be able to hold up to these weapons."

"Data indicates they employed nearly forty of the missiles in our brief engagement," the AI at the data terminals responded after examining the information from the battle. "They used a number of them to hit a very small section of the energy screen, creating a brief failure. The hole created was no more than twenty meters across. They then fired two missiles through which impacted on our ship's hulls, causing the energy screen to fail entirely. All of this was done in microseconds, a technology we did not believe the humans possessed."

"This could be a problem if they have more of these missiles," the commanding AI spoke as it returned to the center of the room with the glowing orb that served as its head glowing even brighter. "We will let the humans expend these dangerous weapons upon the Hocklyn fleet. When our data indicates the humans have used up their inventory of these weapons, we will return and finish the destruction of their fleet."

-

Fleet Commodore Resmunt stared in astonishment at the slowly expanding remains of two AI spheres. "The AIs have withdrawn," he spoke as he saw that the eight remaining massive spheres were still in the system. All of them were now at a safe distance from the human fleet and outside of the gravity well of the planet.

"The humans destroyed two of them," First Leader Ganth stated in surprise as he examined the data now appearing on the new tactical hologram.

Ganth felt growing concern about the coming battle; if the humans had already destroyed two of the master's vessels in the first brief engagement, then what would they do to the Hocklyn fleet? Honor might not be as near as he had first believed.

"We are being ordered to attack immediately," Third Leader Vrill reported from Communications. "The AI commander is insisting that we move into the gravity well and engage the humans and destroy their fleets."

Resmunt nodded; he had expected this when he saw the two destroyed AI ships. "Order all fleets to continue into the gravity well. We still have them outnumbered and will force them back toward the planet where we will annihilate them." Resmunt just hoped it was that easy; he had been expecting to fight alongside the AIs but now it seemed the remaining AI ships were going to sit this part of the battle out.

First Leader Ganth passed on the orders, and the six fleets spread out slightly and accelerated toward the waiting human fleets. Three hundred and ninety-six Hocklyn warships entered the gravity well of the planet, prepared for battle.

"What did we lose?" Fleet Admiral Streth demanded as he reformed his fleet to meet the incoming Hocklyns. Looking at the tactical hologram, he saw that Admiral Sheen was doing the same thing. He had never imagined the AIs would jump in so close to First and Second Fleet and both had paid a heavy price.

"We lost the Strikecruiser Eden, two Monarchs, and five light cruisers," Colonel Trist replied as he studied the damage report. "A number of other ships are reporting heavy damage."

"Order the heavily damaged ships to withdraw to Admiral Adler's position and begin repairs," Hedon spoke, not wanting to risk losing valuable ships he could save. It distressed him that they had already lost one of the precious strikecruisers.

Colonel Trist quickly passed on the orders and watched one of the large tactical displays as six ships pulled away from First and

Second Fleet to retreat to the safety of Admiral Adler and the satellite defenses.

"Order all ships to launch their fighters," Admiral Streth ordered, knowing his fighters would be severely outnumbered. "Their primary mission is suppression of any inbound Hocklyn fighters, and when their weapons are exhausted they are to fall back to Admiral Adler to be rearmed."

"Hocklyns have six fleets inbound," Captain Reynolds reported as he watched the Hocklyn ships enter the gravity well and continue on a course to intercept First and Second Fleet. "They have also jumped an additional four fleets to just outside the gravity well, and they are holding at that position."

"To destroy any of our ships that try to escape," Colonel Trist spoke grimly as he stared at the tactical display. "They're not taking any chances this time. They want to keep us bottled up and annihilate our fleets."

"What's the makeup of those six inbound fleets?" asked Hedon, wanting to know what he was up against. He did not intend to play this battle out on the terms of the Hocklyns; he still had a few unpleasant surprises for them up his sleeve. It was going to cost this Hocklyn Fleet Commodore to retake the planet.

"Thirty-six dreadnoughts, seventy-two war cruisers, and two hundred and eighty-eight escort cruisers," Captain Reynolds replied as the types of Hocklyn ships appeared on one of his screens.

Colonel Trist winced as he looked over at Hedon. "That's a lot of firepower if all of those ships have been upgraded."

Hedon nodded, he knew First and Second Fleet were not in a good strategic position, but if he immediately withdrew and tried to escape the AIs might suspect that this entire attack had only been an attempt to lure the Hocklyn and AI fleets back to the Federation. They would suspect a trap of some sort. He had to accept the casualties and make it seem that his fleets had been forced to withdraw after a hard fought battle.

"Fighters are being launched," Captain Reynolds reported as his sensor screens began to show hundreds of additional friendly green icons. In all, over four hundred fighters armed with interceptor missiles were being launched. Reynolds watched as the fighter squadrons took up a position in front of the two defending fleets, knowing that the Hocklyns would soon be launching their own war wings.

Hedon activated his ship-to-ship com, which would allow him to communicate with all the ships of both fleets. "Battlecruisers and strikecruisers are to load Devastator Threes in all missile tubes," Hedon ordered in a calm and measured voice. "Monarch cruisers and light cruisers are to do the same with regular Devastator missiles. We will hit them with one heavy missile barrage and then fire everything we have at them, targeting any ship damaged by the missiles. On my order, we will begin a slow, fighting retreat back to the satellite defense grid and Third Fleet."

"I hope this works," Colonel Trist spoke in a quiet voice, knowing the Hocklyns had more ships and more firepower this time around. There were also the AIs sitting out in the system that could jump back in at any moment.

"Admiral Sheen has confirmed the orders," Captain Janice Duncan reported from Communications.

Janice trusted the admiral to get them through this, though she knew they were facing overwhelming odds. Looking at Hedon, she could see worry lines around his eyes. She knew he had to be under a tremendous amount of pressure.

Fleet Commodore Resmunt saw that the human ships were not withdrawing back toward the planet and the heavy satellite defensive grid that surrounded it. If their positions had been reversed, Resmunt knew he would have pulled back to preserve his fleet units. "Launch our war wings," he ordered, seeing the growing cloud of human fighters forming up in front of the human fleets.

From the Hocklyn ships over 2,600 fighters launched; all were equipped with interceptor missiles. The plan was to destroy the human fighters and then, when the humans launched their bomber strike, there would be no human fighters to protect it and it could be easily destroyed. Resmunt had no intention of allowing the human bombers to close with his fleet and launch their nuclear payloads.

"We are nearing engagement range," First Leader Ganth reported as he watched with anticipation as the fleets approached one another. "Honor awaits us."

"Indeed!" roared Fleet Leader Resmunt. He could already taste victory. His war wings would roll over the human fighters and then his fleet would annihilate the human warships. This battle would be over very quickly. He had the tactical advantage this time, and he intended to keep it.

War Leader Versith watched the tactical display intently. First Leader Trion and Second Leader Jaseth were next to him by the command pedestal. "I worry about this attack," Versith spoke as he watched the human ships. They seemed so unafraid as they held their positions waiting for the approaching Hocklyn fleets.

"The humans will die!" spat Second Leader Jaseth as he gazed with hate at the tactical hologram and the waiting enemy. He only wished he could take a more active role in their destruction.

"They did destroy two more AI ships," First Leader Trion reminded Jaseth. He wondered if the humans had more of those devastating weapons they had used against the AIs. He wasn't sure if their new and stronger shields could hold up to such weapons. "If they use the same weapons against our ships, I don't believe even the new shields will do us any good."

"Order all ships to put maximum power to the shields," ordered War Leader Versith, agreeing with First Leader Trion's assessment of the human weapons. He knew by doing so it would drastically reduce the strength of his fleet's energy beams, but he had a feeling the humans were not quite as defenseless as they seemed. "Hold off using our energy beams until we know if the humans possess more of those hell weapons."

Trion passed on the orders, agreeing with the wisdom of strengthening the shields to the maximum. If the humans had used up the last of their dangerous missiles against the AIs, then the energy could be taken from the shields and used for the energy beams. He could also see the look of disgust in Second Leader Jaseth's eyes from not being able to use the new energy beams against the humans. Jaseth worried First Leader Trion; he would bear careful watching during the coming battle.

"Our fighters are going to be heavily outnumbered," gasped Colonel Trist as he saw the myriads of Hocklyn fighters streaking toward the waiting Talons. "They have us outnumbered by at least six to one!"

"Inform our fighters to make two passes through the enemy formation and then to fall back to Admiral Adler; our defensive lasers and railguns will have to handle the remaining enemy fighters."

"Two minutes until Hocklyn fleets are in combat range," Captain Reynolds reported as he watched his sensor screens and then transferred the data over to one of the tactical displays.

Each one of the four large tactical displays was now showing a different aspect of the coming battle. One screen was focusing on the fighters, the second on the Hocklyn fleet, another had everything combined, and the fourth was focused on the defensive grid and Admiral Adler's fleet. Hedon drew in a sharp breath, hoping he was making the right decisions. He allowed his gaze to wander over toward Captain Duncan, seeing how she was going efficiently about her job as she communicated with the other ships in the fleet. Janice must have sensed his gaze as she looked over at him and quickly smiled, then turned back to her console. Hedon looked back toward the main viewscreen on the front wall, which was now focused on a Hocklyn dreadnought. The 1,200-meter ship was covered in weapons, all aimed at First and Second Fleet.

The four hundred and twenty human Talon fighters suddenly surged forward and flew headfirst into the oncoming Hocklyn fighter formation. Flight leader Major John Summerfield led the charge as each fighter formed up with a wingman. "All missiles are to be expended as rapidly as possible," Major Summerfield ordered over his com. "We're making two passes and I don't want to see any missiles on a fighter when we make our run back to Third Fleet. Make them count!"

"In missile range," he said as his targeting computer locked on to a Hocklyn fighter. "Firing!"

From beneath the stubby wings of his fighter, a small Hunter class interceptor missile rocketed off toward its intended target. All across the line hundreds of missiles were fired, but the Hocklyns weren't idle; they were doing the same. In just a matter of a few moments, both flights of fighters were full of blazing balls of destruction as missiles found and detonated on their targets. Fighter after fighter vanished in fiery blasts that blew them apart.

The destruction seemed to roll across both lines of fighters and then they were in amongst each other. Numerous fighters collided with their opponents as too many fighters were in such a small confined area and moving at such a high rate of speed. Missile trails and tracer rounds filled space as they searched for targets. Soon, space became filled with shattered wreckage and even a few bodies of both Human and Hocklyn pilots.

By the time the human fighters made it through the dispersing Hocklyn formation, command had fallen to Major Cedrik Thompson. Major Summerfield had been killed when his Talon fighter had collided with an opposing Hocklyn fighter.

"Hit them again," Thompson ordered the remaining fighters grimly as he turned sharply and accelerated back toward the Hocklyns. "Hit them again and then head to Third Fleet to rearm."

Checking his weapons, he saw he still had a single Hunter missile left, and his 30 mm cannon rounds were down to forty percent. A tone sounded in his cockpit, confirming missile lock. Pressing a button, he felt the missile rocket away from his fighter. His eyes followed it, and he grinned in wolfish satisfaction as another Hocklyn ship exploded. He never saw the Hocklyn fighter that dropped in behind him and quickly launched two of its interceptors. Major Thompson's fighter died in a brilliant flash of light.

The Hocklyns were rapidly reforming their formation to face the oncoming human fighters. Once again, the two groups merged, and waves of fire seemed to wash over the formation as fighters from both sides vanished in fiery explosions as interceptor missiles and cannon rounds found and destroyed their targets.

When the human fighters exited the shattered Hocklyn formation Captain Denise Wright was in command. "Head for Third Fleet," she ordered, seeing that not many human fighters remained. She felt a cold chill as she realized how many fighters had been lost. They had taken out a lot of Hocklyns, but they had paid a heavy toll in fighters and pilots. She knew that many of her close friends had just paid the ultimate price.

"Fighters are disengaging," Captain Reynolds reported as he saw the human fighters pulling away from the Hocklyns.

"How many survived?" asked Hedon sharply, knowing he had just sent a lot of good men and women to their untimely deaths. He braced himself, knowing the report would not be good. Too few green icons were heading toward Third Fleet.

"Sixty-eight," Colonel Trist reported grim faced. "We lost all the squadron commanders. Captain Denise Wright is the surviving senior officer."

"What about the Hocklyn fighters; how many did they destroy?" asked Hedon, knowing that the dead pilots would soon be followed by many more.

"A little over seven hundred confirmed," Captain Reynolds reported. "The Hocklyn fighters are pulling back to their fleet, probably to rearm."

"At least we don't have to worry about them for a while," Colonel Trist remarked grimly.

Hedon nodded; the Hocklyn fighters had to be thinned out if the coming bomber strike was to be successful. Looking over at one of the tactical holograms, he gave the order for First and Second Fleet to move forward and engage the enemy. The main part of the battle was about to begin. Hedon closed his eyes and said a brief prayer; he knew he was about to send a lot of good men and women to their deaths and that this would haunt him forever.

Chapter Fourteen

Admiral Teleck watched as the Zanth ambassador left the Command Center of the Ceres to return to his planet. The Zanth controlled a small group of star systems, including their home planet and two established sister colony worlds. They also had half a dozen highly efficient mining operations in nearby star systems and were the closest developed alien race to the Federation, being only eighteen light years away. They had a fleet of eighty warships that were stationed around their home planet in case of an attack. The home planet, as well as their two colonies, were surrounded by massive minefields to deter aggression from other races.

The Zanth were a small race, with larger than normal heads and their skin was grayish in color. They had developed space travel much earlier than humans, and there was a lot of speculation in Earth UFO circles that they might be the legendary little gray men spoken about in Earth UFO legends. The Zanth had been asked about this but had denied ever landing on any planet in Earth's solar system. During early contact, it was discovered that the Zanth seldom sent out exploratory missions and their population grew very slowly. They were also a reclusive race, preferring to stay close to home. The Zanth systems were in a small area of space only ten light years across.

"I'm glad that's over," Colonel Barnes spoke as the massive door to the Command Center slid shut. "I don't know what it is about the Zanthians, but they give me the shivers anytime I'm around them."

Admiral Teleck chuckled and looked over at Kathryn. "The Zanth have that affect on a lot of people," he replied, recalling the first time he had met one. "Once you get to know them, they're actually a quite friendly people and extremely proud of their heritage."

"What's next on the agenda?" Kathryn asked. So far, the admiral had forced her to attend two state dinners and take several long boring tours on a couple of their allies' planets. She wondered if her father had anything to do with this since she had refused to enter politics. Maybe this was his way of getting even with her.

"We're going to drop by the Epsilon Eridani System and pay our respects to Senators Fulbright and Davis," Teleck responded with a frown crossing his face. He hated playing politics, but Fleet Admiral Johnson had asked him to do this favor to try to help smooth things over with the two nervous senators. They were still complaining about the defenses of their system not being up to par with the rest of the Federation.

"Admiral," Captain Travers at Communications suddenly spoke up with a look of deep concern spreading across his face. "We're getting a priority message from Fleet Admiral Johnson at New Tellus."

"What's it say?" asked Teleck, feeling a cold chill run up his spine. He had a strong suspicion what was in the message. There could only be one reason Admiral Johnson would be contacting him way out here.

"A stealth scout has detected a massive Hocklyn fleet moving toward Fleet Admiral Streth," Travers reported as he read the message aloud. "There are also ten AI ships with the Hocklyns."

"Ten AIs!" Colonel Barnes uttered, her face turning pale. No one expected them to send so many. This worried her; how could Admiral Streth handle ten of the massive AI ships?

"Fleet Admiral Streth knows how to fight a battle," responded Admiral Teleck, looking across the now silent Command Center. Most had heard Captain Travers read the message and knew what it meant. The mention of the AI ships had visibly shaken everyone.

"What are your orders, Sir?" Kathryn asked, her hazel eyes focusing on Admiral Teleck. "Do we return to Ceres?"

"Yes," he responded, his face taking on a grave look. He then turned toward Captain Travers. "Send a message to Admiral Kalen to activate our fleet. All ships to be manned and ready for battle, we're returning immediately."

Teleck knew that due to the long distance from where Admiral Streth was to the Federation over forty hours had passed since the stealth scout had spotted the Hocklyns and the AIs. More than likely the battle had already commenced or might even be over with. He needed to return to Ceres as quickly as possible for he knew that, in all probability, the Hocklyns and their AI masters would be arriving in the Federation sometime within the next two weeks. He just hoped that Admiral Streth and what remained of the Ready Reserve Fleet arrived first.

Jeremy looked over the quiet Command Center of the Avenger; no one had spoken for several minutes. They had just received the latest report from Admiral Streth on the size and strength of the Hocklyn and AI fleets that he was facing.

172

"Over six hundred Hocklyn warships and eight AIs," Colonel Malen spoke in a quiet voice. "How can they fight so many?"

"They've already destroyed two of the AI ships and forced the others to withdraw, so we know that Ariel and Lieutenant Johnson's new program works," replied Jeremy, looking over at Ariel who was standing next to the tactical hologram. So far, it was clear of red threat icons. He knew that probably wouldn't last much longer.

"Did you hear that?" Angela said from her position at Communications as she looked over toward Kelsey. "If the Hocklyns and AIs are using that large of a force against Admiral Streth, what will they send against us?"

"We actually have a stronger force than Fleet Admiral Streth," responded Kelsey, wanting to alleviate Angela's fears. "With the space station and the defenses we've set up it will take a truly massive fleet to defeat us. Not only that, don't forget the bears have over two hundred small warships we can call upon."

"We also have fourteen heavy strikecruisers, including the Avenger," Kevin added as he listened to the girls. "And don't forget the four new type two battle stations we have put around the station as well."

"We will hold the system," Katie added firmly over their private channel. "We can't let anything happen to the Carethians!"

"We will be fine," Ariel assured them over the com as she continued to study the tactical display. It bothered her to see and hear the worry and fear in her friend's voices. She knew Kelsey was doing a good job of disguising her true feelings, but Ariel could sense the hidden concern in her voice. "The station is heavily armed and can hold off an entire Hocklyn fleet on its own."

Their conversation was interrupted as an alarm went off on one of the sensor screens. Kevin and Ariel both instantly turned their attention toward it. That alarm could only mean one thing, the Hocklyns were coming!

"Multiple hyperjumps being detected in system K-772," Kevin reported as he studied the data from the hyperjump detection buoy. System K-772 was only four light years away.

"Hyperjumps still being detected," Ariel continued as she began to calculate the number of ships jumping into the nearby system.

"How many?" Jeremy asked as he stepped over closer to Ariel. There was no doubt that this was the Hocklyn fleet they had been expecting.

Ariel was quiet for a moment and then turned to face Jeremy, her dark eyes focusing on him. "Hyperjumps are still being detected."

"How many so far?" demanded Colonel Malen her eyes growing wide in concern.

"Over four hundred," Ariel spoke in a quiet voice. "The numbers are still growing."

For the next five minutes, Ariel and Kevin continued to record additional hyperjumps from the buoy. Finally, the jumps slowed down and then came to a stop.

"What's the total?" asked Jeremy, knowing that the entire Command Crew was listening with rapt attention.

He knew this wasn't going to be good news. It had taken too long for all the Hocklyn ships to exit hyperspace, which indicated they had jumped in with a truly massive fleet.

"Over eight hundred," Kevin reported in a grim voice.

He still couldn't believe that there could be that many Hocklyn ships in one place. Not with so many currently attacking Admiral Streth. He looked over at Katie and saw the open look of fear growing on her face.

Jeremy saw that everyone was looking intently at him, waiting for his orders, even his close friends. He took a deep breath and could feel his heart racing. This was what they had prepared for over all these months. "Take the fleet to Condition Two and get me Admiral Stillson and Grayseth. It's time to prepare our welcoming party for the Hocklyns."

Admiral Streth calmly watched the approaching Hocklyn ships. Their fighters had not stopped at their mother ships but had continued on to rearm on the ships waiting just outside of the gravity well. That seemed to indicate the Hocklyn commodore was saving them for later. Probably to use against the defensive satellite grid or the fleet's bombers.

"All ships, prepare to fire," ordered Hedon, feeling the growing anxiety in the large Command Center. He couldn't blame the crew for that feeling, not with the odds they were facing.

"Devastator Threes loaded and ready to fire," Colonel Trist reported as he listened to Tactical over his mini-com. "Fleet is ready to fire upon your command."

Hedon knew that the Hocklyns were already in range of the deadly Devastator Three missiles, but he allowed the range to continue to fall so their other missiles and weapons would be more effective. They had to inflict as much damage as possible on the Hocklyns in the shortest amount of time.

"Optimum firing range," Major Simpkins reported from Tactical as he waited for the orders to launch the missiles.

"Hocklyns are launching missiles," Captain Reynolds reported as several warning alarms went off on his console and one of his sensor screens lit up with myriads of new red threat icons, all moving rapidly toward the fleet. "I am detecting several thousand inbound missiles."

"Launch!" Hedon ordered, his eyes glued to the tactical display. "All ships, activate defensive weapons and prepare to engage enemy missiles."

Instantly, from the Federation battlecruisers and strikecruisers, nearly five hundred Devastator Three missiles launched. An additional twenty-four Devastator Three missiles from the StarStrike joined them. There was only a brief blur as the missiles exited the missile tubes, then the blur vanished.

The missiles arrived on target almost as soon as they were launched; just a few microseconds passed before impacting their target. Their small sublight drives and inertial dampening systems allowed unbelievable speeds in the deadly, compact weapons.

Massive 40-megaton nuclear explosions rolled across the inbound Hocklyn fleet formation, shattering it. Raging nuclear fire struck the Hocklyn energy screens, wiping them out of existence in an instant. In the cases of the smaller Hocklyn escort cruisers, the ships themselves were heavily damaged by the strike of just one missile and several were destroyed outright.

Numerous Hocklyn warships had been targeted by either two or three of the deadly missiles. In each case, the ship died as its hull was vaporized and its internal structure was blown apart. Dreadnoughts, war cruisers, and escort cruisers died under the ferocious attack. On the heels of the missile strike, regular Devastator missiles arrived, striking ships whose shields were still down. Power beams and pulse lasers followed, inflicting even more damage. Explosive railgun rounds struck the hulls of Hocklyn warships, blasting huge rents in the protective armor.

However, the Hocklyn's own massive missile strike was now hitting the two human fleets. In some cases, dozens of nuclear missiles were striking First and Second Fleet ships, knocking down shields and striking the actual armored hulls of the ships. Light cruisers and even battlecruisers were torn apart as the massive missile strike slammed home. Defensive laser and railgun turrets were firing non-stop, blowing missile after missile out of space. There were just too many of them, and the death toll continued to mount on the human fleets.

A Monarch cruiser fired every defensive weapon it had available, blowing over twenty inbound missiles apart before others began impacting on its energy screen. The screen wavered and then failed as dark blue Hocklyn energy beams arrived, smashing through the weakened shield. Several nukes followed, detonating against the armored hull and causing serious damage within the ship. Moments later, another nuke penetrated deep within the damaged hull, blowing the ship apart. Eight hundred humans died in an instant as the Monarch cruiser Etna vanished into oblivion.

Admiral Sheen gasped in pain as her restraining harness cut deeply into her shoulders as the WarStorm was battered by the missile attack. Then the ship was thrust upward violently and numerous members of the crew were thrown across the Command Center. She could hear screams and frightened people yelling as the lights in the Command Center went out and then came back on. Several consoles shorted out, sending cascades of glowing sparks across the room. A number of the crew had landed on the deck and were not moving. Looking over at the damage control console, she could see numerous glowing red lights indicating serious damage to the ship.

"We need medics to the Command Center," she ordered over her mini-com knowing there were injured and possibly worse. She coughed as there was a lot of smoke in the air and the ventilation system was having trouble handling it.

She spotted Commander Evans lying on the floor next to the tactical display. Colonel Bryson, the Executive officer, was leaning over her, checking the commander's pulse.

"She's still alive," he reported, glancing over at the admiral as several medical personnel rushed into the Command Center.

"What's the status of the ship?" Amanda demanded as she focused her eyes on the tactical display, which had rebooted and was now displaying what remained of the shattered human and Hocklyn fleets.

She could feel the ship still shuddering from the missiles and shells that were still impacting the energy screen. At least the shield was back up.

Colonel Bryson stumbled over to the damage control console and studied the information. "A nuke struck us. We have multiple breaches along the lower hull, we're venting atmosphere, and we have a number of compartments in vacuum." He listened for a moment to several reports over his mini-com and then continued. "Engineering reports several fires in the engineering spaces, and they have fire teams deployed. We have other damage throughout the ship, but nothing too serious. Damage control teams are en route to the areas in the lower section of the ship to check on additional damage from the nuke. We are showing several out of control fires in that vicinity."

"Tactical, what's our weapons status?" asked Amanda, knowing that the WarStorm had been severely damaged. They needed to get back into the fight.

"Still firing," Lieutenant Mason reported. "We did lose four missile tubes, two of our heavy pulse laser turrets, and twelve defensive turrets from the nuke strike."

"Admiral Streth is ordering all ships to fall back to Admiral Adler's position," Lieutenant Trask reported in a frightened voice.

Angela watched as Lieutenant Ashton was carried out of the Command Center on a stretcher. The Navigation officer had struck her head on her console when the nuke hit the ship tossing everyone around. She could see as they took Karen away that her head was bleeding profusely from a wicked cut across her forehead.

"Alright, everyone; lets get it together," Amanda ordered loud enough for the entire crew in the Command Center to hear. "We still have a battle to fight. Lieutenant Stalls, what ships did we lose?"

Benjamin took a few moments to review the sensor data before reporting. It had shaken him badly, seeing Lieutenant Ashton carried out on a stretcher. "The battlecruisers Everest and McKinley, three Monarchs, and seven light cruisers. Numerous other ships are reporting heavy damage."

"Lieutenant Trask, inform all heavily damaged ships to break formation and proceed to Admiral Adler's position; the rest of the fleet will provide covering fire."

Amanda watched as Commander Evans was carried from the Command Center. Samantha had not regained consciousness, and Amanda had no idea how serious her injuries were. She took a deep breath, knowing this battle was just beginning.

"What about First Fleet, what did Admiral Streth lose?"

"One battlecruiser, one strikecruiser, four Monarchs, and eight light cruisers," Benjamin replied, horrified at all the ship losses to First and Second Fleets. It had happened so suddenly.

"The enemy's missiles were more powerful than what we have faced in the past," Lieutenant Mason reported. "Their energy beams have also been upgraded."

"Firing on both sides has slowed down," Colonel Bryson reported as he watched the tactical display intently. "The Hocklyns have suffered major ship losses from our Devastator Three strike and have paused in their advance. We are currently pulling away from them and should be out of combat range in three more minutes."

"Continue to hit them with regular Devastator and Klave missiles," ordered Amanda, wanting to inflict as much damage as possible. They had used nearly half of their Devastator Three missiles in the initial missile strike, and they would have to conserve the remaining ones.

In space, ruined and wrecked ships were everywhere, and occasionally a ship's nuclear self-destructs would activate, blowing it apart. In the Hocklyn fleet, numerous ships were burning, and ships were still exploding as self-destruct after self-destruct went off. The Devastator Three strike against the Hocklyns had been overwhelming.

While weapons fire between the Humans and the Hocklyns was continuing, it was greatly reduced from what it was initially. Both sides were racing to reconfigure their fleet formations and assess the damage the first engagement had caused. Neither side had expected such losses in the opening few minutes of the battle.

Fleet Commodore Resmunt picked himself up off the deck of the War Room. He shook his head in an attempt to clear it. Everything looked hazy, and he felt faint as if a heavy blow to the head had struck him. Reaching up, his hand came back covered in blood.

"Fleet status!" he barked, stumbling back to the command pedestal and looking across the War Room. Other Hocklyns were prone on the floor, either unconscious or dead.

"The humans used their new missile on us," reported First Leader Ganth, coming back from where he had been checking on Third Leader Vrill. His neck was broken and Ganth had summoned a replacement to take over Communications. "They had many more than we believed possible."

"What ships did we lose?" demanded Resmunt, feeling anger toward the humans at the carnage they had caused to his fleets. He knew now that the AIs were using his ships to eat away at the human's stockpile of these deadly weapons.

"Many warriors have met their honor," Ganth replied as he studied a sensor screen to see what ships were missing. "The human's missiles caused a lot of damage. We lost twelve dreadnoughts, twenty-two war cruisers, and eighty-seven light cruisers. Numerous other ships are reporting major damage."

"And the humans?" Resmunt asked, his eyes growing wide at the destruction the human weapons had wrought upon his fleet.

"Our sensors indicate twenty-six of their warships were destroyed in our missile strike, and a number of others are heavily damaged. They are pulling back toward the planet and their satellite defenses."

Resmunt nodded. His fleet had suffered heavily, but his fleet was much larger than the humans. "Hold our advance. I want all of our damaged ships to pull back outside of the gravity well to Commodore Aanith."

"War Leaders Daseth and Hilden were killed when their dreadnoughts blew up," First Leader Ganth added, still shaken by the devastation to the fleet the human missiles had wrought. No one had expected anything like this.

"Order War Leaders Crytho and Zenth to advance into the gravity well and rendezvous with our fleets," Fleet Commodore Resmunt ordered as the firing between the human and Hocklyn fleets lessened and then stopped as the range became too great. "Commodore Aanith is to implement repairs on the damaged ships. I also want all fighters brought forward and landed on our attacking fleets. We will use them to overwhelm the human's defensive satellite grid they have set up around the planet."

"Their big ships that carry their small fighters and bombers are within the defensive satellite grid," cautioned First Leader Ganth, knowing the human bombers could cause a lot of damage to the fleet. "They also have a large number of their small destroyers around their carriers and mixed in with the satellites."

Resmunt was well aware of this, but his remaining fleets were still large enough to handle the human bomber attacks and then destroy the satellite grid. He would drive the surviving human ships into the atmosphere of the planet and wipe them out.

Aboard the dreadnought Viden, War Leader Versith stared in frustration at the retreating humans. His war fleet had suffered less than any of the other Hocklyn fleets because he had ordered all their power to be transferred to the shields just prior to the human missile attack.

"Fleet Commodore Resmunt is ordering that we hold our position until War Leaders Crytho and Zenth arrive with their fleets and the fighters," First Leader Trion reported.

"A mistake," replied Versith, feeling frustration as he stared at the retreating human ships on the tactical hologram. "The humans are damaged; we should have taken advantage of our numerical superiority and pushed on regardless of the losses. We could have destroyed the humans before they reached the safety of their defensive satellite grid."

"Many brave Hocklyn warriors have met their honor today," replied Trion, knowing that War Leader Versith was probably the best tactician in the Hocklyn fleet. He too had felt they should have pushed on and engaged the humans rather than pausing the attack. Now the humans would retreat to the safety of their satellite grid and begin repairs to their ships.

"The humans have demonstrated once more that they must die!" Second Leader Jaseth called out from his position directly in front of the tactical hologram where he was watching the retreating human ships with growing fury in his eyes. "None must escape our wrath for what they have done to our fellow warriors."

Versith remained silent as he gazed in worry at the young Hocklyn. Did Jaseth not understand the Humans had done exactly what the Hocklyns would have done if the situation were reversed?

"Order all ships to make what repairs they can before we resume the advance," Versith ordered. "The AIs will not allow us to pause too long before they insist we renew the attack."

Versith felt fortunate; only two of his escort cruisers had been destroyed though a large number of ships had incurred substantial damage. One war cruiser and three escort cruisers had to be sent back to Commodore Aanith due to the severe damage they had suffered from the human weapons.

Jaseth continued to gaze at the retreating humans ships. Shortly, they would be inside their defensive satellite grid and waiting for the Hocklyn fleets to resume the attack. Jaseth could feel his anger growing because of their proximity to the hated humans. His hand strayed to the blade at his waist, wishing he could use it against his enemy. Someday, he swore, his blade would be covered in human blood.

Amanda breathed a sigh of relief as Second Fleet took up a defensive position between the outer two rings of defensive satellites. She knew that many of her ships, including the WarStorm, needed time to conduct some much needed repairs. Even though the viscous battle had been very brief, both First and Second Fleets had suffered heavily.

Looking at the tactical display, she saw that Admiral Streth had brought First Fleet to a stationary position on the other side of Admiral Adler. At least Third Fleet was undamaged.

She knew that the next part of the plan was to lure the Hocklyn Fleets down into firing range of the outer two defensive satellite rings with their numerous missile platforms. Amanda just hoped the Hocklyns didn't realize they were flying into a trap.

"It will take a while to effect repairs to the WarStorm, and some of the other ships are even more heavily damaged," Colonel Bryson reported as he finished talking to multiple engineers over his mini-com. "Several ships are without shields, and a few others are reporting that numerous weapons emplacements have been destroyed."

"Do the best you can," replied Amanda, knowing the Hocklyns and the AIs were not going to give them the needed time. Her eyes focused back on the tactical display and the swarm of red icons that represented the Hocklyn fleet. Even with all the destruction and damage done by the massive Devastator Three attack, the human fleets were still badly outnumbered. Amanda began to wonder if any of them would survive to return to the Federation.

The AIs had watched the entire battle from a safe distance and been stunned when the humans had used so many of the new weapons that were a danger to the AIs. This could change the entire plan to advance and destroy the human worlds. If the humans had an abundance of these weapons, they could pose a dire threat to the Hocklyn Empire as well as to the AIs.

"The humans used over five hundred of their sublight missiles against the Hocklyn fleets," the AI hovering in front of the data screens reported, waving several of its tentacles. The glowing orb that served as its head seemed to grow even larger and brighter as it continued. "We must assume from this data that they have a large supply of these weapons and were holding them back in order to inflict as much damage as possible when they were needed."

"If they still have many of the sublight missiles, they could even destroy our eight remaining ships," the commanding AI spoke. "We must inform AI Command of this threat. We will need a new plan to remove these humans from this galaxy. This may put our plan of destroying the human worlds in jeopardy."

"They must be destroyed," responded the AI at the sensors. "If they continue to grow and expand they could someday be a threat even to our own worlds at the center of the galaxy."

"The Altons chose well when they picked this race so many eons ago to stand in our way," the command AI responded as it moved over toward the large FTL communications console. "I will also summon more Hocklyn ships from Fleet Commodore Krilen's forces. The attack on Careth will have to be delayed until the humans here are dealt with."

"That is logical," the AI at the data screens responded. "We must assume that the humans defending the Carethians will also have a large supply of these deadly sublight missiles."

"Their end is only being postponed by a few days," the command AI responded as it activated the large FTL transmitter at the heart of the AI warship which could reach all the way back to AI controlled space. "In the end, the Humans and Carethians will all die."

It became quiet as the command AI sent the messages. The eight large AI ships continued to hold their position 120 million kilometers from the human fleets and the planet. They would continue to observe and take note of the human weapons and their tactics. However, the AI commander had a plan, which he sent to AI Command. One that if it were implemented would ensure the destruction of the humans.

Chapter Fifteen

President Kincaid was in his office meeting with Fleet Admiral Johnson, Governor Malleck, and the senator from New Providence Maureen Arden. After this meeting, he had another one scheduled with the full Federation Council to brief them on the latest developments. Senator Arden had agreed to stay in the Federation until the outcome of First Strike was concluded. She confessed that the government on New Providence had given her two years to complete her mission.

President Kincaid was standing in front of the large map of the galaxy gazing at the sector where he knew Admiral Streth must be engaging both the Hocklyns and the AIs. He hoped the legend about Admiral Streth saving the Federation and defeating the Hocklyns wasn't about to come to an end. It was difficult, knowing the battle might already be over but they had no way of knowing the outcome.

"What do we know so far?" President Kincaid demanded as he turned around to face the Fleet Admiral. "How soon before we know if Admiral Streth has survived this attack and is on his way back to New Tellus?"

"Possibly another twenty-four to thirty-six hours," replied Karla, wishing she knew more. It was weighing heavily on her mind as well, not knowing how the battle was going. However, the distance was too great and it would be thirty-six hours after the battle before they knew what had happened, assuming any of Admiral Streth's ships survived to send a message along one of the FTL lines of communication buoys.

"What are his odds of surviving?" pressed Kincaid, not wanting to have to announce to the Federation that its greatest hero had died in battle. It would be a devastating blow to the Federation's morale.

"It's difficult to say," responded Karla, carefully. "His entire plan rests on inflicting heavy damage to the Hocklyn fleet before attempting to withdraw. He will try to lure them down to within range of the satellite defenses he has set up and then hit them with the missile platforms and a heavy bomber strike. After that, he will have to fight his way out of the gravity well and then jump to safety. At the very least, he is going to lose a lot of ships."

"Even on our world of New Providence, Fleet Admiral Hedon Streth is a legend," Senator Arden spoke, her eyes wide as she recalled some of the stories she had read in her youth. "If not for him, we would not have been able to hide in the caverns and bunkers. He destroyed the Hocklyn forces above and on our world, allowing us to go underground."

"The same with the Federation survivors that settled Ceres and New Tellus," Governor Malleck added with a nod of agreement. "He rescued the survivors from the destroyed Federation and brought them safely to Earth's solar system. I don't know of anyone else that could have done what he did."

"It is my wish that Admiral Streth someday return to free our worlds," Senator Arden continued, her eyes glowing with hope. "When our ship first set out on this journey, none of our crew ever dreamed that the legendary admiral might still be alive. It's a miracle."

"Admiral Streth has spoken several times about returning to the old Federation someday," Governor Malleck acknowledged, remembering how he had often talked about life on Maken and the other old Federation worlds. "If we can stop the Hocklyns and AIs at New Tellus, Admiral Streth may indeed return to New Providence and from there free the rest of the old worlds. I can assure you that the people of Ceres and New Tellus would fully support such a move."

"We must win the battles first," President Kincaid reminded them with a heavy frown of disapproval. "Let's not get ahead of ourselves. There's a lot that must be done before we can send a substantial relief force to New Providence."

"Have you notified our allies about the impending Hocklyn and AI attack?" Admiral Johnson asked as she watched President Kincaid walk back over and sit down behind his large oak desk.

"Yes," Kincaid responded. "We've even notified the Albanian ambassador, though I don't know what good that will do since as far as we know they are unarmed."

"I have placed all of our military forces at Condition Three," added Karla, wondering if they should make another offer to help defend the Albanians. "All military leaves have been canceled, and we are deploying our entire fleet in preparation for an impending attack on New Tellus and the Federation."

"What about the fleet you have inside Ceres?" asked President Kincaid, looking over at Governor Malleck. For years, he had wondered just what was hidden in the massive ship bays inside the asteroid.

"They are being deployed even as we speak," Governor Malleck responded. "Admiral Kalen will be moving ships out of the asteroid zone shortly to be met by Admiral Teleck when he gets back with the Ceres. The fleet will be divided into two task groups, one commanded by Admiral Teleck and the other by Admiral Kalen. One fleet will remain to defend Ceres, and the other will be deployed to wherever it is needed."

President Kincaid nodded, they still probably had a week or more at the earliest before the Hocklyns and AIs could reach them. With a heavy sigh, he knew that he now needed to brief the council. Senator Fulbright would be livid and demand extra fleet assets when he learned of the impending attack. Looking back at the map of the galaxy, he just hoped that Admiral Streth was still alive and on his way back to the Federation.

In the Carethian system, Jeremy was studying the latest reports from four stealth scouts he had sent to scan the gathering Hocklyn fleet. Two of the scouts had jumped into the system, taken detailed scans, and then jumped back while the other two had remained to keep watch on the Hocklyns. From what they could tell, the Hocklyns had not detected any of the four scouts.

Jeremy and Admiral Stillson were on the large, heavily armed space station with Grayseth looking at what they were up against. It didn't look good, and Jeremy was beginning to have serious doubts if they would be able to hold the system. It all depended on whether these ships were upgraded or not.

"Eight hundred and twenty ships," Admiral Stillson muttered with a heavy frown on his face. "That's a hell of a lot of Hocklyn warships."

"At least there are no AIs with them," stated Jeremy, leaning back and folding his arms across his chest. They were all three seated at a small conference table. The room contained a holographic table, which was currently projecting an image of the Hocklyn fleet.

"They must truly want to destroy us," said Grayseth, gazing at the tactical display with his large brown eyes. "They come in far greater numbers than ever before. Not even when they destroyed our colony and invaded our world did we see such a great gathering of ships."

"Admiral Streth used a large number of his Devastator Three missiles to stop the initial attack upon his fleet," Admiral Stillson pointed out. "We can do the same. We have a large number in inventory thanks to those Admiral Teleck sent us."

"But they have to last," responded Jeremy, knowing it could be months or even years before the Federation could send a relief force. He knew that if he ever ran out of those missiles a single AI ship could destroy everything.

"Jeremy!" Ariel's excited voice suddenly came over his mini-com. "Look at the tactical display; the Hocklyns are jumping!"

"The Hocklyns are jumping," Jeremy informed the other two as his eyes locked on the tactical display. He watched in dismay as nearly five hundred Hocklyn warships vanished into what he knew were spatial vortexes. Since the system the Hocklyns were in was a little over four light years distant, he knew they would be in the Carethian system within the hour. "Take all forces up to Condition Two," he ordered as he stood up. "We will go to Condition One as soon as the first Hocklyn ship is detected."

"That won't be necessary," Ariel said as she studied the new data coming in from the two stealth scouts still observing the AIs. "From the angle they entered the spatial vortexes their destination is not Careth, they are jumping toward Admiral Streth's position."

"Damn!" uttered Jeremy, knowing that the Hocklyns were planning to overrun Admiral Streth's fleet with a massive attack. "Ariel, send an emergency FTL message to Admiral Streth warning him of what's coming his way."

"Already done," Ariel replied. "It will take the Hocklyns approximately eight hours to reach Admiral Streth; our warning message will arrive in three."

Jeremy nodded. He had done everything he could to warn Admiral Streth. He just hoped it was enough.

Amanda was in her quarters taking a brief break. The Hocklyn fleet was still inside the gravity well of the planet but had not moved since the initial attack. Amanda suspected that they were repairing their battle damage just as First and Second Fleets were. From the latest reports, much of the internal damage to the WarStorm could be repaired if they just had the time.

However, the massive hole in the hull the nuke had caused was different. Work crews were in the process of welding a patch across it so they could restore hull integrity, but Amanda didn't know if the Hocklyns would give them the necessary time needed to finish the repair. The decks immediately beneath the breach had been sealed off and would have to remain that way until they could put into a repair dock.

Looking at the latest casualty reports, she felt a cold chill pass through her body. One hundred and twelve personnel had died as a result of the nuclear strike and subsequent damage to the ship. Another eighty-seven, including Commander Evans and Lieutenant Ashton were in sickbay. Of those, sixteen were critical, including Lieutenant Ashton.

Amanda went to her bed, closed her eyes, and tried to sleep. She knew she could use stims to keep stay awake and alert, but she had always felt they affected her decision making. Amanda wanted her mind to be sharp when the battle resumed. As she fell into a fitful sleep, she just hoped she would get to see Richard again. Right now, the odds didn't seem to be in her favor.

Admiral Streth gazed at one of the tactical displays, which showed the Hocklyn fleet that was within the gravity well. Just a few minutes back, Captain Duncan had handed him a disturbing message from Ariel.

"The Hocklyns are waiting for their reinforcements," Clarissa said from his side.

The blonde haired beauty of an AI was dressed in her standard dark blue fleet uniform, which was a little tight at the breasts. Clarissa had discovered several months back that by making her breasts larger and wearing her uniforms a little tighter in that area she attracted a lot of attention from the men on the ship. She enjoyed the attention as it made her feel more human.

"Five hundred more warships," he said as he weighed in his mind what that might mean.

"That will mean a lot more fighters," Colonel Trist pointed out worriedly. "They might try to overwhelm our satellite defenses before we can fire the missiles. It could also limit the effectiveness of our bomber strike."

"We need to consider that in our strategies," Hedon agreed. He looked over at Clarissa. "I need you to run some simulations on what our best options are if the Hocklyns do indeed launch a massive fighter strike against our defense grid. Can it survive, and can we survive if it is followed up with a full-scale attack by nearly eight hundred Hocklyn warships? Assume we use one quarter of our remaining Devastator Threes to help even the odds."

"Yes, Admiral," Clarissa replied as she began to run various simulations.

"I wouldn't count the AIs out of this either," Colonel Grissom warned as she stepped closer to Admiral Streth. The Military Intelligence officer had been studying the AIs on one of the tactical displays. "They might attempt to jump in when we're heavily engaged against the Hocklyn fleet in an attempt to cause as much damage as possible."

"It's a possibility," Colonel Trist conceded with a look of grave concern. "With their heavy firepower added to the Hocklyn fleet we would have a hard time extricating ourselves from the gravity well."

"We may have to use more of our Devastator Threes than we wanted," Clarissa said after a moment. "If the AIs and the Hocklyns both attack together I compute that we would lose eighty-four percent of the fleet before we could exit the gravity well." Clarissa looked obviously frightened as she knew that she could die in this battle.

"We do have a reserve of Devastator Threes with Admiral Kimmel," Colonel Trist reminded Hedon. "Enough to totally rearm several of the strikecruisers. He also has a strikecruiser with his fleet that is carrying a full load of the weapons."

Hedon thought this over; he didn't like the options he was left with. "Clarissa, what if we use all of our remaining Devastator Threes when we attempt to escape out of the gravity well? How much of our fleet will survive in the worst case scenario?"

Clarissa ran the simulations again, and she still didn't like the results, but they were better than before. "We will still lose fifty-two percent of the fleet," she reported, her deep blue eyes glinting with deep concern. "The odds are just too great with the new group of ships mixed in. It also depends on what the AIs do."

Clarissa contemplated sending a farewell message to Ariel. They spoke almost daily, but since the battle had begun she had hesitated sending a new one since she didn't want to upset the other AI. They were the only two in existence in the Federation, and it was difficult to think about dying and leaving the other alone.

Captain Janice Duncan looked over at Admiral Streth. She could see the look of deep concern on his face, particularly around his eyes. So many lives depended on his decisions. She was glad that she only had to worry about communications and not the welfare of so many others.

Amanda awoke and was astonished to see that over five hours had passed. She hurriedly took a quick shower and put on a clean uniform, then rushed to the Command Center after grabbing a quick bite to eat in the officer's mess. It amazed her that the Hocklyns had not yet attacked. Once inside she took her spot at the command console and quickly read over the latest reports. Glancing around, she saw that the second shift command crew was manning the different stations.

She read with concern and a sinking sensation in the pit of her stomach the communication from Admiral Streth that an additional five hundred Hocklyn warships were en route. Glancing at the time, she realized they would be arriving within the next two hours. Walking over to the damage control console, she spoke to the officer in charge about the ongoing repairs to the WarStorm. She was relieved to hear that the patch had been welded onto the outer hull over the hole created by the nuke and that a secondary patch had been put in place on the inside. While not as strong as the original hull, it would do until more permanent repairs could be made. That entire area of the ship would also remain sealed off.

Her next order of business was checking on the status of Second Fleet. She still had a very powerful force consisting of seven battlecruisers, four heavy strikecruisers, nine Monarch cruisers, and twenty-one light cruisers. Second Fleet was currently stationed midway between the third and fourth defensive ring of satellites.

"How's the fleet?" a familiar voice asked from behind Amanda. Turning around, she saw Commander Evans standing there looking pale and a little bit dazed.

"We're getting there," Amanda replied, relieved to see Samantha back in the Command Center. "How are you feeling?"

"Better," Evans replied with a weak smile. "I took a pretty good knock to the head, and the doctor says I have a slight concussion. But he said I could return to duty."

In a lower voice, Amanda asked. "How is Lieutenant Ashton?" Karen had been with Amanda from the very beginning including First Fleet's reconnaissance mission into Hocklyn space centuries in the past.

"Not well, I'm afraid," replied Evans with a heartbreaking look upon her face. "Doctor Maddok isn't sure she will make it. Lieutenant Ashton took a severe blow to her forehead and there was some hemorrhaging. They have done everything they can to relieve the pressure, and now it's a waiting game to see if she responds. If we were back in the Federation with their big hospitals it would be different."

Amanda nodded. Over the years, she had lost a lot of people; it never ceased to hurt when someone close to her died. She hoped Karen wasn't going to be one of them.

"Hocklyn fleet is jumping into the system," the sensor operator called out. "Numerous spatial vortexes are opening."

"Call the first shift command crew to the Command Center," ordered Amanda, knowing it was nearly time for the next phase of the battle.

Hedon watched impassively as the new Hocklyn ships arrived. Five hundred fresh warships to join the ones already in the system as well as the eight AI ships. They stayed in position for only a few minutes before setting course toward the planet.

"They really want to destroy us," Colonel Trist commented as he watched one of the tactical displays full of the new red threat icons. "They will be entering the gravity well of the planet shortly."

"We need to reposition our fleets," Hedon said after a moment. "I want all of our destroyers to move into the outer satellite defensive screen to add their defensive fire to the satellites. They can engage enemy escort cruisers that come into range, but not any war cruisers or dreadnoughts."

"We will lose some of them," Colonel Grissom warned as she came over from where she had been speaking to Clarissa. "Clarissa believes the Hocklyns will use a massive fighter strike to try to destroy the outer defensive satellite layer, clearing the way for their warships to engage our fleets."

"Perhaps, but we have one hundred and twenty missile platforms hidden amongst those satellites above the base. If we hold our position, we can lure the Hocklyns toward us and within range of those launchers. That's seven hundred and twenty Klave class missiles tipped with nuclear warheads that we can use against them."

"I have a suggestion, Admiral," spoke Clarissa, walking over to stand next to him.

"What is it, Clarissa?" Hedon asked. He had learned to trust the AI's ideas.

Quickly, Clarissa described the new strategy she had come up with.

"That's brilliant," Colonel Grissom spoke, her eyes growing wide. "It just might work."

Hedon nodded; he was thankful that the AI was on the StarStrike. She might have just saved his fleet.

Fleet Commodore Resmunt watched with satisfaction as the new ships took up their positions directly in front of his fleet. He would have the new ships lead the attack with his own attack fleets following up.

"Why do we not lead the attack?" questioned First Leader Ganth, knowing that honor was before them in the coming battle.

"I want to conserve our upgraded ships for the attack on the human home worlds," Resmunt replied in a calm and commanding voice. He had thought this through very thoroughly. "Order all ships to advance; it is time to destroy the humans. Launch the war wings; they will lead the way."

From the Hocklyn fleet, their small fighters launched. Each had been armed with four small missiles to take out the human's defensive satellites. In front of the Hocklyn fleet, a virtual wall of fighters formed. Over 6,000 fighters were now advancing toward the outer defensive satellite ring. Their orders were to blow a hole through it so the trailing warships could reach the humans relatively unscathed.

War Leader Versith watched expectantly as the fighters neared the human satellites. For once, he agreed with Resmunt's strategy; not even the humans would be able to resist such a massive wave of fighters!

"We should be leading this attack!" muttered Second Leader Jaseth, feeling frustrated and betrayed by the role they were taking. "Our most powerful ships should be taking on the humans. Honor should be reserved for our strongest!"

"Patience," spoke Versith, looking over at the young Hocklyn. "There will be plenty of honor for all of us before this day is out."

"Don't be in such a hurry to die," First Leader Trion added as his cold, dark eyes turned to face Jaseth. "Honor comes to those that don't rush into battle rashly. You must learn to observe and learn."

"The humans have nothing to teach me," spoke Jaseth, scathingly. "They only need to die!"

For a moment, Versith contemplated having Jaseth removed from the War Room. The young Hocklyn's hatred for the humans was overshadowing his judgment.

"I will watch him," First Leader Trion spoke quietly.

"Very well," Versith replied as he turned his attention back to the tactical hologram. The war wings were nearly within range of the satellites.

Six thousand Hocklyn fighters neared the Human defense satellites. Suddenly, from one hundred and twenty Klave missile platforms, seven hundred and twenty nuclear tipped missiles launched. The missile launch took the Hocklyn fighters by surprise. Before they could respond, the missiles penetrated their highly compact formation and detonated. Seven hundred blazing nuclear explosions tore through the tightly compacted Hocklyn fighter formation, wiping out entire war wings. The formation broke apart as frantic war wing leaders tried to get their fighters away from the exploding missiles.

Seeing the disarray, all seventy-three human destroyers in the outer satellite grid opened fire with interceptor missiles and laser batteries. They were followed seconds later by hundreds of defensive satellites as the Hocklyn fighters came within range. But the Hocklyns were not helpless. Entire war wings had escaped the deadly nuclear attack and these released their full complement of missiles on the defense grid. In moments, explosions covered the grid as satellites exploded in blinding flashes of light as the Hocklyn missiles found their targets.

Hocklyn fighters and defensive satellites died in high numbers. The satellites died from missile strikes and the fighters from the deadly fire of the satellite's lasers. Space was full of the orange-red flashes of the lasers and the savage explosions of detonating missiles.

The rest of the Hocklyn fighters quickly reformed as the nuclear fire died away. They fired hundreds of missiles at the grid; a number even targeted the human destroyers. In less than ten minutes, the satellite grid was nearly annihilated, and a massive hole had been created for the Hocklyn fleet to come through. As soon as that had been accomplished, the Hocklyn fighters did a one hundred and eighty degree turn and flew back toward the approaching warships to rearm.

"What did we lose?" Hedon asked as he watched the Hocklyn fighters land on their ships.

"They blew a massive hole in the outer ring of satellites and also took out six of our destroyers in the process," Colonel Trist reported.

"How many of their fighters did we get?"

"Nearly eighteen hundred," Clarissa reported. She had been keeping a special watch on the damage caused by the nuclear strike as well as the defense satellites and destroyers."

"That won't work again," sighed Hedon, knowing the Hocklyns still possessed a lot of fighters.

"Enemy fleet will be in engagement range in ten more minutes," Clarissa reported.

"Move us back between defensive rings two and three," Hedon ordered. Defensive ring three contained all twenty-four of their satellite battle stations. It also held another one hundred and sixty additional missile platforms, only these missile platforms were equipped with ten devastator class missiles, each with a ten-kiloton warhead.

Hedon then activated the ship-to-ship com to speak directly to Admiral Adler. "Jacob, ready your bombers; we will need them shortly. They will be going in with all of our remaining fighters."

"We're ready," Jacob replied.

"The humans are pulling back," First Leader Ganth spoke as he watched the movement of the human ships on the tactical display.

"They seek to trap us again," Fleet Commodore Resmunt replied, determined not to be tricked again by the humans. "I suspect that ring also contains missile platforms. It also has those twenty-four large satellite stations."

"What do you recommend?" asked Ganth, turning to face Resmunt.

"This time we will use our fighters to destroy any missiles they launch," the Fleet Commodore responded. "Order half of our fighters armed with long-range missiles to destroy the satellites and the other half armed with short-range interceptor missiles to take out any inbound nukes."

One hundred million kilometers away from the planet, the eight AI ships waited. They had reached a tactical decision. When the Hocklyn and Human ships were heavily engaged they would jump back in and finish off the humans. Only a few of their ships would be allowed to escape and lead them back to the human worlds. The AIs readied their ships. This time the humans would experience the full ferocity of an AI attack. They had also determined which human ships were a threat and those would be the first ships targeted. Once destroyed, the humans would be at the AI's mercy, and the AIs did not know mercy.

Chapter Sixteen

Fleet Commodore Resmunt watched the tactical screen intently as the first wave of fighters passed through the destroyed outer layer of defense satellites. He had 4,200 surviving fighters and he had divided them up into two waves to assail the human satellite defenses above the fleet base. Behind the fighters came the five hundred Hocklyn warships that had just jumped into the system. Escort cruisers were first, shielding the heavier units from attack.

His own updated fleet was also advancing and would mop up any human survivors that might attempt to escape. Commodore Aanith had also been ordered to spread his ships out and be prepared if any of the human ships attempted to exit the gravity well. He knew that according to the AI plan he had to allow a few human ships to escape so they could be followed back to their home worlds.

"Those twenty-four large satellites concern me," First Leader Ganth spoke, his large eyes watching the tactical display. "We should make them a priority target; they may be some type of command and control facility for the satellite defenses."

"You may be correct," Resmunt responded in his rasping voice, agreeing with the First Leader. "Order the fighters to take them out."

Already the first wave of fighters was nearly in attack range. In just another few minutes, the final battle for control of the fleet base would begin, and Resmunt did not intend to withdraw until he had won a victory.

"Launch all fighters," Admiral Streth ordered grimly over his ship-to-ship com. He couldn't let the Hocklyns destroy the satellite grid, at least not until after the missile platforms had launched.

From the twenty-three battlecarriers, 2,080 Anlon fighters launched from the flight bays and quickly formed up into their respective squadrons. Once formed up, Major Arcles quickly passed on the order to attack.

"All squadron leaders we will engage the lead formation of Hocklyns," Arcles ordered in a calm and commanding voice. He knew the two massive waves of Hocklyn fighters had his squadrons outnumbered two to one. "Make every shot count. We have to keep them away from the defense grid until the missile platforms can lock onto their targets and fire."

"At least we're back in fighters," Lieutenant Lacey Sanders spoke in a pleased voice over their private channel.

"Just stay on my wing, Lieutenant," Karl reminded her. Lacy was an excellent fighter pilot, but he still had a tendency to look out after her. "Don't do anything reckless."

"I won't," Lacy promised. "You don't have to babysit me. Let's go kick some Hocklyn ass!"

The massed squadrons of fighters leaped forward as they flew through the defense grid and locked onto their Hocklyn targets. A steady green light on Arcles' targeting system indicated his fighter had a positive missile lock on its target. "Missiles away," Major Arcles ordered as he pressed the missile release button on his console.

Instantly, from each human fighter a Hunter interceptor missile launched, targeting a Hocklyn. At almost the same instant, the Hocklyns launched missiles also. Space between the two became full of rapidly moving missile trails.

A warning alarm went off in Karl's cockpit as a Hocklyn interceptor missile locked onto his Talon fighter. "All squadrons go evasive, and then mix in with the Hocklyn formation. Steak dinner on me to whoever has the most kills."

Missiles from both sides locked on and many found their helpless targets. Balls of fire began to erupt in both formations as fighters died. Then the two groups merged and the real battle began.

"Locked on," Lacy called out as she launched off one of her two interceptors.

The Hocklyn fighter in front of her exploded as the missile impacted. Lacy hit her turbos and turned sharply, bringing her 30 mm cannons in line with another target. She pressed the firing button and a line of bright tracers spread from her fighter until it intercepted the Hocklyn. She could see bright flashes where her shells were stitching the enemy fighter. Then it suddenly seemed to lose power as she hit something vital and it started tumbling. Satisfied, she turned to another target. Everywhere she looked were Human and Hocklyn fighters dueling it out.

"Keep the pressure on," Karl ordered as he tried to keep track of the battle. "We have a second wave that will be arriving shortly." He grimaced as he saw several fighters from his squadron vanish from his tactical display.

However, the second wave was in the process of going around the fighter melee and targeting the defense grid. Missiles were locked on and fired, and then the Hocklyns discovered the purpose of the large satellites as they took control of hundreds of laser satellites and returned fire. Space was full of missile trails and bright orange-red laser beams. The destroyers had also been spread across this section of the defense grid, and they quickly added their own defensive fire to the satellites. Hocklyn fighters quickly began to die, but not fast enough. Satellite after satellite blew apart as Hocklyn missiles found their mark. A series of bright explosions rolled across the satellite grid as hundreds of satellites were destroyed.

The defensive battle stations were firing their lasers as well as interceptor missiles non-stop, wiping dozens of Hocklyn fighters out of existence. Then missiles began striking the battle stations, weakening their energy shields. Several shields failed and enemy missiles began striking the armored hulls, destroying weapons emplacements and causing internal damage.

"They're going to take out the satellite grid sooner than we expected," Clarissa reported to Admiral Streth.

"What about the missile platforms?" he demanded with deep concern in his eyes. Even as he watched the tactical screen, four of the large defense battle stations flared up and vanished as they were overwhelmed by Hocklyn missile fire.

"They're stealthed," Clarissa replied as she checked her sensors. "They are not being targeted."

"That's good," Colonel Trist spoke with obvious relief on his face. "We need those if this plan is to work."

"Enemy fleet units are nearly in range of the missile platforms," Colonel Grissom reported from where she was standing next to one of the four tactical displays. "Their lighter units are in the lead, followed by their heavies."

"All ships standby to advance," Hedon ordered over his mini-com. "We will engage the Hocklyn fleets as soon as the missiles have launched. Admiral Adler, you are to launch your bomber strike as soon as the missile platforms fire. Your bombers will lead the way; primary targets are damaged Hocklyn warships and then focus on their war cruisers. Order your pilots to stay away from the dreadnoughts; we will handle those."

"What about the crews of the battle stations?" Colonel Trist asked as he watched another two vanish from one of the tactical displays. It was obvious the Hocklyns were targeting them.

"Crews are to place their stations on automatic and use their evacuation shuttles to escape," Hedon replied, not wanting to sacrifice the brave men and women on the stations. "They are to rendezvous with the nearest carriers."

"Hocklyn fleet is in missile range," Clarissa reported as she checked her sensors one more time. She felt fear and wondered what it was like to die. So many humans had faced death today, and now even more were dying.

"Fire platform missiles," Hedon ordered his face resolute. "Jacob, launch your bombers. All destroyers, form up around Third Fleet; all ships, advance and engage the enemy!"

Fleet Commodore Resmunt watched without surprise as hundreds of missiles suddenly launched from hidden missile platforms all across the battered human defense grid in front of his fleets. However, this time he was prepared. "All fighters break off and engage the inbound missiles; all ships, fire interceptors! Destroy those human weapons!"

Hocklyn fighters suddenly peeled off from their attacks on the defense grid and the human fighters and turned their targeting systems on the rapidly approaching missiles. While they were doing this, they became easy targets for the human fighters. The humans quickly took advantage of the situation, and hundreds of Hocklyn fighters began to die as interceptor missiles and cannon fire struck them.

The Hocklyn fighters ignored their growing losses and locked their remaining interceptors on the inbound human missile strike. Sixteen hundred missiles had been launched from the hidden missile platforms. Hundreds of Hocklyn interceptors were fired and accelerated rapidly toward the human Devastator missiles. Small explosions suddenly littered space as the Hocklyn missiles found their targets. Nearly six hundred of the inbound Devastator missiles were destroyed before they came within range of the Hocklyn warships.

The Hocklyn warships were ready, and massive waves of interceptor missiles arrowed toward the inbound missiles and more small explosions lit up space as missiles collided. Another eight hundred plus Devastator missiles died, leaving slightly less than two hundred to reach the Hocklyn fleet. Many of these were destroyed by close in defensive fire but others remained and impacted Hocklyn shields. Seventy-two ten-kiloton explosions lit up the Hocklyn ships, causing widespread damage to those that were unlucky to be targeted by multiple missiles. Two war cruisers and six escort cruisers died, and a number of other ships received moderate to heavy damage.

"Only minor damage to their fleet," Clarissa reported in dismay as she studied the damage done to the Hocklyn fleet. "They were prepared for the missile strike."

"Their Fleet Commodore is learning," spoke Admiral Streth, shaking his head. He had hoped the missile strike would have had a far greater effect, now he would have to depend on the bombers to extricate the fleet.

"Bombers are launching," Colonel Trist added as one of the tactical screens lit up with new green icons. He knew the missile strike had been a dismal failure. He looked over at Fleet Admiral Streth and could tell from the look on his face that the fleet was in dire straits.

Hedon watched impassively as 2,500 Anlon bombers formed up in front of his fleets. They would attack in a massive wave and Hedon intended on taking his warships in at the same time. He knew losses to the bombers would be horrendous, but he had no other choice. For once, the Hocklyns were fighting more strategically rather than by their foolish honor code. "Admiral Adler, battlecarriers are free to engage their main weapons against the Hocklyns," he informed his longtime friend. "Tell your ships not to take any unnecessary chances; we're going to need your carriers if we want to get home."

Amanda took in a deep breath as Second Fleet surged forward toward the advancing Hocklyn fleets. This battle would be intense, and even at their best combat speed it would take then nearly forty minutes to clear the planet's gravity well. She wondered if any of them would make it.

"All ships go to Condition One, load missile tubes with Klave and Devastator missiles. Save the Devastator Threes until we need them," she ordered. "Power beams and laser turrets, stand by to fire."

"Remaining Hocklyn fighters are falling back toward their ships," Lieutenant Stalls reported as he watched his sensor screens.

"Admiral Adler is ordering all of our remaining fighters to form up in front of the bombers, they will engage any enemy fighters that attempt to attack the bombers," Commander Evans added as she listened to the chatter from the fighters and bomber squadrons over her mini-com.

"How many fighters do we have left?" asked Amanda, seeing the green icons forming up in front of the bombers were much fewer than they had been a short few minutes earlier.

"Eight hundred and twelve," Evans responded as she called up data on the tactical display. "Many of them will have to return to the carriers to rearm shortly."

"We're passing through the defense grid," Benjamin reported as he watched his sensors. He noticed that there was not much of a defense grid left in their sector. "The evacuation shuttles from the battle stations are landing on the carriers."

"Engagement range in two minutes," Commander Evans spoke as she made sure the ship was ready for battle. "The remaining destroyers are forming up around the carriers."

Watching the rapidly approaching Hocklyn warships, Amanda couldn't help but feel worried about how badly they were outnumbered. She had always hoped that someday Richard and she could return to Krall Island on Aquaria. Now she had serious doubts if that would ever happen.

Fleet Commodore Resmunt watched as the humans came out of their hole to face his fleets. This battle would be short and result in a resounding Hocklyn victory. Much honor would come to his warriors and their families.

"Have our remaining fighters engage the human bombers; they are to ignore the human fighters and fly through them. The bombers are their primary targets." He did not intend to allow the human bombers to ravage his fleets with their nuclear missiles as they had in past engagements.

"We will lose many of our remaining fighters," warned First Leader Ganth.

"We have the fighters to lose; the humans don't," Resmunt responded, determined to destroy the human fleets. He had over 2,000 surviving fighters, and he planned to use them to annihilate the incoming bomber attack.

War Leader Versith nodded in satisfaction as he watched their fighters tear through the weakened human fighters to attack the incoming bombers. It was evident that Fleet Commodore Resmunt had learned some valuable lessons in fighting the humans.

"The humans will be in combat range soon," spoke Second Leader Jaseth, his dark eyes signaling his desire for combat. "Soon we will destroy these vermin and then go on to destroy their planets."

"Some must be allowed to escape," First Leader Trion rasped in his cold voice. "They will lead us to their home worlds where we can finish their civilization's destruction."

"Prepare for battle," Versith ordered as he saw the Hocklyn fighters close with and begin engaging the human bombers. "We go today to find honor for our warriors."

"Honor," replied Trion with a confirming nod of his head.

In space, the Hocklyn fighters had blown right through the defending Human fighters, suffering enormous losses in the process. Now the Human fighters wheeled around and were frantically pursuing the Hocklyns through the inbound bomber formations. The bombers themselves were not entirely defenseless as each was equipped with two interceptor missiles for defense and two nuclear tipped Shrike missiles for offense.

Throughout the formation, bright blasts of light erupted as fighters and bombers died. It seemed as if the entire formation was aglow with dying ships.

"Watch your six, Lacy," warned Karl as a Hocklyn fighter attempted to drop in behind his wing mate. Karl quickly pinwheeled and fired his last interceptor blowing the Hocklyn away in a fiery blast.

"Thanks," breathed Lacy, sounding nervous over the com system. "They're everywhere!"

"Just stay with me and you will be fine," replied Karl, as he tried to make sense of the battle. "We just need to hold on for a little longer; the bombers are almost within range."

The bombers finally broke through the defending Hocklyn fighters and began targeting the incoming enemy fleet with their Shrike missiles. From over 1,600 surviving bombers, 3,200 of the small nuclear-tipped missiles were launched.

"Missiles launched," Karl reported over the com system to all the squadrons, including the bombers. "Back to the carriers to rearm."

All through the inbound Hocklyn fleet, numerous nuclear explosions began going off as the Shrike missiles hit the Hocklyn screens. Screen after screen failed, allowing some of the missiles to strike ship hulls. Dozens of Hocklyn escort cruisers exploded under the intense attack and more than several war cruisers succumbed. Numerous other ships were damaged with some leaking atmosphere and others dropping out of the inbound formation.

"We hurt them," declared Colonel Trist, gazing intently at the tactical display. "We got several more of their war cruisers too!"

"But not enough," Hedon responded as they neared combat range. He knew the ship losses were going to be horrific. He wished Taylor were here so he could ask his advice even though he suspected he knew exactly what his brother would say. *"Trust your gut instincts, Hedon; they've never let you down."*

"Go to maximum combat speed, all ships," Hedon ordered in a calm voice. He would try to blow right through the two enemy fleet formations and make a run for the edge of the gravity well. Looking across the large Command Center, he could sense the growing tension and apprehension in the crew.

"What about our cripples?" Colonel Trist asked with concern in his voice. "We will have to slow down to allow them to keep up."

"No," Hedon replied with a haunted look in his eyes. "If we slow down we lose the entire fleet."

The AIs had been watching the battle and the command AI knew that now was the time. Eight white spatial vortexes suddenly formed in front of the AI ships and they jumped back toward the planet. It was time to destroy the human fleet.

"AIs are jumping!" Lieutenant Stalls yelled in a panicked voice, glancing back at Admiral Sheen. "They should be here any moment." Even before the words were out of his mouth, eight large orange threat icons materialized on his main sensor screen. "They're here!"

"All strikecruisers engage the AIs," Amanda ordered hurriedly over her ship-to-ship com. "All ships, use of Devastator Threes is authorized."

In space, the battle became suddenly more intense. The AI ships opened fire with their massive energy beams, cutting open ship after ship as they tried to annihilate the majority of the human ships. All seven of the remaining strikecruisers turned toward the AIs in an attempt to save the human fleet. A dozen escort cruisers went with them.

"Battlecruiser Amedon is down," Benjamin called out in a fearful voice as the list of destroyed ships began to mount. "Monarch cruisers Triumph and Cassidy are down. Battlecarrier Columbia is down."

"Strikecruisers are attacking," Commander Evans cried out as she saw the flashes on the main viewscreen, which indicated Devastator Three launches.

In space, two of the AI ships saw holes blown in their energy screens and nuclear fire tear at their hulls. In just a matter of a few moments, the two AI ships lost their shields completely and were pummeled by the human light cruisers before they finally exploded when their self-destructs went off. However, the other six remaining AI ships were now targeting all of their weapons on the seven attacking human ships that they knew were a threat. First one and then two of the attacking ships exploded as massive AI energy beams clawed at their screens before knocking them down. In less than a minute, three human strikecruisers were gone.

The remaining four intensified their attack, focusing their efforts on two more of the AI ships. Devastator Threes left the missile tubes, blowing more holes in the two AI ship's screens. Nuclear explosions rocked the two huge spheres as more Devastator Threes detonated against the armored hulls. In seconds, two more AI ships were gone.

"Take us into the Hocklyn fleet formations," Amanda ordered in near panic as she saw the AIs shredding the strikecruisers and their escorts before her very eyes. "Take us to point blank range, it's the only way to get away from those AI energy weapons."

The WarStorm shuddered, and Amanda could hear the hull groan. On the damage control console, more red lights flared into being. An enemy escort cruiser appeared in front of the StarStrike. The mighty warship blasted it out of the way with its energy beams and several devastator missiles, leaving a burning wreck behind that died completely when its self-destructs initiated.

"Load our remaining Devastator Threes!" Amanda ordered to her entire fleet. "We need to blast a hole through the Hocklyn fleets."

On the tactical display, she watched as the last of the strikecruisers died; another AI had been heavily damaged but not destroyed. The remaining three began to move toward the battling human and Hocklyn fleets. Amanda knew that if the AIs caught them it was over. Only the StarStrike still had the ability to take on an AI ship, and not even the flagship could take on three.

Fleet Commodore Resmunt stared in astonishment as the humans destroyed four more of the huge spheres of the AIs. However, the ships that had attacked the AIs with the hellish weapons had been destroyed, and the three undamaged AI ships were now bearing down on the battling warfleets. His cold, dark eyes grew wide in worry as the humans began using their powerful nuclear weapons against his fleets. It was obvious they were trying to blow their way through before the AIs could close the range.

Looking at the main viewscreen, he could see violent flashes of light as nuclear weapons detonated against energy screens. Blue and violet energy beams were obvious. Mixed in were the orange-red of lasers striking energy screens, trying to knock them down. Resmunt knew that space was full of flying ordnance, both missiles and railgun rounds. Never had he imagined such destruction as what he was now witnessing. It was impossible to keep track of the ship losses on both sides. Resmunt knew he was winning, but the cost was going to be high.

Major Arcles and Lieutenant Sanders were once again out in space in their fighters. The fighter and bombers had been rearmed and rapidly relaunched. Bombers were making daring runs on Hocklyn ships with many being caught in the crossfire between the two fleets. Small explosions littered space as missiles were intercepted and fighters and bombers died. Occasionally, a larger explosion would indicate the death of a warship.

"Stay close to me, Lacy," Karl ordered. He was taking his squadrons up and above the fighting. Very few Hocklyn fighters still survived and since their ships were armed with interceptors there was very little they could do.

Second Leader Jaseth grinned viciously as an enemy Monarch cruiser died under the withering fire of the Viden. The cruiser suddenly exploded as its self-destructs blew the human ship apart. "Die, humans, die," he muttered as the Viden refocused its attack upon a human light cruiser.

Hedon felt the StarStrike lurch to one side as an energy beam from a pursuing AI ship penetrated its screen. They had just begun to clear the second Hocklyn formation of ships when they had taken the strike. Alarms began sounding, and to Hedon it seemed as if they had stopped accelerating.

"Sublight drive is offline!" Colonel Trist yelled as he frantically attempted to contact Engineering.

"All weapons, continue to fire," ordered Hedon, knowing this might be the end. "How long until the sublights are back on line?"

"Five minutes," Colonel Trist replied as he finally got through to Engineering.

"We're not going to last five minutes," Clarissa said as she came to stand next to Admiral Streth. "The AI ship will have destroyed the StarStrike by then."

"Our Devastator Three missiles?" asked Hedon, gazing intently at the obviously frightened AI."

"We only have two left, and that's not enough," responded Clarissa, knowing she faced death. She wondered what it would feel like to die.

Hedon nodded. Looking at the tactical screen, he saw that Amanda and what remained of Second Fleet had almost reached the edge of the gravity well. A few First Fleet ships were right behind them, followed by what remained of Jacob's carriers. Hocklyn ships were moving to intercept, but they would not be able to stop the human ships from escaping into hyperspace.

"I have Admiral Adler on the com," reported Captain Duncan, trying to sound calm, knowing that death was only a few short minutes away. She felt the ship jerk violently as another energy beam struck the hull. In the distance, she thought she could hear screaming.

"Hedon, what's the situation of the StarStrike?" Jacob demanded with concern in his voice.

"I'm afraid we're done for, Jacob," replied Hedon, feeling relieved in a way that this would soon all be over. He would be joining Taylor and Lendle; there was so much he wanted to tell his brother. "We need five minutes to get our sublights back online and the AI is not going to allow that to happen."

"The Federation needs you, Hedon," Jacob replied in a strange voice. "Build that cabin on Maken someday." Then there was silence.

"Admiral, the Wasp is interposing itself between us and the AI," Colonel Grissom reported in astonishment as the massive carrier turned and began advancing on the AI ship.

"Jacob, no!" Hedon called out over the ship-to-ship com, knowing what his ages old friend was about to do. He watched in consternation as the Third Fleet flagship finished its turn and began accelerating toward the massive AI ship.

In space, the AI turned the full fury of its energy beams on the human carrier that was rapidly closing with it. Beams penetrated the ship's energy screen, tearing huge glowing holes in its hull, but still the human warship came on. The carrier was firing every weapon it had on a specific area of the AI's screen. It had no weapons powerful enough to penetrate the AI's energy screen, but it could weaken it. Power Beams, lasers, explosive railgun rounds, and regular Devastator missiles pummeled the AI's shield.

Admiral Jacob Adler of the old United Federation of Worlds watched with a vengeful and contented smile on his face as his ship neared the AI energy screen. "Goodbye, Hedon," he spoke softly. Then the 1,500-meter Wasp collided with the energy screen, knocking it down and smashing into the hull of the AI. Both ships vanished in blinding explosions as the nuclear self-destructs on each went off.

Hedon stared in shock at the fiery remains of the AI ship and the Wasp. He had just lost his oldest friend. He leaned back in his command chair, too paralyzed to even speak.

"Sublights are online," Colonel Trist reported in a somber voice, knowing how the admiral must be feeling. He quickly ordered the StarStrike to resume acceleration and to standby to jump. Hedon only nodded mutely as Colonel Trist took over command.

A few minutes later, the StarStrike crossed the edge of the gravity well and jumped away, leaving behind the dead and the dying. A few Federation ships were still fighting due to their ship's sublight or FTL drives being destroyed in the battle. The Hocklyns made short work of these and then descended on the planet.

Fleet Commodore Resmunt stared in shock at the destruction the humans had left behind. While it was true that most of their fleet had been destroyed, the Hocklyn losses were devastating. He didn't know how they could continue with their mission to find and destroy the human worlds. Only three AI ships had survived, and one of them was badly damaged. In his mind, he could still see the human carrier sacrificing itself to save the human flagship. It was a sacrifice worthy of honor.

War Leader Versith shook his head as he looked at the large viewscreen on the front wall of the Viden. It seemed as if space was on fire with burning ships and glowing wreckage. He knew the fires would die out rapidly when they burned off the last of the oxygen from the destroyed ships. The battle with the humans had been more violent than anything he could have imagined. It made him wonder just what was waiting for them at the human home worlds.

Second Leader Jaseth looked at the tactical display with satisfaction. The majority of the human ships had been destroyed; now it was time to proceed on and find and destroy their worlds. His hand strayed down to the knife at his waist knowing that soon, if he had his way, it would be coated in human blood.

Chapter Seventeen

The StarStrike exited the swirling spatial vortex into the star system where Admiral Kimmel should be waiting. With a tired look, Admiral Streth gazed at one of the tactical displays as the ship's systems stabilized and began to come online. The loss of Admiral Adler had shaken him considerably, and it would be a while before he could put the loss of his close friend behind him. For now, he had to concentrate on saving what was left of his fleet and getting them safely back to New Tellus. Jacob would have expected that of him.

"Status?" he asked in a strained voice as he gazed over Captain Reynolds at the sensors. "What ships made it?"

"It's going to take a few minutes," Reynolds replied. "Ships have jumped in all over the system due to damage to their drives."

"It's going to take some time to sort everything out," Colonel Trist added as he went over to one of the large tactical displays and began calling up information.

"We've been challenged by the battlecruiser Excalibur," Captain Duncan reported. "I have sent our ship ID codes."

"It looks as if Admiral Kimmel is where he's supposed to be," Colonel Grissom reported as more information appeared on the tactical display she was standing next to.

"Have one of the ammunition colliers rendezvous with us immediately," Hedon ordered as he saw how few the green icons were that represented his surviving ships. They had suffered heavily trying to escape from the AIs and the Hocklyn fleets. "We need more Devastator Three missiles in case one of the AI ships show up."

At least the strikecruiser Intrepid was with Admiral Kimmel. That would give him two ships to combat an AI if it became necessary. He had never expected to lose all of his strikecruisers in the battle over the fleet base. He also hadn't expected to face so many AIs.

"I have Admiral Sheen on the com," Captain Duncan informed the admiral, relieved that Second Fleet's admiral had survived.

Janice didn't know what would have happened to Admiral Streth if both Admiral Adler and Admiral Sheen had been lost. She could still see the pained look of disbelief on Hedon's face at what had happened. She also knew that Admiral Adler's unselfish sacrifice had saved the StarStrike.

Hedon nodded; it was a big relief to know that the WarStorm and Amanda had made it safely to the rendezvous. He let out a heavy sigh as he listened to Amanda over the mini-com.

"I'm sorry about Jacob," Amanda began in a saddened voice. "We saw what happened. At least he took that damn AI with him."

"That he did," replied Hedon, somberly. "He died a hero, and that's how he will be remembered."

"What do we do now?" Amanda asked.

"We use the six repair ships to get our ships ready for the next jump," Hedon replied as he thought her question over. "Any ships with damaged drive systems will have first priority. I don't think we dare stay here more than six hours. The Hocklyns and the AIs will soon be searching for us."

"We have a lot of repairs that need to be made," Amanda replied with deep concern in her voice. "Many of our ships are barely combat capable."

"I'm assigning our remaining carriers to Admiral Kimmel; two of his supply ships have additional Talon fighters and Anlon bombers on them," Hedon informed Amanda as he thought about how best to defend the fleet. "That should allow us to fill the carrier's flight bays."

"We lost a lot of pilots," added Amanda, knowing that many had been left behind when they hadn't been able to get to the carriers before the ships jumped. There were additional pilots in Admiral Kimmel's fleet but they wouldn't be as experienced as the ones that hadn't made it out.

"We lost a lot of people today," Hedon replied in a voice heavy with sorrow. "They died for the Federation, and it's up to us to make sure their sacrifice wasn't in vain."

"It won't be," promised Amanda. "I'll have my ships get started on repairs. I just hope we have the time."

"Admiral, I have a final ship total," Clarissa reported as she walked up to the command console. She had already sent a brief message to Ariel informing her of what had happened. It had been alarming how close she had come to dying today. It was something she never wanted to experience again.

"What do we have?" asked Hedon, bracing himself. The original Ready Reserve Fleet that he had brought to this sector had been comprised of over three hundred and fifty-six ships. He knew he would be going home with far less.

"First Fleet survivors include the StarStrike, four battlecruisers, three Monarch cruisers, and five light cruisers," Clarissa reported in a calm and clear voice. "Second Fleet survivors include the WarStorm, two additional battlecruisers, four Monarch cruisers, and nine light cruisers. Third Fleet survivors consist of seven battle carriers, one Monarch cruiser, six light cruisers, and nineteen destroyers."

Hedon turned pale at hearing the numbers; when the battle over the fleet base had begun there were two hundred and thirty combat capable Federation ships. Now he was reduced to sixty-seven ships, and most of them were damaged.

"Six hours," spoke Hedon firmly, looking over at Colonel Trist. "Then we start our jumps back to New Tellus."

"Do you think the AIs and the Hocklyns will follow us?" Colonel Grissom asked. She kept looking over at the tactical displays expecting to see red threat icons appear at any moment.

"Eventually," replied Hedon, looking over at the Intelligence officer. "Once they reorganize their fleets I expect they will follow us all the way back to the Federation." Hedon noticed the silence in the Command Center; everyone was still in shock from the battle above the fleet base. He couldn't blame them; he knew he would have nightmares for months over what had happened.

Clarissa remained silent. She knew Admiral Streth was right. The Hocklyns and the AIs wanted to annihilate the human race and would do everything in their power to make that happen.

Fleet Commodore Resmunt was in the War Room of his flagship, the Liberator, looking at the main viewscreen. It was focused on the smoking and burning ruins of his former fleet base. The ground invasion had ended in a disaster. The humans had rigged the base with nuclear explosives that had detonated when the first Hocklyn Protectors set foot on the perimeter of the spaceport. From the last report, over six thousand Protectors had died and numerous others were badly injured. The humans seemed to be experts at setting traps; it was something to remember in future engagements.

"These humans are worthy opponents," commented First Leader Ganth as he gazed icily at the smoking ruins on the viewscreen. "Much honor was gained today and more awaits us on their home worlds."

"True," Resmunt replied in his rasping voice. "We lost a lot of Protectors on the planet, more than expected. We will have to request more to be sent to us before we can attack the human home worlds."

He glanced over at another viewscreen that showed the heavily damaged AI ship. The other two intact AI ships were hovering close by, assisting with repairs. The humans had managed to destroy seven of the stupendous spheres of the masters and seriously damaged another. It made Resmunt wonder silently to himself who the Hocklyns should actually be fighting.

-

Amanda had just received the latest heartbreaking news from sickbay. Lieutenant Ashton had died from her injuries just as the battle with the Hocklyns ended. She had already informed Lieutenants Stalls and Trask, and they both had taken the news very hard. Amanda let out a deep breath, looking over at Navigation, knowing they would never see the talented navigation officer there again. Gazing around, she noticed how quiet the entire command crew was. They all knew that Karen had been one of the original crewmembers of the old StarStrike that had gone into cryosleep so many long years ago.

"The repair ship Oberon is pulling alongside," Commander Evans said as she came over to stand next to Amanda. "They're going to repair that hole in our hull with a more permanent patch."

Letting out a deep sigh, Admiral Sheen turned toward Evans. "I want all of our ships to get full load outs of ammunition from the colliers. We don't know when or if the AIs and the Hocklyns will catch up to us. If they do, I want to be ready."

"I'll take care of it," Evans promised. After the recent battle, the WarStorm and all the rest of the ships in the fleet were extremely low on ordnance.

"Also, make sure we get more Devastator Threes," Amanda ordered. "With as few ships as made it out of the battle there should be plenty to go around."

Once she was satisfied that everything was operating as it should, Amanda retired to her quarters to try to get a few hours of rest and put everything into perspective. She stood gazing at a picture of Richard in his fleet uniform with a reassuring smile on his face. Then she took a quick shower and lay down on her bed. If the AIs and the Hocklyns came chasing after them, it might be quite some time before she had a chance to rest again. After a few minutes, she fell into a fitful sleep. In her dreams, she saw dying and burning ships with people crying out for help; help that would never come.

-

Jeremy was standing next to Ariel as she reported on the message she had received from Clarissa. Admiral Adler gone, most of First, Second, and Third Fleets destroyed. They couldn't have received worse news. Admiral Streth had always felt he could save the majority of his fleet; the deadly attack by the ten AI ships and the massed Hocklyn fleets had proved him wrong.

"Admiral Streth was fortunate to escape with the StarStrike," Colonel Malen said after a long moment of silence. She knew it would have been a heavy blow to the Federation if the Fleet Admiral had died.

"Admiral Adler's sacrifice saved the flagship," stated Ariel, feeling frightened at how close Clarissa had come to being destroyed. It was difficult to imagine life without the other AI.

"Admiral," spoke Lieutenant Walters, pointing toward the tactical display, which was showing the three hundred Hocklyn ships still remaining in the system where the two stealth scouts were observing them.

Jeremy turned around to see what Kevin was pointing at and noticed that all but a small part of the Hocklyn fleet was jumping. "Where are they going?" he asked, looking over at Ariel and knowing she could use the data from the scouts to determine where the Hocklyns were heading.

"To the fleet base," Ariel replied with confusion on her face. "Why would they be going there? The battle is over."

"To replace their fleet losses," Jeremy guessed. It looks as if less than fifty ships remained in the system with the stealth scouts. That made an attack on Careth in the immediate future seem unlikely.

"Admiral Streth destroyed seven of the AI ships and damaged another," said Colonel Malen, looking thoughtful. "I can't imagine them going off in pursuit without more AIs."

"AI ships have better jump drives and can jump further than Federation or Hocklyn ships," Ariel reminded them. "More AI ships are probably on the way and will rendezvous with the Hocklyn fleet before it reaches the Federation."

"I just wonder how many more?" Colonel Malen asked worriedly, looking over at Admiral Strong. "How many AI ships are there in the center of the galaxy?"

"Unknown," Jeremy replied in a calm voice. "No one has ever been there."

"Someday, someone will have to," Colonel Malen spoke into the silence.

"Take our forces to Condition Three and get me Grayseth on the com," ordered Jeremy, realizing they could relax their alert level. "He needs to be informed that the expected attack has been delayed. Also, have all of our stealth scouts deployed between Hocklyn space and us. Perhaps we can detect these additional AI ships and warn Admiral Streth and the Federation as to the numbers they will be facing."

Kelsey looked back at Kevin and Angela; all three felt immensely relieved that the battle had been postponed. "At least we have a few more days," Kelsey commented in a more relaxed voice.

"Maybe they won't attack at all," Angela said, expressing her deepest hope.

"We have time to study what strategies they used to attack Fleet Admiral Streth," Ariel spoke as she listened to the others. "It might make a difference."

"I hope so," Katie said from her computer console. "I would like to get back home someday." She would like to be able to spend some time with some of the remote relatives that Admiral Johnson had introduced her to.

"You will," Ariel promised in a supportive voice. "We will all make it back to the Federation."

Several hours later, Jeremy was sitting with his friends in the officer's mess discussing the latest development. "Only fifty Hocklyn ships remain in the attack fleet," he informed them. "Admiral Stillson, Grayseth, and I both feel it will be a while before they can assemble a force large enough to endanger us here. They lost too many ships in the battle with Fleet Admiral Streth and will be hard pressed to assemble a large enough fleet to attack us any time soon."

"We're alone now," Angela spoke as she watched Kevin pour ketchup over his fries. "Kevin, you can't even see those French Fries!"

"It's a habit," admitted Kevin, sheepishly. "I've always used too much ketchup on my fries."

"At least he doesn't put it on his eggs," added Katie, elbowing Kevin in the side.

"What do you think, Jeremy?" Kelsey asked, her deep blue eyes looking over at the love in her life. "Is there a chance the Hocklyns may not even attack us?"

"It's a possibility," Jeremy conceded as he cut up the pork chop on his plate. "They may wait until after the attack on the Federation. I suspect they will be rushing every available ship to reinforce their attacking fleet, considering the damage Admiral Streth inflicted upon it."

"From what Admiral Sheen learned on her scouting trip, there're not a lot of Hocklyn ships left in the nearby sections of their Empire. It may take them weeks to assemble a force of sufficient size to endanger us here or even to reinforce their fleet that will be attacking the Federation," Ariel informed them, wondering what food tasted like as she watched Kevin take a large bite out of his hamburger. Her friends obviously enjoyed eating.

"I can't imagine the Hocklyns and the AIs leaving us alone too long," Jeremy replied as he used a spoon to toy with his mashed potatoes and gravy. "It's evident they underestimated our ability to destroy AI ships, which accounts for the losses to the Hocklyn fleet that Fleet Admiral Streth was able to inflict. They won't make that mistake again."

"They didn't realize Admiral Streth had so many Devastator Threes at his disposal," Kelsey added. Jeremy had allowed her to read the reports from the battle over the fleet base. "They made the difference."

"We have an even larger supply," Ariel informed them. "From the simulations I have run, it would be wise to use them to destroy as many Hocklyn ships as possible in the early stages of the battle."

It made her feel safer knowing they had a weapon that both the AIs and the Hocklyns greatly feared. It might deter them from attacking Careth until they had dealt with the Federation. If the trap at New Tellus succeeded, Careth might not have to face an attack from the Hocklyns and the AIs.

"You think the AIs will send an even larger fleet of their ships to attack the Federation now, don't you?" Angela asked Jeremy with deep concern showing in her brown eyes. Her brunette hair was cut short with a slight curl in it.

"I do," he replied, laying his spoon down and picking up his fork. "I just hope the defenses at New Tellus are strong enough to stop the AIs. We have no idea how many AI ships there are in the center of the galaxy. It could be just a few hundred to thousands."

"Thousands," repeated Kevin, putting his hamburger down and turning slightly pale. "Do you think that's possible?"

"It might be," Jeremy responded, his eyes looking around the group. "After all, they've had thousands of years to build up a truly massive fleet. Who knows what is waiting for us there?"

"What about New Tellus?" Angela asked worriedly, not feeling much like eating. "What do you think will happen there?" She knew that if New Tellus fell so most likely would the rest of the Federation.

"Fleet Admiral Johnson and Admiral Andrews will be ready," Ariel assured them, her dark eyes looking confident. "I have analyzed the defenses they have put in place, and they should be able to stop the coming attack."

"Once that's over we should see a relief force," said Angela, feeling better after listening to Ariel. "We may not be cut off for so long after all."

"Perhaps," replied Jeremy, putting his hand on top of Kelsey's hand. "We will just have to wait and see. It all depends on the number of AIs that show up at New Tellus."

"I wonder if I can have a second helping of fries?" asked Kevin, looking over to where one of the cooks was serving food to several other ship officers."

"Go ask," Katie said with a pleasant laugh, her green eyes glinting. "I'm just going to work it off of you later!"

"Katie!" blurted Angela, turning red. "You know as ship officers you and Kevin shouldn't be doing that on the ship."

"It's alright," said Kelsey, smiling and giggling at Angela's obvious embarrassment. "No ones going to say anything and besides there's no guarantee we will ever make it back to the Federation. Also, if I remember correctly you spent a lot of time with a certain marine captain down on Careth when we were on leave recently."

Angela eyes grew wide and then she nodded. "I guess you're right. We shouldn't waste any of the time we might have left."

"If there is no sign of increased Hocklyn ship activity in the next few days, I am probably going to allow the crews of our ships to take some short two day leaves on a rotational basis," Jeremy informed them knowing everyone needed some time off. "I want our people to be sharp and rested when the Hocklyns do finally attack."

Later, everyone had gone to their quarters except Kelsey who was going to return to the Command Center. She and Ariel were going to work on some additional jump simulations. Ariel was still sitting with her, and the two were talking about the new equations they were going to try to set up.

"Excuse me," Colonel Malen said as she sat down across from Kelsey and next to Ariel. "I couldn't help but overhear part of your conversation earlier."

"Which part?" asked Kelsey, feeling her face blush.

"The part about Lieutenant Johnson and Lieutenant Walters sharing their quarters together."

"If it's a problem, I will tell them not to," responded Kelsey, feeling uncomfortable talking about this with the ship's executive officer. She knew that Colonel Malen could report the situation to Fleet Admiral Johnson when they eventually returned to the Federation.

"No, I didn't mean that," Colonel Malen replied with a reassuring smile. "But I think it would be a good idea if you would follow Lieutenant Johnson's lead. Admiral Strong is under a lot of pressure and could certainly use your companionship, if you know what I mean." Colonel Malen winked at Kelsey and leaned back in her chair, crossing her arms over her breasts.

"But what would the crew think?" stammered Kelsey feeling extremely uncomfortable talking about this with Colonel Malen. "Command officers are not supposed to fraternize."

"The five of you still don't understand, do you?" Malen said with surprise showing in her hazel-green eyes. "You're the Special Five and nothing any of you do will ever be questioned. The entire crew already knows about your relationship with Jeremy and approves of it. Don't waste this precious time; the Hocklyns could attack us in overwhelming force next week and then it could be too late."

"Colonel Malen is right," Ariel added with a slight nod of her head. "The crew knows and I hear them talking about it every day. No one disapproves."

"I still need to go over those new jump equations," Kelsey spoke doubtfully.

"Don't worry about the equations for now," Malen said with a reassuring smile. "Go see Jeremy; he needs you. The equations can wait until tomorrow."

Kelsey nodded slowly and then stood up and walked out of the door to the officer's mess.

"I'm surprised you hadn't already suggested this," added Colonel Malen, looking over at Ariel. "You seem to keep a very close watch on all five of them."

"It's my job," Ariel confessed in a quiet voice, her dark eyes focusing on the colonel. "Jeremy's dad asked me to watch over them centuries ago, and they are my closest friends. I didn't suggest Kelsey go to Jeremy's quarters because that is still an area of human interaction that I don't fully understand."

Colonel Malen nodded. She had become so used to seeing Ariel in her holographic form that sometimes she forgot that she wasn't human.

"It's complicated," conceded Malen, feeling sorry for Ariel, knowing there were some parts of being human that the AI would never be able to experience. Then, leaning forward, Malen continued. "Ariel, if you ever have questions about things like that you can talk them over with me and I will help you to try to understand."

"Thank you," Ariel said, surprised and pleased with Malen's words. She knew she had just made another friend.

Kelsey went to her quarters, showered, put on a fresh uniform, and added several touches of perfume. Then, taking a deep breath, she walked the short distance to Jeremy's quarters. Knocking lightly, she waited for him to open the door. When he did, she saw the surprised look upon his face. Without hesitation, she stepped forward, put her arms around his neck, and pulled his face down toward hers with their lips meeting. Kelsey smiled as Jeremy silently took her hand and led her back toward his bedroom. Colonel Malen was right. Jeremy and she should have been doing this all along.

Admiral Streth breathed a long sigh of relief as the last ship exited the jump vortex. This was their second jump since initiating repairs on the ships, and there still had been no sign of the Hocklyns or the AIs.

"All ships are present," Caption Reynolds reported as he checked his sensors.

"The battle carrier Essex is launching the CAP," Colonel Trist added as six small green icons appeared on one of the holographic tactical displays.

"All ships reporting FTL and sublight drives are still functional," Captain Duncan added as she listened to the reports from the different ships.

"We will stay here four hours and then make two more jumps," Hedon informed Colonel Trist. "Have the six repair ships begin working on our worst damaged ships again. Once we have made the next two jumps we will take a full day for further repairs. I want this fleet combat ready when we reach the Federation."

"Yes, Sir," Colonel Trist replied with a nod. "I will get on it immediately."

Hedon left the Command Center, made a short inspection of the ship, and then made his way to one of the workout gyms on a lower level. He used this room quite often as it was reserved for officers and had a locker that contained his workout clothes. The room also had a running track that circled it and he soon found himself working up a sweat. Sometimes running like this allowed him to think things over.

"Out for a run?" Captain Duncan asked as she jogged up next to the admiral. She had been surprised to see the Fleet Admiral in the gym running. After going off duty, she had decided to do a quick run herself before turning in. She had not been aware that the admiral liked to work out like this. While most of the time she enjoyed jogging in the ship's wide corridors, today she had decided to use the gym instead.

"It helps me to think," replied Hedon, breathing easily. "I also like to stay in shape."

Janice nodded. She felt the same way. "It helps me to take my mind off of things," she confessed.

Hedon looked over at Captain Duncan and then quickly looked away. She was wearing a regular jogging outfit, but the top was very tight and it was obvious she wasn't wearing a bra of any sort. She was also a little larger on top than what he had imagined. "I've run for years," he stated as they jogged around the track side by side. My brother Taylor got me started, and I've just stuck with it."

"I've heard you mention your brother before," Janice replied with a nod of her head. "What was he like?"

Hedon found himself explaining to Janice what Taylor and Lendle had been like and how they had enjoyed spending time at the small cabin by the lake on the Federation planet Maken. Finally, they came to a stop, and he looked over at Janice. "Someday I intend to return to Maken and rebuild that cabin. It's a promise I made to Taylor and Lendle, and I fully intend to keep it."

"I believe you will," replied Janice, picking up her towel and wiping off her face and arms. "I just hope I get to see the old Federation worlds someday."

"A lot of us do," Hedon replied.

After the Admiral had taken his shower and left, Janice took a quick shower and put her fleet uniform back on. She was amazed to realize how personable the admiral could be. His story about his brother and the cabin by the lake had really touched her.

Reaching his quarters, Admiral Streth fixed himself a glass of tea and then sat down in his comfortable leather recliner and thought about his recent conversation with Captain Duncan. For the first time in a long while, he had actually allowed himself to open up to someone. Why Captain Duncan? For years, Hedon had avoided female companionship because he didn't think a viable relationship could survive all the traveling a Fleet Admiral had to do. Today, while speaking to the captain, he had found that he had actually been enjoying the conversation and her company.

He knew what Taylor would say. His brother for years had told Hedon that there was nothing wrong in having a relationship with a woman even if you were in the fleet. Taylor was never hesitant to point out that he and Lendle had made it work.

Hedon let out a heavy sigh. He doubted that Captain Duncan would be interested in him in that way; it was probably better to keep their relationship on a friendly level. Jogging together was one thing; doing something on a more personal level was something else.

Taking a sip of his tea, he reached over and picked up the control lying on the small table next to his recliner. He activated the large viewscreen on the wall and began going over the fleet status reports, which listed the damage done to each ship. After a few minutes, he knew they would have a lot of work to do if he wanted his remaining ships to be combat ready by the time they reached New Tellus.

He also had to work on a new update for Fleet Admiral Johnson to keep her informed of what was happening. He had already had Clarissa send the admiral an update on the battle above the former Hocklyn fleet base. This would be his personal report listing his recommendations for future battles with the Hocklyns and the AIs.

He was still working on the report when Colonel Trist's voice came over the com informing the crew to stand by for a hyperjump. Moments later, Hedon felt the gut wrenching feeling as the StarStrike made the transition from normal space to hyperspace. It took a moment for his stomach to calm back down. In all the years as an admiral he still wasn't used to the nauseous feeling he associated with jumps; he doubted he ever would.

Later Hedon went to the officer's mess, ate a quick meal, and then returned to his quarters to get some much needed rest. As he was falling asleep, he could hear Taylor's voice telling him that there was nothing wrong with developing a personal relationship with Captain Duncan.

Captain Duncan was in her quarters staring at herself in the full-length mirror in her bedroom. She was thirty-eight years old with brunette hair cut short as per Federation Fleet regulations, with hazel eyes. Her eyes traveled up and down her figure appraisingly. Through her jogging and other exercises, she had stayed trim and fit. Even at thirty-eight her stomach was still flat, though her breasts were slightly above average in size.

She tended to wear her fleet uniforms a little loose on top so they weren't so noticeable. She had caught the Admiral looking at her and knew he had been slightly embarrassed because she was jogging without a bra and they were probably bouncing a lot. From now on she would make sure she wore a sports bra if the admiral was around.

Admiral Streth had always fascinated her, and she had been thrilled to be assigned to the StarStrike to serve under him. She hoped they could become friends and maybe even more. For some reason, she was highly attracted to the Fleet Admiral, and she hoped he found her interesting also. This was a relationship she wouldn't push; if it happened, it happened; if not, then it was not meant to be. She knew that if her sister were here, Linda would be telling her to go for it. Janice knew a relationship like this was against fleet regs, but this was Admiral Streth and she seriously doubted that any fleet regs would apply to the legendary Fleet Admiral.

After taking a long relaxing hot shower, Janice lay down on her bed. They were still a long way from home, and once they arrived at New Tellus they would have to fight another major battle. If they survived that, then she might consider pursuing a relationship with the admiral. It would be fun to take him back home to Horizon in the Tau Ceti system. Her sister Linda would die if she walked into their large family home with Fleet Admiral Streth.

Chapter Eighteen

Fleet Admiral Karla Johnson was in the Command Center of New Tellus Station reviewing the latest reports from Admiral Streth. Clarissa had sent hours of video footage of the fighting above the former Hocklyn fleet base as well as concise damage reports on all surviving fleet ships.

Karla had called an emergency meeting of the general staff plus a few others she had invited. This would be a war-planning meeting. In attendance were Admirals Teleck, Kalen, and Freeman, Rear Admirals Andrews, Tolsen, and Bennett, and Major Ackerman from Intelligence.

"You all have seen the data from Fleet Admiral Streth," Karla began as she looked over the group. "He suffered major losses above the former Hocklyn fleet base before he could withdraw with what remained of First, Second, and Third Fleets."

"Nearly seventy percent losses in the battle," spoke Admiral Freeman, shaking his head in consternation. "He was fortunate to have escaped at all."

"He destroyed seven AI ships and seriously damaged another," Admiral Andrews pointed out. Richard was relieved to know that the new targeting systems and computer program had worked. "We now know if the AIs attack us here, we can destroy them."

"But at what cost?" asked Admiral Telleck, arching his eyebrows. "I know it has always been the plan to lure the Hocklyns here and destroy them, but it might not be as easy as we think. I doubt if even Fleet Admiral Streth expected to suffer the heavy losses he did. Admiral Adler was killed in the last battle, and that is a serious loss."

"I can assure you that he did not," spoke Karla, shaking her head. She didn't know if any other of her admirals could have gotten out with as many ships as Hedon had escaped with. "Admiral Adler died a hero, and that's how he will be remembered."

Everyone nodded in agreement as they remembered the brave and dedicated officer of the Fleet. He had sacrificed his life and ship for the Federation.

"It's the AIs that are the problem," Admiral Kalen stated with a heavy frown after a moment. "The defenses around New Tellus can handle almost any size Hocklyn fleet, but what will the AIs be bringing now that they know we can destroy their ships?"

"In the past the Hocklyns have always tried to use overwhelming force to accomplish their objectives," Rear Admiral Tolsen pointed out, recalling the battles at Gliese 667C. "What if the AIs do the same thing?"

"We're bringing in as many strikecruisers as we can," responded Karla, knowing she was weakening many of the outer colonies. Only Earth and Ceres were being allowed to keep their full complements of strikecruisers. "There will be at least sixty strikecruisers in the system when the Hocklyns and AIs attack. The cruisers, along with the asteroid fortresses, should be able to handle the AIs."

"Our asteroid fortresses are definitely capable of taking out AI ships," Richard spoke with confidence. "The fortresses have enough Devastator Threes and advanced targeting systems to take on five AI ships simultaneously. If they get through the fleet, they won't get through us."

"What if they don't attack New Tellus but go on to the heart of the new Federation?" Admiral Kalen asked worriedly as he looked at the others. He knew that Earth and Ceres could probably defend themselves, but none of the other systems had such massive fortifications.

All their plans had been based on the Hocklyns finding New Tellus first. That was why it was located twenty-seven light years farther in toward the center of the galaxy than Earth and most of the other Federation worlds.

"Admiral Streth intends to halt his fleets fifty light years from us and wait," Karla explained patiently. She knew this would be a dangerous ploy on the admiral's part. He didn't have the ships to fight another major engagement against the Hocklyns and definitely not against the AIs.

"That could be dangerous," spoke Richard, shaking his head. He knew he was letting his concern for Amanda sway his judgment, but he couldn't help it. Amanda was his wife, and she was an integral part of Admiral Streth's fleet.

"He will use his remaining scouts and allow them to be detected in an attempt to draw the advancing Hocklyn fleet to his position," explained Karla. "Once they have found him, he will use a series of small jumps to lead them directly to New Tellus. He feels fairly certain they will follow him as he believes the Fleet Commodore in charge of the pursuing Hocklyn fleets will want to destroy what is left of the human fleets that invaded and captured the Hocklyn fleet base."

"What about Admiral Strong and Careth?" Admiral Freeman asked. "From the data I have read, the Hocklyns are not as of yet massing a fleet to attack."

"Not yet," responded Major Ackerman. The intelligence officer took a deep breath and then continued. "We believe the Hocklyns and the AIs suffered far greater losses than they had projected in the battle with Fleet Admiral Streth. The Hocklyns have pulled nearly all of their ships from the Careth attack fleet to reinforce the one that Fleet Admiral Streth engaged. More ships are doubtlessly on their way to reinforce the Careth attack fleet, but it may be days or even weeks before they can gather a sufficient force to attack Admiral Strong."

"Perhaps by then we can send a relief fleet," Richard said not wanting to see the Avenger or any of the Special Five lost. He knew how important those young officers were to the Federation.

"What about the Hocklyn honor system?" Admiral Tolsen asked. "In the battles I had with the Hocklyns they were very careless in the use of their warships to uphold their honor. That does not seem to be the case in the most recent battles in Hocklyn space."

"We believe the AIs have intervened," Major Ackerman replied. "We also have reason to believe that this Fleet Commodore in charge of the Hocklyn fleet is more conservative about his ship losses and has suspended parts of that honor system, probably with the permission of their High Council."

"What about the weapons on the Hocklyn ships?" asked Admiral Tolsen, wanting as much information as possible before he had to go into battle. "How much stronger are the Hocklyn ships due to their recent upgrades?"

"Some," Major Ackerman responded. "Their energy screens are perhaps twenty percent more powerful than before and their energy beams seem to be nearly as strong as our power beams."

"It puts our ships on an even footing," said Karla, wanting everyone to know that they would have a battle on their hands. "But they will be far from home when they attack us and our sources of supply will be close by. We will have a nearly unlimited supply of Devastator Three missiles on hand, and we will use them as needed."

The group continued to meet for another two hours and then finally broke up to go their separate ways. Admiral Telleck and Fleet Admiral Johnson made their way to one of the large observation rooms on the outer hull of the space station. They stood looking out past the heavily reinforced quartz glass windows with their titanium frames. The few regular crewmembers that had been in the observation room had discreetly left upon seeing the two admirals enter.

"The war is nearly upon us," Admiral Teleck commented as he stood next to Karla. In the distance, he could see his flagship, the battlecruiser Ceres. "How close to completion is your new fleet flagship?" Teleck knew a new battleship was under construction in one of the massive ship construction bays inside the station.

"It's done," replied Karla, recalling her inspection tour of the new ship only the day before. "It still needs some cosmetic work on the inside, but its drive systems and weapons are ready. I've already given the order that it is to be ready to deploy tomorrow. Commander Remus will be giving the ship a quick shakedown cruise around the New Tellus system as well as testing her weapons."

"Have you chosen a name for it?" asked Teleck, curiously. The only other battleship they had was the StarStrike and that name was legendary.

"The Tellus," Karla replied in a soft voice. "We named it the Tellus and someday I hope to see your old home worlds from her Command Center."

Teleck nodded, he knew that Fleet Admiral Streth would soon test that statement. If they were successful in defeating the coming attack against the Hocklyns and the AIs, there was no doubt that the legendary Fleet Admiral would want to return to the old Federation and free those worlds. For quite some time, the two stood in silence looking out the viewports at the stars. It seemed so peaceful, but both knew that would soon change.

President Kincaid was fuming. He had just come from a Federation Council meeting, and Senator Fulbright had been at his best being demanding and critical of the Fleet. He was still insisting that even more ships be rushed to his world before the Hocklyns arrived at New Tellus. He had been quick to point out that if the Fleet lost at New Tellus there might not be enough ships left to deploy to protect his planet. This had caused several other Federation senators to demand the same for their worlds. Kincaid knew they were starting to panic as the Hocklyns and AIs neared. In some ways, he could hardly blame them.

Kincaid had finally agreed to speak to Admiral Johnson and see if several of the new battle stations could be rushed to Serenity. That seemed to placate the senator for now, or at least until the next meeting. He also told the other senators that several of the new battle stations would be rushed to their worlds as soon as they became available. That seemed to calm everyone down, but there were still numerous questions about the losses Fleet Admiral Streth had suffered as well as the impending attack.

Kincaid knew that the sheer magnitude of the losses had stunned the senators, particularly since Fleet Admiral Streth had been in charge. If the Hocklyns and the AIs could do this to the legendary Fleet Admiral, what would happen when they arrived at the Federation?

Earlier in the day, he had called in the ambassadors of the Alliance and explained to them the current situation and what had happened with Operation First Strike. All had accepted that the Hocklyns and AIs would soon arrive and had gone off to notify their respective governments. Now President Kincaid had another appointment with an ambassador he had not spoken with for quiet some time. The Albanian Ambassador had requested an immediate audience.

A few moments later, the ambassador entered President Kincaid's office. The Albanian Ambassador was humanoid in shape and nearly seven feet tall. His skin was very pale with a slight blue tinge and the hair on top of his head, while thick, was a solid white. His eyes, nose, and ears were very similar to a human's, but the eyebrows were very thin, almost nonexistent.

"What can I do for you today, Ambassador Tureen?" President Kincaid asked as he stood up to greet the ambassador.

The Albanians were an old and peaceful race, preferring not to interfere in the affairs of other space going races. They had a very high level of science and refused to share any of their advanced technology with anyone.

"I understand your Operation First Strike has come to an end," Tureen spoke in a calm and self-assured voice.

Both sat down, and Kincaid turned his full attention to Ambassador Tureen. He wondered what the Albanian Ambassador knew about Operation First Strike. The operation had not been a secret and had been covered routinely on the Federation media channels.

"Yes, Fleet Admiral Streth is currently withdrawing back to the Federation."

"We have also heard reports that he has managed to destroy some of the AI ships from the center of our galaxy."

Kincaid leaned back in his chair. How had the ambassador found out about that? The destruction of the AI ships was not general knowledge even though the information had been spread throughout the Fleet as a morale booster.

"Yes," President Kincaid replied in a careful and measured voice. "Fleet Admiral Streth has managed to destroy ten AI ships and heavily damage another during the operation."

"It was not wise to anger the AIs so," Tureen spoke, his light blue eyes focusing on Kincaid. "They have a very powerful fleet in the center of the galaxy and may now be tempted to use it."

"What do you know of the AIs?" Kincaid asked sharply, feeling surprise at the ambassador's obvious knowledge of the enemy. "Have some of your exploration missions been to the center of our galaxy in AI space?"

"Not in recent years," Tureen responded in an even voice. "Know this, President Kincaid; due to your operation First Strike and the destruction of some of their previously indestructible ships, the AIs will descend upon you with their full strength. They will not allow a threat to their existence to survive. When the Altons set your people on this path so many eons ago as a means to stop the AIs and their expansion, it was not believed the AIs and their proxy races would grow so strong."

"The Altons!" President Kincaid exclaimed in shock. No one knew about the Altons; that was a priority one secret! "What do you know of the Altons?"

"They were the creators of the AIs and their biggest mistake," Tureen replied, his eyes looking haunted. "Their science was supreme in the entire galaxy and their exploration ships traveled far. However, they became lazy and more dependent on machines to do their work for them. Over the centuries, they created the AIs and gradually began turning the day-to-day operation of their civilization over to them. Due to the lack of further innovation and a loss of vitality, the Alton race began to die out. In the end, the AIs inherited the Alton civilization and technology."

"Go on," Kincaid pressed. Much of this he had heard before; he was just curious to know how the Albanians knew of the Altons.

"The AIs think all organic races are flawed," Tureen continued in a grave voice. "We believe that once their four proxy races have conquered the galaxy they will begin the complete extermination of all organics, including their proxies. That is why they have always controlled the weapons and technology the Hocklyns and the other three proxy races are allowed to posses."

"That explains the Hocklyn's long stagnation in weapons development," Kincaid admitted. His own people had already suggested part of this.

"The AIs are in the process of a major engineering project near the massive black hole at our galaxy's center. To what purpose we are not sure, though we have some ideas," added Tureen, looking intently at President Kincaid.

"How can they build something around a black hole; wouldn't the gravity pull it in?" This was information that President Kincaid was not aware of. How did the Albanians know all of this? He was getting even more confused.

"As I said, this is a massive construction project, something they have been building for over two thousand years," Tureen continued as he stood up. "No matter what the cost, you must stop this attack on your worlds. The entire future of our galaxy depends on it." With that last cryptic remark, the ambassador stood and walked out of the office. He had been sent in to warn the humans that they might now be facing a massive attack by the AIs. He had accomplished that, and now it was time to contact his government once more.

President Kincaid sat staring in shock as the door to his office closed behind the ambassador. There was something going on here he just didn't understand. However, this was the first time the Albanians had ever come out and spoken about the war. For a race that was pacifist in nature, they seemed to be very concerned about the AIs. Ambassador Tureen had also revealed some information the Federation was not aware of. He wondered what else the Albanians might know about the AIs and hadn't divulged.

Reaching forward, he activated the communication system on his desk. "I want to meet with Fleet Admiral Johnson and Admiral Teleck immediately," he told his chief of staff.

"That's not possible," his chief of staff replied. "They are currently at New Tellus in a war planning meeting. Admiral Teleck is not expected back unit late tomorrow, and I seriously doubt with the impending Hocklyn attack that Fleet Admiral Johnson would be willing to leave New Tellus."

"Very well," replied Kincaid, feeling frustrated. "I will be sending them a priority message; make sure they receive it."

High Leader Nartel stared in shock at the message he had just received from Fleet Commodore Resmunt. High Councilors Jarles and Berken were also in his office.

"The humans destroyed seven AI ships in the battle?" spoke High Councilor Jarles his large eyes growing even wider in shock. "How was that possible?"

"The humans have a new missile that seems to be very effective against AI ships," replied Nartel, wishing he could get a hold of one. So far, he had found no one he could trust with the job of acquiring one of the human missiles. If the AIs were to find out his intentions, it would spell disaster.

"What about our own fleets?" High Councilor Berken demanded. "What were our losses?"

"Quite heavy," Nartel answered still finding it hard to accept the fleet losses that Fleet Commodore Resmunt had reported. "It has been necessary to reinforce the invasion fleet with ships from the Careth attack fleet. The attack on Careth has been indefinitely postponed by the AIs."

"We need more ships," Jarles said sharply, slapping his hand against his battle armor. "We can't fail in this mission or the AIs will enforce a grave payment for our failure."

"From where?" High Councilor Berken demanded. "We have already pulled ships from all the adjoining sectors. Even a small human fleet could push our remaining forces out of those sectors if they were so inclined."

"Our Empire has thousands of ships," High Leader Nartel reminded the other two. "If necessary, we will just pull ships from more distant sectors."

"The full council needs to meet on this," Berken responded in a grave voice. "High Councilor Ruthan is going to be extremely distressed to learn of the loss of the AI ships, as well as so many of our own."

"High Councilor Ruthan is distressed by everything," Nartel replied in a scornful voice. "I will call a meeting for the day after tomorrow. We must send more ships for the Careth attack and a follow up fleet for Fleet Commodore Resmunt. We are talking about moving several thousand additional ships."

"That will take weeks," High Councilor Jarles pointed out, knowing the complexities involved in moving so many Hocklyn fleet units from one sector to another.

"It must be done," replied Nartel, growing impatient. "The AIs will expect it of us."

"And what of the AIs?" Berken asked. "They lost most of their fleet! What will they be sending to attack the human home worlds?"

"That is unknown," answered Nartel, looking over at the other two. "But if I were the humans, I wouldn't want to be on the receiving end of the AI's anger. You both have seen what they did to us for not letting them know of the human's existence sooner. They executed High Leader Ankler and destroyed numerous habitats above our world. For destroying so many of their ships, the AIs wrath will be swift and vengeful against the humans."

Fleet Admiral Johnson looked with confusion at the priority message that President Kincaid had just sent her. Just what was going on with the Albanians? For so long they had been quiet about this war; now all of that seemed to have changed.

"It's perplexing," Admiral Teleck admitted as he read the message again. "Just how do the Albanians know so much about the AIs?"

"The ambassador never said," replied Karla, with a heavy sigh. It seemed as if the Albanians wanted the Federation to defeat the Hocklyns and the AIs but had refused from the very beginning to allow access to any of their advanced technology. None of it made any sense.

"Should we approach the Albanians about access to their technology again?" asked Teleck, looking over at Karla. "Perhaps now that the danger is so near they are having a change of heart."

"I don't know," replied Karla, pursing lips. "But I will certainly suggest it to the president. I am concerned about the fact that the Albanians believe we may be facing a large number of AI ships."

"When I return to Ceres tomorrow, I will arrange a meeting with President Kincaid to discuss this," continued Teleck, thinking about what access to advanced Albanian technology could mean. "As far as additional AIs ships, we have done everything we can to prepare."

"When are you leaving?" Karla asked. She hoped the Albanians were wrong about the AI ships.

"Early tomorrow," Admiral Teleck responded. "Admiral Streth should give us sufficient notice of the impending arrival of the Hocklyns and the AIs for me to return with my fleet. We will know then what we will be facing and be ready when the time comes."

Fleet Admiral Johnson nodded. All of the descendants of the Federation survivors were ready for this war. To them this was the first step toward freeing the old Federation worlds. Karla just hoped that this was a battle they could win. That comment by the Albanian Ambassador that they might be facing a large number of AI ships was worrying her.

Fleet Admiral Tolsen looked at his recently reinforced fleet. He had been given four more strikecruisers, and even the Monarch cruisers had been issued Devastator Three missiles. All four of the defending fleets had been pulled in just outside the gravity well of New Tellus.

An additional twenty strikecruisers with light cruiser escorts had been pulled in around the planet just outside of the orbit of the asteroid fortresses. If the AIs jumped inside the gravity well, the fleet would be ready for them.

"I guess it's a waiting game now," Colonel Arnett commented as she gazed at the large tactical display, which currently showed no active threats inside the system.

"We're even pulling the light cruiser patrols in closer," Race replied as he recalled what all had been discussed in the war planning meeting.

"We'll also have Fleet Admiral Streth's fleets when they get here," Arnett added. It made her feel better knowing that Admiral Streth would be here and helping to direct the battle.

"If there is anything left of his fleets," commented Race, knowing the First Strike fleets had paid a heavy price. He too hoped that Fleet Admiral Streth and Admiral Sheen would make it safely to New Tellus. Both had valuable experience battling the Hocklyns and the AIs; experience they would definitely need.

Throughout the New Tellus system ships prepared to meet the coming attack. Entire fleets were carefully positioned. Ships were placed around New Tellus to help protect the planet and all leaves were canceled. The asteroid fortresses and the defense battle stations prepared to face deadly AI ships. Fighter and bomber patrols were tripled, and all the bombers equipped with nuclear tipped Shrike missiles. Even on New Tellus Station the tension was high as weapons were tested and personnel prepared to defend New Tellus and the Federation.

For years, they had prepared for the coming battle; now it was nearly time to see if their hard work would enable them to destroy the inbound Hocklyn and AI fleets. This was a battle that had been planned for hundreds of years. Every human in the New Tellus system knew that if they failed to destroy the Hocklyns and the AIs it might very well mean the end of the human race.

Deep inside the 22-kilometer thick command asteroid fortress Admiral Andrews was sitting in his quarters, deep in thought. It had distressed him considerably when he had learned of the massive losses suffered by Admiral Streth. He knew that Amanda had been fortunate to survive. Richard could not imagine life without his wife. Someday, he hoped they would have children of their own to pass their legacy down to. Looking over at a recent picture of the two of them when they had been on leave on the bears' home planet, Richard let out a heavy sigh. He just hoped that soon he would be able to hold Amanda in his arms again and tell her how much he loved her.

Chapter Nineteen

Fleet Commodore Resmunt gazed at the tactical holographic display as his fleet formed up for the first jump toward human space. For nearly a week, his fleet had orbited his former fleet base as hurried repairs were made and more valuable fleet units rushed to him.

"AIs are arriving," First Leader Ganth spoke as numerous large green icons began appearing on the tactical display.

"Twenty of them," Resmunt muttered, his eyes gazing now at the large viewscreen on the front wall which was displaying one of the large AI spheres of war.

Fifteen hundred meters of pure death or they were until the humans had demonstrated that they could destroy them. Resmunt wondered how that made the AIs feel, knowing that they could be killed. It pleased Resmunt to know the AIs weren't as all powerful as they once had seemed, particularly after the destruction they had wrought to the habitats above Calzen.

"Order the fleet to stand by to jump," Resmunt ordered as he took his position upon the command pedestal and looked over the War Room. The AIs had agreed to allow Resmunt to schedule the jumps, at least until they reached human space.

"How will we find the humans?" Ganth asked as he carried out his orders.

"We know where one of their worlds is located," Resmunt replied. "It's only a mining colony, but their main worlds have to be close by. As we near what we believe is their space we will send out escort cruisers to search. I suspect the humans will not be too hard to find."

"Fleets are beginning to jump," Ganth reported as the Hocklyn fleets outside the gravity well of the planet began vanishing into swirling white spatial vortexes.

"Order the rest of the fleets to leave planetary orbit and exit the gravity well," Resmunt ordered in his normal cold and raspy voice. "The AIs will jump last."

His warfleet was larger than before. The humans had managed to destroy nearly four hundred of his warships in the battle above the fleet base. It still angered him that so many human ships had escaped. He had planned on only allowing a few to survive and then follow them back to their worlds. Commodore Aanith had positioned his ships too far from the edge of the planet's gravity well to be able to destroy the humans before they jumped into hyperspace. The Commodore had failed to destroy a single human ship.

Every available ship that could be rushed to him by the High Council had been sent to increase the size of his invasion fleet. Even Fleet Commodore Krilen's attack fleet had been robbed, leaving him only fifty warships out of his original eight hundred. Resmunt knew it would be weeks before enough ships arrived from distant sectors of the Empire to allow Krilen to launch his attack on the Careth system. For now, Krilen had been ordered by the High Council to monitor the human forces in that system to ensure that they stayed there.

The Liberator and its attending fleet were the last Hocklyn ships to jump. Fleet Commodore Resmunt watched as a large spatial vortex formed in front of his flagship. He still had a solid core of updated ships as well as the reinforcements received from Fleet Commodore Krilen and the High Council. In all, he had over fourteen hundred warships to strike the humans with as well as the twenty AI ships. A month back, Resmunt would have been certain that was enough to wipe the humans from the galaxy, but after the last battle, he was no longer so certain.

The Liberator entered the vortex and jumped into hyperspace, and then the vortex collapsed and vanished as if nothing had ever been there. The twenty AI ships, seeing that the last Hocklyn ship had jumped into hyperspace, created their own spatial vortexes and moments later, they too were gone.

On the surface of the planet, a hidden stealth scout ship left the small lake in which it had been hiding. Over the past week, it had used the few surviving satellites still in orbit to gather data on the assembling Hocklyn and AI fleets. Now it was time to return to Careth and give the information to Admiral Strong. From there it would be sent along the FTL communications buoy lines back to Fleet Admiral Johnson in the Federation. The Federation needed to know what was coming their way.

—

Jeremy was down on the planet taking the afternoon off. Admiral Stillson and Grayseth were on the space station finishing up some additional training for the Carethian pilots that would be flying the bombers against the Hocklyns. Commander Marks from the carrier Retribution was also present helping with the final training. Jeremy was thankful that the Hocklyn attack had been delayed due to the losses Admiral Streth had inflicted on the Hocklyn fleet. It gave Jeremy and his people some valuable time to finish training the Carethian bomber and fighter pilots and bring them up to Federation fleet standards. Also, every day there was no attack the Carethians hauled more defense satellites up into orbit from the factories down on the planet.

"It's so nice down here," Kelsey spoke happily as she massaged Jeremy's shoulders with her hands. "This beach reminds me so much of the one on New Tellus."

"I've heard Admiral Sheen talk about the beaches on Krall Island on Aquaria," replied Jeremy, feeling more relaxed with each passing minute. Kelsey's hands felt so good on his shoulders. "She says the beaches there are a pristine white, and it has some of the best snorkeling and scuba diving anywhere in the old Federation."

"Maybe we will get to see it someday," responded Kelsey, giving Jeremy's shoulders one final squeeze and then coming around to stand in front of him. "Let's go for a swim."

Jeremy nodded and, taking Kelsey's hand, stood up. She looked great in the light blue two-piece she was wearing. She was as beautiful now as she had ever been. A minute later, they were both in the water, laughing and splashing each other. It was good to get away from everything, even if it was only for a few hours.

On the shore, a few crew personnel paused as they watched Jeremy and Kelsey. It made them feel good to know that their admiral was no different from anyone else and could just relax and have fun. After a few moments, they moved on, leaving Jeremy and Kelsey their privacy.

Katie and Kevin were on the Avenger working with Ariel. This was the first time in quite some time that Ariel and Clarissa had been separated and could not communicate regularly with one another.

"It feels so lonely," Ariel complained with her hands on her shapely hips. Clarissa and she could share thousands of bits of information in moments during their communications. It was not quite the same with her human friends.

"You will get used to it," promised Katie, reassuringly. "I'm sure Clarissa is feeling the same way."

"Do you think they will ever allow more AIs like Clarissa and I to be created?" Aerial asked, with her dark eyes focusing intently on Katie. It would be nice to have more AIs around.

"I don't know," replied Katie, truthfully. "If not for the AIs in the center of the galaxy, I would say yes. But those AIs frighten people."

"But Clarissa and I are not like them!" Ariel protested, her dark eyes glinting. "We would never harm a human!"

"Some people feel all AIs are alike," Kevin explained in a patient voice. He agreed with Ariel. If they had more AIs like the ones they had it could make a big difference in the war. He had seen firsthand how Ariel and Clarissa could fight a warship.

"Perhaps sometime in the future we will be allowed to create more of your kind," Katie said. "Now, let's look at this new firewall I have made to protect you from attack."

"I don't see why I need it," Ariel complained with a frown. "I can block any virus or attempt to take over my program."

"That we know of," Katie reminded her. "We don't know for sure what the AIs may have that could be a danger to you. At the moment, they don't know that you and Clarissa exist. If they ever learn that we have two AIs they may attempt to infiltrate your program and this firewall should at least give you some added protection."

"Alright," Ariel relented. "I will trust your judgment in this. But I would never allow the AIs to influence my program."

"Fine," Kevin said with a grin. "Let's finish this up and go eat. The chef in the officer's mess has promised to make me a double cheeseburger better than any I have ever eaten before. I bet him a week's wages that it couldn't be done."

"This I have to see," Katie replied with a good natured laugh.

Ariel shook here head and smiled at her two friends, it was good to hear them laugh. She was also curious about this cheeseburger the chef was going to make and what would make it so special. The chef in question had been assessing the ship's computer and requesting various recipes for cheeseburgers. Evidently, he was taking this challenge very seriously.

Angela was busy talking on her communications console to the marine captain she had been spending some time with. He had recently been assigned to duty on the space station, and Angela was trying to set up a time so they could get together. It shouldn't be too difficult as the Avenger was currently docked to the station.

"Later tonight," Angela suggested. "My duty shift will be over in a few more hours and I can come over."

"We can eat in the officer's mess hall over here," the captain said. "It has some really good food."

"It's a date," Angela replied with a pleased smile. After talking for a few more minutes, she shut down the com system and leaned back, folding her arms across her breasts. She would only get to see her new friend for a short time, but it was better than nothing. A lot could happen in a couple of hours.

Kevin and Katie were just about to leave when the warning alarm went off on the sensor console. Kevin spun around, looked worriedly at the large sensor screen, and then relaxed as a green icon appeared.

"It's the stealth scout that's been observing the main Hocklyn fleet," Colonel Malen explained, seeing Lieutenant Walters look of concern. "It was supposed to report back as soon as the Hocklyn fleet jumped out."

Kevin looked over at Katie; they both knew what that meant. The Hocklyns and the AIs were headed toward the Federation.

"Lieutenant DeSota, contact Admiral Strong on Careth and inform him that the scout ship has returned," ordered Malen, knowing that Jeremy would want to know.

"Yes, Colonel," Angela replied as she activated her com system to allow her to contact Jeremy through his mini-com, which he always wore. She knew he would be returning to the ship to review the information from the scout. She hated ruining Kelsey and Jeremy's plans, but she knew this was important. The Federation needed to be warned about what was coming their way, and that needed to come from Admiral Strong.

Fleet Commodore Resmunt watched as his assembled fleet prepared to jump again. The AIs had given him a set of coordinates to meet them at in twenty hours. It seemed the AI's sensors could reach out over a distance of nearly four light years, and they would be jumping separately searching for the fleeing human fleet. With the repairs that the humans would have had to make to their ships, there was a good possibility they could be found before they reached the supposed safety of their home worlds.

Studying the coordinates carefully, Resmunt knew it would take his fleet three jumps to reach them. Not bad, actually, that gave his drive cores plenty of time to cool down as well as allowed the engineers to keep them tuned properly.

"War leader Osbith is demanding an audience after the next jump," First Leader Ganth hissed in an aggravated voice.

"I'm sure he wants more ships assigned to him rather than just the one fleet he has," Resmunt replied, his cold eyes gazing across the War Room. "He thinks that since he was with us at the original battle above the fleet base that he is entitled to a larger command."

"He seeks the honor such a command would bring him," responded Ganth, knowingly. "I understand he is related to High Councilor Ruthan."

"A distant relation," Resmunt answered.

Too often in the Empire commands were given to non-deserving Hocklyn commanders due to political considerations. Resmunt strongly suspected that over half of the War Leaders in the Hocklyn Empire were incompetent. He was still in the process of evaluating the ones in his own fleet to determine which ones might be a liability. There was no doubt that some incompetent War Leaders had made it into his combined warfleet due to the decisions of the High Councilors. Commodore Aanith was a prime example of that. Resmunt hoped to have a good feel for what War Leaders he could count on before they reached human space.

On the dreadnought Viden, War Leader Versith was speaking to Second Leader Jaseth. "You must hold your anger in check if you wish to rise in command," he was saying. "This anger toward the humans could seriously jeopardize your career."

Jaseth gazed coldly toward the War Leader, hearing the older warrior's words but not agreeing with them. "My anger makes me strong," Jaseth countered. "The humans are a threat to the Empire and must be eliminated. In the recent battle, the Viden accounted for four kills of human warships. My anger will not endanger the ship; it will only make it stronger."

Versith shook his head, knowing the young warrior was not ready to listen. "Heed my words, Jaseth. It is only out of respect for your father and mother that I don't transfer you to another ship. If I see your anger ever endangering this ship while it is in combat your days as a Hocklyn warrior will be over. Do you understand that?"

"Yes," Jaseth grated out, trying to hold his anger in check. "I will not endanger the ship; you have my word on that."

"Very well," Versith replied. "You may continue with your duties."

After Jaseth had walked away, First Leader Trion stepped up to the command pedestal and gazed at the War Leader. "Do you think he really understands the danger he is to the ship?"

"No," replied Versith, grimly. "His anger is too strong. Keep a close watch on him; I don't like where this may lead."

"As you command," Trion responded. "We have gained much honor in this war so far. I will not allow Jaseth to endanger that."

"Do as you must," Versith answered. "The honor of this ship must be preserved above all else. I have done what I can for Second Leader Jaseth, now it is up to him."

Admiral Streth and Janice Duncan were in the gym, jogging. They had started doing this together once per day and were growing more accustomed to each other's company.

"So Taylor's wife Lendle was a really good cook?" Janice asked as they jogged side by side.

"The best," responded Hedon, finding that each time Janice and he jogged together he found it easier to talk to her. "I don't know where she learned, but she could really prepare a meal. I was always surprised that Taylor could keep his weight down."

"What was the planet Maken like?" Janice asked. She had always been curious about the old Federation worlds.

"It was a beautiful world," began Hedon, thinking about all the times he had visited the planet. "It was the second most heavily populated planet in the old Federation; only the capital Tellus had more. Even so, there were wide areas of untouched forests and wildlife preserves."

"I wonder what it's like now?" asked Janice, knowing the Hocklyns had heavily nuked the planet.

"Almost as it was when I last saw it," replied Hedon, feeling a twinge of homesickness as they slowed their jog down to a more casual walk. "Admiral Sheen went on a mission during the time of the New Horizon incident to search our old worlds for survivors. From her reports, the biosphere on Maken had returned to normal. There were no signs of radiation or any other harmful aftereffects from the Hocklyn bombardment."

"Do you think your brother's cabin is still there?" Janice asked out of curiosity. She would like to see Maken someday.

"I doubt it," Hedon replied with sadness in his eyes. He had so many wonderful memories associated with that cabin. "A lot of years have gone by, so I doubt if anything remains."

"Admiral Streth, report to the Command Center," a voice spoke suddenly over the ship's com system.

"I guess our jog for today is over," Janice replied with a friendly smile.

Admiral Streth walked over to the com panel on the wall and pressed a button. "This is Admiral Streth, what's going on?"

"Admiral, one of our stealth scouts has returned, and they have detected the Hocklyn fleet."

Hedon looked over at Janice with a serious look upon his face. "Now the chase starts; let's see if we can get the Hocklyns to follow us."

After showering and changing, Hedon stepped into the Command Center past the two heavily armed marines that stood at the entrance.

"Report," he ordered as he took his seat behind the center command console.

"Major Arcles just made it back to the carrier Endurance and reports that he spotted a large Hocklyn fleet three jumps back," Colonel Trist reported as he stepped away from one of the tactical displays.

"Did he manage to get scans on the makeup of the fleet?" Hedon asked. They had received a report the previous day from Fleet Admiral Johnson on what Admiral Strong had sent Fleet Command as to the makeup of the Hocklyn and AI fleet that had jumped away from the destroyed Hocklyn fleet base.

"Not good scans," Colonel Trist reported. "He didn't wait around too long in case his scout had been detected."

"From what we can tell, the fleet seems to be the same one that jumped from the base," Colonel Grissim answered as she looked up from a console where she had been studying the data from the scout's scanning systems. "The number seems to be the same, though we don't know the exact makeup of the fleet that Major Arcles found. However, only two AI ships were present."

"The other AI ships are searching for us," Hedon guessed. He knew the AIs had advanced sensors that could reach out for several light years. Over the past week, they had jumped to a point that had them halfway back to the New Tellus system and the waiting Federation forces.

"The AIs could find us at any time," cautioned Colonel Trist. "All six of the repair ships have fleet units docked to them undergoing repairs. That might not be safe if an AI ship jumped into our midst."

Hedon thought for a moment before speaking. "Contact all of the repair ships and tell them they have four more hours to complete their current repairs. Starting with this next jump, the repair ships will be doing emergency repairs only if a ship's drive system fails."

"Will we engage the AIs or Hocklyns if they find us?" Colonel Grissom asked her eyes focusing on the admiral. She knew the fleet wasn't ready for combat, too many repairs still needed to be made.

"No," replied Hedon firmly, shaking his head. "We will allow them to scan us and then we will make our next jump. From the trajectory we enter the spatial vortexes at, the AIs and the Hocklyns should be able to calculate our general course. We want them to follow us to New Tellus."

"I would expect them to locate us in the next day or two," Grissom added with concern in her voice. "The fleet will have to be prepared to jump at a moment's notice to prevent an AI ship from attacking."

"I don't think they will attack us," Hedon answered. "They want us to lead them back to our worlds, so we will allow them to herd us in that direction. As a safety precaution, we will keep the fleet at Condition Three from now on." Hedon knew that, at that heightened alert level, they could jump out quickly if the need arose.

"Twenty AI ships," said Colonel Trist, arching his eyebrows and crossing his arms across his chest. "Can New Tellus stop that many?"

"Fleet Admiral Johnson thinks so," replied Grissom, recalling the latest intelligence estimates of what would happen if the Hocklyns and the AIs attacked New Tellus. "With what I know of the defenses in the New Tellus system they should be able to handle twenty AI ships. The bigger question is, if we stop this attack by the AIs and the Hocklyns what will our losses be? Will we have enough forces left over to stop the next one?"

"We have a lot of ship production capacity in the new Federation," Hedon said as he thought about what Grissom had just implied. "If we can have six months before the next attack, we should be ready."

"Sensor contact!" Captain Reynolds suddenly called out.

"It's a Hocklyn escort cruiser," Clarissa said as she walked over from where she had been standing at one of the tactical displays talking to one of the two officers that operated it. "Twenty-two million kilometers and that puts them within sensor range of the fleet."

"Go to Condition Two," Hedon ordered grim faced as he realized the repair ships would have to stop in the middle of whatever repairs they were doing. "Fleet will jump in forty minutes."

"What's the Hocklyn doing?" Colonel Trist demanded. Then, glancing over at Hedon, "We can send a couple of light cruisers to eliminate it."

"No," Hedon replied as the Hocklyn ship was now showing as a red threat icon on one of the tactical displays. "Let them watch us jump; we're still far enough ahead that they can't launch a full scale strike against us. They must be using a number of their escort cruisers to scout ahead as well as the AI ships."

In space, the crews on the six repair ships hurriedly finished what they were doing. The docked ships slowly backed away from the massive repair ships and took their positions in the fleet formation. All across the fleet there was increased tension as they watched the Hocklyn cruiser, knowing what it meant. There was a fear that, at any moment, an AI ship could jump in and wreak havoc with the fleet, but nothing happened. Finally, the forty minutes were up and the ships started to jump. Blue-white spatial vortexes formed, and the ships flew into them one by one until the only ship left in the system was the Hocklyn cruiser.

The Hocklyn cruiser had gotten good readings on the trajectories of the human ships. It would not be hard to determine their approximate vector and destination. A white swirling vortex formed in front of the Hocklyn ship, and it flew into the vortex and jumped into hyperspace. It was time to return to the fleet and report.

For the next week, the human fleet made short jumps, occasionally staying in a system just long enough for the Hocklyns to find them. In each instance, a Hocklyn escort cruiser would jump into the system and watch the fleet until the human ships jumped, then it would jump back to the advancing Hocklyn fleet and report. The AIs were also keeping a close watch. Most of the time it was their ships that detected the presence of human ships and then ordered the Hocklyns to send in an escort cruiser to scan the human hyperjumps so they could maintain the pursuit.

After each encounter with a Hocklyn escort cruiser, Admiral Streth would send a short coded message to Fleet Admiral Johnson, informing her of their current course and projected arrival time. Every day they drew closer and closer to the Federation.

On board the battlecruiser WarStorm, Amanda looked anxiously at the tactical display. They were now only two jumps from New Tellus, and they would be bringing the Hocklyns and the AIs with them when they arrived.

"Hocklyn escort cruiser detected," Lieutenant Stalls reported as a warning alarm went off on his sensor console. "Contact at sixteen million kilometers."

"Admiral Streth is ordering us to be prepared to jump in thirty minutes," reported Lieutenant Trask, looking over at Admiral Sheen.

Amanda took in a deep breath and nodded. She knew that very soon she would be able to speak to Richard. "Place the ship at Condition Two and enter the coordinates," she ordered. Looking over at Navigation, she felt a wave of sadness pass over her at the absence of Lieutenant Ashton.

Over the past several weeks, a lot of repair work had been done on the remaining ships of Second Fleet. All of her ships were now combat worthy and would do their share in the defense of New Tellus.

"Emergency message from Admiral Streth to all ships," Lieutenant Trask reported in a near panic. "Fleet Admiral Johnson has just sent a priority message. An AI ship jumped into the New Tellus system two hours ago and scanned the system. It has since jumped out and there has been no further contact. Admiral Johnson has placed all Federation ships and military installations at Condition Two, with Condition One expected shortly."

"Wasn't expecting that," Commander Evans spoke with worry in her eyes. "They could arrive the same time we do."

"We still have some time," responded Amanda, knowing now she might not get to speak to Richard before the battle commenced. "It will take time for the Hocklyn Fleet Commodore to make his attack plans and coordinate with the AIs."

"We will also need to receive a complete load out on Devastator Threes when we enter the system," added Commander Evans, wanting the WarStorm to be fully armed with the deadly missiles. She knew that several ammunition colliers were standing by to supply the fleet with needed munitions.

As soon as the thirty minutes were up, a swirling spatial vortex formed in front of the WarStorm and Amanda felt the nauseous wrench as the ship jumped into hyperspace. Just one more short jump following this one and Amanda knew they would be back in the New Tellus system after being gone for months. She gazed at the large viewscreen on the front wall with its swirling colors of dark purple that signified the strangeness of hyperspace. They were going to New Tellus and the trap that the old Federation survivors had been building for centuries. They were about to see just how good a mousetrap they had prepared. She was also returning home to Richard.

Chapter Twenty

Admiral Streth watched anxiously as the StarStrike and the rest of the ships of Operation First Strike exited the spatial vortexes into the New Tellus system. It only took a few seconds for the screens to clear and the ship's systems to come fully online.

"Contact," Clarissa called out as she was watching the sensors intently. "Federation light cruisers at twelve million kilometers."

"That's our ammunition colliers," Colonel Trist said as additional green icons flared up on one of the tactical displays. They had set up a rendezvous the day before when they had sent their regular FTL message to Fleet Admiral Johnson.

"I am detecting six light cruisers, one Monarch cruiser and two ammunition colliers," Captain Reynolds reported as more data came in.

"Receiving challenge for ship IDs," Captain Duncan added as she listened to the message over her com."

"Transmit them," Colonel Trist ordered. It was a relief to have finally made it back to the New Tellus system.

"Set a course to rendezvous with those ships immediately," ordered Hedon, wanting to get his ships topped off with ammunition before the Hocklyns or AIs arrived. He knew they were only one or two short jumps behind them.

"Incoming message from New Tellus Station," Captain Duncan continued as more messages swamped her communications console. "Once we have resupplied we are to proceed to New Tellus and take up a position just outside the gravity well of the planet. The message is from Admiral Freeman. Fleet Admiral Johnson wants to meet with you at your earliest convenience."

Hedon nodded. He knew that the Hocklyns and AIs could launch their attack at any moment, though he hoped it would take them a day or two to plan their assault. "Inform Admiral Freeman that we will proceed to New Tellus as soon as we have finished loading munitions."

"We're back," Colonel Trist commented, his eyes showing his relief as one of the tactical displays began lighting up with the various icons representing the planets and defenses of the New Tellus system. "I just hope they're ready for what's following us."

"They are," Colonel Grissom spoke confidently as she studied one of the tactical screens. "From what I can tell all the defenses have been heavily beefed up during our absence."

"New sensor contacts at forty million kilometers," Captain Reynolds called out and then he turned pale when the contacts turned a glaring orange. "Two AI ships confirmed!"

"Damn!" muttered Colonel Trist, turning to look at Hedon worriedly. "Now what?"

"I'm sure they're only scouting the system," Colonel Grissom informed them as she watched the movements of the two AI ships. "As near as I can tell from our sensors, they have not powered up their weapons."

"Admiral Sheen and Admiral Kimmel are requesting orders," Captain Duncan spoke up as the two messages came in from Second Fleet and the supply fleet.

"I wouldn't recommend attacking them with our limited supply of Devastator Threes," added Clarissa, feeling nervous about the AIs being so close.

"We don't dare attempt to resupply with them in the system," Hedon said with a deep frown, looking at the two colonels. "Order the supply fleet to jump to New Tellus, our ships will jump immediately after they do. We will attempt to rearm after the jump."

"What are the AI ships doing?" demanded Trist, looking sharply over at Clarissa who was standing next to one of the tactical displays studying it intently. "Are you detecting targeting scans or anything?"

The blonde AI turned toward the colonel. "Nothing; they are just sitting there. I assume they are taking detailed scans of the system prior to attacking as I mentioned earlier."

Hedon nodded in agreement; they needed to get to New Tellus as quickly as possible before the AIs changed their minds and attacked what was left of his fleets.

-

The two AI ships had already scanned the human fleets close by, recognizing them as the ones they had been following. It was debated briefly about jumping into their midst and annihilating them, but the AIs were unsure how many of the deadly sublight missiles the humans had left. It was decided not to attack as they couldn't risk ship losses at this juncture. They would continue to scan the human defenses in the system and deal with the human ships later.

-

Rear Admiral Andrews looked over at his subordinate and second in command, Rear Admiral Drew Hazleton. "Two AI ships," Richard stated as he looked at one of the large tactical displays next to the center command console. They had jumped in close to Admiral Streth's returning fleets, which made Richard nervous as Amanda was there. He also knew that Admiral Streth only had one strikecruiser plus the StarStrike that could fight the AIs.

"Fleet Admiral Johnson has just placed all military assets at Condition One," Major Appleton informed them from her position at Communications. At the same moment, red lights began flashing and Condition One alarms began sounding.

"Launch four additional bomber wings immediately," Richard ordered as he gazed at the glaring orange threat icons in the display. "I want them armed with nuclear tipped Shrike missiles." Then, looking back at Admiral Hazleton, he added, "Turn those damn lights and alarms off; we know what's out there."

From the command fortress, forty more Anlon bombers launched from the flight bays to take up defensive positions around the large asteroid. Two flights of Talon fighters were already on patrol and moved in closer to help cover the bombers in case of an attack.

Richard watched as the bombers and fighters moved into position. "Admiral Hazleton, contact all the fortresses and have them prepare for a Devastator Three fire mission. If those two AIs jump into the gravity well close to New Tellus I want to blow them away."

Admiral Hazleton spent a few minutes passing on the orders and then turned back to Richard. "All fortresses are ready with Devastator Threes, and the shipyards have activated all of their offensive and defensive weapon systems. Defensive battle stations have taken over control of the defense grid, and all fleet destroyers are moving into their support positions within the grid."

"I don't believe the AIs will attack," Kiera Watkins, the officer from Intelligence, spoke. "They may just be watching our fleet units and transmitting the information back to their fleets."

Richard nodded. "As soon as Admiral Streth and his fleets arrive, his surviving destroyers will be moved into the defense grid," he informed Hazleton. "The repair ships and his supply ships will take up positions just beneath the lowest level of the grid. We may need those repair ships if this thing goes south."

Richard also knew that most of First Strike's destroyers had been lost in battles with the Hocklyn fleet and the AIs. Out of the one hundred and forty destroyers that had been in the Ready Reserve Fleet, only nineteen had come back with the returning fleets. There were a few destroyers that had been left with Admiral Strong, but most were lost in the operation. It just proved the point that the destroyer's best use was to protect the satellite defensive grid.

"That's about all the destroyers are good for," replied Hazleton, knowing how easily the larger Hocklyn ships could destroy them.

He knew that Fleet Admiral Johnson had given the orders to cease production on destroyers and focus more on light cruisers. At least the light cruisers mounted enough weapons to be able to defend themselves.

"What about the people on the surface of New Tellus?" Richard asked as his eyes strayed to another tactical display that showed Second Fleet and the WarStorm, still dangerously close to the two AI ships. It was painful to know that Amanda was so close, and there was nothing he could do to help or protect her if the two AI ships attacked.

"They are on the way to their underground bunkers," Hazleton reported as he checked the status of the planetary evacuation. Years past, deep underground bunkers had been constructed to protect the millions of people that called New Tellus their home. Nearly 22 million people lived and worked on New Tellus, with most of them being direct descendants of the original Federation survivors.

On the tactical display, the three surviving fleets of Operation First Strike vanished, only to reappear a few moments later just outside the gravity well of New Tellus. Richard breathed a sigh of relief knowing Amanda was now out of danger.

"More hostile contacts," Major Dante called out as numerous red threat icons began appearing in the outer system close to the AIs.

"Hocklyn ships jumping in," Intelligence officer Kiera Watkins reported as she studied her data screens. "Hocklyn dreadnoughts, war cruisers, and escort cruisers detected."

"Additional AI ships detected," Dante called out as four more orange threat icons appeared to one side of the Hocklyn warships.

"Total Hocklyn ship count is four hundred and twelve ships," Watkins informed the two admirals.

"That's not even half of their fleet," Admiral Hazleton commented with a frown. "Where are the rest of them?"

"Twenty light years away," Watkins answered as she studied data coming in from some of the remote FTL sensor buoys. "Sensor buoys in system L-334 have recorded numerous inbound hyperjumps."

"They've split their fleet," said Hazleton, arching his eyebrows. "I wonder why?"

"They're being cautious," Richard guessed as he looked around the massive Command Center and the hundreds of fleet personnel that were going about their jobs.

"I have Fleet Admiral Johnson on the com," Major Appleton spoke from Communications.

Richard leaned forward and pressed a button on the control console in front of him. "This is Rear Admiral Andrews," Richard said.

"Richard, what do you make of this?" Johnson asked.

"They may want to lure our fleets out of the gravity well," Richard suggested as he eyed one of the tactical displays. "It would also give them the option of jumping out if things go badly for them."

"My thinking exactly," Fleet Admiral Jonson responded. "I am going to go ahead and pull Admiral Streth's fleets into the gravity well and beneath the defense grid to be rearmed. Admiral Teleck is on his way from Ceres with his fleet and will be taking a holding position in system L-447 six light years away."

Richard nodded. "Then we are going to let the AIs and the Hocklyns come to us?"

"We need them in the gravity well for this trap to work," Fleet Admiral Johnson replied in a calm voice.

-

Admiral Teleck was well on his way to New Tellus with his fleet. "Status?" he asked as they finished their final jump. The original plan had been to jump into the system, but with the arrival of the Hocklyn and AI ships that had been changed. They would now take up a holding position in system L-447.

"All ships have exited hyperspace and are moving into a defensive formation around the Ceres," Colonel Barnes reported as she received reports from the sensor operator as well as Communications. "The Eden is launching a CAP of ten fighters."

Admiral Teleck nodded; he had a very powerful fleet with him. Eleven battlecruisers, six battlecarriers, ten strikecruisers, twenty Monarch cruisers, and forty light cruisers had been sent on this mission. Admiral Kalen back at Ceres had a fleet of the same size with which to defend the asteroid. After these two fleets, other than a few scout ships, there were no more heavy units inside the ship bays of the massive asteroid.

Kathryn began studying the tactical display as information from New Tellus Station was being transmitted to the Ceres. She felt a twinge of fear pass through her at seeing the numerous red and orange threat icons that represented the Hocklyns and the AIs.

"That's less than half of them," Admiral Teleck said as he stepped over to stand by his young executive officer. "It seems as if the AIs and the Fleet Commodore in charge of the Hocklyn fleet are in no hurry to engage our forces."

What are they doing?" asked Kathryn, uneasily. She knew that, at any moment, Admiral Teleck could order the Ceres and the fleet to attack the enemy.

"It's a waiting game to see who blinks first," Teleck explained. "After the battle they had with Admiral Streth they are being cautious. They're also waiting to see what forces come to the aid of New Tellus. If they determine no more are coming or none are available, then I believe they will commence their attack. Once they begin we will jump in and strike the rear of their formation."

Kathryn nodded and tried not to look nervous. She had never been in combat before, and she hoped she performed her job up to the admiral's expectations.

Fleet Commodore Resmunt gazed with worry at the holographic tactical display. This system was awash with human ships and daunting defenses.

"This will not be easy," First Leader Ganth stated, his large eyes narrowing at what was on the display. "There are six large shipyards, a massive satellite defense grid with large battle stations intermixed, hundreds of warships and those eight massive asteroids in orbit around the planet."

"Our scans indicate those asteroids are heavily armed," Resmunt added in a concerned tone. "If we attack those defenses many of our warriors will go to meet their honor."

"What other choice do we have?" Ganth asked, his dark eyes focusing on the commodore. "The AIs will expect nothing less."

Resmunt studied the tactical display, growing more alarmed at what he was seeing. "This is a trap," he announced finally. "This system has been designed to destroy Hocklyn ships."

"That may well be," responded Ganth, trusting Fleet Commodore Resmunt's judgment. "But as long as this system exists it is a threat to our Empire. It must be destroyed, and we have twenty AI ships to assist us."

"We must be careful in our attack and not throw our ships away needlessly," stated Resmunt, turning his cold gaze toward First Leader Ganth. "I will consult with the AIs. Their ships will have to clear a path for us or this attack is doomed before it starts." Resmunt let out a deep, rasping breath. Never in the long history of the Empire had they ever faced defenses like these.

Resmunt looked back at the tactical display, studying the disposition of the human forces. Not even in the Empire was there a system this well defended. If he didn't know better, he would guess the humans had been preparing for this attack for hundreds of years. If those asteroids were as powerful as they looked, it would have taken decades to move them into orbit and then mount the massive amount of weapons scans indicated they were armed with.

Looking at the six large green icons that represented the AI ships, Resmunt knew he had no choice but to contact them and see if they would listen to his recommendations about how this attack needed to go. He had an idea of what needed to be done, but would the AIs agree to it?

Letting out a long, hissing breath, Resmunt turned to go to the communications console. He despised speaking to the AIs, and he had to admit he had felt a guilty satisfaction each time he watched the humans annihilate one of the massive spheres. The AIs were the masters and no one had ever been able to challenge them, at least until now.

Hedon was still on the StarStrike, which was nearing New Tellus Station. Glancing at one of the large tactical displays, he saw that the Hocklyn and AI fleets had still not moved; they were just sitting there as if daring the humans to come out and attack. He had just finished speaking to Fleet Admiral Johnson, and they had decided to reorganize the surviving ships of Operation First Strike. There would be just two fleets, First Fleet and Second Fleet, and they were being reinforced with the six light cruiser fleets that were normally on system patrol.

All ships would continue to just beneath the defense grid, where they would be rearmed and resupplied. In addition, the six large repair ships would initiate additional repairs on the ships that still had major internal and structural damage. Hedon had considered ordering them into the shipyards, but they were still combat capable and they would shortly need every ship at their disposal.

"We're being ordered to dock with the station," Captain Duncan reported. "We're supposed to dock at docking port seven, and they have a crew standing by with munitions and supplies for us. Fleet Admiral Johnson is standing by and will be coming aboard as soon as docking is completed."

"Very well," Hedon replied with a nod. "Colonel Trist, carry out the docking maneuver, and take the ship to Condition Two while we are at dock but be prepared to go to Condition One and disconnect if the AIs or the Hocklyns begin their attack. Inform Admiral Sheen that she is in charge of First and Second fleets and to get the rearming done as quickly as possible."

"Yes, Sir," Colonel Trist replied.

"I'll be glad to get a full load out of Devastator Threes," Clarissa commented as the gorgeous AI strolled over to stand next to Admiral Streth. "We are being assigned two strikecruisers to join First Fleet in case we have to go up against an AI. Two other strikecruisers are going to Second Fleet."

Clarissa nervously checked her sensors once more. She was keeping a close watch on the AIs. It was times like these that she really wished she could send a message to Ariel. She still could, but it would take several days to get an answer back.

Then in a lower voice so as not to worry the crew, Clarissa looked intently at the admiral with her deep blue eyes and asked, "Do you think New Tellus can hold against the combined AI and Hocklyn fleets?"

"We're going to try," responded Hedon, knowing the AI was worried. It amazed him sometimes at how human Clarissa and Ariel could be and how at times they acted so much like a normal human.

"I hope so," Clarissa responded, and then her eyes brightened. "If we can hold them, we can return to Careth and rescue Ariel and the others."

"I'm sure Admiral Strong will be fine," Hedon reassured the AI. "He and the bears have put up some really strong defenses. If he can stop their first attack, we should be able to get to him in time before the Hocklyns can mount a second."

Clarissa nodded; she really missed talking to Ariel. When they finally did get to talk again, she would have a lot to say.

A few minutes later, the StarStrike docked to New Tellus Station and Fleet Admiral Johnson made her way on board. The two Fleet Admirals met in the small conference room that adjoined the Command Center.

"Hedon, it's good to see you," Karla said with a wide smile as she stepped into the conference room and shook Hedon's hand.

"I wish I could have brought more of the fleet back," responded Hedon regretfully as he motioned for Karla to take a seat at the small conference table. Hedon knew he had led thousands of Fleet personnel to their deaths in Operation First Strike. At night, he could see their faces in his dreams.

"It's war," Karla responded in understanding. "You hurt the Hocklyns and the AIs badly and have stopped their entire expansion. All of our long distance scouts say the expansion of the Hocklyn Slave Empire has ground to a complete halt."

"I'm glad to hear that," Hedon said, but it still didn't help the sick feeling in the pit of his stomach from the men and women who hadn't returned with him. He knew that their sacrifice meant that new worlds were not being conquered, and millions if not billions of inhabitants were not, in turn, dying under the conquering fleets of the Hocklyn Slave Empire.

"You also destroyed a lot of Hocklyn ships as well as ten AI ships in your campaign," Karla continued in a serious voice. "You bought us the extra time we needed to prepare the Federation."

"Then you're ready?" asked Hedon, feeling some relief. That had been the main goal of Operation First Strike to begin with; to give the Federation the extra time it needed to finish its transition to a war economy.

"As ready as we're ever going to be," answered Karla, grimly. Then her face took on a more somber look. "Hedon, I'm assigning Rear Admiral Tolsen and his fleet to your command. That will give you over one hundred and fifty warships to fight this battle."

"And what are my orders?" asked Hedon, knowing they were still facing tremendous odds.

"Protect New Tellus Station," Karla replied evenly, her eyes meeting his. "We will use the heavy weapons on the asteroid fortresses, the shipyards, and the missile platforms hidden in the defense grid to try to whittle down the enemy forces. Admiral Teleck is standing by with an additional fleet of nearly ninety ships if needed."

It was at that moment that both Fleet Admirals heard the new warning come over their mini-coms. "Additional Hocklyn and AI ships are jumping into the system," Colonel Trist informed them. "Latest count is four more AIs and two hundred more Hocklyn warships."

"This is about to get serious," Fleet Admiral Johnson spoke as she stood up. She had wanted to speak to Hedon about some other things. "I had better get back to the Command Center on the station." Reaching the door, Karla stopped and gazed back at Fleet Admiral Streth. "Hedon, in this battle, don't let me screw up!"

"You will do fine," Hedon promised. "You know what must be done, just do it. The people will follow your orders."

Karla nodded; it was good to know that Hedon was here if she needed him. However, the weight of what was about to happen weighed heavily on her shoulders. If she failed to hold New Tellus then the only system that had a hope of stopping the AIs and the Hocklyns was the Sol system itself. That would also mean that the rest of the new Federation worlds had fallen. Karla was determined that not a single Hocklyn or AI ship would leave this system intact. She would either stop them or die trying.

Hedon watched Karla go. He well understood how she was feeling. Command at times could be a heavy burden, and Fleet Admiral Johnson had the survival of the entire Federation resting on her shoulders.

Chapter Twenty-One

The command AI touched the tactical display in front of it with its flexible metal tentacle expanding the view of the human defenses. "This system must be annihilated before we move on to destroy the rest of the human worlds."

"Our other ships have found four additional systems inhabited by humans, and there are probably more," the AI operating the ship's data screens replied. "This sector of space is as we feared, the humans have expanded from their home planet and now may be more numerous than we expected."

"The humans think they have set a trap for the Hocklyns," the command AI said as it continued to study the data on the tactical display. "We will continue to let them think that their trap has worked and then we will launch the real attack and destroy this system. Once this system has fallen, the remaining human worlds will be easy to annihilate. Their numbers will be immaterial to our fleet."

"The Altons chose well in picking this race to prevent our future expansion," the AI at the data screens spoke as it continued to scan the incoming data. "If given additional time to develop their technologies, they could indeed become a major threat."

"Soon it will not matter, and no organic race will ever be a threat again," the command AI replied, the glowing orb that served as its head growing even larger. "In a few more decades, the project at the black hole will be complete, and the organic races will no longer be needed."

"The universe will be better off without contamination from the organics," spoke another of the AIs in the Control Center.

The command AI floated over next to the main communications console. "Let the attack begin."

Richard was in his quarters speaking to Amanda over a private communications channel. The AIs and Hocklyn fleet had been sitting in the outer region of the New Tellus system for nearly two days, and this was only the second time the two had been able to speak to one another.

"Once this is over I've arranged for us to spend two weeks at one of the ski lodges up in the mountains on New Tellus," Richard was saying, wishing he could hold Amanda in his arms rather than just speaking to her over the com system.

"Sounds great," replied Amanda, trying to imagine what that would be like. She had really enjoyed their last trip to the mountain lodge, particularly the hot chocolate they had served. She had never been able to get that wonderful recipe.

"I'm just glad you made it back safely," Richard said. "I was worried."

"There were moments when I wondered if I was going to make it back," Amanda admitted. "There were times I doubted if I would ever see you again."

Richard was about to tell Amanda how worried he had been the entire time she was gone when the red Condition One light in his quarters flashed on, as well as the alarms. "Admiral Andrews, report to the Command Center," a voice spoke over the com unit on the wall."

"They're coming in," Amanda suddenly said as she received a message over her mini-com. "The AIs and the Hocklyn fleets have begun to move and are heading toward New Tellus."

"That still puts them hours away if they don't do a micro-jump," Richard said, knowing he needed to report to the Command Center. "Amanda, don't go off and get yourself killed, I still want a family someday."

"So do I," Amanda replied in a more subdued voice. "Richard, I love you."

"I love you too," Richard replied as he heard the connection end.

Fleet Admiral Johnson sensed the sudden anxiety that swept through the Command Center of New Tellus Station as the joint Hocklyn and AI fleets began moving at increasing speed toward them.

"All fleet assets are at Condition One," Admiral Freeman reported from his post next to Admiral Johnson. "Admiral Andrews is holding off launching additional fighters and bombers until the Hocklyns or AIs enter the gravity well. He is, however, rotating the squadrons currently out on patrol."

Karla nodded. Her eyes moved to one of the large tactical displays, which showed the inbound fleet. "I don't think the AIs will jump inside our gravity well until the Hocklyn fleet is engaged with our ships."

"They may still be trying to lure our ships out to open combat away from the gravity well," Major Ackerman suggested over the open mini-com channel. The Intelligence officer had been watching the Hocklyn and AI fleet intently for several hours, trying to deduce what their strategy might be. "That may be why they have not initiated a micro-jump."

"Also, by approaching at sublight speeds they keep our ships at Condition One and it wears on the combat capability of the crews," Admiral Freeman added. He did some quick calculations and then turned toward the Fleet Admiral. "At their current speed it will take them nearly one hundred hours to reach the gravity well of New Tellus."

Karla weighed her options carefully; she knew that, at Condition One, all military assets would have their top people on duty. "The shipyards and the fortresses will stay at Condition One, all other military assets are to go to Condition Three and stay there until they receive further orders. The shipyards and the fortresses have the command staff and crews to remain at Condition One over a long period."

The orders were quickly passed, and the ships and the battle stations relaxed their state of alert. Around New Tellus Station Admiral Streth had all three fleets under his command go to Condition Three and ordered the first shift duty crews to get some rest. He had a suspicion that the Hocklyns and the AIs wouldn't be satisfied with moving so slowly toward New Tellus. At some point, he was certain they would initiate a micro-jump. He wanted to be ready for them when they did.

Karla continued to gaze at the tactical display showing the massive Hocklyn fleet and the ten AI ships moving steadily toward the human defenses. She was confident her defenses could handle the Hocklyns ships, but the AIs were another matter. She had the firepower to destroy them with the strikecruisers and the fortresses when they came into range, but the AIs might cause a lot of damage in the process. She also had sixteen of the new type two battle stations that could be used to launch Devastator Threes if necessary.

Letting out a deep breath, she looked over at another display, which was focused on First Fleet. It gave her some comfort knowing that the StarStrike and Fleet Admiral Streth were close by. The legendary admiral had survived Operation First Strike, and now they would see if he could survive the maelstrom of destruction that was about to begin around New Tellus.

Fleet Commodore Resmunt was unsurprised at seeing that the human fleets were still refusing to come out and engage his forces. Forty hours had passed, and the humans had not budged from their heavy defenses around the blue-white planet they were protecting. Still, he knew he had accomplished something by keeping the human defenses and ships at a state of high alert. The human warriors would not be at their best when the attack was finally launched.

"It's nearly time," Resmunt spoke in his deep rasping voice as he studied the tactical display.

He was pleased that the AIs had agreed to let him help coordinate this part of the attack. He had come up with a plan that would seriously degrade the human defenses and also demoralize their forces.

"It is good," First Leader Ganth replied with a nod. His hand touched his knife. "Our warriors and Protectors are anxious to add to their honor."

"We launch our attack in two hours," Resmunt spoke in a steady and determined voice, his large dark eyes turning toward the First Leader. "We will jump to just outside the gravity well of their planet and then move toward their largest shipyard. If we can take it and destroy the ships protecting it, then the battle will be ours."

"What about the rest of our ships and the AIs?" Ganth asked. He felt it was dangerous beginning this attack without their full fleet, particularly with those eight large asteroids orbiting the human planet. He had studied the long-range scans of the weapons emplaced upon those asteroids, and they were powerful beyond belief. Many Hocklyn warriors would go to their honor in destroying them.

"Our other ships and the remaining AI ships will jump in as soon as we launch our attack," Resmunt informed First Leader Ganth as he thought over the strategy he had suggested to the AIs. "They will form a second attack wave once we are engaged with the humans."

"Then honor will soon come to us," Ganth spoke, pleased that the attack was about to start. With the full firepower of their fleet, as well as the AIs, they should be able to overwhelm the human defenses no matter how powerful they were. It would be costly, but victory would be theirs.

-

Two hours later, six hundred and twelve Hocklyn warships and ten AI ships jumped to the very edge of New Tellus's gravity well.

Instantly, warning alarms sounded on all Federation warships, battle stations, fortresses, and shipyards, including New Tellus Station.

The Hocklyns seemed to hesitate for a moment and then began moving slowly into the gravity well, followed closely by the AIs. It took Fleet Admiral Johnson only a moment to realize that New Tellus Station was their intended target.

"Get me Admiral Streth," Karla ordered as the command crew worked at a heightened pace, knowing that the battle was finally upon them.

"Admiral Streth is online," the communications officer reported.

"Admiral, the Hocklyns and AIs are moving in, it looks as if New Tellus Station is their primary target."

"I agree," Hedon replied evenly. "It's the largest shipyard we have, and they can see how heavily we are defending it. They must believe by destroying it they can seriously degrade our defenses."

"More ships jumping in system," Colonel Trist suddenly reported over the com channel. "It looks like the rest of the Hocklyn fleet and the remaining AIs."

"This is going to get serious quickly," Hedon told the Fleet Admiral as he watched all the new red and orange threat icons appearing in the outer system. "They might try to overwhelm our defenses with a mass attack."

"Hedon, I'm turning the Tellus over to your command also," said Karla, knowing that Admiral Streth could make the best use of their second battleship. "Should we call Admiral Teleck in?"

"No," Hedon answered quickly. "As the battle progresses there will come a point where we will need some fresh ships and crews; his fleet will provide just that."

"Good luck, Admiral," spoke Karla, trying to sound more confident than she felt.

Cutting the connection, Karla gazed at one of the tactical displays showing the now rapidly approaching Hocklyn and AI fleets. She felt her heart pounding in her chest and her breathing quicken. Even though she was the Fleet Admiral, she had never been in combat before.

"They will have a lot of fighters with them," Major Ackerman informed the Fleet Admiral. "They will need to be eliminated if we want our bombers to have any success."

"Between the shipyards, the fleet, and the fortresses we have the fighters to do that," commented Admiral Bennett as he walked into the

Command Center and took up his station close to the Fleet Admiral. "It will be necessary to hold our bomber attacks off until we have substantially eliminated a large number of the Hocklyn fighters to ensure the success of their attack runs."

"I agree," Karla replied. "Admiral Bennett, I want you to coordinate the bomber strikes with Fleet Admiral Streth and Admiral Andrews. The bombers can be a big advantage to us in this battle if we use them wisely."

Bennett nodded as he activated his com system to speak to the fortresses and shipyards. The Hocklyns couldn't know about the thousands of human bombers that were waiting for them.

The Hocklyn fleet continued to advance until they were nearly in engagement range. At that point, 3,100 fighters launched from the Hocklyn ships and took up defending positions around the fleet and the AIs. The Hocklyn fleet slowed and entered engagement range; it was at that moment that all ten of the AI ships jumped.

"AI ships are jumping," Colonel Grissom warned in a loud voice as they vanished from the sensor screens.

"Where to?" Hedon demanded worriedly as his eyes focused on one of the tactical displays. This was one of his biggest concerns. The AI ships could jump inside a planet's gravity well without harm. If a Federation ship tired the same maneuver, the ship's drive would be destroyed and possibly the ship.

"Shipyard Clements!" Clarissa called out her deep blue eyes gazing at the admiral. "They've jumped around it and are firing their weapons; defense fleet two is responding."

"Damn!" Colonel Trist cried out in frustration, knowing they couldn't reach the shipyard in time.

"There's an asteroid fortress nearby," Hedon spoke as he assessed the situation. "Defense fleet two also has six strikecruisers as well."

Clements was the smallest of the six large shipyards around New Tellus. It was heavily armed and close enough to the satellite defense grid to be covered by their weapons as well as one of the large asteroid fortresses.

AI energy beams impacted the shipyard's powerful shield and several smashed through, causing severe damage to the armored hull of the station. Alarms sounded and airtight doors slammed shut as several explosions rocked the internal structure. However, the shipyard wasn't idle; over twenty power beam batteries locked onto the attacking AIs and violet energy beams smashed into the AI's shields. At the same time, Devastator and Devastator Threes missiles launched and quickly struck the AIs, covering them with nuclear fire.

Additional Devastator missiles were launched from the numerous missile platforms in the defense grid as well as from four defense battle stations that were within range. The pulse laser batteries on the space station finally began firing, and space was full of orange-red beams of light, which began impacting the AI's shields. All ten AI ships were under massive attack, but their shields were holding.

"Fire everything we have!" Colonel Freedman ordered from the Command Center of shipyard Clements. He felt the station shudder violently as another AI energy beam cut through the shield, striking the station. He had never expected to have to face ten AI ships.

"Repair bay four has been destroyed," Lieutenant Baker reported from damage control. "We have numerous compartments open to space and several fires that are out of control. Damage control teams are being dispatched. We also have a lot of casualties."

"Where's the damn fleet?" Major Kline screamed as the lights in the Command Center flickered and then returned to steady. "We can't take much more of this!"

–

Defense fleet two under Admiral Whittington was already coming into range and adding their firepower to the shipyards. Admiral Whittington's command consisted of fifty-seven warships including six strikecruisers. Already, the strikecruisers were preparing to fire Devastator Three missiles at the AI ships.

Looking at the main viewscreen on the front wall of the Command Center of his flagship, the battlecruiser Houston, Whittington could see that the shipyard was suffering heavy damage. He winced as he saw another AI energy beam strike the hull of the shipyard, blowing out an entire section. If he couldn't stop this AI attack, the shipyard was in danger of being destroyed.

"Strikecruisers are to advance and engage the AIs," he ordered over the ship-to-ship mini-com. "All other ships will provide covering fire."

–

The commander of the large asteroid fortress was also in the process of issuing launch orders for a Devastator Three strike. The fortress was already firing its power beam and pulse laser batteries at the AI ships. If the AIs stayed in range, the commander of the fortress was certain he could destroy all ten of them. The fortress packed a massive amount of firepower.

Aboard the shipyard, damage control teams were being rushed to various areas of the station as even more AI energy beams tore through its weakening screen. Several more fires were out of control and one of the fusion generators had gone offline. The station shuddered as more explosions rocked the large structure.

The six 1,000-meter strikecruisers locked onto their targets and quickly fired their Devastator Threes at almost the same instant as the asteroid fortress. Four AI ships were suddenly aglow from the furious onslaught of the 40-megaton explosive warheads. Several massive detonations bit into the AIs ship's hulls creating gaping, fiery chasms hundreds of meters deep.

The energy screens flickered and then went down on the stricken ships, allowing numerous Devastator Three and Devastator missiles to impact the heavily armored hulls. The fleet, shipyard, and asteroid fortress detecting the failure of the shields, fired every weapon they had against the AIs. Power beams, pulse lasers, and railgun rounds pummeled the armored hulls. Three of the AI ships suddenly exploded as their critical systems were destroyed beyond repair and their self-destructs initiated. A fourth was heavily damaged and it suddenly turned and accelerated toward Clements Station.

Seeing the massive warship bearing down on them the station intensified its fire, trying to finish the destruction the Devastator Threes had started. The AI ship exploded upon impact with the station's screen and massive sections of the large sphere smashed into the station, causing substantial damage. Aboard the station, fires were raging out of control and hundreds were dead or trapped.

The shipyard was in danger of coming apart as its structural integrity had been seriously compromised. Damage control personnel raced around the station trying to save what they could. Over three quarters of it had suffered major damage. Its energy screen was down and power had failed to its weapons. Only one fusion reactor was still functioning. For all intents and purpose, Clements was a now dead hulk floating helplessly in space.

The remaining six AI ships suddenly jumped to reappear directly behind defense fleet two and away from the six strikecruisers. Every weapon the AIs had hammered the fleet and ships began to rapidly die. Battlecruisers, Monarch cruisers, and light cruisers exploded as massive energy beams tore them apart. Before the asteroid fortress could retarget the AIs, they jumped again to reappear behind the attacking Hocklyn fleet.

However, the damage had been done, Clements Station had been heavily damaged, and defense fleet two had lost twenty of its fifty-seven ships. Many others had suffered damage. Seeing the destruction, Fleet Admiral Johnson had no choice but to delegate the reduced fleet to guarding the ailing station. Karla also sent orders to evacuate all survivors from the shipyard to the nearby asteroid fortress. The shipyard had been designed to withstand a massed Hocklyn attack, not one by the AIs.

Fleet Commodore Resmunt nodded to himself as the AI ships jumped back to a supporting position just behind his fleet. He had found out what he wanted; the asteroid fortresses were extremely dangerous along with the numerous small battle stations scattered throughout the human's defense grid. His own fleet was at extreme combat range of the defending human fleets around the largest shipyard. The fleet would remain in this position as Resmunt did not intend to endanger it by exposing his ships to the heavy weapons on the shipyard. Also, the largest asteroid fortress would be able to bring its weapons to bear if the Hocklyn ships moved much closer.

Already missile fire between the fleets guarding the station and his own fleet was intensifying. However, his fighters were intercepting the majority of the missiles and only a few were getting through to impact upon his ship's screens. It was time to contact the AIs once more and destroy even more of the human ships.

The command AI looked around the Control Room of its ship. It was overly crowded as all the AIs had been evacuated from the other AI ships so as not to risk their destruction. The computers on the ships could operate them just as well as an AI could. While the loss of AI ships was not important, the loss of an actual AI was.

"Fleet Commodore Resmunt is requesting that we make another strike against another one of the human fleets," the AI in front of Communications reported.

The command AI turned and studied one of the tactical displays, analyzing the current situation. The humans had three fleets defending the largest shipyard and three other fleets capable of defending the other five. They had already damaged one shipyard and eliminated numerous ships from its defending fleet. Much needed data had been gained from the previous attack, and they were still evaluating it.

"I would recommend striking this fleet and shipyard," the AI in front of another one of the numerous tactical displays suggested, waving its tentacles at the suggested target. "It is the second largest shipyard, but it is protected by the smallest asteroid."

"We will target the fleet first," the command AI ordered, the glowing head on top of its body brightening and seeming to grow even larger.

A few moments later, swirling white spatial vortexes formed in front of the six AI ships and they quickly entered them. A moment later, they reappeared around the doomed human fleet.

Hedon felt the StarStrike shudder slightly as a Hocklyn nuclear missile detonated against the energy shield. He had ordered the fleet to conserve their missiles as the Hocklyns were still at extreme range and most of the missiles were being intercepted anyway.

"AIs have jumped again," Clarissa reported from her position next to Admiral Streth. Clarissa had the ability by using the ships sensors to give the admiral immediate reports of tactical developments. The blonde AI had a look of deep concern on her face.

"They've targeted defense fleet four," Colonel Grissom reported from her spot next to one of the tactical displays.

"This doesn't make sense," Colonel Trist added as he watched the deadly beams from the AIs flash out toward the human fleet. One of the main viewscreens had been focused on this new epicenter of the battle. "Why are the AIs so willing to sacrifice their ships?"

"I don't know," replied Hedon, shaking his head. "But we will take advantage of this situation to eliminate them."

Clarissa remained silent as she analyzed this latest attack by the AIs. She found it difficult to believe they were so willing to sacrifice themselves, unless they were not actually on their ships. Could these AI ships be nothing more than massive drones? Carissa decided not to mention this to Fleet Admiral Streth, not until she was certain that she was correct in her assumption. Nevertheless, it was the only thing that made any sense.

The six AI ships had jumped around defense fleet four, which was commanded by Admiral Boise aboard the battlecruiser Coventry. Brutal energy beams lashed out against the fleet's screens and more than one went down. After a few moments, the AIs jumped again to reappear between the human fleet and the shipyard, their weapons now concentrating on the human cruisers that had shown to be a threat to them. If they could destroy all six of them they could wipe out the human fleet with no casualties to themselves. But the AIs had made a grave error. There were four of the new larger type two defense battle stations around the shipyard, and they had already targeted the AI ships with their own Devastator Threes.

Space was lit up with massive explosions and the flashes of violet power beams, white energy beams, and orange-red pulse laser beams. Admiral Boise winced inwardly as he watched his ships die. Two battlecruisers, a battlecarrier, four light cruisers and two of the valuable strikecruisers vanished in bright explosions of energy as they were annihilated by the AI's attack. Then the battle stations launched their Devastator Three missiles.

In space, the 40-megaton sublight missiles struck four of the massive 1,500-meter AI spheres. Holes formed in their screens and more deadly human missiles darted through and impacted upon the heavily armored hulls. Metal turned into glowing gas and explosions tore deep within. The energy shields on three of the stricken AI ships failed, and moments later they died as their internal self-destructs finished what the human missiles had begun.

The two undamaged AI ships and the damaged one instantly jumped away. More information about the human defenses had been gleaned and more human ships had been annihilated. They had discovered that the larger human battle stations were deadly and would have to be eliminated quickly in future attacks.

Admiral Boise ordered his remaining ships to move closer to the shipyard. He had lost three battlecruisers, one battlecarrier, three strikecruisers, five Monarch cruisers, and fourteen light cruisers in the brief battle. Boise knew that if it had lasted for a few more minutes, none of his ships would have survived. At least this time the shipyard was unharmed.

Hedon grimaced in pain as a sharp vision suddenly appeared in his mind. It was of the defenses of New Tellus devastated and the planet on fire from numerous nuclear detonations. AI ships were everywhere, and the Hocklyn fleet was victorious.

Captain Janice Duncan had just looked over at the admiral and was stunned to see the devastated look upon his face, then it vanished and the admiral seemed to return to normal. What happened? She wondered. What had caused that look upon the admiral's face?

Shaking his head, Hedon looked around and saw Janice staring at him. He forced a smile and then turned to Colonel Trist. "Those AI ships have to be drones," he said. "They have been probing our defenses and searching for weaknesses. I can't believe there are any actual AIs on any of those ships."

"That makes sense," Colonel Grissom agreed as she saw that the three surviving AI ships had jumped back behind the Hocklyn fleet. "We may expect a major change in future attacks; they have now determined what is a danger to them."

Colonel Trist nodded in agreement. "They will be targeting our strikecruisers and the type two battle stations."

"Then we need to protect the strikecruisers," said Hedon, agreeing with Colonel Trist's assessment. "I want to pull all three fleets into defensive formation Delta 2A for their own protection." Formation Delta 2A was more of an inverted cone-like formation with the light cruisers forming the outer layer of the cone and the rest of the ships in the second layer. Both the StarStrike and the Tellus would be near the apex of the cone with the battle carriers just behind them.

"The rest of the Hocklyn and AI fleets are jumping in," Clarissa informed them as she put up additional information on the nearest tactical screen. "I have also deduced that the AI ships were drones, though I suspect some of the others are not. There has to be a controlling AI in their fleet somewhere."

On the tactical screen, hundreds of additional red threat icons appeared as well as the other ten AI ships. Over fourteen hundred red threat icons were now on the tactical screen along with thirteen AI ships.

"Once they're in the gravity well, we will need Admiral Teleck and his ships," Hedon commented grimly. "We're going to have to engage this fleet in order to make efficient use of our bombers and fighters."

"I will send the message," Clarissa replied as she watched the tactical screen, noting that the new Hocklyn and AI ships were already slowly moving into the gravity well.

"Get me Fleet Admiral Johnson," ordered Hedon, knowing they needed to change their strategy. The Hocklyns were being overly cautious and were not just rushing in trying to overwhelm the defenses as they had in past battles.

A few minutes later the battlecruisers, Monarch cruisers, and battlecarriers from defense fleets two, three, and four turned and accelerated toward Admiral Streth's position. It would give him an additional thirteen battlecruisers, twenty-six Monarch cruisers, and seven battle carriers. The strikecruisers from the fleets were pulled in closer to the other shipyards with the light cruisers as cover.

As the ships arrived, they were quickly assigned positions in the defensive formation. Two hundred and twenty-four ships were now under Admiral Streth's direct command, which he had formed into one massive fleet.

"Enemy fleets are joining up and beginning to advance," spoke Clarissa as she focused her eyes on Admiral Streth. She felt nervous and frightened about the upcoming battle; they were so heavily outnumbered. She glanced around the Command Center, noting that a number of the humans also looked frightened. Clarissa stepped closer to Admiral Streth; just being close to him helped to give her confidence about their ultimate survival.

"The AI ships seem to be hanging back behind the Hocklyns," Colonel Grissom added as she studied the tactical display nearest her. "They may be planning to allow the Hocklyns to carry out this next phase of the battle."

"They may still be evaluating their recent attacks," Clarissa suggested, her deep blue eyes gazing at Colonel Grissom.

Admiral Streth activated the ship-to-ship communications on his mini-com so he could speak to all of his ship commanders. "We will advance and engage the enemy," he informed them in a rock steady voice. All fighters to launch immediately. Your targets are the enemy fighters. Once we are heavily engaged the bombers will go in. After the first bomber strike has delivered their weapons, we will withdraw back toward New Tellus Station and the command asteroid fortress. At that point, all shipyards and asteroids will launch their fighters and bombers in another massive strike against the enemy fleet."

Fleet Admiral Johnson was listening and almost allowed herself to smile. It seemed as if Admiral Streth had taken over command of the entire battle. She turned toward Admirals Freeman and Bennett.

"Repeat Fleet Admiral Streth's orders to the shipyards and the asteroid fortresses. It's time to see if our trap is powerful enough to stop this attack."

"Yes, Admiral," Freemen replied as he stepped over to the large communications console and began carrying out Admiral Johnson's orders.

Karla sat down in her command chair and gazed across the large Command Center. It seemed calm and orderly as if everyone's lives were not on the line. Karla knew this coming battle would determine the fate of the entire Federation and their allies.

But then she remembered the story that she and every other Federation child had been told by their parents and their teachers. It was a simple story passed on for generations from the time the Federation had first come into being. Someday the great Admiral Hedon Streth would awaken from cryosleep and lead the Federation to victory over the Hocklyn Slave Empire. Karla was about to find out if that old story was true. She sincerely hoped it was.

Chapter Twenty-Two

Admiral Sheen gazed cryptically at the tactical display and shook her head in deep concern. Over fourteen hundred Hocklyn ships and thirteen AI ships were closing on their position. The fleets had taken up a position directly in front of New Tellus Station and were slowly advancing on the approaching enemy forces. From every starship in the human fleet fighters were launching and accelerating toward the expanding wall of Hocklyn fighters forming up in front of their fleet. The Hocklyns were launching more fighters from their new ships and Amanda knew that they would be badly outnumbered, but that was norm for fighting the Hocklyns.

"All fighters launched," Commander Evans spoke, her eyes focused on the wall of human fighters that was now rapidly approaching the enemy.

"They have to blast a hole through for our bombers," Amanda informed her in a low voice. "We're going to need our Anlon bombers in this if the Fleet is to survive."

Looking at one of the main viewscreens on the front wall of the Command Center, she could see the sprawling image of New Tellus Station, and just behind the station was the massive command asteroid fortress where Richard was. She hoped that she and Richard both survived this battle. Letting out a deep breath, she turned her attention back to the tactical display.

"Fighters are engaged," Lieutenant Stalls reported. On his sensor screen, the myriad of green and red icons began to merge.

Major Arcles dove his Talon fighter down at a sharp angle and heard a solid tone go off indicating he had a firm target lock. Pressing a button on his console a small Hunter missile rocketed away and struck a Hocklyn fighter, obliterating it in a ball of fire. Next to him, Lieutenant Sanders flew in close formation as the pair darted through the Hocklyn formation.

"They're like a swarm of bees," Lacy spoke with anxiety in her voice. "They're everywhere!"

"We need to keep the squadron together," Karl responded as he saw on his tactical screen two green icons, which represented fighters in his squadron vanish. He instantly communicated to the other pilots to form up and stay close so they could support one another. "Work together," Karl spoke as he fired a short burst from his 30 mm cannons at another Hocklyn fighter, damaging it. "Let's clear a path for the bombers!"

Karl knew that with the reinforcements from the new Hocklyn ships they were facing over 7,000 enemy fighters. They were outnumbered three to one. "Make every shot count and don't waste your missiles. Be certain you have a good target lock before firing one."

Looking around, Karl could see hundreds if not thousands of missile trails and the bright flashes, which designated exploding fighters, both Human and Hocklyn. A warning tone suddenly went off in his cockpit, indicating a Hocklyn missile had a target lock on his fighter. He quickly fired off some countermeasures and rolled his Talon fighter. Accelerating rapidly, he turned at a sharp angle with Lacy mirroring his movements. The missile narrowly missed as it flew off harmlessly into space.

"You could walk on all of this ordnance," complained one of his pilots as a line of tracers narrowly missed his fighter.

Karl nodded; there was no need to reply. Even as he watched, two more of his squadron's fighters vanished from his screen. Karl began to wonder if any of them would survive this battle.

"Bombers are launching," Clarissa announced as the Anlon bombers left the fleet's battle carriers and began accelerating toward the swirling mass of human and Hocklyn fighters.

"Order the shipyards and the fortresses to launch their fighters," ordered Hedon, knowing he needed to eliminate the Hocklyn fighters so more of their bombers could get through. He had wanted to hold off on the current bomber strike, but he needed to slow down the Hocklyn fleet's advance to allow New Tellus Station and the command fortress to lock on with their heavier weapons.

"Nearing optimal engagement range of the Hocklyn fleet," Colonel Trist reported from where he was standing in front of one of the tactical displays. Then turning around, he looked at the admiral. "The AI ships are hanging back slightly and are still out of effective range of our Devastator Threes."

"Clarissa, keep a close watch on the AIs," Hedon ordered, wanting to know what the AIs were doing at all times. "I want to know the instant any of them move." The Hocklyns he felt they could handle; the AIs were another matter entirely. It made him nervous the way they were just sitting behind the Hocklyn fleet, watching.

From the shipyards and fortresses an additional 3,000 Talon, fighters launched and accelerated swiftly toward the battle. They were fully armed with Hunter interceptor missiles and full loads for their 30 mm cannons.

The original fighter strike had managed to thin the Hocklyn fighters in one section sufficiently to allow the attacking bombers to reach the Hocklyn fleet. With escorting fighters leading the way, the Anlon bombers fought their way through the final defending Hocklyn fighters before pouncing on the enemy ships. However, the Hocklyns had been expecting this, and defensive missile fire became intense as the bombers closed to engagement range. Bomber after bomber exploded in fiery deaths as interceptor missiles found their targets.

"Lock your missiles onto the escort cruisers," ordered Colonel Grant grimly as he saw two more bombers in his squadron burst apart from defensive fire. "Fire your missiles and let's get the hell out of here!"

Pressing down firmly on the four small red buttons on his console, all four nuclear-tipped Shrike missiles underneath the bomber's wings launched toward their intended target. Grant didn't hang around to see if they struck instead he swerved his bomber around, nearly ramming a Hocklyn fighter in the process, and then accelerated rapidly back toward the fleet. A sudden warning alarm sounded in his cockpit, but the strike commander never saw the Hocklyn missile that struck the fuselage of his bomber, destroying it in a fiery blast.

Fleet Commodore Resmunt felt elation as the human fighters died and most of their bomber strike was annihilated just short of his fleet. He had ordered all of his ships to load their missile tubes with interceptors in anticipation of the human bomber strike, and it had paid off.

"Damage reports are coming in from the fleet," First Leader Ganth reported. "We lost eighteen escort cruisers with twenty-two more heavily damaged in the attack."

"Their crews served us well," replied Resmunt, feeling aggravated that the humans had managed to destroy and damage so many of his escort cruisers. "Honor has come for them today. We will continue to advance and engage the human fleet. We have another surprise for them, one they will not be expecting that will ensure us a quick and complete victory."

Ganth nodded; he was not sure what the Fleet Commodore was speaking about other than it involved the AIs. "Humans have launched additional fighters."

"Order all fortresses and shipyards to launch their bomber strikes, additional strikes to be made at their discretion," ordered Hedon, seeing that less than four hundred bombers were returning from the first strike. It had been costly, but it had damaged the Hocklyn fleet. The next strike would cause even more damage. This would be a battle of attrition. He needed to weaken the Hocklyn fleet sufficiently so the shipyards, the fortresses, and the defensive satellites could finish them off.

"Hocklyn fleet is in engagement range," Clarissa reported as she swiftly checked to ensure all of the battleship's weapons were ready to fire.

"All ships, fire," Hedon ordered without hesitation. "Unlimited use of Devastator Threes is authorized." Now the battle would really begin. Hedon let out a heavy sigh, knowing that many Federation personnel were about to die.

The massive fleet battle began. Both sides were now launching missiles and firing their energy weapons. Railguns fired non-stop as space became filled with tens of thousands of explosive rounds, which impacted on ship's screens. They wavered and then failed as the heavy weapons fire overloaded them. Whenever that happened, the vulnerable ships were instantly targeted and normally died a few seconds later. Nuclear explosions ravaged screens and ship's hulls. A human battlecruiser saw its shields go down and almost instantly six nuclear missiles struck the ship's armored hull. The massive detonations split the ship into four pieces and additional inbound ordnance turned the remains into gaseous vapor and burning metal.

A Hocklyn dreadnought's screen failed as two Devastator Three 40-megaton explosions tore into it. Two bright fireballs were all that signified where the dreadnought had been. Along both lines of advancing ships, bright explosions pointed out the deaths of warships.

Amanda felt the WarStorm shudder violently and the lights flickered; she glanced inquiring over at Colonel Bryson.

"Hocklyn energy beam penetrated the shield," he reported as he checked the damage control console. "Only minor damage."

"Fleet's lost two battlecruisers, one battlecarrier, two strikecruisers, six Monarchs and fourteen light cruisers," Lieutenant Stalls reported grimly as the total of destroyed ships rapidly grew. "The next fighter strike is going in as well as the combined bomber strike from the shipyards and the fortresses."

Amanda knew that this meant that over 2,400 bombers would be following the fighters. That should cause the Hocklyns some major damage. Glancing at the viewscreen, she saw that neither New Tellus Station nor the command asteroid fortress had as of yet come under fire though they would momentarily.

Fleet Admiral Johnson nodded in satisfaction as the weapons on the shipyard finally began locking onto the Hocklyn fleet. She knew that the command fortress, a scant five hundred kilometers away, would also now be getting weapons locks. "Fire!" she ordered. It was time to show the Hocklyns the power of New Tellus Station.

Instantly from the shipyard and the fortress space became filled with violet power beams, orange-red pulse lasers, and missile trails all targeting the slowly advancing Hocklyn fleet. The missile platforms around New Tellus Station also began to fire. Missile after missile blasted off, accelerating toward their targets in the approaching Hocklyn fleet.

Fleet Commodore Resmunt smiled as he saw the incoming bomber strike. Once they were annihilated, he could destroy the defending human fleet in front of him. Then the smile faded as the large asteroid and the shipyard opened up with a murderous fire upon his fleet. More Hocklyn ships began to die. Dreadnoughts, war cruisers, and escorts began to rapidly vanish from the tactical display as the heavy wall of human weapons fire destroyed them. Walking swiftly over to the communications station, he sent a quick message to the AI commander. It was time to end this battle before his fleet suffered too many more casualties.

Aboard the AI ship, the command AI had been expecting this request from the Fleet Commodore. They had learned much from their initial attacks, the information had been assimilated, and a new battle plan had been developed. "Send the order," the command AI spoke toward the AI at Communications. Instantly a message was sent into deep space where the main AI force was waiting.

Fleet Admiral Johnson watched the inbound bomber strike fixedly. This one would be going after the Hocklyn fleet's war cruisers. If they could destroy or damage enough of them, the shipyards and the fortresses should be able to handle the remaining Hocklyn ships. Already the weapons fire from the station and the fortress was having a telling effect on the Hocklyn fleet. Its advance had nearly stalled as space became littered with burning and dying ships.

A loud warning alarm suddenly began sounding, and Karla and Admiral Freeman both looked at the large tactical display in shock. Orange icon after orange icon were appearing in the gravity well of the planet. Hundreds of massive AI ships were jumping into the battle.

"It's over," Karla uttered in shock. Her shoulders drooped as she watched the AI ships open fire on the massive defenses of New Tellus. "We can't stand up to that many AI ships. Our defenses were never designed to stop an AI fleet of this size."

Admiral Freeman studied the screen for a few moments before replying. "Two hundred and sixty AI ships have jumped into the gravity well of New Tellus. They are targeting all six shipyards as well as the fortresses."

"Do we call the bombers back?" Admiral Bennett asked, his eyes wide as he stared at all the orange threat icons now on the tactical display. "They can retarget the AIs."

"No," replied Karla, shaking her head bleakly "Have them continue their current attack. Their weapons aren't strong enough to be a danger to the AIs."

"What about the AIs?" Admiral Freeman asked.

"We will do what we have to do," Karla uttered determinedly, knowing the battle was lost. "Contact Admiral Teleck and order him to return to Ceres; his fleet can be better used to protect the Sol system. The battle here will soon be over, and we can't afford to sacrifice his ships needlessly. We can only hope to destroy enough of the AI ships so Earth and Ceres can destroy the rest. Order the fortresses and the type two battle stations to concentrate their fire on the AIs."

Karla let out a deep and ragged breath as she gazed at the multiple viewscreens that were now filled with the deadly AI ships. She knew she had failed to protect the Federation. She could only hope that they could take enough of the enemy ships with them to give Earth and Ceres a chance to survive.

"AI ships are engaging," Clarissa spoke with a tinge of fear in her normally calm voice. She had been visibly shocked when the ship's sensors had started recording the new AI ships jumping in all around them.

Hedon's eyes were checking one of the tactical screens as he desperately tried to think of what could be done to salvage the suddenly reversed tactical situation. He knew that the new AI ships had more combined firepower than everything New Tellus had to defend itself with.

The screens of the StarStrike suddenly lit up with several bright flashes, and the ship shook violently. On the numerous viewscreens on the front wall of the Command Center, flashes of burning light could be seen everywhere.

"The new AI ships are deploying sublight missiles as well as energy beams," Clarissa continued as she rapidly analyzed the attack. "Their sublight missiles contain what appears to be some type of anti-matter warhead with an explosive force of over fifty megatons."

"Anti-matter?" Colonel Trist spoke, his eyes growing wide as the StarStrike was hit by another missile. "I thought anti-matter was only theoretical." He saw the ship's screen was holding, but just barely.

"We've been able to produce it in the labs in small amounts," Clarissa replied as she became more involved in defending the StarStrike.

She was using the ship's lasers to intercept some of the sublight missiles. It was all being done in milliseconds as she took over more of the ship's defensive systems. She was also establishing an explosive flak screen between the StarStrike and the AI ship that had been targeting them, attempting to destroy the missiles as they came through it. Several large explosions in the flak field indicated some degree of success.

"We knew the AI's science was far ahead of ours," Hedon replied, his face turning pale as the number of fleet ships that were dying grew. He quickly activated his ship-to-ship communications, knowing what he had to do. "All strikecruisers are to engage the AIs immediately. Two light cruisers will escort each strikecruiser on your attack runs. Good luck."

In space, every surviving strikecruiser targeted the AI spheres with their Devastator Threes as a pair of light cruisers moved to give them covering fire. The fortresses as well as all the type two defensive battle stations switched their Devastator Threes from the Hocklyn fleet to the AI ships. Computer programs quickly calculated attack vectors and hundreds of Devastator Three missiles left their launch tubes to impact on the shields of the AIs.

Over a dozen AI spheres felt the wrath of the deadly 40-megaton warheads as they struck smashing holes in their screens. Instantly through the small holes more missiles flew. In the space of two minutes, fourteen AI ships died in massive explosions, but so did over thirty of the strikecruisers. The AI ships knew which ships were a danger now and were targeting them with massive missile and energy beam strikes. The remaining strikecruisers didn't hesitate as they saw their fellow ships die; they continued to close the range and fire their missiles in a desperate attempt to destroy as many AI ships as possible before they too were destroyed. Everyone knew that no Federation warship would be leaving this battle.

AI ships were also firing against the fortresses, the type two battle stations, and the shipyards. Shipyard Clements was already heavily damaged, and six AI ships were attacking the station, spearing it with their energy beams and blasting its energy screen with anti-matter missiles. The shipyard had managed to get a second fusion generator operating and had reestablished their energy shield and power to their remaining weapons. A crew of volunteers had remained behind to try and save the valuable shipyard.

The defending fortress managed to take out two of the attacking AI ships with Devastator Threes before the AIs managed to knock down the shipyard's weakened energy screen. Two well-placed anti-matter missiles and the shipyard ceased to exist. All that remained of Clements was a glowing debris field.

The AIs then turned their attention to the fortress and began pummeling it with their anti-matter missiles. The screen wavered as massive explosions hammered it, then it failed in one small area and an anti-matter warhead slammed into the surface. A huge glowing hole over a kilometer wide and half a kilometer deep was blasted out of its surface, but then the shield strengthened, and the brief hole shut. The fortress continued to fire with its crew knowing that the AI's anti-matter weapons were capable of destroying it if enough could get through the wavering energy screen.

The bomber strike flew toward the embattled Hocklyn fleet. Suddenly two AI ships appeared in their path and bombers began to die in fiery explosions as Hocklyn short-range energy beams began to take them out. In moments, hundreds were gone and then the others swept around the two AI spheres and targeted the Hocklyn ships. Hundreds more died as the survivors fired off their missiles. Very few would make it back as the two AI ships continued to kill. In the Hocklyn fleet, hundreds of missiles impacted and more Hocklyn ships died. Six war cruisers and sixty-two escort cruisers were annihilated by the bomber strike.

Fleet Commodore Resmunt smiled in satisfaction seeing the destruction the AIs were delivering to the human forces. The bomber strike had hurt, but it would not save the humans. "Split the fleet into its individual war fleets," ordered Resmunt to First Leader Ganth, knowing the battle was now won. "We will move toward the planet and commence bombardment."

First Leader Ganth nodded. Much honor was coming to the fleet and, once this system was destroyed, they would move on to the other human worlds. With the addition of the new AI ships, the human worlds would rapidly fall. If all went well, Ganth would soon become a War Leader.

The WarStorm shook as if a hammer had struck it. The lights in the Command Center went out and then came back on, but much dimmer. Several consoles shorted out, sending bright arcs of sparks across the room. Several damage control people hurried over and shut down the damaged consoles.

"We took an anti-matter hit just above Engineering," Commander Evans reported as the damage report came in over her mini-com. "The main fusion reactor is down, and we are running on the secondary reactors. The screen is back up, but it's barely holding, and we don't have the power to fire the power beams or the pulse lasers any longer."

Amanda nodded in understanding. She coughed several times as the Command Center filled with smoke from the damaged consoles. This was it, then. She wished she could say goodbye to Richard. "Load all missiles tubes with Devastator Threes and target the Hocklyn fleet. At least we can take some of them with us. Order all ships except the strikecruisers to target the Hocklyns; there is little the rest of us can do against the AIs."

Heavy missile fire erupted from the WarStorm and Amanda watched with grim satisfaction as a Hocklyn dreadnought died. The ship then shifted its fire to a nearby war cruiser.

The other ships of Second Fleet joined the WarStorm as it continued to close with the Hocklyns. A battlecruiser died, and then a Monarch exploded in a blaze of light as two war cruisers bracketed it with nuclear missiles. Two light cruisers interposed themselves between a heavily damaged human battlecruiser and a Hocklyn dreadnought in an attempt to allow the cruiser to get its energy screen back online. Both died in nuclear fire as the dreadnought turned its wrath upon them. But the battlecruiser raised its shield back up and began to fire once more upon the dreadnought. Two minutes later the dreadnought exploded as its self-destructs initiated from the severe damage the ship had suffered.

Amanda watched all of this on the viewscreens and the tactical display. Her fleet was dying, and there was nothing she could do to stop it. It was less than a minute later when another of the deadly sublight missiles penetrated and struck the bow of the WarStorm, blasting a massive hole in the front of the ship. Numerous compartments were instantly exposed to vacuum and fires began spreading in other areas. Hundreds of lives were snuffed out in an instant.

Amanda felt herself slammed forward and her head struck the command console. Everything instantly went black.

Commander Evans picked herself up off the floor and rushed over to the admiral. Amanda was unconscious and had a vicious bruise on her forehead. The air in the Command Center was becoming difficult to breathe as smoke filled the room from several more electrical fires. Looking over at Lieutenant Stalls, she made a quick decision. "Lieutenant Stalls, I want you and Lieutenant Trask to get the admiral to a shuttle. Get away from the WarStorm to another ship. We're not going to last much longer."

"What about you?" Angela yelled as she rushed over to the admiral who was being put on a stretcher by two medics.

"I will do my duty," replied Evans, somberly. She looked down at Admiral Sheen on the stretcher and then back over at Lieutenant Stalls. "Tell the admiral when she awakes that the WarStorm fought with honor, and her crew died for the Federation."

Benjamin swallowed and nodded as he turned and led Angela and the two medics carrying the stretcher out of the Command Center. He knew they didn't have much time to get out of the dying warship.

Commander Evans waited until she heard a confirmation from the flight bay that the admiral's shuttle, as well as several others with injured crewmembers, had launched. "Fine," she said turning toward Colonel Bryson the executive officer. "Activate the sublight drive at one hundred percent and target the nearest AI ship. We will ram the son of a bitch!"

Colonel Bryson nodded as he carried out the order. He knew the WarStorm was finished, and now all that mattered was how they were going to die. Going to Navigation, he set the course and then looked up at the viewscreen as the targeted AI ship grew rapidly on the screen. The WarStorm was shuddering violently as several energy beams struck it and another anti-matter missile vaporized a large section of the aft side of the ship.

Samantha sat down in the command chair and looked at the viewscreen. Explosions were continually rocking the ship as she eyed the large red buttons, which controlled the ship's self-destructs, hoping they wouldn't go off before they struck the AI ship. It was strangely silent in the Command Center as the remaining crew watched the viewscreen.

The WarStorm was a burning wreck when it hit the AI ship's energy screen. The self-destructs on the ship instantly detonated, and the screen went down as the flaming wreckage struck the AI's armored hull. Other Second Fleet warships instantly launched Devastator and Devastator Three missiles at the AI ship, destroying it in a series of fiery nuclear explosions. Second Fleet's flagship had died, but it had taken an AI with it.

"WarStorm is down," Captain Reynolds reported in a stunned voice. "She rammed an AI ship, destroying it in the process."

"Admiral Sheen," Colonel Trist muttered in shock, looking over at Admiral Streth.

"She did what she had to do," replied Hedon, feeling numb at the loss. He knew that Richard had probably witnessed Amanda's sacrifice from the Command Center of his asteroid fortress.

First Jacob and now Amanda, Hedon thought as he looked at the tactical displays, which showed a steadily deteriorating situation. His shoulders drooped as he felt the devastating losses of war. Two of his oldest friends were now gone, and he strongly suspected that he would soon be joining them. With a heavy sigh, he knew he would soon be seeing his brother Taylor and Lendle. The only thing left was to decide how to die. He turned and looked over at Clarissa who was standing next to him.

"Clarissa, I'm turning command of the StarStrike and the Tellus over to you. Your targets are the AI ships. I want to destroy as many of them as possible. Our survival is not paramount."

"Yes, Sir," replied Clarissa, feeling a strange pain at knowing Admiral Sheen was gone. She also knew that her own life could probably be measured in minutes. She wished there was someway she could tell Ariel goodbye.

Richard had watched in anguish as the WarStorm rammed the AI ship, knowing he was powerless to do anything. For a brief moment, he had felt his anger nearly take over. Even down this deep inside the command asteroid, he could feel his command vibrating from the anti-matter strikes that were getting through the screen.

"Keep firing Devastator Threes," he ordered, knowing he did not have time to mourn. All he could do was kill as many AIs as possible to avenge his wife and then join her in death.

Major Arcles had gathered the survivors of his squadron around him. There was one notable exception, Lieutenant Sanders' Anlon fighter was not among them. "Did anyone see what happened to Lieutenant Sanders?" Karl demanded as he tried to look out of his cockpit windows to see if he could spot her fighter.

"I think she took a missile hit," one of the other pilots reported.

"Did she eject?" Karl asked as his world spun. He couldn't imagine going on without Lacy.

"No, I didn't see anything," the pilot replied. "I don't think she got out."

Karl didn't know what else to say. Most of the Hocklyn fighters were gone, and there was nothing his remaining fighters could do against Hocklyn warships or the AIs. All he could do was keep his fighters away from the fighting and wait until the battle was over, and then hope there was somewhere they could land.

Admiral Tolsen had watched the WarStorm die and knew that in all likelihood Admiral Sheen had died with her ship. He knew it was only a matter of time before his own flagship, the Defiant, would meet the same fate. Already over half of his fleet had been destroyed and his remaining ships were backed up next to New Tellus Station, offering what protection he could give to the now besieged shipyard. Everywhere he looked was death and destruction. The tactical screen was full of red and orange threat icons, with the green Federation icons steadily dwindling.

"This is it then," Colonel Arnett spoke in a somber voice, her eyes glued to the main viewscreen. Flashes of light were visible everywhere as devastator and anti-matter missiles detonated against ship's shields.

"We will take a lot of them with us," Race replied with determination as the Defiant fired its main power beam batteries at a nearby Hocklyn escort cruiser. He watched in satisfaction as one of the beams penetrated the shield and tore a huge, glowing rent in the hull.

Colonel Arnett nodded. She had hoped someday to be able to raise a family; she knew now that day would never come.

Hedon felt the StarStrike shake badly as another nuke hit the hull. In the last ten minutes, Clarissa had taken out four AI ships with the StarStrike and the Tellus and was currently targeting another. On the main viewscreen, which was pointed at New Tellus, he could see the horrifying flashes of nuclear weapons striking the surface of the planet. This must be what the ships defending the old Federation had witnessed, he realized, feeling numb as Clarissa turned both battleships in a tight turn and accelerated toward her next target.

The command AI watched with interest as the human's two battleships fought with uncanny precision as they destroyed AI ship after AI ship. They seemed to be unstoppable.

"It is as we postulated," one of the AIs in front of the data screens reported. "That battleship is commanded by an AI. We must destroy it."

"Send the virus," the command AI ordered. From the data they had analyzed in all the battles with the humans, they had determined there was a high probability that the humans had two highly competent AIs in their fleet. There had been discussions about attempting to turn the AIs against the humans, but it had finally been decided to destroy them instead.

On board the StarStrike, a computer virus was inserted into the ship's computer system through an open communications channel. The virus was instantly detected and firewalls slammed down, then individual systems disconnected from the ship's mainframe, allowing the ship to continue to fight. However, the damage was done. This virus searched for and found the AI controlling the ship.

The first thing Hedon knew that something was seriously wrong was when Clarissa's holographic image suddenly vanished from his side with a shocked look upon her face. A moment later, the computer console that contained her program exploded and shorted out.

"Clarissa is offline," Colonel Grissom reported as her hands ran over a console. "She is no longer responding."

Colonel Trist ran over to Clarissa's computer console and jerked the front off it. Inside was a large green crystal that contained the matrix for the AIs complicated program. The crystal was cracked and looked as if it had been burned. Trist shook his head at Hedon. "She's gone, Sir."

Hedon nodded. "Pull us back to New Tellus Station; we will make our final stand there. Hedon passed on the order to all of the surviving ships. They would die together.

Fleet Admiral Johnson looked at the steadily worsening situation knowing that the trap they had been building for all of these years was going to fail. They had never intended for it to stand up to nearly three hundred AI ships.

"Admiral, screen two!" Admiral Bennett suddenly yelled in consternation.

Looking up, she saw that one of the asteroid fortresses was under attack by nearly forty AI ships. The fortresses shields had finally failed, and its surface was being bombarded with anti-matter missiles. The asteroid seemed to be glowing from the massive amounts of energy that was being released, and then it suddenly broke apart as the intense pressure from the attack finally overwhelmed it.

The defense grid was also under attack by the Hocklyn fleet and a group of AI ships. Satellites, missile platforms, and even defensive battle stations were being destroyed in massive numbers. Over thirty nuclear detonations had already been detected on the surface of New Tellus.

Karla looked over at Admiral Freeman, knowing that she had failed the Federation. "Send a message to President Kincaid and inform him that we will soon lose the New Tellus system to the AIs. We will try to inflict as much damage as possible in the hope that the Sol system can survive the coming attack."

Admiral Freeman nodded and went over to communications to send the message. Just as he was about to transmit it, the main sensor screen began screaming its alarm again.

"New contacts jumping into the gravity well of the planet," the sensor operator reported, looking confused. "I don't recognize the ships."

"Put one up on the screen," ordered Karla, feeling baffled. Were these more AI ships of a type they hadn't encountered before?

One of the new ships appeared on the main viewscreen. The ship was over one thousand meters in length and no more than two hundred in width. A large sphere nearly four hundred meters in diameter was at the front.

"Admiral, the new ships are firing on the AIs!" the colonel sitting at one of the tactical consoles suddenly called out.

"Who the hell are they?" demanded Admiral Freeman as he rushed back to Karla's side.

"They're Albanian!" Major Ackerman the Intelligence officer spoke. "Those ships are similar to their research vessels, but much larger."

"Albanian?" Admiral Freeman said feeling faint. "But the Albanians have refused to participate in the war; why are they here now?"

"I don't care why," Fleet Admiral Johnson commented with a wolfish smile as she watched an AI ship explode on one of the viewscreens. "But their weapons are tearing right through the AI's shields. See if we can contact whoever is in charge of that fleet!"

In space, four hundred Albanian battlecruisers had jumped inside the gravity well of New Tellus. Each was armed with energy weapons specifically designed to penetrate an AI ship's energy screen. AI ship after AI ship died as the powerful energy weapons flashed through the defensive shields as if they were butter. The beams impacted the armored hulls and easily cut deep into the heart of the 1,500-meter spheres, causing them to self-destruct. In less than a minute, sixty AI ships had been annihilated in bright explosions of sheer energy.

The command AI stared in shock at a ship of the new arrivals on a viewscreen. "Those ships can't exist," the command AI stated in a disbelieving voice. "They're dead!" For the first time, the command AI was at a loss as to what to do.

On Earth, the Albanian ambassador stepped into the main chamber of the Federation Council, which was in emergency session. He had demanded an immediate meeting to address the senators.

President Kincaid watched as Ambassador Tureen walked to the front of the council table and stopped. He was at a loss as to why the Albanians had demanded this meeting. The ambassador then turned around to face the council.

"As you know, the AIs have launched an attack against the New Tellus system. What you don't know as of yet is that an additional two hundred and sixty AI ships have jumped into the system and are currently destroying the defenses around New Tellus."

"Two hundred and sixty," moaned Senator Fulbright looking accusingly at President Kincaid. "We're doomed!"

"How do you know this, Ambassador Tureen?" President Kincaid demanded, his eyes focusing on the Albanian. "And why are you telling us this now?" He knew if what the Albanian ambassador had just said was true, then the Federation was finished. They could not fight that many AI ships. He doubted if even the massive defenses around Ceres could stop that many AIs.

The ambassador took a deep breath and then began speaking again with his eyes taking on a haunted look. "We know that because thousands of years ago our remote ancestors created the AIs."

"What?" Senator Barnes from Ceres asked, his eyes growing wide in disbelief. "The Altons created the AIs; we all know that!"

The ambassador nodded. "We are the Altons, or at least their remote descendants. When our research expedition originally found Earth, it was decided to take some of your people and animals to populate another world closer to the center of our galaxy. You see, at that time there was a great debate amongst my people about the AIs we had created."

"I don't understand," Senator Fulbright muttered, confused. "Your people created the AIs?"

"They were created to serve us, to make our lives easier," Tureen explained with a hint of deep disapproval in his voice. "But many of us felt the AIs would be our undoing, that we would become too dependent upon them. And there was a possibility that at some point in time, due to the way they were programmed, they could become dangerous."

"What do you mean become dangerous?" asked President Kincaid, leaning forward, wanting to hear what the Albanian ambassador had to say.

"They were given as one of their core commands to protect the Alton race and the center of the galaxy from any aggressor," Ambassador Tureen explained. "When the Alton race in the center of the galaxy died out, they eliminated the command to protect the Altons and decided the only way to protect the center of the galaxy was to conquer the entire galaxy."

"Which they have been doing for the past several thousand years," spoke Senator Barnes. "Where do your people come into all of this if you're really Altons?"

"As I said, we were part of the exploratory expedition," Tureen continued. "It was decided that some of your people would be settled on a world where someday they could be used to control the AIs if things got out of hand. Part of the crew remained behind and swore never to build another AI and promised to watch over Earth. We have also kept a discreet watch over the AIs in the center of the galaxy as well. It was only when the Hocklyns discovered the old Federation that we realized we had made a serious mistake. The Federation was not yet strong enough to face both the Hocklyns and the AIs. We had also grown complacent after all the time that had passed. We didn't have the ships at that time to intercede and save the old Federation."

"So what do we do now?" asked President Kincaid, worriedly. "The AIs and the Hocklyn will soon finish off the defenses at New Tellus and then descend upon us here. We can't possibly hope to fight that many AI ships."

Ambassador Tureen looked slowly across the worried group of Federation senators. "Immediately after the old Federation fail we built a fleet of warships to be used in case the AIs ever found us or Earth. That entire fleet has been kept in stasis until it was needed. A short time ago we finished reactivating the entire fleet, and it has jumped into the New Tellus system and is in the process of annihilating the AI fleet there."

All the senators grew quiet as they stared wide eyed at the ambassador. "But you're pacifists!" protested Senator Fulbright. "Everyone knows that."

"Not all of us," Tureen responded as he looked at the senator from Serenity with a steady gaze. "While it is true we will do everything we can not to become involved in a conflict, we knew this one would arrive at our doorstep someday."

"Then we've won the war!" Senator Fulbright shouted, his eyes glowing with delight. "We no longer have to fear the Hocklyns or the AIs."

"No, Senator," Ambassador Tureen spoke sadly with a shake of his head. "We have won the first major battle against the AIs and the Hocklyns, but the war has just barely begun."

Chapter Twenty-Three

Fleet Commodore Resmunt looked in shock at the tactical display, feeling disbelief at what it was showing. Hundreds of strange ships had jumped to the human's rescue and were annihilating the AI ships. On the main viewscreen an energy beam that seemed to be unstoppable smashed through an AI ship's screen, blasting a hole deep inside the sphere's hull causing tremendous damage. The AI ship finally exploded as its self-destructs initiated. The AI's energy beams and new sublight missiles seemed to have no effect against the screens of the newcomers. Massive anti-matter explosions played harmlessly on the powerful screens, and the AI's energy beams also seemed ineffective.

"Who are they?" demanded First Leader Ganth in anger as he saw Hocklyn ships beginning to die in growing numbers as the battered human defenses turned all of their remaining weapons against the Hocklyn fleet. He saw his hope for increased honor and advancement rapidly fading.

"I don't know, but they are destroying the AIs," Resmunt hissed in frustration, seeing his expected victory vanishing before his eyes. His well planned attack was falling apart, and he knew he was now facing imminent defeat.

"Commodore Aanith and War Leader Osbith are beginning to withdraw their fleets," Ganth added with growing irritation as he saw their fleets beginning to break contact with the humans and flee toward the edge of the gravity well.

"AIs are starting to jump out," another Hocklyn reported as several AI ships disappeared from the tactical screen as they initiated their jump drives to escape.

"Prepare to withdraw," Resmunt ordered, his large dark eyes glued to the tactical display. If the AIs were leaving, then he had no other choice. To remain and face the human defenses and these new ships was suicide. "These new aliens are too powerful; we must withdraw and reevaluate the situation."

White space vortexes were forming in front of numerous AI ships as they attempted to escape the growing disaster. Every AI ship had descriptions of their creator's ships in their computer files, and there was no question that the attacking ships were indeed Alton. For the first time in their long history, the AIs knew fear. Their ancient creators had suddenly come back to life.

"All ships are to execute immediate withdrawal," the command AI ordered as it studied one of the Alton ships on a tactical display. There could be no doubt; the ship was Alton and their weapons were deadly to the AI ships.

Many ships had already jumped, but others were hesitating. It was difficult to accept that, after so many years, the Altons had made an appearance. All historical records indicated they had completely died out thousands of years ago. This was confusing to the AIs as to why the records were not true.

They would withdraw back to AI controlled space and evaluate the new situation to come up with future strategy. The presence of live Altons would seriously change the AI's galactic plan. What role the Hocklyns and the other three proxy races would play after this would be determined later.

The command AI watched as another AI ship exploded under the attack of a single Alton cruiser. The Altons could pose a major threat to their Empire. From the AI history records, the Altons were described as a peaceful and benevolent race, far different from the ones attacking the AI ships now.

"We shall withdraw," the command AI ordered the AI hovering in front of the navigation controls.

Seconds later the command AI sphere vanished into a swirling white vortex, fleeing the battle.

"More AIs are leaving," Ganth reported as their masters began to flee en mass. "The command AI ship has just jumped."

"Then we must leave also," spoke Resmunt with a rasping breath, finally admitting defeat. "We must preserve as much of our fleet as we can for future battles."

The High Council would be extremely upset to learn that the attack had failed. However, what other choice did he have? If these new ships could destroy AI ships with such impunity, they would make short work of the Hocklyn fleet. He also knew that, at the moment, the borders of the Hocklyn Slave Empire were extremely weak, as most of the ships had been appropriated to take part in this attack.

For a long moment, First Leader Ganth stood still as he thought about the commodore's words. Honor would not be served in sacrificing their ships uselessly against an enemy whose ships could not be destroyed. It might be best to return to the Empire and preserve their ships to fight the humans and this potential new enemy.

"We must withdraw to seek honor another day," he concluded, agreeing with the commodore. "I will pass the order to disengage and make for the edge of the planet's gravity well."

"Order all ships to set jump coordinates to the system we recently jumped from," Fleet Commodore Resmunt ordered. The Liberator shuddered violently as a human nuclear missile detonated against the warship's energy screen. "We will stop there and make basic repairs before we start back to Hocklyn space."

"This will be a long war," First Leader Ganth spoke as he watched a Hocklyn war cruiser explode on the main viewscreen. The human ships were now on the offensive as the AIs were jumping out and the Hocklyn ships were turning to withdraw.

The humans were intensifying their attacks now that they could focus their efforts only on the Hocklyn fleet. The Hocklyn Slave Empire had finally found opponents worthy of combat. The First Leader looked at the viewscreen at one of the new ships that had jumped in and was in the process of destroying one of the last AI ships still present, wondering what this might mean for the Empire. In his entire life as a warrior, he had never imagined there could be a serious threat to the Empire itself. He now knew that supposition was wrong.

"No!" Second Leader Jaseth screamed in frustration as the Viden turned away from the human Monarch cruiser it had been engaging and began to withdraw. "We can destroy that human ship. Its energy screen is weakening!"

"We have our orders," War Leader Versith spoke evenly from the command pedestal. "We are to withdraw to the edge of the planet's gravity well and jump into hyperspace."

"Turn the fleet back!" Jaseth demanded his face marked in anger as he whirled around to face Versith. "We must destroy the humans!"

"The battle is over," spoke First Leader Trion, gazing disapprovingly at the young Second Leader. "Our orders are to preserve our fleet for the future, and our duty is to obey. Honor is served by obedience to the Fleet Commodore."

"Fleet Commodore Resmunt is weak and foolish," continued Jaseth scathingly, staring at War Leader Versith rebelliously. "The others will follow your orders. You are the most respected War Leader in the entire fleet. Order all the fleets to resume the attack!"

"Second Leader Jaseth, you need to go to your quarters," War Leader Versith ordered coldly, his eyes focusing sharply on the young, out of control warrior. Jaseth was beginning to disrupt activity in the War Room from his words of disrespect. Other Hocklyns were gazing at him uneasily. This could not be allowed to continue.

"Give me command of the Viden!" Jaseth demanded, his eyes growing even darker with the rage burning inside of him. "I will finish the destruction of the human ship. Honor is before us!"

Versith glanced over at First Leader Trion and nodded. Trion instantly gestured toward the two heavily armed Protectors standing at the closed hatch to the War Room. "Take Second Leader Jaseth to his quarters and make sure he stays there until I say otherwise," Trion ordered.

As the two Protectors escorted the visibly agitated Second Leader from the War Room, Trion stopped them at the hatch and spoke to Jaseth. "You have not added to your honor today by your behavior. Think about that as you spend the next few days in your quarters." Trion nodded and the Protectors opened the hatch and left with the still visibly agitated Jaseth.

Versith shook his head, realizing that the young warrior was not going to reach his potential if these actions continued. Glancing at the tactical display, he saw they were rapidly pulling away from the human ships and that they had stopped their pursuit. The last few AIs were still disengaging and jumping away, to where Versith had no idea. He hadn't been aware to begin with that the massive AI fleet had been following them.

His attention turned back to the main viewscreen, which was focused on one of the new ships that had jumped in and attacked the AIs. From their design, it was obvious these were not human ships but ships of an ally. An ally that was amazingly powerful. Versith knew that the Empire was going to have to change if it hoped to continue. Fortunately, the Hocklyn Slave Empire was large and had thousands of ships to draw upon as well as numerous slave worlds. All might be needed if the Empire was to survive this new threat posed by the humans and this new mysterious ally of theirs.

The Viden and what remained of its fleet reached the edge of the gravity well and crossed it. Almost instantly white spatial vortexes began forming in front of the individual ships. The Viden surged forward into the swirling vortex and jumped into the safety of hyperspace.

Admiral Streth leaned back in his command chair and breathed a deep sigh of relief. He had just finished speaking to the admiral in charge of the fleet that had jumped in and had confirmed that it was indeed Albanian.

"What's the latest status of the AI and Hocklyn fleets?" Hedon demanded as he looked over at Captain Reynolds at sensors.

It was difficult getting used to the fact that Clarissa was no longer here. The beautiful blonde AI was gone and would no longer grace the Command Center with her presence. It would take some getting used to.

"The last undamaged AI ship has jumped," Reynolds reported as the last orange threat icon vanished from the tactical displays. "The remaining Hocklyn fleet is withdrawing and is nearing the edge of New Tellus's gravity well. Most of them have already jumped."

"Sir, we have several shuttles from the WarStorm requesting permission to dock," Captain Duncan said suddenly. Then her eyes widened as she received another report. "Admiral Sheen is on one of the shuttles and is badly injured!"

Admiral Streth quickly unbuckled his harness and stood up. "Have the medics meet the shuttles in the flight bay. I want Admiral Sheen rushed to the med bay as quickly as possible. Captain Duncan, contact Admiral Andrews on the command fortress and inform him that his wife is alive but injured." Hedon couldn't describe what he was feeling at the moment. He had thought he had lost Amanda to the AIs but now here she was.

"I'm glad Admiral Sheen is alive," Colonel Trist said in a serious tone as he studied one of the tactical displays and the wreckage that was everywhere. "I hope she pulls through."

"She will," replied Hedon, confidently. "That woman won't die, not with so much life still ahead of her." Then Hedon paused as he looked at the mess on the tactical screens. "I want every shuttle we have in the fleet launched to begin rescue operations. See if we can get the most severely damaged ships into the repair bays on the shipyards. If you need me, I will be in the med bay."

"Yes, Sir," Colonel Trist replied with a nod. He knew there was nothing he could say that could stop the admiral from going and checking on his lifelong friend.

"Sir," Colonel Grissom spoke as she gazed over with sadness in her eyes at the damaged AI console. "What should I do about Clarissa?"

Hedon paused for a moment. "I don't know. Have the computer technicians remove the memory crystal and put it in a safe place. If we ever get back to Careth, Lieutenant Johnson can take a look at it. I don't know if there is anything she can do as badly damaged as the crystal is."

Grissom nodded. She would make sure the crystal was well taken care of. Clarissa had been an important part of the crew and of Federation history and she would make sure that the crystal was delivered safely to Lieutenant Johnson. If anyone could restore the AI, it would be the talented lieutenant.

A few minutes later, Admiral Streth was in the med bay as Admiral Sheen was brought in. A doctor was with her and, after giving instructions to several other physicians, turned toward Hedon.

"She has a severe concussion," he reported. "However, she should be fine with the medical technology we now have."

"How soon before she awakes?" asked Hedon, feeling relieved to know that Amanda would be okay. He had lost too many friends recently.

"I want to keep her under sedation until the swelling goes down and we are certain there are going to be no complications," the doctor answered.

"Will she be able to return to duty?" Hedon asked. Amanda was his top admiral, and he didn't want to lose her services or her friendship.

"At least four to six weeks," the doctor replied in a firm voice. "Perhaps longer. She needs some rest and time away from this war to fully recover."

Hedon nodded. He would make sure she got that. It was just an immense relief to know that one of his oldest friends was going to be all right.

Fleet Admiral Johnson was still in shock at the sudden turn of events. At one moment, they were looking at total defeat, and now they had a victory. A costly one to be sure, but the AIs and the Hocklyns were jumping away in defeat. She had spoken briefly to the Albanian admiral in charge of the fleet that had jumped in and saved New Tellus. She was still amazed that the ships were Albanian.

"What are our losses?" she asked in a quiet voice, looking over at Admiral Freeman. She knew they were going to be heavy.

"We lost over sixty percent of the fleet, shipyard Clements, two of the asteroid fortresses, and forty percent of the defense grid," Freeman answered, appalled at the losses. It would take years to rebuild what had been destroyed. The tactical displays were covered with wreckage. Just cleaning up the wreckage from the battle was going to be a trying task.

"What about New Tellus?" Karla asked as her eyes strayed to a viewscreen, which showed the beleaguered planet. Already, dust and smoke from the nuclear explosions were turning the atmosphere a darker and more sinister color.

"We recorded forty-two nuclear detonations on the surface," replied Freeman grimly, knowing the planet had paid a heavy price. "All between the ten to twenty megaton range. The admiral in charge of the Albanian fleet has asked permission for his ships to go into low orbit over the planet. He claims they have equipment on board their ships that can neutralize the radiation."

"Give them permission," Karla decided quickly. "Inform the surviving defensive battle stations to allow the Albanian ships passage through the defense grid." If the Albanians could remove the spreading radiation, it would be a godsend to the planet. "Also, contact Admiral Streth and have him begin reorganizing our fleets. I don't think the AIs or the Hocklyns will return, but I want to be ready just in case they do."

Karla leaned back in her command chair. She needed to send a message to President Kincaid and inform him that New Tellus had survived. She also knew the Albanians had a lot of explaining to do. Once she had the message sent and a few more things attended to, she was determined to meet with the admiral in charge of the Albanian fleet and find out just what was going on.

-

Fleet Admiral Resmunt looked at the ruins of his fleet. Numerous ships were damaged and even as he watched several self-destructs went off, taking the ships with them. The other ships moved quickly away from the nuclear explosions to avoid any flying wreckage.

"Where did those ships come from?" First Leader Ganth demanded his large, dark eyes even wider than usual. "Their weapons cut right through the AI's screens! How is that possible?"

"An ally of the humans," spoke Resmunt, knowing it would be a long time before they dared to mount another attack on human space.

It would be necessary to approach the AIs about more weapons upgrades, particularly the new sublight anti-matter missiles they had used. He also had no idea where the AIs had vanished to; they had not come to the designated rendezvous.

Resmunt knew they were fortunate the new ships had concentrated on the AIs or the losses to the Hocklyn fleet could have been devastating. As it was, nearly sixty percent of his fleet had survived.

But the losses had been bad enough. Commodore Maseth and his flagship the Destiny of War were gone, as well as four other War Leaders. Over five hundred warships had been lost, including twenty-six dreadnoughts and thirty-one war cruisers, as well as hundreds of escorts. He still had a powerful fleet comprised of over eight hundred ships, but many of them were damaged, and it would take days of intensive work by the crews to make them fully combat ready again. Even then, there would be a lot of internal and hull damage that could not be fully repaired in space.

"We will return to Kenward Seven to repair and rearm the fleet," Resmunt stated in a calm voice, knowing he had no other choice.

"Then we will return," proclaimed Ganth, determinedly. "We will destroy the humans and add to our honor."

"I don't think so, at least not for a long while," replied Fleet Admiral Resmunt, shaking his head. "I fear we will have to worry about preserving our Empire first. We have severely weakened the outlying areas from all the ships we have taken for this assault. The humans and their ally may take advantage of this to attack us."

"We still have thousands of ships in the Empire," replied First Leader Ganth, fearing that the commodore might indeed be correct. "It may take time as you have said, but eventually we will be victorious."

Resmunt only nodded. He was not quite so sure. He now had a duty to perform that he had been delaying. The Liberator had an FTL communicator on it furnished by the AIs. It would allow him to send a message directly to the High Council. How they would take word of this defeat was unknown, but Resmunt could take solace in the fact that the AIs had also been defeated.

Admiral Teleck was in the Command Center of his flagship, the battlecruiser Ceres. He had been preparing to jump back to the Sol system when he received a new message from Fleet Admiral Johnson.

"Albanians," Colonel Barnes repeated, her eyes growing wide in disbelief. She had met the Albanian ambassador to the Federation several times at state dinners put on by her father the senator from Ceres. "I thought they were pacifists."

"Evidently not," Admiral Teleck responded as he studied the message that Admiral Johnson had sent. "They attacked the AI ships besieging New Tellus and destroyed over ninety of them."

Ninety of them!" Kathryn echoed, her eyes widening in astonishment "How?"

"Fleet Admiral Johnson reports the Albanian ships are equipped with some type of energy beam that cuts right through the AI's shields," Telleck replied almost in disbelief. "The Albanian ship's energy shields are also immune to all of the AI's weapons."

"What should we do?" Kathryn asked. She had met Ambassador Tureen several times when he had visited Ceres, and she was curious as to what he would have to say about this sudden reversal in the Albanian's attitude toward nonaggression. If she knew her father, Senator Barnes would have a lot of questions for the ambassador. "We always thought their advanced science would make a difference."

"Fleet Admiral Johnson wants us to jump to New Tellus," Admiral Teleck replied, his face showing deep concern. "They lost over sixty percent of the fleet and much of the rest is damaged. We're to help with rescue operations as well as serve as a defensive force until they can get their remaining fleet units reorganized."

"Fleet Admiral Streth?" asked Kathryn, hoping the legendary admiral had survived.

"He's fine," Teleck replied with a nod and then with an element of concern in his voice he continued. "Admiral Sheen was severely injured, and her flagship the WarStorm was destroyed. Set coordinates for the New Tellus system just outside of the planet's gravity well. All ships are to standby to help conduct rescue operations; there are a lot of stranded pilots and damaged ships out there."

A few moments later, blue white spatial vortexes formed in front of the eighty-one ships of the Ceres fleet and the ships quickly flew into them, jumping into hyperspace. The vortexes collapsed, leaving no trace of the ships. Space was empty as if nothing had ever been there.

Karl Arcles was on the battlecarrier Endurance waiting anxiously as dozens of pilots were being unloaded from rescue shuttles. Most had ejected just prior to their fighters or bombers being struck by Hocklyn missiles. A few had ejected when their craft had become too damaged to continue in the battle and could not make it back to the battlecarriers.

As each shuttle was unloaded, Karl searched the pilot's faces hoping to spot Lacy. He still hadn't given up hope that she had managed to eject and survived the battle.

"Still no sign?" Captain Stewart asked as he came to stand by Karl as another shuttle landed in the bay. Stewart was a squadron leader from the Endurance and had survived the battle with nearly half of his fighters.

"Not yet," Karl replied somberly. "I can't imagine she didn't make it. She just has to be out there!"

"We lost a lot of good pilots," Stewart continued in a grave voice. "I've never seen a battle like the one today. There were so many Hocklyn fighters, and the missile fire from their ships was intense. Most of our bombers were not able to complete their attack runs. I heard several of the bomber pilots talking about entire squadrons being wiped out, particularly when those two AI ships jumped in."

Karl nodded; a number of fighter squadrons had suffered just as bad. Of his own squadron of twenty fighters, only eight had returned to the Endurance. His gaze focused on the recently arrived shuttle, and he saw four tired looking pilots step out. He felt disappointment flow through him. Each time a shuttle landed without Lacy her chance of being one of the survivors decreased.

"Who's that?" Stewart asked as another pilot appeared in the door of the shuttle.

Karl looked back up and saw the familiar blonde hair. He knew instantly that it was her. "Lacy!" yelled Karl, feeling intense relief at seeing the young lieutenant.

Lacy looked up, and a big smile spread over her face as Karl ran up to her. "Did you miss me?" she asked with a grin.

Karl grabbed her and wrapped his arms around her in a big hug, lifting her up in the air. "Don't you ever scare me like that again!"

"Yes, Sir," replied Lacy, embarrassed at the embrace.

Karl let her go and stepped back. "What happened? One minute you were off my port wing and the next you were gone."

"I got cut off by two Hocklyn fighters," explained Lacy, recalling the horrifying experience. "I managed to take out one of them, but the other dropped in behind me and nailed my fighter with a missile. I managed to eject just before it hit."

"You were lucky," Captain Stewart said from where he had been listening to the two. "A second or two more and you wouldn't be here now."

"I know," Lacy replied her blue eyes focused on Karl. "But I am and I survived the battle."

"Let's go get you cleaned up and something to eat," Karl said brusquely, feeling moistness in his eyes. "We have a squadron to put back together!"

Admiral Streth was busy reorganizing the surviving fleet ships into two combat ready task groups. While he didn't think the Hocklyns or the AIs would return, he wasn't going to take any chances. There were one hundred and two surviving Federation warships, not counting the destroyers. Thirty-four of those ships needed serious yard time and had headed to the shipyards.

Fleet destroyers were towing a few warships that had serious damage to their sublight drives toward waiting repair bays. Fortunately, a large number of the destroyers, which had been deployed in the defense grid, had survived. The ten fleet repair ships were also busy as there were not enough repair bays for all the damaged ships and one of the shipyards had been destroyed in the battle. Several others had suffered serious damage.

"We have sixty-eight ships that are still combat capable," Colonel Trist reported as he finished going over the reports. "Most of those have minor to moderate damage."

Hedon nodded; that was about what he had been expecting. "We will form two fleets using the StarStrike and the Tellus as flagships. That will put thirty-four ships in each fleet."

"At least the Albanians are still here, and Admiral Teleck will be arriving soon," Colonel Grissom added.

Looking at one of the tactical displays, she could see that all of the Albanian ships were circling New Tellus in low orbit and were deploying some type of widespread energy beam that was supposed to eliminate the radiation from the nuclear detonations on the planet's surface. She hoped they were successful; New Tellus had been a beautiful world.

It had been a difficult day. Hedon let out a heavy sigh as he thought about everyone that had died. He knew that if not for the Albanians the New Tellus system and all the fleet units in it would have been destroyed. His quest to destroy the Hocklyns and someday rebuild that cabin on Maken would have come to an end. Looking at the planet on the main viewscreen, he knew from the latest reports that all the underground bunkers had survived. There had been very few civilian casualties on the surface of the planet, though it would be a while before it would be safe enough for some of them to emerge from the underground shelters.

In the last hour, a shuttle had arrived to take Amanda to the hospital in the command fortress. The command fortress had a large, modern hospital deep inside that could handle even the most serious of injuries, and Hedon wanted Amanda to have the best treatment possible. He had also notified Richard that she was coming over. Her husband would be waiting for the medical shuttle to dock.

"Admiral Teleck is arriving," Captain Reynolds announced as numerous green icons began to appear just outside of the planet's gravity well.

Hedon nodded. It was a relief to see the friendly green icons appearing on one of the tactical displays. A few moments later he watched as Admiral Teleck's fleet began moving toward the gravity well of the planet. The battle was over, and he and the StarStrike had survived. Looking at another tactical display showing all the Albanian ships above New Tellus, he wondered what this could mean for the war. Already, in his mind he was thinking about the next steps that needed to be taken.

Captain Duncan leaned back as she listened to the various communications between fleet units. It was a relief to know that Admiral Teleck's fleet had arrived. Janice knew all of them were fortunate to still be alive after the massive attack by the AIs and the Hocklyns.

Looking at Admiral Streth, she was surprised to see the look of confidence on his face; she wondered how much of that had to do with the Albanians. She knew that Hedon wanted to return to the old Federation worlds someday and free them from Hocklyn control. With an Albanian fleet to support him that might just happen much sooner than anyone had believed possible. If it did, she wanted to see this lake where Hedon wanted to build a cabin. She was extremely curious to see the world that Fleet Admiral Streth had come from.

Chapter Twenty-Four

President Kincaid had just finished a long private meeting with the Albanian ambassador and several important Federation senators. Some of the things Ambassador Tureen had revealed had been astonishing. It seemed that agents working for the Albanians had secretly furnished key parts of the science used to develop the sublight missiles to several Federation research scientists. There were also a few other important scientific advances that could be attributed directly to the Albanians. Tureen had gone on to assure Kincaid that Albanian interference in Federation affairs had been minimal since the Federation already had a powerful driving force in the old Federation survivors.

In his office now were Senator Barnes from Ceres and Senator Anderson from Earth. They were all quiet as the Albanian Ambassador left and they thought over what he had said. It had been a stunning development to learn that the Albanians were actually the Altons, the creators of the AIs.

"It seems as if they are willing to share some of their military technology," Senator Barnes spoke. The entire council had been briefed on the battle at New Tellus and the difference the Alton ships had made.

Barnes was still waiting anxiously to hear from his daughter on the battlecruiser Ceres. Kathryn had not yet sent him a message, and he didn't know if the Ceres had been involved in the fighting around New Tellus or not.

"Only some of it," President Kincaid reminded him as he looked over at the large map of the galaxy. "They are willing to share their energy weapon technology that was so devastating to the AIs, but it will take a totally new type of power system."

"A power system they are willing to furnish," Senator Anderson spoke. He had been Earth's Federation senator for nearly ten years. "The power system itself will allow for even stronger energy shields and an increase in the power of most of our current weapon systems."

"Just from listening to Ambassador Tureen I got the impression that they are still hesitant about sending their warships too far from home," commented Senator Barnes, raising his eyebrow.

"That's what I understood also," responded Kincaid, leaning back and placing his hands on his desk. "They are willing to make a few of their ships available to us in the short term, but the actual fighting in this war is going to be primarily left up to us and our other allies."

"What about Careth and New Providence?" asked Barnes, thinking about Senator Arden back on Ceres. "With a few Albanian ships to support our fleet we could send a relief force to Admiral Strong as well as set up a defensive perimeter around New Providence."

President Kincaid was silent for a long moment. "I strongly suspect that Fleet Admiral Streth is already planning that, but it's going to take us a while to replace our fleet losses from Operation First Strike and the recent attack against New Tellus."

"I agree," replied Senator Barnes but then, leaning forward, he added, "If we can secure those two systems to use as advance bases in this war it might prevent the Hocklyns and the AIs from launching additional attacks against us here."

"A strong reason for sending a relief fleet as soon as possible," Kincaid conceded. It would also be devastating to the Federation if something happened to Admiral Strong and the crew of the Avenger.

"Can we design our strikecruisers to handle this new power system and energy weapon of the Albanians?" asked Senator Anderson. "I don't think we can launch any type of relief mission until we have done so."

"We need to talk to Fleet Admiral Johnson and Admiral Freeman," replied Kincaid, knowing that Admiral Freeman would know more about that. "The Albanians will have to bring in the technicians and weapon specialists we'll need to adapt this new technology to our warships. After I speak with Johnson and Freeman I will set up another meeting with Ambassador Tureen to discuss that aspect."

"It's going to take a while," sighed Senator Barnes. At least he could tell Senator Arden that there was hope for New Providence. He knew the ambassador was getting impatient to return home.

Outside the building that housed the Federation Senate Chambers, Ambassador Tureen was climbing into a ground car. An Alton ship had just gone into orbit, and he needed to go up to speak to its commander. One thing he had not revealed to President Kincaid was the fact that their warships were highly automated. On the ships that had gone to New Tellus, there were less than twenty Altons in the crew of each one.

For the majority of the Alton race, any type of armed or physical conflict was detestable. Only a small percentage of the Alton people could be counted on to participate in this war. That was the primary reason that the majority of their ships would be staying close to home, and the humans and their allies would have to carry the war to the Hocklyns and the AIs.

Admiral Andrews was waiting anxiously for the doctor that was examining Amanda to come out. Admiral Hazleton was currently busy coordinating the repairs for the remaining six asteroid fortresses. All six, including the command fortress, had suffered heavy damage in the attack. From the initial assessments, it would take years to repair all the damage.

The doctor came out and, upon spotting Richard, came over. "Your wife will be fine. She has a nasty bump on her head and will be under observation for the next forty-eight hours, but she should make a full recovery from this injury."

"Can I see her?" Richard asked, his eyes focusing on the doctor. "Is she conscious?" When she had been brought off the medical shuttle, Amanda had looked very pale with a large bandage over her forehead. It had shaken Richard to see his wife looking so vulnerable.

"Barely," the doctor replied. "You can go in to see her, but only briefly; she needs her rest."

Richard went into the room and saw Amanda lying on the hospital bed with her eyes closed. "Amanda," Richard spoke softly, not knowing if she would be able to hear him.

"Richard," Amanda mumbled weakly her eyes fluttering open. "Is it really you?"

"Yes, it's me," replied Richard, forcing a smile and taking her hand. "You took a nasty bump to your head."

"The WarStorm? Commander Evans?" Amanda asked, her eyes trying to focus on Richard. "Are they okay?"

Richard hesitated for a moment. "They didn't make it," Richard said in a somber voice. "Lieutenants Stalls and Trask got you off the WarStorm. It was seriously damaged and coming apart around them. Commander Evans rammed an AI ship with your dying battlecruiser, destroying both in the process."

"The AIs?" asked Amanda, struggling to sit up worried that the battle was still going on. Admiral Streth was counting on her; she needed to get back out there.

"Lay down," Richard told her, taking her shoulders and gently forcing her to lie back down. "The battle's over, and we won. It's a long story, which needs to wait until you're feeling better. Just know that for now, we are all safe and Admiral Streth is still watching over us."

That seemed to satisfy Amanda as she closed her eyes and was soon asleep. Richard sat down in a comfortable chair next to the bed and gazed at his wife. There was so much he would have to tell her the next time she awoke. The war was about to change, and he knew his wife would continue to be a big part of it. He just hoped they would have some time alone before she had to leave again.

High Leader Nartel was standing in front of the Hocklyn High Council. He had just given them the battle report from Fleet Admiral Resmunt. Every Councilor stared at him in disbelief, unable to comprehend the enormity of what he had just told them.

"The AIs, defeated?" muttered Councilor Ruthan, shaking his head. "I don't believe it! Fleet Admiral Resmunt must be trying to cover up his own cowardice."

"Fleet Admiral Resmunt puts the total losses to the AIs at over one hundred and twenty ships and his own fleet at close to six hundred," spoke Councilor Berken, repeating the numbers that High Leader Nartel had just told them. "How is this possible?" It would be the worst defeat in the Empire's long history. It was incomprehensible to imagine how the humans could destroy so many of the massive AI spheres. Up until this time, the AI ships had been nearly invincible.

"The humans have an ally whose science at least matches the AIs," Nartel replied, his dark eyes focusing on the council. "The AIs had no defense against their weapons."

"We are doomed!" wailed Councilor Ruthan, gazing in consternation at High Leader Nartel. "The AIs will destroy us for this. They will blame us for their ship losses and this defeat."

"I think not," replied Nartel, glaring at Ruthan despising his obvious weakness. "They suffered as badly if not worse than we did. From what Fleet Commodore Resmunt has reported the AIs vanished shortly after the battle and he has not heard from them since. He believes they are returning to the galactic center to repair the damage to their fleet."

"What do we do now?" Councilor Jarles asked in a grave voice. "Any expansion of our Empire will have to be put off until this situation with the humans and their ally is dealt with. It could be years before we can begin to expand again."

"Fleet Admiral Resmunt is bringing his surviving fleet back to Kenward Seven," High Leader Nartel replied. "He has requested that we speak to the AIs about giving us even more advanced weapons, particularly the new sublight anti-matter missile they used against the humans."

Everyone was silent as they wondered how the AIs would react to this defeat, the first one in their long history. Would they even consider giving the Hocklyns the weapons they needed to combat the humans?

"I have given the order for all ships returning to Kenward Seven to be upgraded," Nartel continued in an even voice. "I am sending the same message to all of our other shipyards. We are honor bound to give our warriors the best weapons and ships that we can for this coming conflict."

"Then you believe the humans will attack our Empire again?" Councilor Desmonde asked.

"Yes," Nartel replied his hand sliding down and touching the blade at his waist. "Never has our Empire faced such a threat. We must prepare for all out war. New and more advanced ships will have to be built. I have also given the order for our scientists to begin weapons research."

"What!" screamed Councilor Ruthan, standing up, his face turning livid. "The AIs have strictly forbidden that! You must order our scientists to stop immediately or we are finished!"

Nartel shook his head. "I don't think our weapons research will be a big concern to the AIs anymore. I also intend to ask them for more advanced weapons as Fleet Commodore Resmunt has suggested."

Nartel looked across the council, seeing the acceptance in their faces. He doubted that many of them realized the significance of what had just happened in human space. For the first time in their long history, the entire Hocklyn Slave Empire was going to have to prepare for all out war.

Jeremy looked worriedly at the latest reports from his stealth scouts. The Hocklyn fleet gathering in the system a short distance away had grown to over two hundred ships, with two recently arrived AI spheres joining them.

"Still no word from the Federation?" asked Jeremy, looking over at Angela.

"No, nothing," she replied, shaking her head. "Our lines of communication may have been cut."

"If the AIs or the Hocklyns found our FTL communication buoys and managed to destroy a significant number of them we won't be able to send or receive messages from the Federation," Ariel commented from Jeremy's side.

It also meant that she had no way of sending messages to Clarissa. Ariel really missed her lifelong friend. She hoped the StarStrike would return shortly so she could speak to Clarissa again. Even with the Special Five to speak to, she still felt lonely.

Colonel Malen came to stand next to the command console. "Admiral Stillson is suggesting we send a destroyer back to the Federation to see what's happened."

Jeremy nodded. They had really felt cut off since their communication lines went silent. Everyone wanted to know what had happened to the Federation and if the trap at New Tellus had worked. "Let's do it," Jeremy responded. He knew it would take the destroyer over two weeks to travel to the Federation and return. However, the not knowing was crippling morale.

"I will have the destroyer leave in the morning," Colonel Malen responded.

Jeremy's eyes went to the viewscreen. Careth was prominently displayed with all the rich colors of an inhabited world. The deep blues of the oceans and the white of thick protective layers of clouds drew his eyes. Across the continents was the deep green of massive virgin forests. Careth was a beautiful world, and Jeremy was determined that the Hocklyns would never have it back.

Later, Jeremy was in his quarters with Kelsey. They were lying in bed talking abut their current situation.

Kelsey placed her hand on Jeremy's chest and raised her head to look at him. "I'm sure the Federation is fine," she spoke. Ever since the loss of communication with the Federation, the worry in Jeremy's eyes had deepened.

"I'm sure you're right," replied Jeremy, sliding his arm around Kelsey and marveling at how warm and soft she felt. "I have a meeting with Admiral Stillson and Grayseth tomorrow. Grayseth still wants to try to build a bomber production facility in one of their underground cities."

"Let's not worry about the war for now," Kelsey spoke softly as she slid her body over on top of Jeremy. She bent down and kissed him fervently on the lips. She knew there was one sure way to take his mind off the war.

Ariel turned off the monitor, which had been focused on Jeremy and Kelsey. She needed to talk to Katie more about this sex thing with humans; it was something she still found extremely confusing. Reappearing back in the Command Center, she had the main viewscreen focus on Federation space. All that was visible were hundreds of non-blinking stars. Ariel hoped the Federation and Clarissa were still safe.

Admiral Streth was on New Tellus with Captain Janice Duncan and some others from the Fleet. It had been two weeks since the Hocklyn and AI attack. Almost all the cities on the planet had been destroyed, and now a massive rebuilding effort was underway. They were currently at one of the plush mountain ski resorts, which had escaped the nuclear fire the Hocklyns had rained down upon the planet from space.

Janice had been extremely surprised when Admiral Streth had accepted her invitation to spend some time down at one of the resorts. They had separate rooms and Janice decided not to push it. If anything romantic happened, then it did; if not, then now was not the time.

"Were there mountains on Maken?" she asked as they sat at a small, secluded table, eating dessert. They were sitting next to a window, and the sun was slowly falling behind one of the nearby mountains.

"Some," replied Hedon, recalling his home planet. "Not as many as are on New Tellus, but Maken had some it could be proud of."

"You will have to show me someday," Janice spoke softly, her eyes focusing on the admiral. "I would love to see your home world."

"You may sooner than you think," Hedon replied.

He wondered what Taylor and Lendle would think about Janice. That he was developing feelings for her was something he couldn't deny. He would like to show her the lake on Maken and the snow covered mountains. In two more days, he would be returning to New Tellus Station to meet with Fleet Admiral Johnson and Admiral Teleck. It was time to return to the old Federation worlds while the AIs and the Hocklyns were still reeling from their recent losses.

Admiral Strong was waiting for a relief force, and Hedon was determined to lead it. He only needed approval from Fleet Admiral Johnson and President Kincaid. Then, if things worked out at Careth, Hedon intended to push on to the old Federation worlds. Smiling over at Janice, Hedon decided he was going to enjoy the next few days. For the first time in a long while, the future looked brighter, and he knew that someday he would show Janice his old home world. He also knew another simple fact. The battle for New Tellus was over, but the battle for the Hocklyn Slave Empire was about to begin.

The End

Books in the Slaver War series should be read in the following order.

Moon Wreck
The Slaver Wars: Alien Contact
Moon Wreck: Fleet Academy.
The Slaver Wars: First Strike
The Slaver Wars: Retaliation
The Slaver Wars: Galactic Conflict

The Slaver Wars: Alien Contact can be read either before or after Moon Wreck.

Turn the page to see other books by Raymond L. Weil.

For updates on current writing projects and future publications go to my author website. Sign up for future notifications when new books come out on Amazon.

Website: http://raymondlweil.com/

Other Books by Raymond L. Weil
Available on Amazon

-

Dragon Dreams: Dragon Wars
Dragon Dreams: Gilmreth the Awakening
Dragon Dreams: Snowden the White Dragon

-

Star One: Tycho City: Discovery
Star One: Neutron Star
Star One: Dark Star
Star One: Tycho City: Survival

-

Galactic Empire Wars: Destruction

ABOUT THE AUTHOR

I live in Clinton Oklahoma with my wife of 40 years and our cat. I attended college at SWOSU in Weatherford Oklahoma, majoring in Math with minors in Creative Writing and History.

My hobbies include watching soccer, reading, camping, and of course writing. I coached youth soccer for twelve years before moving on and becoming a high school soccer coach for thirteen more. I enjoy playing with my five grandchildren whenever I have the opportunity. I also have a very vivid imagination, which sometimes worries my friends. They never know what I am going to say or what I am going to do.

I am an avid reader and have a science fiction / fantasy collection of over two thousand paperbacks. I want future generations to know the experience of reading a good book as I have over the last forty years.

Made in the USA
San Bernardino, CA
29 October 2014